A TALENT FOR LOVING...

Evaliño had become utterly transformed. Gone was the withdrawn, innocent, girlish manner. She had thickened spiritually with one deeply-felt kiss into as close an approximation of an emotionally abandoned woman as any anti-débauchée would ever care to say.

Her nostrils quivered. Her scarlet tongue licked at her lips as might that of a test baker at a patisserie, hungrily and incessantly.

Her eyes filmed with the daintiest lust imaginable...

Also by Richard Condon
Published by Ballantine Books:

MONEY IS LOVE

THE WHISPER OF THE AXE

A Talent
for Loving

The Great Cowboy Race

Richard Condon

BALLANTINE BOOKS · NEW YORK

ISBN 0-345-25767-7

Manufactured in the United States of America

First Ballantine Books Edition: July 1978

For

RED, DEBO AND WENDY

who have the talent

The riches I bring you
Crowding and shoving,
Are the envy of princes:
A talent for loving.

THE KEENER'S MANUAL

FOREWORD

THE ACCOUNT that follows is intended to be my grandmother's ultimate grant to the Archives of the Department of Sociology, Pickering Academy for Women,
Pickering City, Texas.

In assembling this history I have had access to those
of my grandmother's diaries covering the years 1868–
1871 which had been titled "The Circumstances
Leading to My Marriage"; to the scrapbooks, *souvenirs
des fromages,* and expense-account vouchers of Mr.
Franklin Heller, first Commissioner of Public Health
of Pickering City; and to U.S. and Mexican newspaper
accounts of the region during that period. The latter
sources, while not reporting in detail, did convey the
sense of community excitement and total participation
engendered among the international population of an
area covering almost 480,000 square miles.

I wish to express my family's appreciation to the
Misses Shiela Mirlis and Rose Reiter, Trustees for the
Mat Sun Benevolent Agency and Tong, San Francisco,
California, for certain records, markers, financial histories, manuscripts, and other statements of transaction which have made it possible for me to piece
together the career of Major William Patten, my maternal grandfather, founder of Pickering City and one
of the conquerors of the West.

In the Republic of Mexico I have been greatly favored with precise historical perspective on *cantinas*
and *bailes* by the social historian Peggy Pena.

To Miss Evelyn Roja Hunt, chief librarian of the
Pickering City Free Library, I wish to express my
profound gratitude for her tireless checking of this
manuscript for errors in the Apache language. To
Counselor Bertram A. Mayers I express my admiring
acknowledgment of his massive thirty-volume work on
the development of jurisprudence in Pickering City as
a county seat.

I am most deeply indebted, however, for contribu-
tions of fact, method, idiom, song, spirit, and place

made to this book by these sources and their authors: *The Cowboy at Work* by Fay E. Ward, *Cowboy Lore* by Jules Verne Allen, *Western Words* by Ramón F. Adams, *The Great Plains* by Walter Prescott Webb, *Life among the Apaches* by John Cremony, *The Lower Rio Grande Valley of Texas* by J. Lee and Lillian Stambaugh, *Vaquero in the Brush Country* and *Apache Gold and Yanqui Silver* by J. Frank Dobie, *The King Ranch* by Tom Lea, and *Shanghai Pierce: A Fair Likeness* by Chris Emmett.

RICHARD CONDON

Mexico City
15 April 1960

BOOK ONE

1844-1851

CHAPTER 1

BAT DONGIN was a professional gunthrower the Moore boys brought in to kill Maurice Hanline. The Moore boys—Hogger, Fred, and Shorty—owned most of the town and most of the land around it, except the Hanline place. The Moore boys had decided they would be able to deal better with the new owner of the Hanline place after she had been made a widow. Shorty Moore would have killed Hanline himself, but the older, wiser brothers wanted the land deal to be clean so they brought in Bat Dongin.

Fort Hill was the center for butchering buffalo that year, and wherever the buffalo butchers were working for steady money, thugs and riffraff skulked in. There were about four thousand people in the town. Sometimes cowhands rode through. If they were sober they generally kept on riding. Soldiers, horse thieves, lost women, cow thieves, and back-shooters were most of Fort Hill that season when the buffalo were being diminished to extinction. Outside of maybe one hundred and ten people, the town was a mongrel's vomit.

The fort itself was up on the bluff. So was the big mercantile store. The tang of the town was down under the bluff in the flats, where every building was noisy and fancy and where the Moore boys owned four of the seven honkatonks. It was no place to go unarmed or to walk in the dark. The moon never seemed to come out over Fort Hill. The whisky didn't taste right. A man could strike a wooden match on the cheeks of most of the drunken dance-hall women while they slept and never wake them. About daylight any morning, anyone who took a stroll down by the river might find another body hanging by its neck from a cotton-wood tree with a sign stuck on it that said *Horse Thief No. 24* or whatever number it happened to be.

The Moore boys' biggest saloon was called The Jefferson House. It was painted red and had gilt porch posts and gold swinging doors. All drinks and seegars were two bits apiece. In front of it drunken Indians staggered around or lay face down in the mud. The thugs who called themselves buffalo hunters would sit on the front gallery to insult any woman who walked past. Inside, any kind of a game any customer wanted to play was available—keno, chucka-luck, roulette, Spanish monte, poker, faro, casino—anything at all. The price of buffalo hides had dropped to sixty cents. The tramp buffalo butchers were feeling hollow. Most of them were on foot. They'd kill a man for a horse or five dollars. They were not only evil and mean, they smelled bad. The whole town stank. Wagon trains were carrying buffalo hides out but acres of ground all around the town were still covered and reeking with them.

Bat Dongin came into The Jefferson House late in the afternoon and ordered himself a heavy dinner. He had been told that Maurice Hanline would come in at nine o'clock. Waiting made him nervous. Dongin was a skinny man with a strong sour smell and a port-wine scar on the left side of his face from hairline to jawline. He whined everything he said. By seven o'clock he was catching cards behind a rank cigar in Major Patten's poker game with three other players: Tom Pryor, the town printer; Hogger Moore; and Frank O'Connell, the lawyer who had come to the town traveling for Mooney & Schmidt, the fancy-food firm.

Major Patten ran a day-and-night poker game. His father had run a big dance hall and gambling hell in Mirlis, Tennessee.

Major Patten had left Mirlis on his twenty-first birthday, 13 January 1834, the day Horatio Alger was born in Revere, Massachusetts. The major's father had died three days before that, leaving him $91,505 in gold, killed by a rattlesnake while running about barefooted during a seizure of *mania a potu*. His mother had left them both when the major had been fourteen, the result of her husband's drinking and oppressive infidelities, to seek peace in one of the Dame Maria Van Slyke Temperance nunneries which were then in spiritual vogue in eastern New Jersey.

The major had moved slowly across the land away

3

from Mirlis from gambling hell to gambling hell, sliding slowly down the map through the Arkansas territory and the Oklahoma territory into the Republic of Texas, engrossed in gaming and making sure he won. When Bat Dongin sat in on his game he was thirty-one years old and sickened by gambling, but he could do nothing to stop his own play. A feeling of mission, of what the religious call *vocation,* had come over him again. His vocation, more and more, was growing to be to save himself from becoming a cipher towering over a sea of empty noughts. He was weary of remaining imperturbable with scum and sitting beside thieves and worse. Sober, his father had instructed the major in the logic of becoming what one would tolerate, then had demonstrated the postulate with his own life.

The major was not, nor had he ever been, a military man. It was legitimate to refer to him as Major Patten, but how and why this was so were secrets the major held close to himself—as he did everything else. He was a slight man, but the desperadoes of Fort Hill were careful to show their respect for him. He had maintained tolerant aloofness even while pistol-whipping the hulking Marvo Frank for shouting insults after the most hideous woman of the town. As the expression went, Major Patten had more guts than you could hang on a fence.

He was a stern man of about frying size with silk-lined hands and the mean-child eyes of a hooked gambler. His voice was pitched so low people had to lean forward to hear what he said. He wore a close-cropped ginger mustache, that length in itself an oddity for the region and the time. He was a handsome man, but his most memorable characteristic was one which he had the brass to cherish well before Dr. Freud had entered his historic practice of surmising in Austria—a passionate and hopeless compulsion to gamble. That he had become a professional gambler was the result of a compromise between his intelligence and his sickness. It was more economical and logical for a man who could not stop gambling to make gambling his profession.

The major spent some time early every morning with Kate Grigson, the youngest and most popular of the calico queens in the Jefferson House dance hall, which put her somewhere around thirty-three. She was a boldly pretty woman with a figure like a girl within a fountain and the eyes of one who hopes deeply. She was dark against his pink-and-white skin. Taller than he when they were standing beside each other, which was seldom, in bed beside him she could make herself seem to herself far tinier and more delicate than he. The major never considered his size. He was her lover. She was his newspaper.

He was the only man she had ever known who paid her attention. She mistook this for touching interest in her person and then, irrevocably, in herself. His absorption with what she did and said was in endearing contrast to the ways of the men with whom she spent the rest of her life. Those men were rough and callous because they had to be, because all others were, because there could be no reason for profit by behaving differently. She screamed at them with laughter and invective more than she spoke to them. She drank with them and slept with them, and it was tiring work. For her customers she had a heart of pure salami. To the major she offered a heart made of small flowers, fresh and fragrant: frangipani, jacaranda, bougainvillea, sweet william. He was her man and she could sing out her days to him. The major listened. He was gentle. He was deft and sure. He was a man but he was not a noisy man.

Kate imagined that Major Patten seemed to sense that there was something quicker inside her, the valuable entreating *her* that shimmered like a humming bird which drank lemon sunshine and darted like a dancer before the sound of music, which was how she lived inside the heavying padding of her flesh. That was how she thought he saw her to be—how she knew herself to be, as a circus fat lady knows she is a mind and feelings, a tankard for tears, not the outer part. Kate Grigson saw the way he looked at her and she hoarded his esteem to pay herself indemnity for every cuff of coarseness in her nights.

The major did listen, with eyes and ears. To him

she was the gazette which roved for its intelligence far and wide while he sat with the anchor chain of chance wound round his legs. She seemed to have seen everything which had happened during the night she had just left behind, all the things which could not be confirmed or noted because of his concentration on the cards. She talked to everyone who rode through the town and remembered what she heard, reported it with economy and with feeling but did not serve it up under the sauces of personal opinion. In short, she kept him informed.

He did not know about the inner self. If he were capable of recognizing that there might be a different spiritual texture under the powder, the sweet breasts, and the soft cradle of hips, he would have expected it to be a reserve power of the same order, more tender equipment for his comfort and joy.

They would lay together in the darkness, as they did on the morning of the day Bat Dongin came into the saloon and after a while the major's cigar would glow and Kate would light a tallow candle, prop herself up on one fleshy elbow, then stare gratefully into his eyes.

"Did you have a good night?"

"The house has to win, little bird."

"Not this part of the house."

"We win money and we lose something else."

She sighed like a housewife. "They are such damn country boys. I grew up in St. Louis."

"A pretty place."

"Not so pretty as that. A sour waft of beer and cats in the garbage is what I saw the minute I said the name."

"Good and bad. We take it all with us."

"Not all."

"No. And a good thing."

"See anybody special tonight?"

"Yes." He puffed on the cheroot. "I did. A jeweler name of Max Stein come all the way from Chicago on his way to Fort Hayworth and he stopped off here to have a losing streak."

She loved to hear that the chumps had lost. "He

6

did? How much, Bill?" In all his life Kate had been the only one who called him Bill.

He reached out of the bed and dipped his hand into his coat pocket. "This much," he said and dropped a brooch which sparkled with shining stones beside her on the bed. "A little pin."

"A little pin?" She picked it up so all the light could find it. "Why, Hogger Moore'd sell you this whole saloon for a pin like this."

"Then—buy it from him."

"Buy it? Buy—Bill, you mean you're givin' this pin to me?"

He smiled at her. He had good teeth. He was not afraid of anything so he smiled well when he was pleased. "Now what else would I do with a lady's pin?" he asked, and Kate began to cry. She laughed while she cried, but mostly she cried and then they made love again.

After a while the end of the major's cigar glowed again and Kate relighted the tallow candle.

"I'll never get a present like that ever in my life again."

"A little pin?"

"The pin, too. Most of all, I meant you. You have a talent for loving, Bill."

He smiled at her and touched the side of her face.

"And you smell so good, all over you," she said.

"What's the news tonight?"

"Man told me they're givin' land away in the Southwest."

"Good news for farmers."

"Not for farmers. The man said there's a million head of wild cattle walking on the land. All there to be taken. The Mexicans left them behind in thirty-six and they been breedin'. Man said if you'll tell them in Austin that you'll raise cattle you can get ten times as much land as if you say you want to farm. And if you still want more, you can spend about two bits an acre—or maybe a nickel is what he said."

"Cattle can be gold in the ground."

"Hell, they're free. Nothin' is gold you can buy real cheap. I know."

7

"Don't you believe that, Kate. You hear?"

"It's funny to hear you talkin' like a workin' man."

The major stared at the ceiling and smoked his cigar. Ashes fell on his chest but Kate dusted them off before they could burn. "You thinking of turnin' cowman, Bill?" she grinned.

The major smiled at her because she pleased him very much. "Who knows, little bird?" he answered.

At noon each day the major had two drinks of bourbon and a talk with Franklin Heller, the Jefferson House bartender. Heller had gone to sea. He'd been almost everywhere oceans touched land. The major would pump him about gambling games, then sip whisky and think how he would bet them. Heller knew how to train crickets for fighting. Heller knew how to bet chemin-de-fer and he knew the right way and the wrong way to handle a fighting cock. The major learned a lot because he asked questions steadily. Heller stood there behind a white apron, polishing glasses, and slowly discovered that he knew a lot more than he thought he knew. That attached him to Major Patten. Sometimes Heller tried to switch the talk to other adventures in the ports of the world but the major discouraged that. He wanted to know only about gambling and methods of play so that, after he left Kate in the mornings and before he went to sleep in the big room on the floor above the saloon, he could stretch out with his hands behind his head and think about what he had learned and, in his mind, make his play.

At one o'clock every day he ate lunch alone at a table in the Jefferson House kitchen, looking out the window at the scrub and talking disconnectedly with Mat Sun, a young Chinese cook who had come to America so recently that he still wore his hair in a queue down his back, plaited and shining.

Mat Sun seemed to listen but maintained inscrutability because he had worked since he was four years old. The major paid Mat Sun one silver dollar after each meal, even though the house provided his meals free, because Mat Sun was a remarkable cook and he worked for greater and greater effects when he cooked

8

for Major Patten's money. For lunch on the day Bat Dongin came to Fort Hill, Mat Sun made a fry-pan full of the breast of wild turkey in gravy and a cobbler of wild plums from the Red River.

The major slept for two and a half hours after lunch. He opened the play at the regular table at six o'clock every day and he played until two o'clock the following morning unless he had some big losers at the table who wanted to play on. The major dressed in the uniform of his trade, perhaps because it made him feel more like a gambler. It was a back-East costume which hewed to the fashions set by the men who worked on the Mississippi river boats. This uniform ritualized the intensity of the ecstasy-anxiety he experienced in play. It was a black frock coat which covered a Walker pistol, a black wool vest crossed with a silver chain, soft boots with gaiters, a white shirt with a black string tie, and a flat black felt hat.

Bat Dongin threw his cards untidily and with no regard for custom. He swore at his bad luck. He crowed when he won. He had a way of spitting too close to the major's boots. In about two hours he would have to gun Maurice Hanline dead and it was much on his mind. He had nightmares too often—nightmares in which, when he went for his gun, the leather would be empty and while he flapped his arms at his sides the other man's gun would come out slowly and the bullet would clap into his chest.

Hogger Moore was there to point out Hanline. Fred Moore was in the crowd somewhere to back the play. The brothers had not told Shorty that this was the night because he got excitable whenever there was shooting and sometimes did things which made his folks feel ashamed of him.

At nine o'clock or thereabouts, Dongin was to walk to Hanline and say loudly, 'I'm a-goin' tuh kill you fer whut you done to my sister,' because this was something that always threw a man off balance. Dongin had been making a living with that single sentence for two years, and he'd shot down eight men. He had worked in a lumber mill for six years but he had been sure he could feel the sawdust getting into his lungs. Then one day, he was doing this. The work made him jumpy. He always fired before he could finish the sentence. He was a sloppy workman all around. As a result, the small flawed things he let himself do made people remember him more than the port-wine scar did.

By seven o'clock the saloon was a mire of noises. On Saturday nights the women's laughter seemed to have more sand and sadness in it. There had never been a killing in The Jefferson House, which was just one year old. There was no law in the town, either.

Ed Simmons was at the piano, behind his beard. On Saturday nights he was backed by a guitar player named Gobel and colored fiddler who had said three years before that he was working his way across Texas to California.

The spittoons gleamed. The sawdust on the floor was pink and damp. The Jefferson House was the only honkatonk within four hundred and twenty miles that had a board floor. The girls appreciated this: it gave the men a gala feeling and they spent more than they ever would from a dirt floor. The steady beat of the music wooed the spenders. Hard legs of sound wound round the room. Stairways of murmurs ascended to moans in the rooms above. The yellow light ran down over all of them, flickering like a drunken stare, and the major had another flash of feeling that he was wasting his life. Poker chips mewed, hard money clinked, whisky bottles were slammed down on top of table and bar. There was constant, hot movement in the low-ceilinged room which held eleven round tables, sixty-six chairs, thirty-two tallow lamps, and a long bar. Talk shuttled, shrill voices of the women over bass rumblings and nasal snarls. Sequins and glass sparklers signaled from the depths of the big mirrors on each wall. They were yelling three-part harmony on 'Utah Carrol' in the back, fighting off the spiny sounds of the band. All the smells were heavy and pragmatic—orange water, tallow, sweat, beer, dead buffalo, cloves, leather, and horses. The women's working dresses were oily colors of stinging red and singing blue, as though they had chosen sides for teams to contest which could separate the men

10

from their money the quicker. Their hair was piled on top of their heads, making it easier to wipe away the sweat which came with the dancing.

Just after eight o'clock Franklin Heller, the bartender, remembered who Dongin was. He signaled to the Head Girl to take over. On a crumpled piece of paper he wrote *Man with scar murdered preacher in Balder last year.* He put the note under a tray, walked to the major's table, cleared glasses from it, and left the note in the major's lap where it was read under the heavy gold fringe which garnished the green baize cloth. When he got back to the bar Heller took a six-gun from the back bar, made sure there were five biscuits in it, and laid it on the bar shelf in front of him. Mat Sun, who was taking a break standing in the kitchen doorway at the near end of the bar, said, "Whassa matta, Flank?"

"If you're always ready, you're always glad," Heller said. Mat Sun reached behind him into the kitchen. His hand came out with a big pistol which he stuck into the waistband of his trousers.

The preacher at Balder had been the third religious Dongin had murdered in six years, almost seven, even before he had taken to steady killing for a living. He hated preachers. They were the only ones he counted when he cut notches. This was something deeply personal, a matter which could not be shared because he would not have known how to explain why he did what he did to them, but whenever a preacher looked at him Dongin got the feeling the man was consigning him to burn in hell and no mere man should have that right.

"How many cards?" the major asked softly.

"Don't hack at me," Dongin answered. His voice sounded as though he should have blown his nose many years before.

The blue cigar smoke which roofed them and lay upon them in soft, horizontal lines made it seem as though they were playing underwater. Dongin's pale eyes behind his scarlet half-mask shifted from face to face around the table.

A woman's voice hurtled from far in the back, protesting. "Why, you filthy son-of-a-bitch!"

11

"Give me five cards," Dongin blurted.

Hogger Moore didn't mean to, but he laughed nastily. He tried to stop but he kept laughing. He sounded like a drunken ram. Tom Pryor just stared at Dongin. O'Connell said, "Five, *Five?*"

"That's what I said," Dongin whined.

The major ignored Dongin's request for five cards. "Two for the dealer," he said, throwing his discards with his left hand and dropping two new cards on his stack with his right.

"Them is my cards," Dongin said, making as if to reach for them. The major stopped him with a stare. Dongin saw then that the major, dressed all in black and white, looked like a preacher.

"Play," the major ordered Hogger Moore—who owned the saloon, the tables, the chairs, and who had rented Dongin's immortal soul for the evening.

"You are a cheatin' yeller bastard," Dongin said loudly with his clotted voice.

Three men and a woman at the table directly behind them got up quickly and moved. O'Connell pushed back his chair. Pryor slipped his poker hand into his left front pocket. Hogger Moore dropped his cards face down on the table. They pushed back at the same time. They kept going backward until their backs touched the wall. Dongin sat and stared. His breath fluttered shallowly. Hogger Moore spoke to him in a low voice, "Easy, Bat. Easy, boy. He's bad. He's bad. Easy, Bat."

Action went dead in the big room. Kate Grigson, sitting on a soldier's lap fifteen feet behind Dongin, wanted to scream *"No!"* but her mind played tricks on her and she began to laugh wildly to think that Hogger Moore could call Major Patten bad. She made shrill cutting sounds. The other soldier at the table slapped her hard across the face, just as the major spoke gently to Dongin, saying, "Ain't you the pervert that murdered the preacher up to Balder?"

Dongin went up, kicking the wooden chair backward under him, clawing at his gun. The major remained seated. He allowed Dongin the security of getting his gun clear before he moved, then a gun went off in his left hand. Dongin never fired a gun

12

again. Franklin Heller shot from behind the bar, his fire going between the major and Dongin. His employer, Hogger Moore, was slammed back into the wall by the force of the bullet and dropped the gun in his hand. The crowd moved its collective head as would spectators at a ball game. When Mat Sun fired from the kitchen doorway and took the top of Fred Moore's head off, their eyes were swung to the kitchen to carom off to discover where the bullet had gone. Not one of the three dying men looked as though he could believe he had been killed.

Across the forty feet of the room the major asked, "What happened?"

"Hogger was fixin' to gun you," Heller said.

"Hoggah brothuh too," Mat Sun said.

The major turned inquisitively to look down at the body of Fred Moore. "He was the worst of the Moore boys," he said, almost to himself. He turned Hogger's cards face up on the table. "Straight," he announced. "Jack high."

Pryor stepped over Hogger's body and walked to the table unsteadily. He dropped his poker hand shakily. "Nines and sixes," he said with a trembling voice. The major reached down and turned over the cards of his own hand. "Full house," he said crisply. "Kings over aces."

"That man should have asked for four cards," O'Connell said. He turned over the two cards which had waited to be dealt next from the top of the pack. They were two more aces.

"Well!" the major said admiringly. "He sure missed out. Chances of drawing to four of a kind are one in four thousand one hundred and sixty five." He raked in the pot, looking down at Dongin with his ripped chest. "Can't be lucky all the time," he said. Then he looked at the faces which were crowding in all around. "Game is closed," he announced, and walked through the bumbling crowd to the bar.

Kate Grigson was waiting for him with Heller and Mat Sun. "You boys was real awake," the major said, "an' I ain't never forgettin' that. You see them work, Kate?"

"Two men rode outta here to the Moore ranch," she answered. "Shorty Moore will be back here inside an hour with a dozen men to kill all of you."

"We'll see about that," the major replied.

"You got to get out, Bill," she pleaded. "Now and fast. An' I'm goin' with you."

"No."

"You got to run, Bill. Please, Bill."

"No, I don't."

"What else can you do?"

"What would anybody do?" He looked levelly at Mat Sun, then at Heller, to see if any faintness had overtaken them. Mat Sun was chewing on something. Heller was polishing a glass.

"These two boys an' me'll ride out to the Moore ranch an' ambush Shorty an' kill him an' his boys before they even think they're set to kill us."

"They'd hang you if you did that."

"Maybe you can tell me who'll be left to hang me. Running is no good. Shorty ain't no good neither. I ain't goin' to ride at night 'ceptin' to stay outta the heat an' I ain't goin' to spend the rest of my life facin' the door wherever I set because of some thief's brother. No, ma'am. We'll kill Shorty an' we'll ride outta here easy. You with me, boys?"

Mat Sun nodded vigorously, his pigtail bobbing like a bell rope. Heller said, "Hell, yes. We're with you."

"Well, good. Take five minutes to get your bedroll together. You pack what you cook with, Mat Sun. I ain't one for roughin' it. We'll meet at the stable." He looked at Kate tenderly and smiled at her, then he walked through the crowd to the back of the saloon and started up the stairs. She was behind him. She didn't speak. A big man with a three-day grizzle of beard and buffalo blood on his pants tried to pull her down to him as she went past but she disengaged herself effortlessly and kept following the major. She didn't speak. Ed Simmons started the piano going again and Gobel took up the beat on the guitar, but the music fell on a different kind of room where everybody talked in low voice, like eager biddies.

The major pulled on heavy boots and looked over what he had. "We'll travel light," he said absent-mindedly.

"Will you take me with you, Bill? Are you going to take me with you?" Kate sat on the edge of the bed. In her spangles with her hair piled up, she looked like a small girl ready for a costume party.

"Little bird, you know I can't do that."

"After Shorty. Will you come back for me *after* Shorty?"

"Let's see first if there is an after Shorty."

"Bill, *if* there is. When it's over and you're safe— are you going to come back for me?"

He walked close to her and touched her hair. "Talk ain't much," he said gently. "We'll wait an' see what happens." He lifted her chin and kissed her mouth lightly, twice.

After that she did not look like a small girl any more. She looked as hard and as old as a dance-hall hooker is supposed to look.

"Kate, do something for me?"

She nodded, looking at the wall.

"I'm goin' to write a letter to my Ma and in case I don't get back here, would you pick it up and see that it gets in the mail?"

"Yes."

He leaned over a chest and began to scratch a letter with the stub of a pencil. While he was writing she left the room. When he finished, he took off a money belt and counted out two thousand dollars in paper money and sealed it in the envelope.

He decided to take Shorty at Bara's Gap. The three men dismounted and picketed their horses.

"Don't shoot 'til I shoot," the major told them, "but when I fire my second shot I want you boys to hit ever'thing that moves but try to miss the horses. We can use them."

"There are folks who'd give us a medal for shootin' the Moore boys but who'd sure as hell hang us for stealin' their horses."

"I go along with that sentiment generally," the ma-

15

jor answered thoughtfully, "but I am not in agreement at the present time."

They were in wooded terrain. The land rolled slightly upward, blending with the night ahead of them. The road which had been a wagon trail for thirty years and which rutted the ground from the Moore ranch to Fort Hill was a straight line through a large, split lump of granite which was known as Bara's Gap. The moonlight was strong. The stars were out. The major made sure his small force remained on the same side of the five-foot granite lift which made the side of the gap so they couldn't nick each other in a crossfire. He seemed to be in a gay, relieved mood.

"We'll be able to hear them a mile away on a night like this," Heller said.

The major stopped whistling. "Sure enough," he said, "and they're comin' now."

The thrum of many horses' hooves and the tinkle of gear sounded faintly off to the right. "Frank, you take them from furthest out. Mat Sun, you handle the middle. I stay here. I'll fire the first shot in the air to stop them. Pay no heed and wait for the second shot."

They separated. It took twelve minutes for the Moore posse to reach the gap. Shorty came tearing through first, about two lengths in the lead. He was ahead of five men. The major stepped into the center of the road in the moonlight, a short, jaunty figure which cocked a pistol indolently, then fired into the air.

The lead horse pulled back so short it seemed to be backing up rapidly into the clump of horses and riders right behind it. There was a lot of concentrated cursing, then everything got quiet.

"Who the hell is that?" Shorty finally got courage enough to bellow. "I'll tear yer goddam ears offen yuh." He had a raw bully's voice and he was scared nearly witless. The riders behind him separated themselves nicely, making clear targets against the night sky, the separation being a natural movement after the jam-up.

"Major William Patten here."

The riders froze into a tableau entitled "The Night Riders of Bara's Gap."

16

"I'm buyin' chips, Shorty." This form of address, in the past at least, had always made the last Moore boy fighting mad: he preferred to be addressed as *Cap'n.* The major was sure Shorty could see him now. In a few seconds one of the riders would draw on him; in true fact it might possibly even be Shorty himself. The moon cleared a cloud. The major was outlined clearly—black clothes against silver sand, a man on foot against horsemen.

One of the riders directly behind Shorty went for his gun and was slammed backward across his horse's rump by the major's bullet. Heller and Mat Sun opened fire instantly and four other riders were shot out of their saddles. Shorty found himself, suddenly, sitting there all alone, quite statuesque, certainly self-consciously, like a figure upon a rented horse within a city park as it waits decorously for a troop of prams to be pushed across the bridle path.

"Get down, Shorty," the major said patiently.

"No!"

"You'll have more of a chance that way."

"Listen, Major. I'm a-goin' to let bygones be bygones, an' you can take a head start to get outta the county."

The major smiled, then began to chuckle. Mat Sun's voice came clearly from Shorty's right. "Get down or I shoot you down." In panic, Shorty turned in his saddle. Heller spoke from farther back on the same side. "Get down, Shorty. You beat up on a lotta women an' you stood right up there an' you outdrew three blind drunks. Now get down an' take your chances with a sober man."

Shorty turned back slowly toward the major and looked at him blankly. The major smiled at him indulgently, his mean-child eyes glittering. Shorty climbed down, slowly and stiffly. "Send your horse back to Frank," the major suggested. Shorty turned the horse, then hit it on the rump. Shorty stood there like a boy under a sprig of mistletoe, like the moon was mistletoe, quite shy, toeing the sand, licking his lips, but they stayed dry.

"You're scared sick an' you never was much," the major said in a kindly way, "so I'll shave the odds

17

for you, Shorty." He took a pack of cards out of his pocket. "This is a little bet we'll have, you an' me. I'll throw these cards in the air. If you can hit me afore I hit these cards, you cash the bet an' them two boys won't shoot you, less you try shootin' them. Fair enough?"

Shorty nodded. He started at a sudden birdcall in the night. He was wet with sweat.

"Now this is our little bet—I bet you those six horses that you don't make it," the major told him, throwing the cards high towards Shorty's head. A gun fired twice. The playing cards splattered like fireworks before they fell to cover the dead man.

Heller and Mat Sun came running. "Nobody can call us horse thieves now, boys," the major stated flatly. "We won them horses fair an' square."

Kate Grigson leaned against the side of The Jefferson House and waited for the major to return. She was dressed for traveling. The clothes were right for it even if her expression was not. Her expression showed she knew she wasn't going anywhere. She was lovely in the moonlight. The worn parts were invisible. The gift of hope she had always cherished now assembled the beauty of her face. She waited for a long time. When it was almost morning she went up the back stairs to get the letter for the major's Ma. When she found it it wasn't addressed to the major's Ma. It had two words written across its envelope: *Kate Grigson*. It was for her.

CHAPTER 2

THE men rode south and west. Three of the horses won from Shorty Moore were used as pack horses. The major guided them. Franklin Heller and Mat Sun each pulled two of the others behind their own. They rode easily, knowing there would be no avengers interested in following them.

When they crossed the 98th Parallel they left the East behind them as distinctly as if they had climbed

18

out of a garden over a picket fence. The green country, the trees, the water, the hills, the coolness and the companionable rains were gone. They rode on land as level as a painting of an ocean, and the land rolled slightly as an ocean does. Trees had been replaced by sagebrush and greasewood, scrub oak and mesquite. The rivers were aggraded and shallow, filled with quicksand and spoiled for drinking by alkali and gypsum. The sun struck from the sky as its burning reflection leaped up from the ground. The wind never stopped; there were no trees to stop it. It was hot and dry, hard and constant. "We could sell a lot of whisky out this way," the major said absently.

They rode over the baked and enormous land, over patch grass and sand, over the tough mesquite grass which would be fuel for beef and which could sleep in the heat for a long time, then perk right up with a little rain. They rode across the great plain between the humid timber behind them and the arid desert far ahead.

They rested when it was hottest. They rode at night and in the mornings when it was coolest. They had taken on full supplies at Fort Wilmot. They ate better than most men in the cities on buffalo meat or bear steaks, on antelope ribs barbecued on a stick over coals, and on consistent triumphs of sourdough biscuits which made Mat Sun a revered man.

On the sixth night, while they were chewing marrowgut lengths and staring into the fire, the major asked Heller:

"What'd you do afore you come to Fort Hill, Frank? I mean way back, before you went to sea."

Franklin Heller was a large man, five inches taller than the major and quite a few feet wider around. He was thirty-six years old. He had champagne-color hair, a deceptively bland disposition, and was one of the few men the major could remember having met who wore eyeglasses. They were nose-clipper spectacles without rims, and they were attached to a black ribbon which Heller wore around his neck. As he rode across Texas in half-range, half-city clothes wearing those glasses under a cream-colored Stetson, he re-

19

sembled a senator being brought home after a two-week drunk.

"Until I was twenty-two years of age," Heller answered, "I was sure my life would have been dedicated to cheese."

"Cheese?"

"Yes. Cheese. The adult form of milk. Hard and soft; new, mature, and overripe. Graced with a spectrum of smells from wispiness to shocking assault upon the nostrils; mild and bitter, salt or sweet, piquant or mellow." He sighed. "I grew up in the North where ever'thing is green except the lakes, which are bright blue even at midnight. The people is all Swedes and Germans. They make the best cheese you'll ever taste."

"I always wanted to try cheese," the major said, "but I never lived near none."

"I had my heart broke. I guess that's how come I feel so good all the time. Got the sad part over early."

"A woman?" the major whispered.

Heller nodded. A coyote howled miserably, shaking itself by its own miserable throat out in the darkness beyond the fire.

"We was both twenty-two years old, excepting that she fibbed about her true age, which was twenty-eight. Ever'body called her Kitten. She had beautiful ears and the lightest touch on a mandolin I ever heard."

"She sounds right nice."

"She was the only daughter of the biggest cheese-maker in the state. I mean, he was *rich*."

"Velly, velly good," Mat Sun said.

"We kept our love a secret until I could learn enough about cheese to have a chat with her Dad, and until I could tell my own father that I wouldn't be carrying forward the family business because I had set my course on bein' a cheese man."

"Did that rile your Daddy?"

"Broke his heart."

"What was the family business?"

"We made Christmas-tree ornaments just the way his father and his grandfather had made them in Germany. He called all his workers The Merry Dwarfs.

20

But that ain't why I quit. I have a feeling for cheese. I purely do."

"I got to try cheese sometime," the major mused. "I like the good things. Mat Sun knows that. But I don't often enough get to set next to them."

"Majuh like food velly good."

Heller, fairly started, did not want the trend of the conversation to veer away and took it up again quickly. "My father an' me had a bad time. A man can say some pretty long curse words in German. He yelled and wept. He threw my table through the window. When he chased me out of his room at the factory all the Merry Dwarfs was sullen because they'd heard what we was shoutin' an' they couldn't believe I could give up Christmas-tree ornaments for cheese. I guess that's what hurt," Heller said bitterly. "My father hated cheese." He shook his head. "He didn't even like butter . . . Anyway, as I walked out the north wing toward the door, a huge Dwarf name of Freddie Goldberg, who'd been our glazin' foreman for sixteen years, stared at me with hard eyes an' held up a Thousand Mirror Star over his head, our most expensive item, an' let it drop to crash to pieces on the stone floor."

"Men lose their heads when they are hurt," the major said.

"The next day was the day Kitten an' me had picked to tell her father that we was in love and that we wanted to marry. I faced him on a Sunday morning—I'll never forget it—in his private cheesery in their own home."

"What's a private cheesery?" The major reached out for more marrow gut. Mat Sun put more wood on the fire.

"Oh, a place where all the natural cheese aromas are sealed in, to blend with hundreds of other cheese aromas over the years. Where a man can feel that the temperatures are right and will not threaten his collection. Where the exotic cheeses of other lands may be stored in cheese vaults for sniffing and tasting on one's day of rest."

"Well, think of that," the major murmured. "I'll have to get me one of those someday."

21

"I sat there an' I looked him in the eye. I told him the way it was with me an' Kitten. He was a tall thin man, as straight as a cheesestick, with cheeks like Cheddar an' teeth like Roquefort. He asked me how I was with cheeses. I told him I had been working nights for two years at Kuhn's Cheese Farms under an assumed name, as I did not want any embarrassment for his family was I to fail."

"What did he say?"

"Well, major, he opened the big cheese vault beside his desk, shielding the combination. "Let's talk cheese," he said to me. Then he went on to explain how he would cut off little wedges from his collection and I would have to tell him what it was and where it was from. He stared at me hard an' told me he was doin' it because Kitten had told him she loved me, an' I near blubbered."

"Right nice," the major said.

"Yes. He told me I could sip Port wine between tastes and he slid the first little wedge at me. 'Course I knew it in one nibble. A soft Turkish cheese called Milhalic. I sipped some wine. He slid me the second wedge. 'Vasterbottensost,' I says . . ."

"What? What did you say?"

"Vasterbottensost. A slow-maturing hard cheese made in north Sweden. Oh, I had figured Kitten's father wouldn't want to give a peach like her up to any Tom, Dick, or Harry and that he had been importing remote cheeses for four months. Hell, I knew 'em all —from Touloumotyri to Domiati."

"What're they?"

"Oh, Touloumotyri is jest one of the names they give to the Feta cheese which is packed in goatskins in Greece, and Domiati is a so-called pickled cheese which is very big in Egypt."

"My, my!" the major said.

"I passed with flyin' colors."

"I should think so."

"I was so good he couldn't stop smilin'. He slid back the big double doors of the cheesery and we popped into the airlock which leads to the regular part of the house. We took off our long, white cheesers' coats and hung them on the knobs of Edam, which is a Dutch cheese made of cows' milk with about forty per cent fat content and bright red outside. We'll have to get you some of that sometime."

"Yes, sir, I'd like to try it."

"Kitten an' her mother was waitin' for us. They was both poached blonde women, complexions like a rarebit. We sat down to the first Sunday dinner I ever had with the Bückelmüllers. There was the most beautiful browned turkey on that table you ever seen an' I durned near yelped I was so pleased because roast turkey is the most favorite dish I ever et. Her daddy carved. He laid out thick slabs of white meat on the plate and spooned on potatoes with brown gravy, then sweet potatoes and some green peas. I'll never forget it. He told me to go right ahead. I took up a piece of that turkey an' began to chew—an' I stopped. I thought I was bein' poisoned. I looked all round me to get rid of it then I pulled the napkin up to my mouth so's I can spit it out an' the three Bückelmüllers look at me like I'd gone loco. 'What're you doin'?' Kitten's daddy says. 'Don't touch that turkey,' I says to him, almost stranglin', '—someone's poisoned it.' Kitten made a terrible sound. '*Poisoned?*' she yelled at me. 'That turkey was molded with Poppa's finest mozarella-type cheese!' "

Heller fell into a moody silence. He held his mouth in a bitter shape for a fraction of a moment before he allowed it to disappear. Molecules of the odor of chaparral drifted along close to the ground ahead of the steady night breeze, but in his memory Frank could still smell the milky blandness of that day, fourteen years before, when he had entered the climax which had changed his life.

"That's pretty hard times," the major said. "It's hard to get beat when you hold a king-high straight flush."

"I still can't believe it. I turned to Kitten but she looked away. There was more than just disappointment in her face. There was a kind of disgust. Then her father told me that it would be best if I left his house, and there were freckles of contempt all over his voice. I lost everything. My father. The biggest Christmas-tree-ornament business in the country. My sweetheart. An enormous cheese opportunity. My way of life."

"An' velly litch girl fathah," Mat Sun said.

"I drifted east after a while. I went to sea out of Boston. I put in at New Orleans after five years an' overslept sailing time. I been a bartender ever since."

"After we get settled," the major told him, "we'll think about stirrin' up some of that cheese you talk about."

"Best thing in the world for you," Heller said. "It sits on your stomach easy and each different kind of cheese is a different kind of friend."

CHAPTER 3

TEXAS won its independence from Mexico following the Battle of San Jacinto in 1836. The nine years which followed were difficult times for Texas. Its heroes quarreled; Mexico, England, and France threw salt on the wounds; very special interests in the United States wheedled and threatened by turn; investors in Texas bonds and scrip rocked with anxiety until, in 1845, Texas had herself annexed to the United States. Mexico viewed that action with alarm.

The Mexican War which followed was fought over a raw strip of land between the Nueces and Rio Grande rivers after Mexico had rejected an offer of forty million dollars for California and New Mexico. When the war was over the troops withdrew. Then the real fighting between Mexicans and Texans began.

The Nueces River was called the deadline for sheriffs. When the General Land Office of Texas mapped the area in 1839, it was noted "of this section of country little is known." Other maps called it the Wild Horse Desert. To *vaqueros* it was known as the *Brasada*. It was the roughest brush country of the southwest. In that brush moved over one million wild horses and cattle, there for the taking. It was a region about 295 miles long by 195 miles wide. A rider could move over fifty to seventy miles of it without seeing a dwelling or another human being. It held fugitives, cow thieves, and tinhorns. It was the bloody playground of bandits and Indians. It had some water. The ancient Mexican families who had held the land since the sixteenth century called the region the Desert of the Dead.

No establishment on that land was feasible without a body of armed fighting men to defend it. Within one month, with four more dead men in the ground after attacks and ambushes, the major understood the situation clearly. He set his base two hundred and sixty miles north and west of Brasada, on the Rio Grande. He made claim to sixty thousand acres of land. He would hunt cattle in the Brasada, then drive them out to his own range. He put together a cow camp beside the strong seep springs that fed into Pickering Creek, two miles north of the river. He built a crude four-room house of adobe brick and rough-laid rock, roofed with wattling packed hard and thick with earth. Around it he alloyed for two large corrals and around that he built a stockade with one tall tower for watching the horizons. He made friends with the Mexican community scattered over the area. They knew cattle, game, horses, and tracking. They had strength and courage. They had survived because they had stayed poor. They were Mexican *vaqueros,* the extraordinary breed who had invented the ways and means of handling half-wild cattle from horseback, who had invented the saddle pommel for use as a snubbing post for the rope, who used a branding iron from Spain to burn the mark of ownership into an animal's living hide. The tools and methods created by the *vaquero* realized the only way of harvesting the grass of the New World.

The major sweated out the work while he sweated out his gambling hunger. The withdrawal pains were as bad as those of a man who stops whisky or narcotics as suddenly. To the south, in Brownsville and Corpus Christi, the wheels were spinning and the cards plopping softly on green baize. He could be there in four days and he could throw himself into gambling until he was fulfilled again, and exhausted. But he

25

knew if he did ride south he would probably never come back to the ownership of things and, in the end, that was what he wanted more than gambling.

The abrupt wrench from the old ways to the legitimate life was not as total as it could seem. Each day he went to work again proved he was taking a bigger gamble than on any tiger he had ever bucked before. He settled down to learn the new play—and he had to learn it from soda to hock.

The family dynamics which ordered the new course were simple. His family had been crooked, all of them, but there had been a tradition to their dishonesty. The tradition demanded accumulation of property and the acquisition of large amounts of money to permit them to hold up their head among the people they had stolen from as well as among their peers, the other distinguished thieves. The Pattens had made their places on other frontiers and the major needed to match their record. In ten years of table gambling he had increased the original legacy from his father by $38,008, a gross yield of $3,800.08 per year which would have been difficult to get in any more respectable endeavor. Including his expenses, gifts, and loans over the ten-year period, adding the net to his legacy, he had been able to put aside $109,564, an enormous fortune.

He held that considerable amount of money but he owned no things—no bricks, no wood, no kine. He had acquired sixty thousand acres of land on which to establish these things and it was his immediate intention to add more land to that as soon as he had stocked it with cattle, buildings, and people. The traditional way of his family had been to get the money first, then steal the things, then legitimize the theft of both; the manner in which he carried his plan forward was nearly reflexive. His grandfather had been run out of Baltimore a rich man. His father had been run out of Ohio a richer man. It had been to some extent with the pride of a great traditionalist who has answered a mystic call that he had left Fort Hill after killing the Moore boys. His family, could they have seen him, would have been proud.

The major understood how to get people who knew how to ranch. He invited twenty-three *vaqueros,* sixteen of them Mexican hands, for a two day cookout at long tables strung out in front of the temporary stockade.

"Boys," he said to them, "ever' time you run cattle you got to bring an' cook your own grub. You bring along your tin cup, some coffee, some salt, some sugar an' maybe a supply of cornbread. Sometimes you take bacon, but mostly you get your meat on the range. Now, I'm fixin' to change all' that. I jest happen to have workin' for me the finest cook in the world an' he's a man who purely loves to cook. Jest to show him off, an' mebbe to show you boys how ranchin' should be done where a man who works hard all day can jest set back an' have delicious food come to him, I have invited all the *vaqueros* in the neighborhood of about a hunnert an' ten miles to stop by for a tastin'. An' I tell you this. If you sign up to ride with my outfit, you're goin' to have food like this ever' day." He stepped aside and the eating started.

Mat Sun served Son-of-a-Bitch Stew the first day; he had put it together with loving care by taking from the carcasses of nine freshly slaughtered beeves the brains, liver, heart, sweetbreads, kidneys, and marrow gut, washing them all well, then cutting them into pieces about an inch square. He put these into Dutch ovens with pieces of suet tallow as big as hen eggs (confiding to Frank Heller that the tallow pulled off the beef kidney was the very best) and enough water to cover them. Mumbling Ning Po incantations, he sprinkled on handfuls of salt and chili powder, then let it all boil until the meat was tender. At each oven he mixed a handful of flour with some of the juices and added it to the stew, levigating like he had four shoulders, and let it cook for another hour or so. The visiting riders couldn't stop eating.

He gave them prairie oysters—split calf testicles fried in deep hot fat, then salted well—and blanket steak, made by cutting fat off the beef and letting it melt in the Dutch ovens, then dropping the steaks in water, salting them and rolling them in flour, then plopping them into the hot ovens with the melted fat.

He piled red-hot coals on the lids of the ovens and stretched the steaks across them until they were done. He put flour into the juice and stirred it smooth with water and salt and pepper, then let it stew until it was a thick gravy. The smells made the guests roll their eyes like mustang stallions and slaver all over everything.

Added to that line of chow were endless quantities of sourdough biscuits and a few hundred sucamagrowl dumplings. The hands were letting out their belts hole by hole, and the thought that they might never have to cook for themselves again seemed to make their hands tremble as they lifted the food from fifth helpings to their mouths. Twenty-three men said they had never eaten that well in their lives. Out of the twenty-three every man pushed to sign with the major. Out of the twenty-three, seventeen were still with him ten years later, still eating with their eyes popping. Of the six who weren't still there, two had died from delirium tremens and four got themselves killed brush-popping.

They moved into the Brasada in the late winter and set the traps. The traps were corrals fifty or sixty feet in diameter with an inlet which was a toothed set of entrances called triggers, and an outlet set of exits which led into holding pastures as big as a hundred acres, more or less, varying in size with each of the stock catches.

The motion of men and animals brought life to the stillness. Antelope bounded away from them. Wild turkey whirred into flights and, far off, bands of wild mustangs galloped toward the horizon, streaming their long manes behind them.

The noise was maniacal. Steers charged riders, cows milled and screamed in the thick dust which rose in clouds twenty feet into the air to be gilded into near-opaqueness by the hammering sun, calves bellowed, and horses bit and kicked. *Vaqueros* cursed, yelled, and sang. The sun piled its weight upon everything in an orange-colored rage.

There were watering places inside the traps to pull the cattle in as they were driven by the riders and the catch dogs. After the stock were in, the men drove staves into the ground, which was tufted with burnt

28

gamma grass over pebbly soil, to make a fence to hold the rest of the beef inside.

Out in the brush there were three catch dogs running with every two riders and the wild cattle couldn't have been brought in without them. They included every breed of dog but were mostly mastiff and deer hound. Man and dog, the two great enemies of history, had banded together to domesticate wild cattle. The major's catch dog was a golden red dachshund named Pepper who trailed up the wild steers and held them at bay until a rider could get to the spot. If the mossyhorns broke out and ran before the rider arrived, Pepper would leap up and catch a great horned beast by the nose and hang on by his teeth until the critter stopped running and learned to stay in one place.

The sun's heat grew more and more intense. Men and animals ate pounds of dust. The beards caked on the riders and their lips cracked and their hands grew horny.

The major let in the first hold-up, a good-sized herd of gentle cattle, to mix with the wild stock. He rode slowly among the cattle to get them used to a moving horse with a man on its back. Gradually he drove the pack around the enclosure until the snuffy stock simmered down and seemed willing to stay in the herd, then moved the other riders in to take over. They would close in gradually, surrounding all the beef but keeping far enough away to give them plenty of air. Cows that kept trying to bust out now were tied down and their upper eyelids cut off; the first brush those cattle ran into to try to hide would be a mite hard on the eyes.

The cattle-trapping was an endless process endlessly repeated. With the major as pilot rider, the herd would be led out of the holding pasture into the corral, held there to get them used to humans, then taken out and driven to the new Patten ranch on the northwest. The major took the point of the herd and his *vaqueros* took the swing. There were no drags, not with that pack of wild, running yaks. It was the work of five men for each man to do his part to hold the herd together and keep it headed in the direction it had to go.

As the season moved along the outfit grew. The major and the expanding outfit of *vaqueros,* cooks, and horse-wranglers were in the thickest brush and the roughest country, where a snake could hardly make a trail, for four separate round-ups of approximately five months each. Every time they brought back four to five thousand head of cattle. At the end of two years of back-breaking work, the major had sixteen thousand cattle which were worth four dollars a head on the range and forty dollars a head delivered to a buyer, wherever the buyer could be found.

The major didn't need the money and he didn't have to ship. He began to buy herds from other spreads during droughts, and his determined stocking of the ranch brought a minor cattle boom to the Mexican states of Tamaulipas and Coahuila.

In 1849, the major negotiated with the state of Texas for the purchase of his largest section of land up to that time. It was a rectangular tract of flat grassland of 34.5 square leagues or 149,250 acres which faced northern Coahuila along the Rio Grande. Counting the small parcels he had added to his original sixty-thousand-acre claim, the Patten ranch encompassed 239,676 acres of range land. Counting the original wild stock of sixteen thousand head of cattle, then adding broken-herd purchases of another fourteen thousand, plus twenty-three thousand he had bought from Los Patteños, the ranch held a basic fifty-three thousand head of cattle. However, the major had not sold off any stock. Cattle increase at the rate of thirty-three and one-third per cent per year, naturally doubling the original stock every three years. Over the six-year period to 1850, this natural increase had brought his total beef-cattle stock to ninety-four thousand head before he decided to begin to sell. To round out that stock figure, he owned 6,285 horses, 6,300 sheep, and 8,300 goats. He employed 197 *vaqueros,* American and Mexican, to work the stock on 686 saddle horses.

In 1850 the big Patten ranch house was finished. It matched the major's expanding ambitions and his deep feeling for greater comfort through greater luxury. The building flung itself out in the shape of a large "Y." One wing was two stories high. It was made of milled lumber and field rock. Its ceilings were eighteen feet high. It was stark white with black shutters. The tips of the "Y" were encircled by high adobe walls, making three expansive patios. Six ranch hands worked full time, watering and gardening in these spaces to create oases of flowers, rug grass, pirul trees, and gushing fountains. The major and Mat Sun lived in the big house. Franklin Heller stayed in the presidential suite at the Pickering Hotel in Pickering City.

In the course of bringing culture, civilization, and a good deal more cash money into the wilderness of southwest Texas, Major Patten founded Pickering City, setting it on the river two miles from the ranch house, in 1849. Pickering City was built in part of the area which had been designated by the surveyors of the King of Spain as *Porción* 180, originally granted by the crown in 1767 to Doña Conchita Castelli Gair y Hombria, Duquesa de Salgado, to settle a quarrel over an extended game of piquet. Major Patten named the city for his maternal grandmother, Martha Irene Pickering, one of the founders of the ladies auxiliary of the Independent Order of Oddfellows in 1817. Within five years as county seat, Pickering City (as shown in the census of 1850) contained 134 inhabitants, 103 of whom were unable to read or write; 151 dwelling places, one church, and one school. Drinking water sold for $1.50 per barrel. The town held 491 registered aliens. By 1910, Pickering City was to become isinglass capital of the Southwest, to remain in that industrial sun for almost seven months.

Pickering City was built where timber was scarce. It was made of sun-baked mud bricks and rough-laid stone. Pickering House, the courthouse, the mercantile store, and the bank were part timber dressed with stone. The major had laid the town out with the large, dusty courthouse plaza bulging out at the middle of the main street. The Pickering House was at the west end of the main street; the livery stable and the Pickering Academy for Young Women were at the east end; they were three hundred yards apart. Abe Weiler's printing office, which put out a newspaper called *The Peecee Times*, was at the middle of Main Street, facing Courthouse Square.

From the day Franklin Heller was named Managing Director of the combination hotel, saloon, and dance hall—the town's first edifice—on 12 February 1850, Pickering City was a growing community. In its way it became a sub-trading center for the region. There were no railroads but people moved with difficulty on riverboats, more sedately on wagon trains, and on horseback. Occasionally, ocean-going vessels reached the small port of Brownsville, Texas. Blood, Fitzgerald & Neal opened a wagon route to New Orleans in 1849; this sometimes brought grass freight to Pickering City. Mail came in bi-monthly from Corpus Christi and weekly from Laredo. There were problems of growth. It was difficult to keep the weevils out of the rice, and it was to combat such things that Major Patten appointed Franklin Heller as Commissioner of Public Health for the city, an office he held for forty-three years—in addition to his other duties.

CHAPTER 4

ON a beautiful morning in the spring of 1850, Major Patten acted upon something of which he had been aware for some time. He knew that some of the Rio Grande families, as the result of old grants from the Spanish crown or later grants from the Mexican government, owned the immense tracts which were registered in his name at the capital in Austin. He knew he had enough guns and men to enforce his possession of that land. Although he had never been approached by any individual, group, or government to accede the land he had paid for in Austin, he thought instinctively in terms of percentages of profit and loss and likelihood, and it seemed to him entirely likely that combinations of circumstances at some future time could cause him to lose all which he had built. He had been considering the probabilities for some time. He knew how little the Mexican families valued their lost property under a foreign flag. He knew how little they would ask for property they considered could not be lived on. He also learned (and this changed all existing odds) that the titles Mexicans had offered for sale farther down in the Rio Grande valley had been upheld by an act of the Texas legislature one month before, confirming the rightful ownership of original Spanish and Mexican land grants to the original heirs and succeeding purchasers.

He began to secure his own position by locating the heirs of a portion of the river south of the ranch house, in the region facing the state of Tamaulipas. Instead of sending an emissary, he rode out himself across the river and rode for two days until he came to the hacienda of the widow of Martínez, her sons, and their wives. He was made welcome. He explained that he had ridden out to them to acknowledge his personal debt to Mexico. He would have been hospitably received in any case, but his intentions were so honorable as stated, his conception so *charro,* that he was made welcome with all doors open.

They told him that none of them even remotely considered a return to that forsaken land. If he wanted to buy it they would sell it, but in any event they had no intention whatsoever of ever attempting to occupy it again. Within two days, which were devoted mainly to eating good food, listening to music, and drinking good brandy, they all set their hands and seals to a warranty deed conveying their property of 15,514 acres on the northern side of the Rio Grande to Major Patten for the sum of three hundred dollars, a unit price of something less than two cents an acre.

The major rode on across northern Mexico. Within two weeks he had acquired all but the largest piece of the land he had not owned, but which he lived upon, for an average price of 1.84 cents an acre. He was honored for buying it. His name and reputation went out before him as he rode.

The largest unit of range and not yet so obtained comprised 34.5 square leagues, or 149,250 acres, of land, which faced the state of Coalhuila along the Rio Grande. The major had no illusions as to his recourse should this final *hacendado* of his journey refuse to sell. If he informed the major that he would, instead, choose to occupy the land, the major was ready to rerturn to the ranch, fortify it, send emissaries to Austin and Washington for Rangers and federal troops, then wait for the Mexican owners to attempt to eject him from the tract.

With this in his mind, at the beginning of the third week of his circuit Major Patten rode into the property of Dr. Don José Vicuña y Arias, the greatest single cattle ranch of the world in its time. Years before the founding of any English colony on the American coast, the ranching ancestors of Dr. Don José Vicuña y Arias were branding forty thousand calves a year on this range.

His ranch had more *vaqueros* than many ranches had *vacas*. It was the home of 2,439 employees, utilizing 326 buildings of varying sizes on 1,843,746 acres of grazing land in the states of Coalhuila and Chihuahua, all of it shaped like a gigantic isosceles triangle upon the map of Mexico. The ranch was stocked with 818,093 head of cattle, 22,161 horses, 89,252 sheep, and 54,517 goats. At times the noise must have been horrendous. It was Don José's boast that within thirty days he could deliver twenty thousand head of cattle, all of them of any one color and any one age, from calves to five-year-olds. He owned more cattle than had ever before been collected on one continent.

As Major Patten had traveled from Mexican ranch to ranch he had been able to compare his own holdings with smugness, but when he had to ride more than two hundred and sixty miles from the eastern boundary of the Vicuña ranch to its *casco,* he felt what he owned was like a matchbox next to a cathedral. As he made the four-day ride to the headquarters buildings he passed such toys as an Egyptian barge on a drying river bed, four great musters of peacocks, a cemetery with a three-story marble mausoleum, and two great stone faces, not Mayan, standing thirty-six feet high, which had somehow found their way from the South Pacific as exotic primeval fetors. He passed large greenhouses. The plants growing within them were the plants of England and Scotland, the flowers of the Lowlands and the bottom coasts. He saw brilliantly varicolored *mañadas* of horses, each a group of twenty-five mares led by a stallion, all divided into different colors, each color a moving unit—mouse-colored, maroons, paints, sorrels, duns, whites, blues, palominos, and blacks.

The outer rim of the Vicuña hacienda was a meandering river. The *casa grande* was the biggest single building the major had ever seen. It was, in fact, the Late Señora Vicuña's ancestral castle. Don José had earned a degree in veterinary medicine from the University of Edinburgh while he steadfastly courted a stubborn Scottish girl he had met at a ball at the British Embassy in Mexico City; she married him five years after the day they had met, the day he received his degree. When the last of the Scottish Gourlays had passed on to the arms of St. Andrew, Don José had had the castle taken down and shipped to Mexico to surprise his wife and cheer her. It had been erected at the ranch headquarters at vast expense while Don José and his bride had wintered in Tangier. When she returned she had wept for joy.

Clustered about the great stone building were the huts of herdsmen and workers; corrals and sheds for livestock; storerooms, granaries, and workshops; a smithy and a high-backed pink church with a lofty cross and a heavy bell. This hive was surrounded by a tall wall, crenellated and loop-holed, with guard towers studding out of each of the four corners. Beyond the stone walls, great pastures were fenced by league upon league of rough rock and by endless rows of spiked, cultivated cactus grown as fences. The herds and flocks of sheep, goats, mules, and horses were penned and guarded by night, pastured only by day.

Inside the wall, at the great door to the castle, Major Patten allowed his horse to be taken from him. He walked bemusedly across the flagstones, under the vaulted ceiling of the entrance hall, through a blessed coolness like that of a brewery, following a beautiful and stately female butler.

As he entered an enormous room, Dr. Vicuña was seated under a half-glass roof, setting the broken foreleg of an Irish wolfhound who was being held down by four small, pretty Indian girls. Dr. Vicuña smoked a long, very black cigar as he worked. Occasionally the silent female butler would hold a small dish under the end of it and tap it lightly to catch the ash.

"Just three more minutes, my dear sir," the doctor rumbled.

"Thank you," the major answered.

If Major Patten could have expressed what he felt, he might have taken off his boots and socks and walked among the furs or reached out for one of the bottles of perfume he could see on the far wall shelves to pour it over his arms and chest. He felt as if he had come home after a journey of seeking across his life-time. He was one with his surroundings, immersed in an ineffably sensual atmosphere. The room was forty feet square. The walls were lined with soft-blue cashmere tweed. Two divans, twenty feet long and seven feet wide, covered with a whispered shade of emerald satin and holding explosions of yellow velvet cushions, stretched along two walls. The carpeting seemed to be stretched puma skin, or perhaps it was the exquisitely tanned hides of *asarajado* fighting bulls, under scattered rectangles of blue fox.

The garments of the five women around the doctor were brown and soft. They did not hang upon the rounded frames of flesh, they clung to them; and each body seemed to have been touched with the terminal fragrances of ambergris, civet, and musk. Major Patten's upper torso was drawn forward and his nostrils opened and shut three times, like a clenching and unclenching fist. At once, the doctor said, "The Greeks regarded perfumes as medicines for curing nervous disorders. The wildest bird may be tamed by rubbing oil of bergamot on its nostrils and it is written that the enchanting houris of the Mohammedan hereafter are created from the purest musk. There is much to say in favor of perfume." The doctor discouraged any reply by returning to concentration upon his work. The major felt a need for rutting, roiling, rubbing, ructating sex explode throughout his liquated hollowness. He was staring at the butler. She lifted her eyelids and stared into his eyes from fifteen feet away, colored, then let herself stare at his trousers. He turned away.

The marble nudes had muscular tonic to their skin;

36

as with Bernini's work, the male fingers seemed to dig into the female flesh. The sun disposed itself softly through the amber-tinted half roof of glass and spotted gleaming notes of light upon row upon row of small bottles of scent that lined the far wall. The shelving was placed so close together as to suggest that the bottles were really gallon jugs seen from hundreds of yards away. From somewhere a chamber orchestra played Mozart softly, tirelessly, and with stirring effect. The major walked to the broad window and looked down upon the streets and buildings of the *casco* and marveled at its industry and size.

"A bull knocked this one over," Dr. Vicuña said, as though in mid-conversation with the major. "Stepped on his leg breaking it cleanly. This one then rose up and raced forward to tear away the bull's *cojones*. Woo! I wince to think of the moment, but what a sense of outrage this dog has. There!" He kneaded the small buttock of the girl standing nearest to him and spoke in Spanish: "Carry him to the stables and speak softly to him, tickling his throat in this manner—" the doctor scrambled his fingers lovingly under the girl's behind, causing all the girls except the butler to giggle with delight, "—before you remove his muzzle." The huge dog attempted to thrash about. Don José leaned down, put his echinated face into the dog's ear and murmured something. The dog became serenely still. "A little flattery goes a long way with an Irish wolfhound," the doctor explained. The girls carried the dog out with pomp, while Don José washed his hands in a white bowl held by the lovely butler. When his hands were dry he powdered them with care, saying, "I hope this doesn't seem over-fastidious to you, sir, but if I do not use the powder my hands seem to stick to everything I touch, for I exude some sort of glue from my palms." He advanced to Major Patten and welcomed him, shaking his hand and guiding him to a group of deep chairs under the glass roof, to seat both of them at a large, low round table which held an enormous bowl of fruit, two bottles of Scotch whisky and a cigar chest.

Dr. Vicuña wore a red spade beard and a country coat of cocoa-brown linen which seemed to be lined throughout with red and yellow stripped material which was rolled over the edges as binding. His capacious trousers were bottle green. He wore soft black carpet slippers. Most of him seemed to be dressed more for a stroll through the Princes Street gardens than to cope with the *mesquitals* of northern Mexico.

He was a formidable man who stood six feet six inches tall, a measure which raised him eleven inches higher than the major. His voice was profoundly deep and its sounds had been tugged, pushed, and pulled into a British line by English and Scottish masters of diction. He spoke English with a royal-family accent. He spoke Spanish and three Indian languages with his staff and ranch workers. He spoke French, Italian, German, English, and Spanish with his only daughter. He spoke Latin with the elderly priest of his late wife, and something strangely different to his dogs and horses. Don José also had a command of pidgin English, Kuan Hua, *bêche-de-mer,* Yiddish, Swahili, and Romany.

Red beard and fair skin notwithstanding, the doctor was Latin in every way. His exophthalmic eyes were dark brown. His square white teeth could have chunked out a cave in a pumpkin. He had a nose not unlike the beak of the eagle on the badge of the Republic of Mexico, and the nose is the eloquent spokesman of every face.

Invertebrates may have their noses almost anywhere. Insects have their noses placed at the ends of antennae. The nose is in pits on the heads of various worms, in the feet of ticks, and near the gills of molluscs, but the osphradium of Dr. Vicuña was placed proudly, as the prow of his being, at the center of his large, strong face, its base like a strong forearm sculpted in rose alabaster as it held the top half of an archer's great bow. "Great is the ornament," John Bulwer said in 1650, "that the face receiveth from the nose." The doctor's nostrils were like the mouths of the cannon which took the charge of the Light Brigade at Balaclava. The nose was not merely fleshy. It seemed to have rippling muscles. It was a nose for smelling, for threatening, and for rooting up the tender tendons of writhing maidens.

His mouth was wide and heavy. His eyes were bulging, and glistening. They bracketed this nose, all of it captured within the foam of red hair, eyebrows, and beard, all corroborating the nose's implicit testimony of virility.

"Have a cigar," Don José said, opening the chest and extending it. Within were the chocolate ridges of tobacco logs of deep mahogany. They were long and thick and resinous. The major accepted one warily.

"While we may agree that there is possible anaphrodisia in tobacco, there are other comforts," Dr. Vicuña said. "When smoking such cigars as these in moderation, I have found, by and large, that all functions improve." He leaned forward to light the major's cigar, then his own. Both men puffed experimentally.

Major Patten had taken on the look of a young religious. "This is a *cigar!*" he sang. "What a flavor! What chewiness!"

"You please me greatly."

"I mean it, sir!"

"Well. These are called *Maduros*. Cuban, of course. The richest cuttings from the top of the plant. Cured by the sun and fairly popping with juices and oils. Very rich."

"Oh very. Very."

"Melted chocolate, in fact. From the loamy soil of Vuelta Abajo. Absorbent clay. Soft sand. Right amounts of sun and air and dampness. After all, Cuba itself is a huge humidor."

"But how can I get some?"

From the instant he met Don José, the major's fleshly spirit was released to dart like a chubby, resplendent bumblebee among the sticky flowers which he had always envisioned as being The Life. It was as though Don José became the major's *chorda tympani,* carrying cargoes of taste impulses to his brain and senses.

Don José strode to a large table which seemed to be held down by a huge vase of many riotously colored flowers. "Naturally it will take a bit of time to effect delivery," he said, "but you will have the joy, as you wait, of knowing that you have given me the happiness of sending twenty-five boxes of these to your house, wherever it is."

The major looked startled but ecstatic.

"But, my word, you don't have a drink!" The doctor sprang into action, clutching the note-paper, and poured three fingers of Scots whisky into a tumbler for each of them. They clinked glasses. "I was educated in Scotland and, to precede the consequences of that training, I shall quote Bunyan: *'The way to the Celestial City lies through this town where the Lusty Fair is kept; and he that will go to the city and not yet through the town must needs go out of the world.'* "

"Bunyan?"

The doctor nodded.

"Who is Bunyan?"

"An English writer."

"Would you mind just noting that name on the same piece of paper?"

The doctor leaped to his feet and strode to the large table, talking as he walked and as he wrote with the quill. "The whisky of Scotland is where the lusty fair is kept. It is the wine of their country. The art of distilling is to be revered. Old, you know. In his *Meteorology* Aristotle said, for he must be first to be quoted on all things, then Shakespeare, but—oh—long before Aristotle they were distilling whisky from flowers in India. At least as long ago as 800 B.C. Scots have been practicing the art since the thirteenth century. In Mexico we have several distillations which are unique and delicious, if you will allow me to say so, but I was a long time in Scotland and I drank a lot of Scots whisky, so there you are. Drink up, sir!"

Major Patten goggled, then they both knocked their whiskies back. The major's sigh was a lasciviously spending thing as he lowered the glass. "That's the smoothest-tastin' likker I ever had in my life," he said with tones of supreme admiration. "It don't grab you by the throat an' pound your head up and down on the floor one bit."

"How appreciative you are!"

"Dee-licious!"

"It *is* rather splendid."

"Where can I buy some?"

"It is necessary that it be purchased in Scotland," the barbigerous veterinary purred as he strode again to the quill pen and paper at the large table. "That takes a bit of time, of course, but my people are most reliable and once you have placed your revolving order you will find that it will be delivered on a regular basis, Indians and bandits notwithstanding, for my wine agents in London are thorough men."

"London?"

"Yes."

"Ah."

"Of course, I will see that you are accommodated until the shipments can begin. I shall send along five cases to get you started."

"Five cases!"

"You have greatly complimented Scotland, a country dear to my heart, and you must accept these few bottles with my compliments." He stared intently at the major. His nose seemed ready to charge. "What is your name, sir? Where may I send the cigars and the whisky?"

"Major William Patten. My place is—"

"*Aaaaah!*" Don José rose to his full height from bending over the note-paper. "You, then, must be the young man who has been insisting that he must pay back to Mexico for the land which is ours." His wide brown eyes were warm with pleasure. His head nodded with admiration. Absentmindedly he reached for the talcum and shook it over his hands. "What a gallant conception for a young man to undertake. Ah, sir," and he waggled his red beard approvingly, "ten cases of whisky it must be. I can do no less."

He wrote rapidly upon the foolscap, dotted all manner of letters enthusiastically, then handed the paper to the voluptuously dressed female butler who was always near him. "My compliments to the Señorita. If it pleases her, tell her that her loving father is presently chatting with the estimable Major William Patten whom she madly admires. Then attend to the delivery of the cigars and the whisky to the Patten ranch, if you will." She took the slip from him and started to leave. "And, oh—Juana. Please include a volume of Mr. Bunyan's *The Pilgrim's Progress* in that shipment." Don José beamed upon the major. He returned to his seat, nearer the whisky. "In an abstract sense," he said, "my daughter's admiration for you and the enormous sense of honor implied by your gesture in offering to pay for that land, is simply boundless."

"Well, I—"

"She, too, enjoys Scots whisky, so you will have a good deal in common."

"Well, I sure thank you, Señor Vicuña, but—"

"Call me Doc."

"Well, I sure thank you, Doc, but that ain't the way it is."

"The way what is, sir?"

"I mean, I been just ridin' around to the ranchos tryin' to tie up a lotta legal loose ends. Jest good business. I mean it may be a little cute, but it sure as hell ain't gallant."

Don José spread his large hands wide. "My dear major," he said, "you know that and, of course, I know that. But this is a most prosaic part of the world for a young woman, and anything which brings to her a feeling of honor among men and valor—indeed, of chivalry—is not to be minimized." He stared steadily at the major. "Do I make myself clear?"

"Why—sure, Doc."

"Have another whisky."

Don José poured four fingers of the Aberdeen ambrosia into each glass. He strode to a cabinet of carved wood, opened it, and removed a tiny crystal vial with a slender crystal stem. He brought it to the table and filled it to its brim with fifteen drops of whisky. "My daughter, like myself," he said, "is abject about Scots whisky."

He sat down to await her arrival, stretching out his legs—which gave the impression that a ship might be launched down their ways.

"I know about your ranch," he said. "You have made a great success in a short time, and that requires a natural stockman. Have you always been in the cattle business?"

"No."

"What did you do?"

Although no one had ever asked him that set of questions before, it did not occur to the major to respond with anything but the true answer. "Six years ago, and for ten years before that, I was a professional gambler."

"A gambler? Where?"

"Oh, around saloons and honkatonks in Tennessee, Oklahoma, an' East Texas."

"Fascinating! Did you ever cheat?"

"Well, sure. Sometimes. Like I said, I was a professional gambler."

"Oh, really! Oh, this is splendid! Do you think you could teach me to cheat at dominoes?" His interest brought him far forward in his chair.

"Well, sure. Any kind of game."

"Priceless!" The doctor fell back again. "And you will teach me?" He leaned forward.

"Any time."

"You cannot know what this means to me. You see, I am burdened, in a sense, with the elderly confessor of my late wife. A good man, you understand; in fact, in very nearly every way a saintly man. He has but two vices: (a) he cheats at dominoes and (b) he crows over whomever he defeats. I cannot detect how he cheats. With your kind help, I shall be able to defeat him, then when I win I shall teach him humility by not crowing. Then I shall defeat him again and again and again to teach him more and more and more humility until—when I am sure he has mastered humility—I shall defeat him again and I shall crow over him." Don José laughed with great power, and shaking the furniture with his bounding body, he caused the tiny, fragile vial of Scots whisky to tremble anxiously. "What a lucky day!" he said, shaking talcum powder into his hands as the lovely butler returned to the room.

She went to Don José's side and spoke to him in soft, rapid Spanish. He listened, nodding sympathetically. "My daughter sends her regrets, Major Patten," he reported. "She will be unable to join us. She is taking her whistling lessons."

"Whistlin' lesson?"

"At the moment she is learning to whistle Handel's

43

'Water Music.' A stunning effect. It is part of the tradition of the women in our family."

"Is that so?"

"Yes. She pleads that you remain to join us for dinner, which is most unusual for her. You would of course have stayed in any event, but my daughter is something of a recluse—in certain areas. She has asked me to tell you that she is filled with emotion at your determination to demonstrate one man's recognition of common justice and courtesy due to a great nation."

"Shucks, Doc. My best offer ain't been but two cents an acre."

"Hmm. Let us dispose of that. First, I would not consider accepting two cents an acre, and that is my final word. One cent is more than the property is worth, but I will accept a cent an acre just to get this business over and done with. Do you accept?"

"Why, hell yes."

"Good. Now, my dear major," the tomentose veterinary leaned forward again to emphasize his point and to pour them each another jar of fine whiskey, "I trust that I need not ever again remind you that the financial side of your acquisition of all Mexican property is to be put aside and forgotten, never to be referred to in the presence of *any Mexican* ever again. Agreed?"

"Yes, sir."

The two men set their glasses upon the table. They reached out and shook hands firmly, smiling at each other, each made happier by their meeting.

CHAPTER 5

THE MAJOR GOT A TASTE OF LUXURY THAT DAY AND that evening which he not only never lost but which widened across the remainder of his life like a sonorous musical note played upon a clutch of oboes.

At nine o'clock that night Dr. Vicuña and Major Patten walked slowly across the great hallway of the castle, following the gynecocentric butler who trailed nodules of spikenard, sweet marjoram, myrobalan fruits, myrrh, and cinnamon. From above them came the sound of skirling bagpipes, muted as though played by sporraned ghosts at a great distance. Before they were more than half-way across the hall to their destination, a thirty-six-foot-high double door into which massive diamonds of purple hardwood had been carved, the bagpipes reached the end of their small journey through tilted noises, and the hastening heat of a single Flamenco guitar—played as by an Andalusian gypsy when either much silver money or many chickens are in direct view—spilled down upon them. The major stumbled because, unwittingly, one of his feet had attempted to dance.

The enchanting butler, her eyes like large charcoal kisses, swung open the huge door and the feeling of a cold stone castle was left behind. The chamber into which they entered was warm with yellow light upon blue damask silk and muted red tones within a Persian carpet. A fire breathed hungrily at them as the wind spoke down the flue. The draperies were pale orange, blue, and beige, flanking blue painted consoles against apple-green walls. An arrogant Velázquez commanded the major from a distant wall and the major thought at once *throw away every stick of furniture in the ranch house and start all over again, if I can only discover how it is done.* He turned slowly at the doctor's voice and looked into the haunted eyes of Maria de Lourdes Vicuña. Despite his control of the Scots whisky and himself, he almost fell forward upon her bosom.

As she held his hand, greeting him, her nostrils quivered like a doe's. "What you have chosen to do," she said to him, "has reached me and touched me deeply." Her ten fingertips ran lightly down the sleeves of his jacket from shoulders to wrists as though the story of the sins of his life had been printed there and this was her method of reading them. The stunning lady butler offered him a sherry. The major sipped it. It was whisky. He looked to Don José, who smiled mildly at him and saluted him simply. The eyes of Maria de Lourdes Vicuña nailed him again. He

45

swayed. "To me, what you have done has more significance than the work of General Molina."

"The bandit?" the major asked breathlessly.

"The patriot."

"It is the same thing, Major Patten, each from a different view," Don José interjected smoothly. The major gulped and bowed his head, stifling any argument which flickered weakly within him. When he looked up, her lovely eyes were still contemplating him gratefully. Her nostrils were agitating rapidly and before him the eyes grew filmy. "Ideals are more important than enemies," she said.

Dinner was announced.

Compared with the enormity of the castle, the great hall, and the drawing-room, the exquisite compartment in which they dined was so small and so perfect in each detail of execution that the major had the dazed feeling of sitting at a table in a room within a ship's model which has been built inside a small bottle. The room had walls of painted wood. The sideboards were red lacquer and ormolu. Around the rich and flawless setting of the table were placed three Louis XV chairs with white frames around Pompeiian-red satin. The draperies framing the single broad window were cloth-of-gold. Over all glowed a heavy rock-crystal chandelier.

Major Patten was thirty-seven years old and he had never dined upon table linen before. He had never eaten more than two courses at any meal. He had never tasted wine. He memorized everything he tasted, touched, or saw that night.

The thick candles in the silver candelabram, too heavy for a woman to lift, caressed the silver damask cloth and placed intense silver lights upon the spoons. The plates were rose quartz. The glasses were carved crystal, four to a place. The first wine was dull gold.

The major sat at Maria de Lourdes' right, facing Don José. Maria spoke to the major, at the major, and even—once or twice—with the major, but he remembered so little of it later that he could not be sure it had happened.

The procession of color and taste began. Pink salmon with finely ground white onions and coarsely

46

ground black pepper; golden soup; pale green cucumber sauce that covered hauchinango; maroon beets, chinese-red tomatoes, purple Burgundy; ivory sauce sparkling with curry over a snow breast of wild fowl; beige bread, amber champagne; many subtle smells.

Sounds which were set internally with odd words flew into his ears and out again. He could not relate the sounds to things he remembered. "I eat to taste, yes. But I eat for the textural pleasures and most of all for my nose."

Don José had said that; then he heard Maria de Lourdes address him. "Do you have an educated nose, Major Patten?"

"I don't know," he answered.

"Papa has a famous nose."

"Yours, Maria, will be the most famous this family has ever known."

"It is a beautiful nose," the major said and Maria de Lourdes laughed with delight, only to stop suddenly and preoccupy herself with eating.

"I am thinking of the Goethe play, *Faust,*" Don José said, "which I read aloud to your mother when we were in Rome in '37. As I recall, in the second part, when Paris enters the Emperor's court he creates quite a stir among the noses of the women. A Young Lady says, "Mixed with the incense-steam what odor precious steals to my bosom, and my heart refreshes?" An older lady responds, "Forsooth, it penetrates and warms the feeling! It comes from him." Then the Oldest Lady tells them, "His flower of youth unsealing, it is: youth's fine ambrosia ripe, unfading, the atmosphere around his form pervading.'" Don José had addressed his performance only to Maria de Lourdes. She would not look at him. He turned his attention to Major Patten. "Someone has written that as we grow older the sense of smell is the first to dull. Not so with me." He raised his glass. The two friends clinked and drank.

The major was aware of but one vibrance in that room: Maria de Lourdes. She shocked and assaulted, caressed and charged, all of his senses each time she moved or spoke. He found himself not only unable to speak but disinterested in speech. Her beauty and her

47

gifts were so exalted that they had no use for comment, so he settled upon staring. He pretended to listen and he stared. The food, the wine, the music, the gleaming linen and silver; the massive movements, sights, and sounds of Don José, the murmured offerings of the servers, all remained as distant to him as the memory of some average morning in a schoolroom would be to a swordsman who was fighting for his life. He stared at her. She was a tiny woman. Her silk dress was black and yellow in alternate bias stripes over a lace flounce by Worth. Her hair was as red as her father's beard. Her chatoyant eyes were gray-black against pale ivory skin. She had worn gold fingernails since her Saint's Day in her fifteenth year when her father had surprised her with the gift. To Major Patten her beauty was like the sight of a light across the open sea to a man who had been adrift upon a raft for forty days and nights, but he saw a piteously urgent call in her eyes which seemed to shout at him in another language. It pained him to look at that petition. He would watch her eyes, hear the clarion, then stare at his plate to try to decipher what the eyes were saying to him. There was desperation in them. There was considerable whimpering fear in them. As he watched her cry out to him with her eyes, the great noise of the call became clearer but—as when a voice calls out from the center of a hurricane—its words are lost and only a vestige of its meaning remains.

She seemed to be gathering impressions, information, and unknown data from him with her nose. Her nostrils would swell or contract when she looked at him intently and sometimes she would close her eyes and lean back in the tall chair as though in sudden weakness.

He concentrated upon finding the meaning she offered him by eliminating all secondary signals. He eliminated his impression of her feeling of fear. She loved her father. She lived in comfort and safety. She had great good health. He threw aside the message of excitement her eyes flamed out at him because he could find no reason for it. What was left within her eyes then, he decided, was a bare need, a supine,

48

frantic need; mute, crushing, chilling, hopeless need.

After dinner Maria de Lourdes whistled Paganini's "The Devil's Trill," utilizing Tartini's third sound, in the drawing-room. Her virtuoso puckering very nearly drove the major's imagination to collapse. When she had finished he marveled, but she said, "Ah, Major, if you could have heard my grandmother whistle the Mozart operas and Haydn's heroic *Creation,* you would have known the whistler's art." Don José nodded in humble appreciation.

The major found himself holding her tiny hand again for an instant as she said good night to him. She touched his wrists and upper arms lightly. She sniffed around him like a tribolite as though cataloguing a thousand fragrances. He watched her small, voluptuous figure grow smaller as it moved away, along the great hall to the massive staircase; to climb, turn, smile, wave, then disappear.

When she had gone, the major wheeled to face Dr. Vicuña, gripping both of the doctor's forearms, almost needing to reach up to do so.

"I ask your permission to ask your daughter to marry me," the major said intensely. The doctor seemed neither surprised nor offended, neither pleased nor startled. He took the major by the elbow and steered him gently to the conservatory. As they moved among the shadows their silhouettes seemed those of an elephant guiding a dachshund.

CHAPTER 6

THEY seated themselves in the soft, low chairs under the glass roof, in the moonlight. The butler stood behind the doctor's chair, at ready. The doctor asked for coffee. She departed into the darkness. The major sat erect and attentive.

"You are a young man to hold the rank of major," the doctor said in a preoccupied manner.

"It ain't a rank, Doc," the major replied hoarsely. "I suppose folks get to thinking it's a rank. I don't do

49

annathing about that except maybe to stand straighter."

"Honorary title?"

"No, sir. It's my name. My first name is *Major,* my middle name is *William,* and my last name is *Patten.* My father was christened Professor Patten. My grandfather's legal name was Doctor Gustave Patten. I have an uncle whose birth certificate reads Admiral Fosdick Patten and a first cousin who has the right to be called Governor Mitchell Patten. It's a family tradition, you might say. My great-grandfather, who had a mite to do with the development of national lotteries, calculated that proper naming could give a boy a head start, as the sayin' goes."

"My word, yes," Don José said emphatically.

They sat silently. They smoked. The moonlight chuted softly into the room. The major gazed out the window at the enormous plaza in front of the castle within the walls of the *casco.* It was entirely paved, as long and wide as the Piazza San Marco or St. Peter's Square. What seemed to be a company of guards had set up camp at its center.

"Doc, if you don't mind my askin'," the major said softly but suddenly, "was that cheese we et tonight?"

"Yes."

"Well, I'm glad I asked. A good friend of mine is purely wild about cheese, and I'll be happy to tell him I finally et some."

They fell into silence again. The beautiful butler returned carrying a silver pot of coffee and two china tankards upon a silver tray. She poured, startlingly lovely in the falling moonlight. The doctor lifted her hand, crushed its palm into his face hungrily, then bade her good night. They could hear the door close behind her.

"We see very few people here, really," the doctor began, shaking talcum powder on his hands. "My wife died seven years ago. While my wife was alive we entertained seldom, because we are so far from the capital and there are so many bandits and Indians in between. We see our neighbors infrequently for that reason. In seven months you are the only visitor we have had with the exception of Don Cyril Solomon, the frontier dentist." Don José seemed to think about

50

Solomon for a moment, for he shook his head in puzzlement. "At one time my wife and I traveled a good deal, in Europe and in Asia. Maria de Lourdes had been in school abroad for six years before my wife died. In Madrid, Paris, and Frankfurt for one year each, then for three years in Edinburgh, but when her mother died she felt she must come home to bring me company. I would have preferred that she had remained in Scotland. I am able to lose myself in my work and, in any event, I had known that neither my wife nor I could have expected to die simultaneously to inconvenience the pain of loss. So, with Maria de Lourdes here working hard to keep me amused, we talked together a good deal, discovered we liked each other very much, and I came to know her even beyond the traditions of my side of the family—which is an extraordinary condition, to say the very least, which perhaps we will be called upon to go into, you and I, some other time."

Don José sipped his coffee. His face, in thought, was as crinkled as the skin of a baked apple. The major did not touch his coffee, but listened to the silence intently.

"Maria de Lourdes is twenty-nine years old. She is greatly gifted and, as you have noticed, a great beauty." The major found he needed to close his eyes as the doctor said that.

"I am her captor," the doctor said slowly. "Up until two years ago we traveled, but seeing people, meeting men, it—it only complicated the problem. I must tell you that Maria de Lourdes has never allowed herself to become interested in a man, and that is the somber truth, Major; but tonight, I felt somehow tonight, from the way she looked at you and touched you, the way her bee-sharp nostrils inhaled your essence—" Don José tugged at his beard. "Coffee is not the drink for a talk like this, my friend. I shall have a whisky while I deny that I have any dependency upon the stuff." He poured three fingers' worth into a glass, then looked over at the major, his eyebrows lifting. The major nodded hastily. The doctor poured another.

"You know, Major, before you arrived today my British phlegm and my Spanish *formale*—the first ac-

51

quired but none the less effective for all that, for the great teachers are with us all our lives—could not have conceived of me sitting here and talking with a stranger who had been a saloon gambler, whose name signified what it was not, in the manner in which I am talking to you tonight."

"I'd change things if I could. It's important to me. But I can't."

"No, no! I stated a most unorthodox condition cruelly in order to set my own perspective. To help me face what I must see. I have decided that I must trust my judgment of myself and of my past. If I cannot feel confidence there—but what is at stake is far more important than my self-esteem. I must tell you what I would have postponed." He sighed. "Maria de Lourdes and I are under a family curse. It was the consequence of brutal ignorance and arrogant folly on my mother's side of the family."

"A curse?" the major croaked.

"Yes. Indeed, yes. Although it is not true that everyone in our family considered it a curse. A handful of them, mostly the single men and two of the women— two at the least—have considered it a blessing."

Don José belted the whisky, coughed lightly, then proceeded with bravery.

"Maria de Lourdes and I are the direct descendants of Don Jaime Arias de Catalonia, a captain with Hernando Cortés. Upon the arrival of the Spanish force at Tenochitlan, our ancestor was sent at the head of an intelligence and reconnaissance patrol to garrison in the south, at the Isthmus of Tehuantepec. Don Jaime was a handsome man with a special but outright taste for Indian women, but lest word of his extraordinary sexual stamina get back to his wife in Cuba or to Spain, where his father-in-law was as close a friend as the King of Spain ever had, he sought a method by which his myriad lusts could be covered up.

"He had been told, as had every member of the Cortés expedition, that they had been mistaken by Moctezuma, the Aztec emperor, for gods, representatives of Quetzalcoatl, the great deity who had been with them in living form three hundred years before. Quetzalcoatl had had white skin, a black beard, and

52

blue eyes. When he had left them he had said he would return to them. The Aztecs thought Cortés' force was the god's advance guard." Don José lighted a cigar carefully, taking much time, as though he were composing his thoughts.

"Cortés reasoned that he who was called Quetzalcoatl must have been a Spanish traveler who had been marooned on the Mexican coast, whose special gifts—due to his European education—had made him seem divine to the aboriginals. The condition, as seen by both sides, suited Don Jaime's plan entirely.

"Some compulsive attitude of historian or aberrant, it doesn't matter which, had him keeping an exact record of the infinite details of each of his hundreds and hundreds and hundreds of sexual adventures with Toltec, Zapotec, Aztec, Mixemeoque, Popolucas, Nahua, Chontal, Mayan, and (according to his own record, although it seems inconceivable) one Iroquois woman. These were women under eighteen years of age. He set down with great scholarship, or enormous perversion, all their paphian reactions, mothers' names, erogenous sympathies, whether they had sisters or girl friends, their physical susceptibilities, their unexpected resiliencies, and his own various methods of adapting to the monumental effort he undertook. Much later he blamed his own uncanny stamina upon having eaten too much boiled iguana. How he loved to eat boiled iguana, once he discovered its powers! It was said by the records of the priests accompanying the expedition that Don Jaime, single-handed, almost made the iguana extinct in that region as though it were nature's irony, for if there were less and less iguana due to Don Jaime, there were more and more Indians to the point where Maria de Lourdes and I may be related to most of the states of Oaxaca, lower Vera Cruz, Tabasco, and Chaipas." Don José shook his head with a wag of almost reverent admiration.

"All of these data were kept as an hourly journal. He wrote it as though it were a secret document kept by Quetzalcoatl. Don Jaime must have been a literary man, a real counterfeiter. He became so carried away with his work—uh, that is the literary portion of his work as well—that in lieu of its publication and the laying on of laurel by his peers, he began to brag to traveling Spaniards in the courier service about having found this great and secret document. He showed some of them the book. They were extremely taken with it, as soldiers will be with such things." Dr. Vicuña coughed delicately. "In no time, word of this catalogue of position, response, and sensation, this treasure map to the—uh—hearts of young Mexican womanhood came to the direct attention of Cortés, no monk himself."

The major sat sunk down in his chair, chewing on his cigar, his brows furrowed into an intense scowl as he seemed to commit every word of the legend to memory. Dr. Vicuña's voice and face were sad.

"Cortés sent for Don Jaime. He asked to see the book, then pored over it. He was extremely impressed with the scholarship and the amount of exhaustive research which the book reflected and therefore did not credit the authorship to Don Jaime but rejoiced that every word of every page had been written and experienced by the god Quetzalcoatl. At this time, as always, Cortés—"

"Excuse me, Doc."

"Yes?"

"Just who was this Cortés?"

"Hernando Cortés was the commander of the military force which conquered the Aztec nation which ruled Mexico at that time. He acted in the name of the King of Spain."

There was silence.

"You have heard Mexicans and Texans speak Spanish?"

"Speak it myself on the ranch."

"Mexicans speak Spanish because of Cortés. He brought Spanish rule and Spanish culture to Mexico."

"When was this?"

"Three hundred and thirty years ago. Exactly."

"Well, I'll be goddamed. Well! Please get right on with your story."

"Yes. Well, Cortés had been pressing the Aztec for conversion to the true faith. The emeror Moctezuma, who believed as devoutly in the savage horror of his liturgy as the Spanish captains believed in theirs,

54

would not submit. The Aztec would give up their land, their government, their gold, their women, and their lives, but they would not reject their religion, which called for such practices as ripping out living human hearts and blood drinking—that sort of thing."

"I ain't got any religion, myself."

"Cortés, a remarkable man who made everything work for his cause, saw immediately how he could use Don Jaime's forgery, not ever even remotely suspecting that it was a forgery. He foresaw a mass conversion to the true faith—but then, he was a military man. Quetzalcoatl was one of the three great Aztec gods. He was sacred to them as The Feathered Serpent, as the God of Learning and the Priesthood, and frequently as the Wind God. Only Huitzilopochtli, the Humming Bird Wizard plus Sun God, and Tezcatlipoca, Smoking Mirror and chief god of the pantheon, were his equals among the forty major Aztec deities. I tell you, Major, what Cortés did turned out to be one of the shrewdest mistakes ever made by the military mind. He reasoned into Aztec theocracy, which he would not have understood if he had lived an additional five hundred years. In Mexico the gods ruled, the priests interpreted and interposed, and the people obeyed. In Spain, the priests ruled, the king interpreted and interposed, and the gods obeyed. A nuance in an ideological difference is a wide chasm."

Don José stared at the major with haunted eyes. It was as though, centuries before, the climax of his own life and of his daughter's life had been reached. "I almost lose my reason when I think of what happened that afternoon. Were the entire affair not so grotesquely and foolishly human, I should have lost it long ago. Seven years ago, in fact." He smoked and sipped in silence. The major held out the bottle and refilled Don José's glass, then his own. "Cortés ordered Moctezuma to call his princes and captains, nobles and priests, to the emperor's palace. The meeting was held in one of the gorgeously decorated ceremonial rooms, an enormous quadrangular chamber which was one of many around the main patio and whose walls were hung with featherwork of delicate workmanship and exciting colors.

"The native ladies of the Spaniards, Doña Marina and the Tlaxcalan belles, had been invited, which is proof that Cortés expected to carry the day—for he needed to appear infallible before the ladies.

"Try to imagine this tableau of two hemispheres. The nobles of the Aztec court were arrayed in rich cotton wraps interlaced with rare feathers. Everyone wore riotous colors. Many wore the *quetzalalpitoal*, an ornament composed of tassels of feathers and gold which hung down the sides of their faces from the tops of their heads. The warrior's hair was combed straight up into a high tuft from which fell bulky jewelry of many colors. All the men wore their false mustaches made of bright blue and green feathers which hung from a hole in their nose partition. Around their necks were *chichiwitls* of golden shrimps or pearls. Some of the men carried long fans in many colors or in dazzling white and smoked tubes of aromatic tobacco. The women walked softly on their bare feet, their purple-dyed hair falling to their waists. Their teeth were dyed pink and their breasts were tattoed with blue marks.

"When the hall was in readiness, the emperor appeared. He was dressed in blue, the imperial color, with a mantle and a diadem. No Aztec looked directly at him, for to do so was to die. He walked through silence. He moved to a platform raised three feet above the floor. He sat upon an *ycpalli*. The precious stones inserted into the holes in the sides of his nostrils glittered exotically. He signaled for Cortés to approach him. The commander went forward, his interpreter at his side. The two leaders exchanged greetings, then Cortés explained that he had asked that the meeting be called to discuss a dire religious matter.

"According to Bernal Diaz, who was there as all this happened, Moctezuma was about forty years old, slender and of good height, not very swarthy but with the golden skin of the Indian. His hair was long enough to cover his ears. His scanty black beard was well shaped and thin. His face was somewhat long, but cheerful. He had good eyes. He was no weakling. He was a prisoner of his religion and his epoch.

56

The day that the god Quetzalcoatl had left Mexico he had prophesied that in the year *Ce Acatl* or One Reed, strange white men from across the sea would conquer his people. The year of *Ce Acatl* was 1519, the year Cortés landed with his forces. When he met Cortés on that dreadful afternoon, he was literally a captive of the Spaniards and yet he had not called his people to revolt.

"This dreadful afternoon was the *key* date in the conquest of Mexico, June 30, 1520. The night which followed this meeting became known as *Noche Triste* because at this meeting the Spaniards revealed themselves conclusively not to be representatives of the gods. The official story, handed out to save face for the military mind, that futile and endless fumbling force throughout history, tends to shift the blame for the revolt to Alvarado, saying he had slain a large number of Indians at a religious feast. Pass that one by. Makeshift propaganda. The revolt happened, as it should never have happened, because of Don Jaime Arias. The Spaniards were attacked in a religious frenzy when they tried to leave the city secretly that night. They lost half their force and most of the treasure they had collected—yet when he called that meeting Hernando Cortés had been sure of a total, bloodless victory for the King of Spain and for The Host of God.

"When Cortés said he wished to speak on a religious matter, the emperor commanded that the two high priests be brought to sit with him; *ycpallis* were provided. They were men of about sixty years, a formidable age. They were called *Quetzalcoatl-Totectlamacazqui* and *Quetzalcoatl-Tlaloc-tlamacazqui*. They bore the name of the god because it was the archetype of the priestly ideal. The second names referred to the War God and the Rain God of their respective cults. The third word meant *priest*. Their skin bore the deep scars of maguey-thorn punctures in all possible stages, from fresh bleeding wounds to old, crusty scars. They wore black cotton mantles clasped on the right shoulder under thick manes of hair which had not been touched by water or comb since they had entered the divine service as boys, and the hair was a heavy, solid mass

57

of dried blood from decades of human sacrifice. They smelled heavily of death, but they smiled cordially at Cortés.

"In most courteous terms Moctezuma asked Cortés to speak. He never commanded the great captain because, to the Aztecs, Cortés was a representative from the gods. Cortés demanded once again that the emperor decree that the people of Mexico renounce their cruel religion and convert to the true faith. Moctezuma and the two priests gazed down at him with pity. Cortés' voice became contemptuous. He demanded to be told how priests of any true religion could dedicate their lives to celibacy when the very god they worshipped was a wanton monster who wallowed in carnal lust. The emperor put his hands on the priests' arms and they remained quiet. Moctezuma asked for Cortés' authority for such a terrible statement."

Don José passed his hand wearily across his eyes. He sipped at his whisky. His shaking hand lighted another cigar.

"Cortés held up the forgery. 'We have found Quetzalcoatl's carnal journal,' he answered arrogantly. 'It is written in the god's own hand.'

"Moctezuma gestured that the book be brought to him. Cortés gave it to a page who brought it forward, his eyes cast down to the floor. The emperor took the book, opened it, stared at it for a moment—then flung the book from him. 'Ah!' Cortés exclaimed. 'You know the book.'

" 'You will read the book to the priests,' Moctezuma commanded, his manner so utterly changed that the Spaniards grouped eight paces behind Cortés became uneasy. The page picked up the book from where the emperor had flung it. Cortés took it and began to read it aloud. He read slowly and steadily so that the interpreter could not lose a word. It was, perhaps, the worst day that interpreter ever had in his life. The book contained the sort of—uh—case histories which one simply does not read aloud to groups of three hundred and more—and with two high church clerics in the room.

"The opening attested, in the flawless literary style

of Don Jaime Arias, that this was an autobiographical document written by the god Quetzalcoatl. I don't remember its wording, but it is still in the Archives of the Indies in Seville should you ever wish to consult it. It then went on to account for the most outlandish sexual experiments—to the point of being very nearly exhausting just to listen to a description of them. I am told that at this point Don Jaime sank back from the front rank of Spaniards and sat on the floor in the middle of his group, either made unduly nostalgic by his own words, as his leader read them, or merely frightened out of his wits.

"It was a significant tribute to Don Jaime that, when Giovanni Jacopo Casanova years later found access to this document in Seville (he gained access by disguising himself as a learned monk) his screams of pique and self-pity revealed his true identity and he was led away, a broken man, for Don Jaime had exceeded his own work in the field by a total of six hundred and twelve partners and eight seemingly unrealizable sexual attitudes." Don José paused and tugged at his beard. "I would venture to guess," he mused, "that the tropics must account for that amount of increased flexibility.

"Each time Cortés' voice would soar to the end of reading yet another enormous feat of amoristics, he would ask the emperor, panting, whether he wished the indictment to continue. Each time the emperor would nod gravely. He and the two elderly priests seemed to be listening with personal rather than ecclesiastical interest. When Cortés finished, almost hoarse, the less ancient priest wiggled his fingers to signal that the book should be brought to him, a contemptuous act of unalterable disrespect. The page took it forward. The priest glanced at it. He handed it across Moctezuma to his confrere, who scanned one or two pages calmly, then returned it to the page who gave it to Cortés.

" 'Let the book be shown to the warriors and nobles in this assembly,' Moctezuma said. Cortés, smiling triumphantly, gave the book back to the page, who held it opened at his chest and who then walked along row upon row of the dazzling, beplumed, and expressionless Aztec aristocracy until at last he returned the book to Cortés. The inspection had taken place in complete silence.

" 'Let us be shown the man who brought you this book,' the older priest demanded. Back in the ranks of Spaniards, at Cortés' command, Don Jaime was lifted to his feet and propelled forward in a gentle manner. The emperor asked Don Jaime where he had found the book. Don Jaime shrugged and said, 'From the women.' The older priest asked him if the women had told him that the book was the true journal of Quetzalcoatl. Cortés lost his temper there. "There is nothing else to say!" he shouted heatedly. 'Do you denounce this lascivious and bestial monster you call a god?' " Don José shook his head sadly. "I tell you that day was *the* triumphant apogee of the military mind."

"What happened?"

Don José shrugged. "The emperor and his two high priests leaped to their feet as one man, their faces working and crumpled with hatred and scorn. Moctezuma spoke. 'The book is written in Spanish,' he said contemptuously.

"The Aztecs wrote in pictographs. Quetzalcoatl had been an Aztec. Because the Spaniards had decided among themselves that Quetzalcoatl was a marooned Spanish mariner they had all accepted the fact that Quetzalcoatl would write in Spanish.

"Cortés stood there dumbstruck, for a moment, when he realized what he had done, but he recovered instantly and turned quickly to get his people out of the palace so that a retreat could be organized.

" 'Stop!' the older priest cried out in a terrible voice. They all turned involuntarily.

" 'You will all die between now and tomorrow's dawn,' the priest screamed, 'many on the altar of the Sun God.' He pointed directly at Don Jaime. 'Before you die, I place upon your head and your blood the curse of the ancients.'

"Women screamed. Warriors fainted. Moctezuma's legs gave way under him like socks whose garters have been severed and he fell down upon the *ycpalli*. The priest's voice shrieked, 'Every life born of your loins, unto the thousandth generation, shall be possessed with such a talent for loving that he shall grow insane for the need of love at the instant of his first carnal embrace!' The old man hacked off his own left hand with three chops of an obsidian hatchet, then ran to Don Jaime and held the stump up over Don Jaime's head so that the blood would cover him."

Don José seemed to collapse within himself. His face was newly dented with grief like a loaf of bread a giraffe has kneeled upon. "That is why my daughter has never allowed herself to be alone with a man. That is the curse upon all who carry the blood of Arias." His head fell heavily upon his chest, but his whiskers tickled so he lifted it again.

"I ask your permission to ask your daughter to marry me," Major Patten said hoarsely.

Don José got to his feet, the cigar clamped by his strong teeth. He walked toward the large window in the moonlight. "I am sixty-seven years old." he said. He spoke absently, as though teaching himself something or probing to find evidence which he might or might not recognize. "As you have seen, we have only women servants in this house. Lest you form the impression that this measure is a form of safeguard for Maria de Lourdes against herself, may I tell you that they are my servants and my concubines, and if they were not there, all of them, always and constantly, to be used by me again and again throughout the day and night, I would go mad without them and perhaps do terrible things." He stared out at the night light upon the vast courtyard, looked without seeing at the campfires of the guard. "Because of the curse all of our senses, mine and Maria de Lourdes', are as sharp as any animal's. In Revelation 5:8, John says that odors are the prayers of saints. I wish it were ever so."

"I ask your permission to ask your daughter to marry me," the major said.

"You have a good smell to your body. You are an honest man, a kind man. You have no fear." Don José did not turn away from the window. He seemed to have displaced again the thought that the major was there. "Tonight I must say that I do not know, really, if such a curse exists or if it ever existed. I was told long ago that it did. My father told it to me because my mother and her sister had achieved a horrid scandal and had ridden away in the night with the men of a traveling circus, leaving behind a stinging note for their husbands that they had chosen to mate with five acrobats. They were both Arias in direct line. *Acrobats*. What an active congress of sin, what a thicket of exhausting lust that must have been for them in the summertimes." He sighed, filled with the thoughts of Mother.

"My father forgave them. A week after they had gone he locked the doors behind us and told me the story of this curse passed down to them and to me by Don Jaime." He laughed with mirthless bitterness. "I was shamed by my mother and, from some source, found a clear understanding. Once, in Spain, I gave my hand to a gypsy crone in Córdoba when I was nineteen years old. She peered into it, pored over it, and with a moan swooned upon my hand. When we revived her she came out of it tearing her clothes off and, smelling of wolf's spittle, tried to throw herself upon me." He walked ponderously back to the chair which faced the major. He fell into it, his eyes hard. "Am I what I am because I wanted to believe my father against my mother who had deserted me, or is it because I am Arias that I live with eighteen concubines, that I was so uncontrolled all of my life that my wife, in a desperation of anxiety, told Maria de Lourdes of the curse? She is in the grip of it now. She is fighting it like a Renaissance saint in her room above us, for she knows she is cursed as I knew it the moment my father had told me." He shrugged. "But not until." He stared at the major levelly. "I give you my permission to ask her to marry you, openly and sadly, praying as I do that I have not made you a gift of tragedy."

"We live on what we believe," the major answered briskly. "You got to back your play."

CHAPTER 7

Dr. VICUÑA showed the major to his apartment on the third level of the castle, then he descended one floor by a turning casement staircase, followed the blue-carpeted corridor to the opposite side of the building, and knocked emphatically upon the high double doors of Maria de Lourdes' room to awaken her *criada,* who slept on the floor of the foyer between the corridor and Maria de Lourdes' chambers. After pounding, kicking, and finally shouting under the door itself, he succeeded in awakening the faithful watcher, who staggered with torpor as she opened the door.

"I am a bandit here to murder your mistress," Don José said. "Where may I find her?"

The *craida* waved in the general direction of the inner door as Don José stepped into the foyer, then she spiraled to the floor in a falling-leaf pattern and was asleep again before she hit. Don José tapped lightly upon the inner door. He heard his daughter's voice call out for an accounting. He gave his proper name, *Papa.* She bade him enter. He did. She was dressed in a long diaphanous peignoir of apple green. She looked haggard. She clutched a rosary in her right hand, held at her side.

"It was almost impossible to get through your outer guard. She kept falling asleep all over my boots."

"Philomena worries because I do not sleep enough, she thinks. She talked to an old woman in her village about it. The woman gave her potions marked with my image and now Philomena sleeps for both of us."

"Ah. In that case I'm sorry I woke her. Did it tire you?"

"Actually, I'm somewhat over-rested. She's been asleep out there for two days."

"You were very beautiful tonight."

"Thank you, sir."

"Especially so, I thought."

"Why?"

"I thought the major stimulated you, heightened the color in your cheeks."

"No, Papa."

"I am always wrong about such things." He sat down daintily, a trying illusion, upon a tiny French chair until she pushed a pale-blue chaise-longue into position. He arose immediately and shifted to full-length comfort. She bit the end off a large black cigar and lighted it. She stuck it between his teeth.

"Shoes?" she said.

He shook his head, smiling slightly.

She sat in front of a triple mirror at a boudoir and brushed her long red hair with regular but slow movements, in a semi-automatic manner.

"I have had a revelation tonight," he said. She continued brushing. He took his time. He puffed at the cigar. "I have become convinced that there is no curse upon us."

"You did?" she replied.

"I think my mother was a slut and that she started this curse."

"Papa!" She wheeled in her seat.

"Or her mother." With his cigar he waved the responsibility to wait in the past. "I am going to talk to some of the old ones. The Arias men *and* the Arias women who live in the capital. I suspect they would sniff at such a curse."

"No, Papa. Not sniff."

"My father was a worm of a man. Anyone could bully him if they were coarse enough to want to bully. My mother was a bold, dominating, and—as I see her now in this context—a cruel sort of woman, I suspect."

"Why?"

"Because she told him about the curse, then went off with five acrobats. *Five!* To be shared by the two of them, she and her wanton sister, my aunt. *Acrobats.*"

"Did he say that she told him that, then left him?"

"No. He didn't say when she told him. He merely said there was this curse. And that he was to tell me."

"But if she told him at all it would have been to save his feelings, to allow him to think that whatever

64

had happened had happened in spite of all she felt for him, that she had to do whatever it was she was going to do, in spite of herself because of the curse."

"Well, yes, I suppose so."

"That wasn't cruel."

"Then my father must have made up the curse. He was a wild-eyed and bookish sort of man. The invention of such a curse would have saved his face after his wife had made such a preposterous decision involving acrobats."

"Why did you decide this?"

"Decide? It was not anything as deliberate as a decision, my darling. It was—as I say—a revelation which burst upon me."

"Tonight?"

"Yes."

"Why not a year ago, or more importantly still, seven years ago. Before Mama—"

"Because it didn't," he answered harshly. "Who can say why these things come and go, or come at all?"

"I can say."

"You can? Why, then?"

"Because of Major Patten."

"Whatever has Major Patten got to do with *our* family curse?"

"I know you, Papa. *I know you so much that I love you with all my heart.*"

"What are you talking about?"

"You worry that you will die someday and that I will be left alone."

"Naturally!"

"You want me to marry."

"I confess that to be the truth, but surely that has no connection with my revelation?"

"You don't want me to be alone. You want the hacienda to go on and on with someone young and strong to cherish it after you can no longer cherish it." She brushed her long, thick hair with regular strokes. "It cannot be, Papa."

He threw his legs to the side of the chaise and sat up suddenly. He leaned forward, his great nose like a battering ram before a buttressed gate, his eyes alarmed. "Why can it not be?" he pleaded. His voice broke. "Maria de Lourdes! Don't believe that curse. It is a shabby, shabby trick."

"It is a shabby trick, Papa, but it is a curse. Do you tell me this so you can believe that what you did to Mama, whom you loved beyond love, was all selfish, meaningless, cheap, carnal indulgence? Did you sell her life for the lips of chambermaids or did you not wish you could have died instead, rather than do what you did—what the curse made you do?"

His face hardened. "I did what I did by my own choice. If she killed herself because of it that was because she—because she—" Maria de Lourdes left the dressing-table to sit beside him, to hold him while he sobbed into his hands in the pink light.

"There *is* a curse Papa. You know it. We have both seen the records and the letters which proved that it happened long before your mother went off with the acrobats."

He regained control of himself. He got to his feet and walked to the large washbasin and poured water into it and washed his face and hands. He opened a cabinet and took out a container of talcum powder and shook some of it over his hands. He walked back to her, dragging a small chair behind him. He pulled the chair up to face her directly as she sat on the side of the blue chaise, then seated himself.

"Then I will say to you that there *has been* a curse. But we do not know that the curse stained every Arias since the Conquest. I say to you that there has been a curse for the weak ones, like me and my mother, but I ask you to consider that there may not be a curse for the strong, for you."

"I am weak."

"No! Maria de Lourdes, let me help you to prove that you are strong."

"How?"

"Tonight we sat in the solarium. We talked for many hours. Before we went into the solarium, the instant you left us at the top of the stairs, he turned to me and he asked for my permission to ask you to marry him."

"Papa!"

"I ask you to think what it would be like if you had been born with a terrible affliction."

"I was, Papa. I was."

"Suppose you had been born without legs, or deaf and dumb, or bald and hunchbacked? Suppose a young man still wanted to marry you. What would you do?"

"He would be able to see my affliction. He would know that I lacked what he could believe he deserved. It would be different. It would not be the same, Papa."

"It would be the same."

"How could it be?"

"Because I told him about the curse."

"Papa!"

"It is the first time the horror has ever been mentioned beyond the chain of mother to daughter, father to son. I let him strain to hear your mute voice. I let him stare into your sightless eyes and when I had done he said he would thank me if I would give him permission to ask you to marry him."

She sat with the knuckle of her forefinger caught between her teeth. Blood ran down across the backs of her fingers, but her father did not move to stop her. All at once, the maimed hand fell into her lap. Her father took it in both of his and began to wrap the finger in a long white handkerchief.

"I want a man, Papa. I want a man like Major Patten who has little parlor charm and perhaps no humor, who isn't sure which form to use, and whose speech is halting but who might kill for one if need be. I want a man with hands like his—soft and long and strong and clean; and eyes like his which are without imagination and therefore without fear. I want a man who trembles when he looks at me but who studies me, seeking my wounds to bind them. I want such a man, Papa!"

"You must test your strength. You must. You must. And you will win."

She looked into his eyes, her own wet. "You said that to yourself once, didn't you, Papa? You saw that lovely girl and followed her to Scotland. You stood upon her doorstep for five years saying those words to yourself, saying that there was no curse and that

67

you were strong. Then she married you and you loved her more than ever before, didn't you, Papa?"

He would not answer.

"If I married him because he is a stranger, this time we would use the callousness of approaching the curse impersonally through a stranger, but it would end the same. Even though I have never seen him before, I am almost thirty years old and I can feel what he is and I can know that I would come to love him, as you loved Mama. Then, afterwards—afterwards, as time dripped upon my body and eroded that stifling need for him alone, afterwards—"

Her father stood quickly. "Good night," he said roughly. "Good night." He walked rapidly but not overhastily to the door which led to the corridor. "Good night, my dear."

CHAPTER 8

THE major was awakened at five-thirty the following morning, according to the large grandfather's clock against the wall of his chamber. His caller was a tiny girl who seemed grossly frightened to be there. She awoke him by tapping upon his shoulder with a five-foot-long twig, and when he opened his eyes she cried out good morning and fled the room. The major dressed at once, inwardly resolving that he would put grandfather clocks all over his own ranch house. He spent time shining his boots. He scrubbed his fingernails. He attended his ginger mustache. Maria de Lourdes, according to her father's best advices, breakfasted at six, rode until nine, and then would most likely disappear until she could reassure herself that the visitor had parted.

As he came down the broad staircase, moving with the suddenness of a short man and the nervousness of a distraught man who could not find the confidence that he would be able to complete some task at hand, he saw the beautiful lady butler waiting for him at the foot of the stairs, staring up at him with a placid absence of expression.

"Good morning," she said.

"Good morning," he answered.

He thought of Don José's tribute to this amanuensis. "She is the perfect woman," the doctor had said. "Entirely mental or physical. No soft thoughts of selfish sentiment. No ropes called love. Something within her makes her need to serve men. Every man should have such a butler and fatigue would disappear. With fatigue would go much of the evil of the world."

The great granite hall seemed like a nave of an unfinished cathedral to be consecrated come Doomsday. The butler wore a plain black dress with a low, square bodice. Her figure was all swells and clutches. He nodded as he came abreast of her, considerably preoccupied, attempting to frame sentences in his mind which would state his intentions persuasively to Maria de Lourdes and having no clue as to where he should begin. The sound of his boots hitting the stone floor startled him.

He was dressed as he had dressed since he had left short pants, in the manner of the professional gamblers who had attended his father's gaming rooms. To those who had never walked through a honkatonk he would have looked like a schoolmaster in a severe black frock coat, startlingly white linen, and a black string tie. He was scrubbed pink and white. His curly ginger hair was wet and combed with unusual attention to thousands of individual hairs. His small boots shone, and the close-cropped hairs of his ginger mustache were graded with precision. There was nothing tentative about his bright blue eyes.

The butler indicated that he would not be risking his life if he followed her, which he did. She walked three steps ahead of him and, that morning, trailed the scent of powdered spicewood, *udi,* and crushed essence of the flowers of the thousands of different kinds of angiosperms. He moved quickly to overtake her. He spoke in a low voice: "Has the señorita come to breakast yet?"

She turned her beautiful head to him, looked blank, and shook her head. He wanted her not to tell the señorita that he was there, but he could not.

The butler guided him to an archway leading to a

broad terrace. A large table had been set with three places. He walked to the battlement and saw that the castle stood upon a bluff which overlooked the green-stubbled sandiness of mesa which stretched to sixty miles where it collided with a ring of purple mountains. The air was cool. The light was strong. The blue top of the sky was near.

"Early, ain't it."

"Not for ranchers, señor."

"I'm a rancher."

She nodded as though she felt it would be impolite to disbelieve.

"What's your name?"

"Juana." She had black hair and grey eyes. She was small and willowy, long by illusion but so full in the figure.

"Are you Scotch?" the major asked distractedly, to fill in the slots of silence as he seated himself because his mind was not on what he said or saw; he spoke as if he wished to keep talking to be sure he was awake and was indeed there and correct in remembering that he could expect Maria de Lourdes to appear sooner or later.

"I am a Frenchwoman," the butler replied. The major began to drink the coffee he had just discovered and to apply butter to a croissant, something he had never seen before, which had materialized under a blue napkin. He studied it for a moment before he decided it was all right to eat.

When he looked up, Juana had gone. He chewed voraciously, marvelling at the many things he had found to his liking in such a short time, absently evaluating the blueness of the morning sky. A mild breeze touched him. The sun was well into its work. The light was investigating everything before it, leaving a fulsomeness of itself behind, then moving along to light the shadowed west.

Juana reappeared, followed by two serving girls who pushed a wheeled cart covered with a silver dome. The major made a mental note to inquire where he could get one. Juana lifted the bell of shining metal. He saw bacon, ham, lamb chops, broiled goat, kidneys, broiled liver, kippers, steak, potatoes, and oatmeal. He smiled at her brilliantly and nodded, not quite perceiving how he was to start. She took the cart away and returned with three large covered dishes containing some of all of it, and their smells mingled with the wonderful morning. The major ate steadily for thirty-five minutes. When he had indeed finished she brought him more hot coffee and a chest of cigars. The serving girls cleaned the table swiftly. He took a thick, resinous cigar and Juana brought a light for it.

"Is Juana a French name?" he asked uncertainly.

"French enough, señor. My name is Janine. Janine Michaud. Juana is close, and easier for Mexico."

"Did you—uh—study your—trade in France?"

"No señor. It is just that I do everything well."

CHAPTER 9

MARIA DE LOURDES, walking rapidly, stepped upon the terrace. She stopped short and stared at the major. Her nostrils quivered. Her face colored. Juana left them. The major rose slowly.

"Mornin', Miss Vicuña."

"Good morning, Major Patten." Her voice was low, choked.

"Lovely mornin'."

"If I seem surprised, please forgive me. I am so used to breakfasting alone. Papa is a late riser." The words came rapidly.

She was lovelier than he had been able to remember her since he had awakened, lovelier than he had dreamed of her the night before. She wore high boots, a buckskin skirt, and a leather blouse. Her red hair was caught up behind in a peruke, tied with a yellow ribbon. He studied the freckles across her nose. He tried to smile, but it wouldn't match. He held a chair for her but, agitating her nostrils, she shook her head and accepted another seat which was upwind from him. She sat down slowly, holding the table. Her long gold fingernails glistened on the cloth. She seemed as unsteady as he seemed.

"Can I get you some chow, ma'am?"

"No. No, thank you. Coffee and a croissant is all I eat. Then I ride. Then a steak."

"Which is the croissant?"

She did not smile. She held one in the air.

"Oh. Them. Mighty good but a long way from corn dodgers."

"Did you sleep well, Major?"

He nodded. He had seen her eyes again. He knew he would not be able to speak lightly like this any longer. "I sat up late with your Pa. We talked."

"Papa adores company."

The major exhaled a nasal sigh. "I'd like to talk to you right serious, ma'am. If you're willin' to hear me."

She nodded. Her nostrils opened, closed; opened, closed.

"My Pa died from drinkin' too much whisky. He was a honkatonk operator and so was my grandfather, in a different place. I come from Tennessee. My Ma pulled up an' left us when I was fourteen years old. I was raised a tinhorn gambler. I woulda gambled annaways because there's somethin' in me that was eatin' at me to keep gamblin'. Since the day I started I've killed four men in self-defense. I've cheated people. That there was the slow part about me. The quick part was that I was able to stop gamblin'. I have myself a spread across the river that I thought was mighty big 'til I seen your Pa's. I own a nice little town called Pickering City with a bank, a courthouse, a big saloon, a mercantile store, an' a newspaper." His voice dwindled off into stalled silence. They stared at each other so fixedly that they seemed to be made of pale wax. He cleared his throat. "We watched you go away at the top of the stairs las' night and I turned to your Pa an' I asked him for permission to ask you to marry me."

She gasped. She wanted to pick up the coffee cup but her hand trembled. "What did he say to you?" she asked harshly.

"He told me about the curse."

A sob broke in an exploding bubble of pain from her lovely throat. She wheeled away from him in the chair. He could see one quarter of her profile. For a warm, flashing moment he thought of Kate Grigson. He wondered where she was and how she was and if she had made it to safety. He wondered if things needed to start sad or to end sad when men and women groped to save each other.

"It may be that the right way for me to ask you these things," he said slowly, "would be to come callin' on you an' court you the way a girl has the right to expect, but the time would all be used up ridin' back an' forth over the two hunnerd an' forty miles between our two spreads." She turned slightly. He had earned her half-profile. "Your Pa gave me permission to ask you to marry me." He lifted her hand for a moment, kissed it softly, then put it back on the tabletop, where it clenched the edge of the table until its knuckles showed puce and white. "I'm asking you now, Maria," the major said.

She spun round to face him. Her voice was thick with ruffianly intensity.

"I thank you, Major Patten. But you heard my family's story from my father and you know that I may not think of such a thing. If I ever married, life could become a prison for two people where it is now a prison for one. Because of Don Jaime, a marriage which might have lasted until death would be burned to a cinder before it had truly known the raptures of its life. I tell you that unless I prevent my own marriage I would bring to the man who would marry me pain, shame, humiliation, disgust, and dishonor because of what I have been cursed to do with my body once I began, so I will not begin." She slammed the table with great force. She glared at him defiantly, breathing hard. She dropped her head into her arms on the table and sobbed bitterly, her long fingers entwined with each other before her.

He pulled his chair close to her so that his mouth was at a level with her ear as he leaned forward. He spoke to her quietly, his lips brushing her hair.

"If there had never been a curse, if there had never been what happened to your Pa an' your Ma, and you would say that you would marry me, and still you did these carnal things which you fear so bad that you will do because of that curse, well, it still couldn't have any meanin' in terms of shame or pain for me." She lifted her head. "As that old Aztec said, once we start lovin' we will love true, with a great talent for lovin', an' if we love true there ain't anything can stop it, for in love there ain't no wrong, for evermore."

His pink cheeks glistened with two lines of tears. His mustache was sopping wet. His hands shook as he touched her. As she turned to him, her face so greatly changed and softened, he lifted her. Standing, he drew her to him. They kissed as softly as the fall of dusk in summertime.

Her face was shining with an emotion so new to her that her head shook slightly in disbelief as she stared at him. "You smell like freshly baked bread upon which honey is being poured," she said. She grabbed his head with violence and pulled it to her mouth.

CHAPTER 10

Upon the bride and groom Don José bestowed a congress of wedding gifts. Heading the long largesse, in unanimous estimation, were four Krushen machine cannon. They were crank operated and their locking systems employed a toggle-joint arrangement that rammed home a fixed charge. The stiff linen cartridge was fed on a tray located on the left side of the breech end of the gun. A very clever method was used to place a percussion cap on the nipple mechanically after the weapon was safely locked. The rate of fire depended solely upon the rate of speed with which the crank could be turned. "They do not aim with particular effect, except by accident," Don José explained proudly, "but it is really not necessary to kill or maim with them. The noise they make will scare the whey out of bandit and Indian alike."

The young couple kept walking around and around the four machine cannon, which were mounted among presents from the Papal Nuncio, from Santa Anna, the exiled President in Cartagena, the Swedish ambassador (with whom Dr. Vicuña played chess by post), Senator Houston of Texas, the governors of nine northern states of the Republic, eleven retired ballerinas, and others. The young newlyweds were simply unable to believe their good fortune, particularly Major Patten. The Krushen cannon were not only beautiful and valuable, but were so extremely useful to the homemakers. "Oh Papa!" Maria de Lourdes exclaimed. "They are exactly what we needed and wanted." Dr. Vicuña beamed.

He gave them a dinner service for forty-eight made of pale-green transparent beryl and a bagpipe with a sable windchest upon which the bride played "The Flowers of the Forest" and "Over the Sea to Skye" at the wedding feast. He gave them a Persian carpet of the Sefavid Dynasty the weaving of which had not begun until the effects of altitude and climate upon the wool of the contributing flocks had been studied and the silks and dyes matched and rematched, for eleven years, to the pure patterns of color and line within the design. He gave them a seven-foot-long miniature of the Birr Castle telescope, which had been sent to him by the Earl of Rosse. He gave them one of the new Erard double-action harps and a large overland eight-horse coach so that they could have reason to make frequent, almost comfortable trips between the two ranches. He attempted to give them his own *chef de cuisine* Pierre Weill, the wizard of Orsay, on whom Don José had spent three years of cunning persuasion by speech, by letter, and by emissary, to cause him to make the journey to Mexico from the Rue Artbuch Wald, winning him over at last by himself cooking for the great *chef* in a Paris restaurant called *Lucien* on the Rue Surcouf a steaming bowl of *mole negro oaxaqueño,* a dizzying stew of tender turkey and spare ribs of pork, two kinds of *chili;* almonds, pecans, peanuts, and avocados; raisins, pepper-corns, cinnamon, cloves, and chocolate, all presenting a bouquet and a flavor so elementally seductive that the gifted *chef* had finished the huge bowl, scraped the pot with a demi-baguette of bread. He had then saluted Don José with devotion, saying that he was ready to travel as far as would be necessary to any country which could think in such astounding combinations.

Fortunately, Don José had told his daughter of this intended gift beforehand, as the present of M. Weill was to have been a surprise for the major's newly found palate. Thus a disaster was averted. With drained face, shaken at so close a call when she told him the secret she was not supposed to tell, Major Patten explained urgently that Mat Sun was not only considered the greatest cook in the Southwest but that he had saved the major's life and would take it as such an irretrievable loss of face that he might shoot M. Weill if the major were to accept the *chef* as a wedding gift. Major Patten was sorely conflicted, for he had developed a gnawing fondness for M. Weill's *beignets de Réchauffé de Dinde à la Créole,* but in the end his loyalty never wavered.

Maria de Lourdes rushed to her father to pour out the story. He comforted her. "I would never be mean to a cook who can shoot," he told her. In the end it was decided that Mat Sun could not object if they accepted (on behalf of the bride's habituation to certain kinds of food) M. Weill's apprentice, a young *saucier* named Smadja who, after Mat Sun had grown used to having him around the chuck wagon, was to make the tactful offer to show him how to prepare *Longe de veau à la Vichy, Pompadour de caneton à la mirabeau, Râble de lièvre a la crême aigre,* and a few other little specialities like that. Then, if Mat Sun wished, he could meet occasionally with M. Weill, under the ruse that M. Weill was requesting a meeting with him to exchange recipes. To provide a lure for the *chef* in the matter Don José asked the major to describe the preparation of *Son-of-a-Bitch Stew à la Brasada* as conceived by Mat Sun. M. Weill, a stew slave of the order of the savant Johannus Starr, wanted to saddle and ride to the Patten ranch at once to taste the dish.

One of the father-in-law's gifts made the major gasp with burbling astonishment. It was an ice-making machine, the newest improvement on the inventions of the Scotsmen Cullen and Sir John Leslie, who had worked concurrently to provide the basis of this machine, by Carré, in whose firm Don José was an eager stockholder. It used sulphuric acid, water, and an air pump and could make a hundred pounds of ice a day at a cost, in northern Mexico of 1850, of not more than twelve dollars a pound. With it came one of the John Perkins ether refrigerators which would work perfectly, Don José guaranteed, if he could persuade the London company to spare them two trained mechanics to maintain it. "It is an extremely sound principle," he explained; "it is only that it does not operate effectively."

Last, the gift which exceeded all gifts was Don José's deeding of the entire hacienda: land, kine, and lakes; mountains, streams, and brakes; horse, sheep, grass, and goat; castle, kirk, wall, and moat, to his beloved daughter.

"Your Pa is an extremely generous man," Major Patten said to his bride at some random moment during the night of their second wedding.

"Papa has always been wildly generous. Once he gave Mama an entire Ukrainian ballet company, which she kept for four months; then, because she could not speak to them as they would not learn English or Spanish, she gave them their freedom in Antofagasta."

"Did she send them back home?"

Maria de Lourdes put a consterned hand over the O of her perfect mouth. She shook her head in dismay. "No. I mean, I really don't know. Dear Mama was so forgetful that I feel sure she didn't."

On the occasion of the night of his daughter's first wedding, Don José had a fifty-mile chain of bonfires lighted upon the mesa to the south of the castle which spelled out the great word JOY, ordered forty-eight hours of celebrations at his expense in all pueblos on the hacienda, ordered that all children born within the calendar year to follow be named after either the bride or the groom, then asked the exquisite lady butler to join him in toasts to the health and happiness of the bride and groom. They broke twenty-one crystal goblets joyously in the fireplace. Don José drank and toasted sitting. The beautiful butler drank and toasted standing behind his chair. For the first time in memory, the beautiful butler got drunk. It was impossible for Don José to notice her flushed sparkle growing and glowing while they were in tandem position. As she bent forward to pour the final cognac she continued to bend, falling into a pocket of blackness. Don José blamed himself. He vowed to have a mirror installed on the wall opposite his drinking chair the next morning so that it could not happen again and went to bed with one of the tweenies.

For reasons well known to father, daughter, and suitor, two separate marriage ceremonies were undertaken. The first was consecrated by the priest of Maria de Lourdes' mother thirty-five minutes after love's first kiss and the major's proposal of marriage at breakfast, at seven-ten in the morning at Don José's immovable insistence, with the father and the fetching lady butler as witnesses.

Dr. Vicuña had watched the major propose marriage, observed his daughter's heated denunciation, witnessed the major's conciliation, and wept over their first kiss from a turret in the crenellated tower far above them. Drying his cheeks, he had lost no time picking his way daintily down the circular stone staircase to the terrace where, not awaiting any announcement from them of their intentions, he proclaimed with a stern voice that the marriage must take place at once, then sat between them while the appetizing female butler was sent off to summon the priest for his office.

Theirs was not to be a long engagement. In fact the rite was performed just in time. Maria de Lourdes had become a totally changed woman within the timing of that dual set of kisses. Gone was the withdrawn, tentative manner; the frightened, needful eyes; the frozen-angel visage. She had thickened spiritually in eleven minutes into as close an approximation of an emotionally abandoned woman as any antidébauchée would care to see. Her nostrils writhed. Her scarlet tongue licked at her lips as might that of a test baker for a patisserie, hungrily and incessantly. Her eyes were filmed with the daintiest lust imaginable. She could not keep her hand off the major but, with enormous effort, kept it from going further than plucking at his sleeve. Don José was not shocked, but he was anxious. He began to believe that the old priest would need to read the marriage rite while running backward up the main staircase and along the corridor toward

78

Maria de Lourdes' chambers while she made her responses and pulled the major after her.

The old priest was tragically aware of the power of the Aztec curse and made no shouts or murmurs of surprise or disapproval concerning the decision for such a sudden marriage, once he had looked upon the transformed young woman. The ceremony took four minutes. The marriage was celebrated in the large four-poster bed in Maria de Lourdes' rooms seven minutes later. They remained in bed for two and one-quarter days. At last, when the bride had fed, bathed, and massaged her husband and had helped him into his clothes, they hobbled downstairs to receive Don José's blessing.

The doctor was in his solarium painting a portrait in oils, from memory, of Pope Gregory XVI, who had granted Don José and his wife weekly audiences in 1841.

He greeted them with a whoop. He lifted Maria de Lourdes high in the air and whirled her about, covering her cheeks with kisses. He clapped the major on the back with such joy that he almost drove the nearly weightless man through the flooring of the castle. Then sat them down around the table which held the whisky and the cigars under the glass roof and plied them with mangoes and Liebfraumilch while he detailed his plans for their formal wedding, to be held three months hence on September fourth, which would be the sixty-ninth anniversary of the founding of El Pueblo de Nuestra Señora La Reina de Los Angeles de Porcicincula in California and therefore a fitting commemorative day for such a significant international wedding between a Mexican and a North American. He apologized that the wedding would need to be held to five hundred house-guests because of the necessity of supplying one armed guard to protect every five guests and as he could not pull in more than that many *vaqueros* from the range at a time when they were getting ready for round-up.

The major did not leave the Vicuña hacienda, or his wife's side, until fifteen months after the day he arrived. His own business affairs were conducted at the ranch and in Pickering City by Franklin Heller and Mat Sun, who alternated their visits to the major every other month. The Lipan Indians were raiding in northern Mexico in considerable numbers so that each time one or the other of the Patten lieutenants made the trip he would be accompanied by five armed riders. "I don't feel as safe as I might," Heller told the major. "I keep remembering how Shorty Moore had five men ridin' right along with him."

"Hell, them Indians can't shoot," the major said. "How're we doin' on whisky sales?"

"Better'n I ever seen it go. Even Miz Lee Schaefer sends over for a tin cup fulla the new stuff."

"What new stuff?"

"By mistake somebody sent along ten cases of a new-flavor whisky from Scotland. I sure hope the salesman comes in soon, 'cause I'll be all out in one more week."

"All out? All out?" The major grabbed his lapels. "You didn't jest happen to get in a few crates of a new kinda seegar, did you?"

"Why, yes. Strong but good. Howdy Hal Shaefer was havin' all kindsa trouble with a new herd of mustang mules but since he's been feedin' them these new seegars they jest foller him around like a little lamb."

It was at that moment that the major realized he had cast his lot for ever with the *cognoscenti*.

The system of making up guards of five riders eventually led to seven marriages with the young women of the Vicuña hacienda, the offspring accruing to the population of the Patten spread as the riders took their new brides home with them. The major was unable to take his bride home because she was so happy in the castle which had rather more to offer in terms of physical comforts and diversions than his own seat, a fact which the bride did not give a thought for she would have gone anywhere with him, but the major was just beginning to get the knack of luxurious living and greatly hesitated to halt his studies while such progress was being made. As he talked to Don José, as he observed what constituted luxury, he passed these pointers along to Heller or Mat Sun and gradually the interior of the big ranch house on the

80

other side of the river began to take on fixtures and fittings which would have delighted the most orectic sybarite.

Working with Don José he learned more about the administration of an enormous castle stand than he would ever have been able to teach himself. Seeing such vast numbers of cattle go only into hides convinced him more than ever that if he could solve the problem of shipment and delivery his cattle and his wife's could go forth to feed the world. When Don José asked him to stay on for a while or for ever, for as long as he could, he stated blankly that he felt it would be most necessary for the major to understand the operation of the empire of beef and land which would become his one day.

CHAPTER 11

MAJOR PATTEN and Don Patricio Reyes, the Vicuña wagon boss, rode through the ranch operations. The major learned a good deal more of what he had not known before. And he made one of the great friendships of his life.

In the sixth week of inspecting, working, learning (never more than a half-day's ride from the *casco* so that his wife could ride out to get him if she needed him), they rode into a pink pueblo which was in sight of the *casco,* two miles away. It held about seventy small adobe buildings, a large general store-cantina, and an immaculately white church whose bell began to peal as the two horsemen cantered down the wide street. As they came to a good-sized ranch building, four small boys and three girls came running out, crying "Papa! Papa!" and reaching up to grab reins and legs. Don Patricio swung off his horse, grinning broadly. "My house is your house," he said to the major with great pleasure. They were pulled inside by the children. The major met Señora Reyes, a small woman who studied him as though he were a calf at a country fair, then disappeared. He was introduced with formality to nine of the eleven children, then

81

Papa spoke sternly and they all scattered. All but one left the room. He was a small boy.

His father pretended to ignore him, guiding the major to a comfortable chair beside a fountain in the small, shaded patio, but the boy followed closely and stood beside his father's chair when Papa had seated himself.

"The others obey their father and go away when I tell them to go away, but not Benito," his father said. "Benito is very fond of my size, my guns, my horses, and that I am the big boss. Is that right, Benito?"

The small boy, who had a firm grip on his father's right hand, grinned with delight and nodded vigorously.

The major coughed with indecision. "How old are you?" he asked the boy, thinking that this may have been the first child he had spoken to since he had been one himself.

"I have seven years, sir. Benito Reyes, at your orders."

The boy stared somberly at the major as though memorizing his features. Señora Reyes appeared carrying a tray which had a thicket of beer bottles upon it. She set it down upon the table between her husband and the major. Don Patricio grinned, uncapped a bottle, handed it to his guest. He uncapped one himself and drank it down as though it were a small cup of tea. Señora Reyes waited for her husband's approval. He nodded, greatly satisfied, then opened two more bottles. "Good. Oh, very good. How is the gringo woman?"

"The same."

She returned to the darkness of the house.

"How is the gringo boy?" Don Patricio asked his son.

The boy nodded.

"The government is a long way from here," Don Patricio said; "Don José often says it would be easier and quicker to get help from Washington because there aren't so many mountains and deserts in between." He swigged at the beer. "In Texas, in the north, they offer a bounty for gophers, because gophers are peaceful little pests. In Coahuila we also have pests, but they are not peaceful." He broke wind. "In fact they are deadly and they are called Apaches and Lipans and Commanches. So the governors of the northern states of our Republic have caused the creation of a new kind of monster. Although that is not always what progress represents."

He opened another bottle of beer for the major. "This monster is the man who submitted his resignation to the human race and now sells scalps to the government." He shrugged. "I have killed many Indians, but I have not had the delight in horror which is the essence of a savage. I cannot maim and torture because he maims and tortures for the reason that I think I am closer to God than he is. But the bounty-hunter smirks at God. He gets two hundred pesos for a male scalp, one hundred and fifty for a female scalp, and if he is strong enough and brave enough to capture an Indian child alive he can sell it into slavery for one hundred pesos." He lifted Benito's hand and kissed it. "The Governor's palace at Sante Fe is beautifully decorated with dried Indian ears, smelling in the heat. Why ears?"

"Why not noses?" asked the boy seriously.

"Of course! Why not eyebrows?"

"Why not chins?"

The little boy smiled adoringly at his father and held Don Patricio's right hand with both of his own.

"The sick woman we have with us is the wife of such a man, a scalp merchant. His name is Oscar Street. He went into this business of murder and scalping the way you went into ranching, thoroughly and efficiently. The wife discovered what he did for a living when she had the joy of opening a trunk filled with blood-soaked scalps one afternoon. He explained them by telling her he was dedicated to protecting men, women, and children from the unholy scourge of the Indian. She left him. She went to New Orleans, where she had his child. He made no effort to stop her. He wanted the money. He was a simple man— he would have said. He wanted the money, nothing more. What could he do with the money? In his course he may have killed and scalped a thousand Indians, earning two hundred thousand pesos, but he stayed in the mountains and in the wastes. People seldom saw him." Don Patricio shook his head. "What could he want with money?"

"There was a story about him. For years in Sonora, Chihuahua, and Durango there has been a story about him. He invited eighty-six Indians to a feast and while they gorged he fired into them with a cannon he had concealed under some saddles and flour sacks. He earned seventeen thousand two hundred pesos that night, at a low cost in shot, but don't think it is an easy job to scalp eighty-six men by firelight all alone, particularly when, although all of them were maimed, not all of them were dead."

"But the wife is not a woman like that?"

"No. A great lady. They met at a ball so long ago, she says. In New Orleans. She opened the trunk. Then she left him. She raised the boy. A good boy—a really good, fine boy." He looked into Benito's eyes and smiled. "Benito likes him." The boy smiled like a flame.

"The mother became sick in the chest. She found out she was dying. Bloody scalps or not, she decided she must see her husband again. Must. She traveled from New Orleans across Texas and into Mexico, bringing the boy with her. He is exactly Benito's age." He sighed. "My wife would not let her go any farther than this. Her husband was caught in an Apache ambush two months ago and very little was left of him beyond a few fingertips. We don't tell her that. She will be dead soon."

"What will happen to the boy?"

Don Patricio grinned, a wonderful sight. "What will happen? He will become Benito's brother. When there is food in the pot, twelve children are much more jolly to have than eleven."

CHAPTER 12

DESPITE the major's half-day forays to learn other ways of big ranching, the bride and groom were almost always together. She whistled the great scores for him or played the harp. For days on end they would remain locked in their apartment in the castle, stretched in pink-whiteness across the green silk sheets. In the spacings Maria de Lourdes smoked *cañamo de India* and read aloud to him from the Kamasutra, frequently interrupting herself to demonstate a Vātsyāyana dictum.

Their formal wedding, on 4 September 1850, was attended by twelve hundred and fourteen guests, counting one-half the employees of both the Vicuña and Patten ranches who had drawn lots for invitations; most of the diplomatic corps from the capital; twenty-six generals, including the extraordinary entourage of General Enrique Jorge Molina, who carried a price on his head equal to the value of two-thirds of the cattle in the state of Tamaulipas, he having driven it there after having stolen it in Texas. His military staff, all in medalled uniforms, were a dazzling consortium. They were the most effective and professional of any staff of any *cabecilla* in the Republic—being brilliant, if unstable, cashiered officers from the British, French, and Polish armies.

The governors of the states of Sonora, Chihuahua, Coahuila, Tamaulipas, Durango, and Zacatecas also attended the wedding, complete with armed guards before and behind. Unfortunately, the governor of Zacatecas was shot in the left heel by a romping bullet from one of the guns of General Molina, who wept piteously throughout the wedding ceremony in the reconstructed Scottish kirk on the mesa and who fired at random when he reached the open air only to relieve the depression of so much sentiment.

The Arias family, sixty-four in all, attended from the Federal District, a journey requiring a certain character and keen interest. A committee of four

85

aunts were delegated to explain to the groom that, should the child or children be female that she, or they, were to be sent to Mexico City for formal education from the sixteenth to the nineteenth year, and then and there required him to sign a paper, so agreeing, which specified the names and addresses of the families with which these yet unborn were to live during that full and necessary unbroken period. They explained that the female children would be Arias, through Maria de Lourdes, and that they had a right to be taught how to protect themselves. He signed at once.

On little stages, decorated with blue-and-white tiles of Granada ware, bright rugs, and rich embroidered *mantones,* rival gypsy minstrels sung plaintive and thrilling *cante jondo.* There were bullfights. There were day-long celebrations of *charreria.* Flowers from the hothouses decorated all approaches to the *casco.* At night high torches were staked into the ground in hundreds of locations. Booths and cafés were arranged among them. Five hundred cases of tequila had been sent by wagon freight from Jalisco. Five of Mat Sun's brothers, who had arrived on a one-a-year schedule from China, were his straw bosses. They worked in Spanish which was as good as their English (which is to say they were as understandable as any five given pekinese dogs) yelling and darting through armies of women cooks. There were no meals hours after the first great wedding feast. Beeves, sheep, goats, and— as a favor to friends—some rabbits were turned on spits under which great coal pits glowed. The taco may have been invented at that wedding.

The guests slept in tents, on hammocks woven by Peña de La Quebrada in Acapulco, eight to a tent. The plaza before the castle, then the plain before the *casco,* was martial with billowing canvas striped broadly with red and yellow, green and blue, changing subtly in the orders of tone called out by the light of dawn, noon, dusk, moon, or torchlight. A picket line of guards on horseback and prone behind bushes in ambush made up the outer circle of the encampment. Sentries patrolled the area between the two. The only bandit most likely to have the force and daring to strike at such an assembly was General Molina, and he was an honored guest. No Indian force would make the attempt any more than a tiger would attempt to dig its way into a deep hole to get at a nest of cobras. Indians didn't operate that way.

Don Patricio presented his respects and those of his family to the bride and groom and to Don José on the day of the wedding and explained that their guest, the gringo woman, was sinking fast and that Señora Reyes was saddened to apologize that she must miss the wedding.

Franklin Heller was to be best man. After the bride and groom had gone to bed to rehearse procedures for the wedding night, he and Dr. Vicuña sauntered into the solarium and opened a bottle each of the Aberdeen ambrosia. Somehow, mainly because Franklin was wedged into a conversation about Argentine dairy products, they began talking about cheeses. It was a fabulously successful evening for both men. Franklin valued it because he seemed possessed with total recall. He sat quite erect, quite portly, his champagne-colored hair pouring down over his coat collar, his pince-nez glasses riding high on the bridge of his purple nose, the figure of a senator and twice as loquacious. Don José could not believe his good fortune in finding such a kindred spirit so far from the cheese capital. They were well into their second quart each when Heller reached the end of his discourse on the home-made Biza or *Fajy* cheese of Iraq and of the effect of its secret ingredient, *caoob,* when Dr. Vicuña became nostalgic.

"Do you know Dunlop cheese, Mr. Heller?"

"Aye."

"Aye?" Don José's voice rose in rapture.

"Ayrshire. Dunlop is a good cheese, Doc, but it sure is a peculiar thing that it's the only cheese the Scotch make when you figure they got such fine cattle and such fine grass." He hiccupped with panomphean resonance.

"I have thought of that often," the doctor pondered.

"Well, hell, it's worse than that, Doc. Dunlop don't keep an' it don't travel." He hiccupped so hard his head was snapped backward, crashing into the wooden frame of his chair. For an instant there seemed to be little x marks where his eyes had been.

"Rub his head, please," Dr. Vicuña directed the lady butler. She crossed behind Heller's chair in an instant and holding his head along the left cheek, she massaged the back of his head gently and soothingly with her right hand. Franklin talked on. "But it's got a great aftertaste, an' it sure is good toasted. I've et it. Sometimes I think the only reason I went to sea was to taste the cheeses that wouldn't travel."

Don José filled another jar with Scots whisky and the two men pulled on it broodily. The doctor stared at his guest, nodding his head slowly with admiration.

"Mr. Heller," he said with a deep tonal profundity, "a man with your figure and presence should really be dressed to the nines for that ceremony tomorrow. You would make it all the more memorable."

"You thinkin' of maybe *charro* clothes? Big hat crusted with silver? Afraid it won't work, Doc. I can't get inta them narrer pants."

"No, sir. I am thinking in terms of a frock coat with an ascot. Of striped trousers and a silk hat. You're a very distinguished-looking man, Mr. Heller. And highly civilized. Have to be to know Dunlop." Dr. Vicuña swayed slightly though seated.

"More moisture than Cheddar. Mild and creamy. Thin rind."

The stunning female butler had returned to her post behind Dr. Vicuña, and he attempted three times to look over his right shoulder to address her, but it would not match. "My dear, would you fetch my wedding suit?" he said straight ahead. She left the room.

"You're about my size, I'd say, Mr. Heller. I keep meaning to put a mirror on that far wall. Could make turning unnecessary."

"Ackshully, Dunlop keeps priddy dam well for three or four months."

"Would you mind standing for a moment?" Don José held tightly to offered protuberances and pulled himself to his feet.

"Cut across a Dunlop an' you'll see a perfiggly close, flat surface."

Dr. Vicuña made it with rigorous dignity to Mr. Heller's side. By wheedling, and by tapping him heavily, although in a friendly way, on the side of the head, he got him to his feet. Heller was some five inches shorter than the doctor, although stomached for two. "I'd like you to try on my wedding suit," Don José said.

"Thass one a the nicest things annabody ever said to me."

"Not at all."

"Yezzit is." Heller took off his jacket and let it drop. "If you ever come on over to Texas, I'd like you to try on a tie my father gave me. I've had that tie for sixteen years." His eyes grew misty. To cover it, he unbuttoned his shirt rapidly and took it off.

"Great Scots," Don José exclaimed. "You're gorgeous!" He walked as quickly as he could, without falling, to bring more light. "Don't move, sir. I pray you. Don't move." He placed lights on the tables all around Heller, every inch of whose skin from belly band to throat, front and back, arms and torso, was incomparably tattooed in many colors. "My dear Heller," the doctor gasped, "how absolutely and completely a work of art you are!"

"My tattoos?" Heller responded foggily.

"Yes, yes."

"My tattoos!" Heller seemed to sober up. His expression was consternation. He placed his hands flatly across his chest as the Sabine women may have done before they sat for the painting. "Where's my shirt? Where's my glasses?" The pince-nez had slipped behind him and were suspended on the black ribbon down his back.

"Do stop turning and jigging."

"How did this happen? How did they get my shirt offen me?"

"Will you *please* be still and let me study this exquisite draughtsmanship?"

Heller hung his head. "Well, Doc, all right. If you can get pleasure outta makin' me stand here like a freak in a freak show, well then you just go right ahead."

"Freak show? My dear Heller, you are a living,

89

breathing museum. You are so absolutely a work of art that I shall have to ask you to reveal to me where you had this done. Even at my age I must have it duplicated, or something like it, on my own chest and back."

Heller stared at him, touched, astonished, and dumbfounded. "You would have this here tattooing put on *you?*"

"And when I do, sir, they will have a difficult time of making me keep my shirt on. Why—I have never seen anything like it on any *canvas!*" He bent over and scrutinized a still life showing three orange mangoes, two bright-yellow and black bananas, and a coconut which rested upon purple shadows and an intricately woven straw mat directly over Heller's liver.

"Is that so?"

Dr. Vicuña turned him around slowly and rose to the right shoulder-blade area, where a thrilling tropical sunset spilt gilt overpainting upon the waters of a lagoon which was remote from all but continuing dreams of men. "Oh! Oh! I have *never!* How utterly magnificent!"

"You mean it? You ain't foolin'?"

"Mean it? *Mean* it? My dear Heller, you should be standing on a turntable in the Royal Scottish Museum this very instant."

All sorts of happy, relieved, grateful expressions attempted to break through upon Heller's face. His lower lip bobbled. "I—I can't believe it, Doc. I been undressin' in a closet for the past eleven years. I—I just thought I was a freak for a freak show."

Dr. Vicuña was gasping at the acharné horror of a Maori devil mask which glared out from a position over Heller's left kidney, then he followed a thick chain of jacaranda entwined with golden chalices around which flew the most exotic butterflies that any passion for beauty had ever conceived. It led to Heller's navel, then cascaded below his belt line. "What an exquisite balance of color!" Don José ejaculated. "This is simply staggering."

"You really mean that? Why, it's been ten years since I kissed a girl without all the lights was turned off an' the shades pulled down."

"Would you mind stepping out of those trousers, old boy?"

"Well—uh—I—"

"Come, come, Heller."

"The right leg is pretty good if I do say so myself." He unbuttoned his trousers slowly and stepped out of them with some effort, assisted by the doctor.

"Ah! Oh! Ah! Oh, my word. Slip out of that right sock, will you, old boy? It's flawing the dolphin's plunge." Three great silver dolphins were breaking water in a tremendous leap up Heller's right leg while crashing along his right thigh there came a long outrigger canoe carrying six exultant Polynesians.

"Mon dieu!"

They wheeled. They were both rather sobered now. The delectable butler stood in the doorway. "What a beautiful, beautiful man!" she sang. Heller had begun to flinch but her words straightened him. She came running to him, carrying the dress suit, then walking rapidly around and around him. She moaned lightly as she saw what she saw. "This is my home," she sang. "These are the people of my father's land, the Tuamotu, where France forgets in the Pacific."

"Well, how did you know that?"

"This is Nukutipipi or Pukapuka." She ran her free hand lovingly over his stomach, which billowed out over the top of his underwear.

"Where did you have this done, Mr. Heller?" the doctor asked insistently. "After the wedding we shall leave at once to have such masterpieces etched into us."

"I—I don't right know," Heller said slowly. "I'd sure tell you if I knew because you've changed a lot of things for me just now, but I was shipwrecked eleven years ago, somewheres in the South Pacific—"

"I knew it! I *knew* it," the lovely butler said.

"They was mighty purty people I lived with. They was good to me, too. One day I was walkin' along the shore an' I seed an old man get pulled out of a boat by a churnin' fish net and then he got tangled in it an' it looked like he was drownin'. I got out there with a canoe, then I went over the side after him, an' a shark come by. I hadda knife. I stuck it in the shark an' after a time I got the old man ashore. Then I blacked out. When I woke up they tell me I'd got the fever. I'd been under three months an' while I was under, to thank me for what I had done for him, the old man had tattooed ever' part of me, including these frangi-pangi petals on the soles of my feet, to make walkin' easier." He held up one foot and the doctor and the butler stared into its gorgeously multicolored sole with fascination. "I was picked up a year after that. Left a lot of good friends back there. But I don't know where I was or how to get back, an' even if I did, I don't think we'd ever find that old man again."

"Art is short and time has flown," Dr. Vicuña said mournfully. "Dust to dust."

The wedding was held on the steps of the small Scottish kirk which had been reconsecrated upon its reconstruction by Dr. Vicuña's dear friend, the Papal Nuncio. It stood alone on a knoll on the mesa. Before it, women weeping, men bareheaded and solemn, stood the friends of the bride and the groom, family, and well-wishers. When they had been pronounced man and wife (although no kisses were exchanged by internal family agreement, as it would not have done to have got the bride inflamed at such a time) the belfry began to sing its iron song, giving a marching rhythm to the procession of twelve hundred wedding guests as they poured across the mesa by carriage, coach, horseback, and on foot to sit at the wedding banquet.

The banquet began at six o'clock in the evening and was expected to move through the night upon the back of its beatitude into the following day. Don José had called in from the pastures the eight shepherds who had accompanied his bride on the voyage from Scotland. They danced with claymore and scabbard in the victory dance called Gilly Callum, then into the Flamborough which straightened out into a longways formation, a ring-and-step, into heys, double-unders, threedling with double overhead arches into the lock on the swords, into a star shape, circling clockwise in the rose, never loosening their hold on the chain of swords held between them, hilt and point. When they finished they stood, breathing hard and weeping while the bride played "Lament for the Macleod" on the pipes. Then seven Negro jugglers from Vera Cruz filled the air with ninety flying pieces of fruit which cascaded in swift patterns of color while an orchestra of guitars and harps played *bombas*. Massed Yacqui Indians in ceremonial dress danced and keened wedding ritual music. Seventy-eight *mariachis* from Guadalajara, Ahualuco, and Mascota shook the skies with their assembled noise. A massive *cuadro flamenco* of forty-four couples moved wantonly through stamping explosions and wild, waving movements; then, to complete the international cultural picture, Major Patten stood on his chair and with full and moving baritone sang "Hell Among the Yearlin's."

As he reached the fourth chorus, a Lipan attack struck the pueblo of Don Patricio Reyes, two miles from the wedding feast. The smoke and light from the fire of the burning buildings was seen first by Don Patricio, who leaped to his feet with a scream of premonition, pointing at the light in the distance. Forty riders, all men from the pueblo, were mounted in six minutes. They rode off. A troupe of tumbling, painted clowns came on the platforms before the guests; with such diversion it was difficult for twelve hundred to miss forty.

CHAPTER 13

MOST of the buildings of the pueblo were ruined. Charred or disembowelled bodies of women, children, and men were strewn across the open ground. Babies had been brained against building walls. Nothing lived. Even the throats of the dogs had been cut. Black smoke hung in the air, spiced with the smell of roasting meat. The *vaqueros* fell to their knees and stared at the past. Don Patricio walked from body to body in a daze, marking his own dead, counting upon the fingers of his grief until he stumbled in a blood-filled rage back to his horse. He mounted and rode off, oblivious of the others. By twos and fives they mounted and rode after him. Soon only a wall of dust as tall as the ghosts in their memories, rose and obscured them.

They trailed the Lipan force for three days. They never caught sight of them. The Lipans knew the mountains well and the highways of rock which left no trail. From the people along the route of pursuit they learned that the leader was the new young, monstrous chief Tortillaw and that he carried a Mexican girl strapped behind him. They learned that eight small boys had been mounted as captives, and each father's heart lifted to think that his son might still live—then it fell again at what the life would mean. The Lipans needed small boys. They could be made into savages. The Apache nation was not breeding males. For two generations there had been many, many more females than males and seed was needed.

The Lipans had driven no stolen cattle or horses ahead of them. They seemed to have raided only to destroy. Don Patricio thought of the ivory matchstick of a woman who had been dying so much more slowly than she did finally die, who had been a silly girl in a banal ball dress who had married a bland fiend who murdered Indians for profit. By signing the marriage register she had killed a village. He thought of his wife. He thought of the fate of Good Samaritans. He thought of God, then he remembered he had lost Benito.

On the sixth day the riders returned to the ruins of the pueblo. Each man dismounted and knelt to pray in front of what had been his house. Patricio clasped his hands and bowed his head and began the miraculous process of transferring his grief to his God in minute parcels to be handed over each morning and each night until the past joined eternity, muted and veiled, its daggers fallen from hands which stretched to make a ring of time with the future; endless, each the same, each face lifted toward heaven. He saw the days in his life in that charred house. He heard the voices of his children. He felt the calm beauty his wife had revealed to him when his eyes were sore with the exhaustion of living. They had left him in that house; now he must leave that house and find a way to whirl and spin which would fling off his grief with centrifugal force. The last part of his prayer was an explicit message to his God, stating flatly that he did not blame Him. When he opened his eyes and lifted his head Benito was standing before him, smiling bravely.

Don Patricio could not speak. Benito spoke. "They killed Mama. They took Jacaranda with them."

His father threw his arms around the little boy to hold him close and to weep on him as he knelt in the dust. Benito kissed his father, arms held tightly around his father's neck, and said, "Jim and I were with the cattle in the south corral when they came. It was dusk. We heard the screams. We saw the fire. We saw them take Jacaranda. She fought them but they hit her. We hid among the legs of the cattle all the night. Jim is very sick. He went to find his mother but she had turned black. Her eyes were gone. Because of the smell of the people in the fire he says he cannot eat. He tries, but he cannot eat."

Don Patricio stood up. "Where is he?"

Benito held his father's right hand and kissed it. "The men from the *casco* were here. The *patron* was here. They made a big funeral but they did not see me. I stayed with Jim. I waited for you to come." He led his father to a roofless half-burned barn which was behind the house they had lived in. A thin, pale boy was curled up under a wagon. Don Patricio picked him up in his arms. This is why they are all dead and torn, he thought. This is the son they came to kill, the son of the wife they came to kill, the son of the murderer who had ambushed hundreds of their people. This boy is alive and all the rest of ours are dead. "He has fever."

"He is very sad."

"We will ride to the *casco*," Benito's father said.

Maria de Lourdes took the burning boy from him. The boy moaned and called out Benito's name shrilly and in fright, so Don Patricio sent Benito to stay with him. "Ai, he is wasting away." Maria de Lourdes said, then hastened off with him.

Don Patricio watched them go with his dull eyes and thought that the fire and fever within the boy had withered all of them, that the disease of spirit had flared and burned to consume a village. He asked the servant to take him to the *patron*. As he walked through the shadows of the castle, his mind had already started to leave the place. When he faced the *patron* it was seen that he had changed his eyes from those which Don José and the major had last seen in his head. They were only guttering lights where there had been suns. They had lost the purpose which had set him apart. His cheeks were sunken. His beard was filthy. His voice was hoarse.

"I cannot stay here for the time, *patron*."

"Are all the men of the pueblo to leave?"

"No. I do not think so. To them the days have brought more grief. To me—the days have brought grief and I know why this has happened. It deranges me."

"Sit down, Patricio. Please. Sit down."

He touched the huge man on the shoulder, causing him to stumble backward and fall into a chair. Don José poured a glass of whisky and handed it to him. He stuck a large cigar in Patricio's mouth and lighted it.

"I have to get away, *patron*. I have to keep moving in the new places. I will fight in the days and leave the nights for prayer."

"Where?"

"With General Molina, I think. When did he leave here?"

"Five days ago."

"Where did he go?"

"San Nepomuceno. Between Reynosa and Matamoros."

"*Patron?*"

"Tell me. Anything. Ask me anything."

"My boy Benito was saved."

The major made a guttural sound in his throat.

"God is good," Don José said.

"He has a brother. The gringo boy."

"Give them to me. Until you can come back."

"I will come back."

"I know that."

Patricio stood up. He held Don José's hand in both of his. "Benito wants with all his heart to grow tall and become *muy charro, patron*. As you are."

"As you are, Patricio."

"If time and God should keep me away—" his voice trembled with indecision.

"He shall be raised to grow a heart like his father's," Don José said flatly.

"The gringo boy, too?" The indecision pulled the words of the sentence far apart and distorted whatever meaning they might have had.

"Do you want that?"

"Yes." All at once the decision had been made and Don Patricio's eyes began to dissemble their darkness. "That is important. It is most important in the eyes of God. If there had been no gringo boy, if we had not sheltered his mother, there would have been no raid, no death." He sighed with an exhausted hiss through his nostrils. "No one must think to blame that boy."

"He will be raised with Benito. Both as my sons."

Don José and Patricio shook hands. Major Patten lifted his hand slowly and then placed it over theirs, gripping hard and staring at them intensely, joining their pledge.

CHAPTER 14

THE two boys were alone. It was early morning. "You must eat. You must will that the food stays within you," Benito said intensely into the pale boy's ear.

"Can't." He was a dark-haired seven-year-old boy and he looked very Mexican.

"Try." Benito was a light-brown-haired, seven-year-old boy and he looked very Irish. He looked tired, too, but each time his friend spoke he seemed limitlessly rested. Only his haggard small face and the red rims of his eyes as much as suggested that he was not wholly stimulated at the opportunity for conversation at five o'clock in the morning.

"You know why?" Jim asked in a whisper. "I know."

"Why?" Benito leaned over his friend for the answer as though there would be no other chance except in this answer.

"They cooked my mother. I can smell the roasting meat."

97

"I can smell it too. Still."

"They cooked your mother, too."

"Yes. But I can eat."

"You know why? I know."

"Why?"

"You didn't see your mother afterwards."

"No."

"I did. I saw mine." He rocked his head feverishly, as though in an effort to shake an awful picture out. He lay still. Irish sat on the chair beside the bed, his head upon his fists, staring and waiting.

"Irish?" It had never bothered Benito when Jim called him Irish.

"Yes?"

"Meat is meat."

"Yes."

"Cows, bugs, and people. Cook it and it's meat."

Benito stood up slowly, supernaturally refreshed. "You are right, Jim. Now I am going to get some tortillas. Tortillas are not meat. We will start you eating again with tortillas."

"No!"

"I will be gone five minutes. You will have time to think about it. Tortillas are not meat." He slipped away into the darkness, closing the door behind him.

Dr. Vicuña had sat with Jim for almost three days, off and on, returning to his bed at all hours of the day and night. Benito slept in the bed which had been put beside Jim's. He always seemed to be awake when the doctor came in. Jim had not eaten for six days. Sometimes his eyes were rolling, wild with fever, but mostly he was weak and torpid. That evening Dr. Vicuña had taken Benito into the corridor.

"He is dying, Benito."

"No, *patron.*"

"Very well. Then I will say to you that if he does not eat soon, he will die soon."

"He will eat."

"How do you know that?"

"Because I always talk to him about eating. Whenever he is able to stay awake."

"Everyone talks to him about eating, but he does not eat."

"But I will find out *why* he will not eat."

"Ah."

"When we know why, we can help him to eat."

"You are, as a boy, like your father, as a man."

The little boy's eyes shone with gratitude for that, then he smiled like the light of sun through a clean morning. "Tell my father, *patron*."

When Benito came back to the sickroom he had a straw mat on which he carried some cold tortillas, some cold frijoles, and a pear.

"Do you think, Jim?" he asked.

"Yes."

"What did the thinking say to you?"

"That tortillas are not meat."

"Yes, *yes!* Here, a very small piece of tortilla." He left the shred in his hand and brought it to Jim's mouth. The boy took it and chewed it.

"Frijoles are also not meat," Benito said.

"I will think about it."

"Good." He sat on the chair beside Jim's bed and rested his head on his clenched fists, one on top of the other. Five minutes passed, then ten. He did not move or speak. Jim lay back on the pillow with his eyes closed as though he were sleeping or dead.

"Frijoles are not meat," he said.

"Oh, *yes!* Yes, Jim. You are right. Frijoles have strength." He plucked a small nugget of frijoles from its solid, dark-brown mass of mashed beans and brought it carefully to Jim's lips. "This is a *vegetable*. This is not meat. Many, many people never eat meat, Jim. They eat corn and frijoles and tortillas and they become very strong." He touched the boy's lower lip with a small morsel of cold beans. The mouth took it. It chewed a little bit. The boy swallowed. They waited for a long time. He did not vomit. In the hour after that he was able to take the rest of one tortilla and two more smidgeons of frijole. He fell asleep.

"You sleep because you have gorged yourself, Jim," the small brown-haired boy said. He grinned at his own joke. He ate the pear himself. He pulled the chair closer to his friend's bed. He pillowed his head on his arms, resting on the edge of the bed. Soon he was asleep.

CHAPTER 15

DR. DON JOSÉ VICUÑA Y ARIAS, gentleman and friend, died on the Fourth of July, 1851. He had been told of the impending arrival of his grandchild some four months before, on 18 March, and this glorious news had sent him off to the farthest reaches of the enormous hacienda, bigger than all but four countries in Europe, to spread the good word and to set off intensive celebrations through which he would ride a galloping stallion shooting six-guns into the air, then eating, drinking, and dancing as though he were running for the presidency of the Republic. He celebrated the arrival of his grandchild some months ahead of time in point of clinical fact, and his joy exhausted him.

His Fourth of July celebration was his last exuberant achievement. It was based upon the view that his grandchild would be half North American and that the Fourth of July therefore held a new significance. Between 18 March and 4 July he had thought much and aloud about what the child should be called. He had reached his decision on the morning of his death. The problem was, on the surface, simple—once the approaches to it had been cleared away. He explained to the expectant parents, and they agreed, that the name should have a North American ring and yet be one which would stir the memories of the Mexican side of the family. If a boy, it was voted unanimously after Dr. Vicuña's nomination the child would be called Joseph, not José. They agreed that the name José Patten did not come together properly. If a girl, the infant would be called Evaliña for no reason at all except that Don José had looked mystical and faraway when he had said it and it may have had to do with some lost spirit of his youth.

For the Independence Day celebration the honored

guests were assembled on the terrace overlooking the broad mesa to the rear of the castle. *Copas* were poured, toasts were drunk, wine flowed, the buffet groaned, and off to the side—to the whimpering ecstasy of Franklin Heller—there stood a sideboard holding seventeen different kinds of cheese.

It was a small, intimate group. Mat Sun and M. Weill talked shop, the major and Mr. Heller chewed cheese, Don José and the old priest hurled toasts to the sky from a chain of cups passed by the enchanting lady butler, and the round mother-to-be beamed upon all and knitted on something, occasionally patting the sides of the burgeoning area at her middle.

Flushed, breathless, and ecstatic, Don José in a trembling voice announced the splendid surprise he had planned to be in keeping with the meaning of the day. He excused himself from their company to produce "a little effect commemorating the entry of the former Mexican territories of California and New Mexico into the flag of the country which will have so shortly a half-claim upon the allegiance of my grandchild."

Forty minutes later, eighty feet below the parapet, they watched move across the area at eight miles an hour, covering a compact area of 274 square yards, the pattern of a living flag of the United States of America formed by *mañadas* of hundreds of varicolored horses: red, white, and blue. White ponies ran among the sea of blue-black mares to represent the stars of the thirty-one states of the Union. The two ponies which represented California and New Mexico, the two stars which had been admitted to the flag that day, wore bridles of gold and cockades of white feathers. The galloping flag was a stirring and beautiful sight; fitting to Don José's human proportions.

Then, eighty feet below the view of the people who loved him most, Don José fell from his horse as he rode directly above the moving flag. They stared, stunned. No one could find the wit to move except the major, who clattered across the flagstones and ran headlong down the stairs to the plaza. He snatched the reins of the nearest horse and cut into it with quirt and spurs as he raced out to find what he feared.

When he reached him, Don José was still alive. Alive as if by will, as if he had known the major would cooperate. He smiled briefly but moved his fingers impatiently for the major to come very close. The major put his ear close to Don José's head.

The broken voice came in gasps. "If the child is a girl you must never tell her about the curse. I—I no longer believe there is a curse." Then he died.

The funeral and the internment in the marble mausoleum in the hacienda's pantheon was quite silent except for the eulogy by Patricio Reyes, who had been summoned from the east, the intoning of the aged priest, and the soft weeping of the hundreds of women whom the departed had favored in his lifetime. Thirty-eight hundred people attended the services. It rained, which Don José would have considered banal.

At the castle after the funeral, Maria de Lourdes retired to pray. Don Patricio told the major he should stay on and take over again as foreman. Pale, her eyes ringed in black, dressed for travel in bonnet and cloak, the lady butler came to the major and resigned. She would return to France. He told her she could not go. She said she could not stay. He pleaded with her, asking how she could think of going when he needed her most, when his child, Don José's grandchild, was about to be born. She stared at him sadly, her eyes slowly changing away from hopelessness. "My mind was with him. I did not know you needed me." She removed her bonnet as she left the room.

Evaliña Patten was born on 13 October 1851. Her mother tired easily and, in attempting to move her head to see her baby, died at the half-turn.

Major Patten left the hacienda for Texas on 17 October 1851. He rode in the eight-horse coach with Janine Michaud, the lady butler who had found the need she sought. She carried the baby in her arms.

Major Patten had lost his beloved; he had been abandoned by his great teacher and friend; he had become master of the greatest juncture of cattle ranches the world had ever known.

102

BOOK TWO

1857-1868

CHAPTER 1

MAJOR PATTEN sent word to Don Patricio in the spring of 1857 that he wanted Patricio's son and the Street boy to be transferred to work on the Texas side of the ranch. They were fourteen years old. Don Patricio had the boys sent to him at the center of the great paved plaza, baked in sunlight, at approximately the place he had first met Major Patten and, hunkering down on their own legs in a tight circle, he told the boys the news.

"But why on the Texas side?" Benito asked. "We know English. Why can't we work for you?"

"The major wants you to learn how they do things on the other side of the river. You boys have to get ready to do the big jobs."

"We will be ready," Benito said.

"When do we go?" Jim asked.

"When Benito and I return from Lalotorres."

Benito studied his father. This was something new. He had never heard of Lalotorres. Jim watched Benito.

"Benito is going to meet the girl he will marry someday," Don Patricio said.

"I am?"

"When?" asked Jim intently.

"We will leave in the morning.'"

"I mean when is he going to marry her?"

"When she is eighteen."

"How old is she now?" Benito pressed.

"She is four."

"*Four?*" both boys exploded.

"That is the best way," Don Patricio said. "It proves the seriousness of the marriage."

"That is true." Benito nodded gravely.

"I'm glad it ain't me," Jim Street said.

The boys were the same long, stringbean size. Jim was scrawnier; Irish had started to fill out sooner. The major had started everyone calling Benito "Irish" years before, and in time everyone came to think this was a natural name—although it had been a long time since anyone within a thousand miles had seen an Irishman, if ever. The boys had been inseparable since the raid on the pueblo. They thought in the same way. Irish was a little quicker to arrive at a conclusion but Jim was more stubborn in holding convictions and was much more sure of what the convictions meant. Jim Street looked as Mexican as Benito Reyes looked Irish. He was classically, aquilinely, brownly Mexican, with large dark eyes and coarsè black hair. Irish was fair. He had sandy hair. He was as aquiline as a gumdrop. His blue eyes were wide with the astonishment at how his small, snubbed nose had snapped back toward himself. He grinned. Jim was impassive.

For two years the boys had been working as *caballerangos*, wranglers in charge of the outfit's saddle horses—called the *remuda de caballos,* which usually ran on a good-sized ranch from one hundred to three hundred mounts. The Vicuña *remuda* was broken down into eight separate units and comprised over twenty-two hundred saddle horses. The boys worked the *remuda* closest to Don Patricio.

A horse-wrangler is the low man in any outfit. His relationship to the top hand is about the same as a dish-washer's at a great restaurant to the customer with the biggest line of credit. A wrangler must know every horse in the *remuda* by name and sight, and know when one is missing. As wranglers they were also the greenest hands. They learned how to work stock, rustle wood and water for the cook, help to set up and strike the camp on a round-up, and hook and unhook wagon teams. Many times when the cook was forced behind schedule by weather trouble, each boy chopped firewood or took up a sack to gather a harvest of dried cowchips for fuel. Both boys knew what they were doing around a ranch from the beginning. The work gave them muscles and seemed to stretch them out at an incredible rate. When they were fourteen they were six feet tall and still growing. Don Patricio saw that they learned to do everything they needed to know. He also saw that they learned to shoot. He taught them himself, then turned them over to Pepe Ferrer, who was the fastest gun in the north of Mexico and who could plait the most magnificent rawhide quirts, called *cuartas de cordon*. They were taught to carry their six-guns low on their thighs and to strap them firmly into position where the hands and arms learn, by practice, to find them instantly. The gun butts swung out midway between their knees and hips, right where their hands fell naturally to touch them without bending the arms. They were taught to carry their guns on a snug-fitting belt about two and a half inches wide and the belt was held up with a pair of shoulder straps if they had to carry the guns for any length of time. Don Patricio was awestruck when Ferrer came to him after four months of working with the boys for one hour in the morning and one hour in the evening to report that they were faster than he was with either hand. "It is good this happened," he said. "Good for me. It keeps my vanity very small which means that I will live longer."

Don Patricio and his son set out for Lalotorres on bay horses before dawn. The ride to the state of Zacatecas was just over four hundred miles. Irish was excited to make such a journey with his father and also because his future father-in-law was the great Don Guillermo Peña B., the greatest gunman ever produced in Mexico history, who had been his father's closest comrade-at-arms during the year he had spent in the forces of General Enrique Jorge Molina while that greatest of all cattle-stealing technicians had bored a hole in the bottom of the map of Texas through which eventually fell over seven hundred thousand Texas steers which were liquidated at once into sound money after shipment from the Mexican Gulf port of Baghdad, in Tamaulipas, to Cuba and other points.

On the third night, after they had eaten and before Don Patricio turned in, leaving Irish to take the first watch, for they were in hostile country where Indians or bandits would be happy to murder them for their gear, Don Patricio began to talk about his friend the great gunman, perhaps to give his son an idea of the traditions of the family into which he was about to be pledged to marry.

"There has never been a gun like him, Benito."

"I know. Oh, I know. Pepe Ferrer has told me."

"Ferrer is fast. But he could draw and Don Guillermo Peña could have time to take a pair of skin-tight gloves off before killing your teacher."

"That is what Pepe Ferrer said. I mean more or less exactly."

"It is an incredible, almost magical, effect which I shall persuade him to show you before we leave Lalotorres."

"Ah."

"If you could have seen how proud General Molina was of his skill. The general would send out patrols to reconnoitre in the various saloons and dance halls as far away as San Antonio. They would listen carefully to all the bullies and the braggarts. They would report to the general and he would make his selection. Then, for each Christmas Day celebration, he would have one of these men kidnapped and brought into our camp. We would have a big feed. The general would let the prisoner eat with us, then he would explain that he had asked his men to bring the prisoner to us because he had been told that the man was one of the great gunmen of the Southwest. They would always admit it. Then the general would ask the bully if he were afraid of gun-fighting with a Mexican. This would make the prisoner laugh and laugh. Then the general would say that because it was Christmas he was going to declare an amnesty and give him his own guns back if he would agree to a gunfight with one of his men. If the man won, the general would say, he would not only be set free but he was going to be given a Christmas present of a thousand dollars in gold."

"A thousand dollars in gold!"

"After all, the general could have said ten thousand. They never collected, these men. Don Guillermo Peña would lean on a hitching-post in the company street, very casual, and as the prisoner was sent out to face him, packing his guns on, his belly full of good, inviting whisky, Don Guillermo would smile at him and whisper something. 'What did you say?' the Texan would bellow. Don Guillermo would make his voice a

107

little louder and he would answer, 'I said good-bye,' still leaning up against the hitching-post while his man went into a stiff, high crouch, his fingers tensing. 'Draw!' Don Guillermo would yell, for that cry was his trademark. The prisoner would draw and then he'd be dead." Don Patricio gave his head a wag of admiration. "They were two of the most marvelous Christmas Days I ever spent," he murmured.

On the fifth day, the night before the day they would reach Lalotorres, Don Patricio began to talk again about the good old days. "I remember a famous time when we had heard about a killer who came from Laredo. We were a long way from Christmas so the man was useless in a celebration sense, but he had upset General Molina because he persisted in saying that although he had seventeen notches on his guns to record the men he had killed, he never bothered to keep count of the Mexicans he had gunned down."

"If a man kills you he can at least have the courtesy to count you," Irish said.

"Exactly. Yes. When Don Guillermo Peña heard this story he did not wait to hear it twice. He told me what he was going to do and I said I would like to ride along with him. We told General Molina and he gave us full leave, as long as it would be necessary, at full pay. He said that if we brought back satisfaction that we would be invited to eat at his mess for one week. General Molina ate the way Don José, God rest his soul, used to eat, and the privilege was accorded only in instances of extreme bravery beyond the call of duty. It was a greater honor than the Molina Medal, which the general awards on Easter morning and on the morning of his saint's day each year, bringing with it five bottles of tequila and a two-day pass.

"We were working further south at the time under maneuvers in San Luis Potosi, robbing banks and holding up the *dilegencias* whenever the general had been informed of gold-ore shipments, so it was a good nine-day ride to Laredo. He had an unusual name—the Sweet Potato Kid was what they called him. Jim Heneghan, the Sweet Potato Kid. I am happy to say he was in Laredo just as though we had written ahead for a reservation to shake his hand, and I say we were happy because the one-hundred-and-fifty-mile stretch between Monterrey and the border in January is the driest, dustiest stretch of country I had ridden through in a long time. We had spent a year in Tamaulipas, near the water. What a verdant, moist, delightful state! Surely it is the prettiest in the Republic."

"But what happened?"

"Oh. Well, as soon as we located him at the center of the bar in the big saloon, Don Guillermo shriveled himself up and approached him most respectfully, his sombrero in his hands, his eyes cast down. What a delightful scene he played. It was the Christmas pageant all over again. He was the cowed and cringing peon who dares to address the great pistolero.

" 'Señor Sweet Potato—please señor,' Don Guillermo entreated for attention.

" 'What the hell do you want, greaser?' the Sweet Potato snarled at Don Guillermo.

"Don Guillermo put on his hat humbly. 'I have come this long way to ask you one question, your grace. All the way from San Luis Potosi.'

" 'Where the hell is that?' roared the Sweet Potato. He was having a wonderful time. The crowd was beginning to gather around. He lived for that."

"He died for that, too, I bet," Irish said gaily.

"He did indeed, my son. Then Don Guillermo said, 'May I ask you one question, estimable Sweet Potato? It is only to settle a bet.'

" 'What question?' the Sweet Potato snarled back, beginning to like this little man because he knew such good manners.

"Don Guillermo smiled a little smile of a poor man who hopes to be forgiven for breathing the same air as the great. 'This is the question, honored señor—of the seventeen people you have murdered—' the crowd stiffened '—how many did you shoot in their backs and how many did you shoot in their sleep?'

"The Sweet Potato looked pop-eyed for an instant. Don Guillermo yelled 'Draw!' Then he killed the man.

"Of course it was a delightful moment but its delight

was to be exceeded because the killing of the Sweet Potato Kid was only half of what we had made the long ride for. The dead man had been a nuisance to the forward-looking business element among the gamblers and whores of the saloon business, and they crowded all around us—that is around Don Guillermo, whom I happened to be standing beside, and insisted upon buying us drinks. They had noticed the many notches in his gun butts and, with much respect, they waited for him to cut a new notch for Mr. Heneghan, but we just enjoyed the free drinks.

"Finally, the sheriff spoke up. 'You are the fastest gun I ever seed, stranger,' looking at Don Guillermo as though he were a folk hero, and out of nowhere four extremely ugly dance-hall girls who were much older than we appeared on either side of us, baring their teeth unalluringly. The sheriff stared tenderly at Don Guillermo. 'Ain't you goin' to notch your gun to score the Sweet Potato Kid?'

"This moment was really what we had made the long ride for," Don Patricio said to Irish beside the flickering fire, his face softened by the pleasure of the memory.

"Don Guillermo shook his head, then he spoke very carefully because his English was not quite as precise as the suave Texan's, but he spoke what he had to say perfectly because I had drilled into him the pronunciation of this one English sentence many, many times during the long ride north. 'No,' he answered, 'I never bother to keep count of the gringos I shoot.' "

Irish and his father stared into the fire for some time before Don Patricio spoke again. At last he said, "Don Guillermo Peña is a man who never forgets a wrong. He is relentless. Always remember that, Benito."

"I will remember, Papa."

"He is a very proud man."

"I can sense that, Papa."

They rode into Lalotorres just after three o'clock the next afternoon, the time calculated by the enormous turnip watch Don José had given to Don

Patricio. They were braced by the invigorating smell of the charcoal and by the sound of the women slapping tortillas. It was a small village. It had red roofs, golden walls, brown streets, and it was dominated by a dazzling pink seventeenth-century church in the stately main square under a stinging blue sky. Geographically, it could be said that the town had everything because it straddled the Tropic of Cancer: one half of it in the Temperate Zone and the other half in the tropics. It had been a silver-mining town years before. It had been an ancient hideout for thieves and highwaymen. Now, the people made tiles and mosaics which were beautiful and durable. As the man and the boy rode into town past an occasional cow or goat chewing apathetically on cactus, beneath circling turkey buzzards which planed across the solid blueness, they were content because they saw Mexico before them repeating its song of life. Don Guillermo was sitting at a table on a small terrace before a fonda in the plaza, facing the pink church. He was the mayor of the village and he had made the table his office. He was eating his second favorite dish, which was tripe. As their horses crossed the sunny plaza with dainty steps, they grinned at each other waiting for him to look up and greet them with a shout of welcome. As they came upon him they watched him eat, waiting for the explosion of his warmth.

They were almost upon him when he looked up, and the look which crossed his eyes almost turned them and their horses to stone; a gun had appeared in his hand and Irish, in reflex, fell sideways out of his saddle. The man caught himself in time, before he shot. He recognized Don Patricio and let out a great whoop of joy to welcome them.

Don Guillermo was a tall, slender man. He was deeply tanned. He had hard, merry eyes and a brown, drooping mustache. The slash of a mouth under it could have made a great matador of bulls shiver. It was the mouth of a man who could keep vultures as lovebirds. He wore a tall, chocolate-color, conical sombrero with a wide brim which was severely upturned in the back. He carried two guns and wore cartridge belts crossed on his chest. His dark brown trousers gripped his legs tightly, *charro* style. He wore cartwheel spurs of silver.

"Patricio!"

"Memo!"

"And this is the son who has ridden across a nation to meet his future wife."

Irish had brushed himself off. He stood by with much deference. His father swung down off his horse and the two men fell into an *abrazo*.

"How good to see you, Patricio. So many years."

"Ah, Memo! How fine! How fine!"

"This boy will be bigger than you."

"He will be bigger than his horse."

"How old is he?"

"Fourteen years."

"That is good. Very good." Standing between the two Reyes, he took them by the upper arms and propelled them forward to the single table in front of the cantina. "Sit down," he said. "You are now in the office of the *alcalde* of Lalotorres. Marco! Marco Reuben!"

A man who could only be an innkeeper appeared instantly. He seemed to be made of circles. He smiled and bobbed, bobbed and smiled behind a huge white apron, standing in the doorway. "Yes, your honor? Tequila? Wine? Pulque? Beer? Water? Coffee? The check?"

Don Guillermo ordered a bottle of tequila and he and Patricio started at once and by midnight they had covered the first three months of their service with General Molina. Irish was fed at nine o'clock. He found a bed in an inn an hour later. When he awoke it was six o'clock. His father and Don Guillermo were still talking on the terrace. That is, Don Guillermo was talking. His father seemed to be sleeping, propped up by one elbow.

When Don Guillermo saw Irish he said, "Well, son, you and your father have been riding pretty hard for six days so maybe you ought to go to bed."

"Yes, sir."

"Tomorrow you will meet Florita. It will be one of the most important days of your life."

"Yes, sir."

"And of mine. Have some rest. I will come for you in the morning." He got to his feet easily, spun slowly around at knee level, then fell forward on his face. The innkeeper took charge of him. Irish slid his wide shoulder under his father's waist and lifted. He carried him upstairs to the room he had just vacated and lowered him gently to the bed. He pulled the boots off, got the gun belt off, then loosened the shirt at the throat.

"You waited a long time for that talk, hey, Papa?" he grinned.

The formal meeting of the affianced couple was held in the patio of the Peña house—which had been built upon the only hill overlooking the town, as befitted the residence of its most famous man and mayor. The bride-to-be was painting a mud mustache on a doll which had fallen out of her favor when she was summoned to her father's side. She arrived in her mother's arms, kicking and screaming, to meet the man she would marry. This aggressive indifference troubled the groom, even troubled Don Guillermo.

"I do not think she understands," her father said.

"She was probably busy," her fiancé answered.

"She is tired," her mother explained. "She is really a very good girl, but she had a touch of colic in the night and it kept her awake for some time."

"Then perhaps you should put her to bed," Don Guillermo said a trifle stiffly.

"In that case we will withdraw," the mother said, and carried the bawling, squirming child into the house.

"She seemed very pretty," Irish said faintly.

"My boy," Don Guillermo pronounced, crashing his chilling gaze into Irish's eyes, "this is one of the great moments. You have just looked upon your future. It seemed to weep upon you and to protest, but that is the best omen for it is written that a bad beginning means a good ending. Am I right in the use of that aphorism, Patricio?"

"You are correct; I have never seen two young people who were so suited to each other."

113

"Furthermore, that is not all the luck which is yours, Benito," Don Guillermo continued. "You will have fourteen golden years to think about this marriage until it grows into a sacred thing before your eyes and one which will become more and more desirable as the years go on, for it is my wish that you return again in six years to meet your bride again, then five years after that, then three years after that for the thrill of the ceremony itself."

"We will be there," Don Patricio said solemnly.

"Yes, sir," Irish murmured, staring at the threatening slash which was Don Guillermo's mouth. "We will be there, God willing."

As father and son rode north that afternoon, Don Patricio said, "Well, what did you think of him?"

"A fine man beyond doubt, Papa. He seems, in the smallest way, to lack but one thing."

"What is that?"

"He is not entirely strong in humor."

Don Patricio considered that for a while, then he said, "Yes, that is true. But I would say it is his only fault."

"I am not sure it is a fault, Papa. After all, if he had humor, how could he have become the greatest killer in the history of the Republic?"

When Don Patricio and Irish made the journey to Lalotorres in 1863, Florita was much more subdued. For one thing, she was ten years older and that can settle a woman.

Her mother had died after a visit to her own mother in California where she had foolishly neglected to boil the drinking water, but a young aunt had put sweet-clover carnations into the plaits of Florita's black hair. She wore a deep lavender dress with a wide skirt and a delicate white yoke and long black stockings in tiny black shoes. She was very pretty. Her smile was of touching excellence. She was ten years old and three feet five inches tall. Irish was twenty years old and six feet five inches tall. It would have been unsuitable had he bent over and picked her up, as they were only affianced. The difference of

114

three feet seemed to emphasize the gap between them and they did not fraternize.

Florita was withdrawn into the house by her aunt. She went quietly and willingly.

"You find her much changed, hey?" Don Guillermo said.

"Exceedingly."

"Come, we will go to my office in the plaza. I wish to show you how my plans for the wedding are developing."

This time all three men drank tequila.

"I will dig an altar with a forty-foot base and twenty-eight feet in height, into the side of that slope over there, which leads to the mountain. In that manner your marriage will be visible to all guests, of every rank, as the ceremony will be held over their heads as it were, and yet we will not have the embarrassment of inviting Colonel Winikus, General Molina's chief of staff who is a Protestant, into our church. Do you approve?"

"Very, very ingenious," Irish murmured.

"And impressive," his father added. "Very impressive."

"He is a Protestant but he is a very good officer, none the less. We must try to be fair."

"Up to a point," Don Patricio stated flatly.

"Naturally. Next year I will have the bids in my hands for the construction of a pipeline from the state of Jalisco to this plaza."

"A pipeline?"

"For tequila. I expect several thousand guests as I am a leader in this state and a national figure and I don't like either the time, the storage problem, nor the sloshing about which would be entailed were we to ship the tequila by oxen. Do you approve?"

"We have eight years," Don Patricio said. "Perhaps it would be wiser to build a distillery right here on your own property and make the tequila here."

"And have my enemies state that I served home brew at my only daughter's wedding? Never, comrade. Tequila is only tequila when it comes from Jalisco."

The talk of the wedding preparations went on for many hours. At midnight, Marco Reuben and Irish picked up the two men and passed them up the stairs to beds.

In 1867, when Irish was twenty-five and his father was sixty-six, they made the journey south in a much more leisurely fashion. They hunted for sport as they traveled. All his life Don Patricio had been a student of the ways of the Indian with nature and his methods of hunting and fishing were as cunning as any Apache's. He demonstrated for Irish a way to catch wild ducks by using gourds. He shot and roasted an antelope and explained how the Lipans would don a deerskin suit and antlers, so that they could not be distinguished from the deer, and make their way right up to the herd to be able to kill at close quarters, with a knife if they chose. To Irish, his father was a man who evoked a new miracle every day. It was the best trip of their lives together.

At fourteen, Florita was such a beauty that Irish could not believe his luck. He was tongue-tied with astonishment. She was dressed in pale blue and flowers made a halo around her head. This time, the two fathers remained at the mayor's office in front of the cantina. Irish rode up the hill alone to make his call.

Florita's aunt brought her out. They sat on a bench side by side, and Irish was by far the more flustered. The aunt sat on a bench close by. Sometimes she gazed sighing at the young couple, for she had never married herself, beaming broadly and extracting a vicarious effusion of feeling from four years in the future. Then, as though she had imagined just a little too much, she would look away quickly and peer at some point on the horizon.

"Only four more years, Benito. How the time consumes itself."

"It is hard to wait."

"It was hard for me until I was twelve. Then I started to work sewing the wedding clothes and the towels and curtains and all of the other things and I have almost been too busy to think of it."

"Your father's plans for the wedding are very exciting."

"Oh yes. He has engaged eight famous carpenters

116

from the village of Santa Carmen de Barajas, where the actual tables for the tribunal which sentenced Emperor Maximilian were made. They are at work now on the tables and benches for the wedding banquet, and he has begun to breed the great-grandfathers of the lambs and goats which will be served at the banquet by feeding them on the tenderest salted grass for four generations."

"How delicious that sounds!"

"The salt for the grass is being imported from Guerrero."

"How thorough your father is."

"It is pride, rather than thoroughness. He is a very, very, very thorough man but he is a very, very, very, very proud man."

"I have sensed that."

"Tell me of your work and what you are doing."

"We are breaking horses now, Jim and I. We are the top hands on the Patten ranch. We get the best horses and the best pay."

"How much pay, if I may ask?"

"If you cannot ask, who can. Sixty dollars a month."

"Ai!"

"That comes to two dollars a day."

"Ai!"

He smirked.

"Who is Jim?"

"Jim is Jim Street. He is my brother since we are seven years old. He will be the best man at our wedding. We do everything we do, always together."

"Is Jim going to get married?"

He grinned at her, delighted to be one up on his friend. "No, Florita. No, he is not."

When Don Patricio and Irish got back to the *casco* of the hacienda, the old man was coughing badly. He climbed upon an ascending fever which turned into pneumonia. He sent for Major Patten. When they were alone, he had wasted away badly and his strength was going fast.

"You were good to come, old friend," he whispered.

"You must rest. You must sleep," the major said.

117

"I will sleep. For a long, long time. Soon." He smiled weakly. "I had to talk to you. About the curse."

"The curse?"

"I know of it. From Don José. I have told no one. You must keep one thing deeply within your heart."

"Yes, my dear friend. What is it?"

"The curse is a Mexican curse. Your daughter is an Arias but she is half American. She has spent her life away from Mexico." Don Patricio's voice was fading and his breath came in gasps. "Never tell her of the curse. I beg of you, as I lay dying, never tell her of the curse then—perhaps—it will—not—happen." He died. His sightless eyes stared at the great stone plaza, paved with sun, over the buildings of the *casco*, over the mesa to the town which had been rebuilt over the ruins of the Lipan raid which had taken his family seventeen years before.

After the funeral Major Patten, Irish, and Jim, three stricken men, had a meeting. Irish was made foreman of the Mexican side of the ranch, succeeding his father. Jim was made foreman of the U.S. side of the ranch, succeeding the major.

"I'm goin' to move up to planning what we do next," the major said. "We're goin' to start to move the emphasis away from the hide business strictly and get deep into the beef business as near to a hundred per cent as we can make it. Feller told me about a big ice ship that took seven hundred slaughtered steers all the way to England. A squaw man name of Jesse Chisholm has showed the boys a straight-on route to get the beef all the way up to Kansas. Now, we'll jest go on over to Pickering City for two or three months and get our moves shaped up so they'll stick real fast then we'll go on out an' do her."

CHAPTER 2

IN 1867, at the time they were made foremen, Jim Street and Irish Reyes were the two top cowhands in the Southwest. They each weighed 185 pounds, probably to the equal milligram. They both stood six feet five inches tall, probably to the equal millimeter. They worked the Patten rough string, cutting out seventy-odd head of salty horses every day. Every one of those horses was a lifetime to sit on and they needed to be smoothed out, cold and regular, for riding by the other hands.

They had been circle riders after two years as wranglers, jinglers as they were called on the Texas side, in the saddle for eighteen hours a day; moving sixty to eighty miles in a day's work depending on the kind of country; rounding up, branding, day-herding and night-guarding; never mind the weather, never mind the terrain. They were rugged men.

Each was the other's peer: *dopplegängers* in spirit and in strength. Any medical check-up, laboratory analysis, astrological forecast, palm reading, aeromancy, handwriting study if they had been able to write, phrenological charting, stress resistance measurement, or reflex-reaction comparison would have shown each man to be the mirror image of the other in every way excepting that Street, who had been born in New Orleans, looked like a Mexican and Reyes, who was a Mexican, looked like a cartoon Hibernian.

By 1867 there had been many changes made at the big ranch house. Major Patten had studied long, well, and with great love at the feet of Don José Vicuña and he had done his level, if not as cultivated, best to carry forward a joint family tradition of great luxury, civilized living, and service to the senses. He had for seventeen years to think about the accoutrements of the good life. He had expended his tastes slowly but in a wide swath.

First off, the ranch establishment itself had had to

grow with the burgeoning stock and the requirements of administrating twenty-three times more land and cattle than he had had when he had wandered on to Don José's hacienda in 1850.

All told, the buildings spread over an area which was almost a mile in diameter. In addition to the ranch house and the cook-house and two corrals which had been there before, the major had had the stockade torn down, had built an office for the transaction of the cattle company's business, two carriage houses, six barns, three saddlehouses, three bunkhouses, a crib, a store, a hide house, a gear and smokehouse, a carpentry shop, a hide press, four hay barns, a potato house, a hoghold, and a goathouse.

He had grown his own olive grove to provide garnishes for a drink which Mat Sun had brought from China which was five parts gin and one part sherry; quite delicious when served very cold. The major aptly christened the drink an "Old Fashioned."

One year after his wife died, the major began to gamble again. To have such a call to gamble and the riches to support it made his geographic location in the world a piteous thing. Had he lived in the East there would have been a militant army of selfless men and women willing to game with him and take his money. Had his place been in Europe there would have been the diversions of the casinos, all willing to remain open twenty-four hours a day for a man of his interests and resources. There would have been endless fatiguing card games and the great racecourses so close, in Paris, to one's hotel. He could have squandered money at *fronton*. There would have been the industrial and commodity bourses and the coin-pitching at Nolan's on Rue de Stockholm. In Asia he could have bet on dogfights, cockfights, and bullock racing or enjoyed shouting *"Banco!"* into the whimpering faces of maharajahs or paling grand dukes. Lotteries in Tangier, fantan in Macao, bicycle racing in Japan, cricket fights in Bali; he could have had all of these.

On his own ranch, however, at the center of that lonely ocean of grass and soil, he had no such opportunities to taste the rare, exciting, and esoteric refinements which would seem to fit a man of his cultivation, so he sweated it out and it kept him mean in spirits and morose for days on end.

There were card games with the ranch hands. He couldn't play against his own bank at the Pickering House. Once a month he played casino with Mat Sun and generally managed to lose a thousand to fifteen hundred dollars. Franklin Heller blandly refused to play.

There were Patten riders who pretended to prefer to ride line all winter in below-freezing weather just to save a few dollars which were sure to be doomed in those games. Of the six hundred and forty-one people on the Texas side of the ranch who could have contributed to fulfilling the anxiety-ecstasy tension which was what the major got out of gambling, only two hundred and sixty-three were old enough or suited by sex to hold cards while sitting upright in a chair, but no more than thirty-six of these were ever within reach at all times, and of those seven objected to gambling on religious grounds and six were drunks.

In 1856, Janine Michaud, the bathykolpian lady butler-cum-bersatrix, was twenty-five years old. She had raised the Patten baby, living at close quarters in the Big House with Major Patten; living through cool afternoons and lime-encrusted evenings in the patios in which pink and white Poinsettias grew; mantequilla roses, bougainvillea, and flame trees. Each patio had a large, spreading *pirul* tree with a stairway winding up its trunk to reach the tree-house which looked down upon perfumed fountains. She could not close her eyes and think of the joyous peace of those patios without amazement over having been twice blessed in her life.

For five years and a little more they each fought off the increasing sense that mourning could not last for ever, that a time for grieving had ended but that the supports and appurtenances of grief need to be kept vital lest self-hatred overtake them for allowing themselves to seem to forget a dead man and a dead woman whom they each had vowed would be the only ones they would ever love.

After five years of being away from the physical

121

movement of what was now only an exultant, an-guished memory of desire, Janine was quicker in re-laxing her grip upon her jealous devotion to the dead man. In the evenings, after the baby had been put down, she would dress carefully, then come out slowly into the patio perfumed and soft-looking, to take a chair near the major. When she spoke to him, or he to her, during the daytime, when there was movement all around them, he was even and pleasant, always polite and always pleased with her. He had told her many times how much he valued what she had done for him, and that he would never know how he could repay her. If she were looking at him directly when he said that to her, she would have to close her eyes tightly. She needed to hear it because she needed to know that she was serving well, more than many other women. She had a deep nature which was engulfed in bottomless love. She had anxiety to give of her abundance. She had always been like this. She had lived with it and had learned, studying it much now that she was so much alone, that prodigality in giving is self-defeating. She needed to serve, but she sur-rounded another terrible need within herself, a physi-cal need for love which could and did contort her body, causing her to repeat over and over again into her pillow at night, "God will understand. God will understand."

It took the major three years to agree to admit to himself that he had detected some change in her, and in his feelings towards her. In the evenings, after the third year, he was brusque and even bitterly reproving when she spoke to him.

"Good evening, major," she would say with her soft voice, so beautiful and more beautiful because it was heard so seldom.

He would grunt.

"Would you like a refreshment?"

"No." He would be staring straight ahead and she would sit a foot or so behind him, to his right. To see her he would need to turn, but he could not bring himself to turn. When the wind changed course it would become unbearable and he would speak to her, almost snarling, but not turning. "Why do you put scent on you? It seems to me every night I tell you that I do not want you to wear scent and yet you do. You wear it. Why do you wear it?"

"It is not scent."

"It is, goddamnit! It *is* scent. Do we live in a barbershop or a whorehouse?"

"It is soap."

"Hah!"

"I will not sit here any longer or at any other time."

"Oh, for heaven's sake, Janine—"

"There are two other patios just as comfortable as this."

"No."

"Why not?"

"There may be snakes. I don't want you sitting alone if there are snakes."

Janine was twenty-five years old when she released the rope she had plaited which tied her to the wrist of Don José as he slept on in the marble mausoleum or as he strode through the halls of the *casco* motored by her memory. The major was forty-one years old.

When he began to be conscious that he was prepared to admit that he could feel her close to him as she sat serenely in the semi-darkness, as a part of the fragrance of the flowers and the sweetness of the scent of her body. When he could conjecture that she was as aware of him and thinking of him intently, he would project across the full reach of his mind an enormous picture of Maria de Lourdes at the instant he had first seen her, or a fully dimensional memory of her panting head, directly under his, when her eyes were a little mad, but he could accomplish that trick of projection less clearly and less fulfillingly each time he tried to do it.

Abruptly, without explanation, he moved to the Pickering House for nine days but the noises of his youth—incessant music, the click of ivory balls on the wheels, the brassy laughter of the women, and the smell of raw booze—were annoying and unpleasant to him. He went hunting alone for five weeks after that and spent most of that time trying to understand why he could not go either backward or forward: he could not live any longer as he had lived for the first third

123

of his life on the top floor of a jumping honkatonk, yet he could not stay on in his own house while she was there.

He was not able to teach himself the full answer. He could only get as far as learning that if he began to think of Janine Michaud as a woman, he felt a hurting coldness and nausea and weakness in his legs because he had betrayed his dead wife and her father.

He had a fine house with great correo chests, tall roperos of carved cedar, velvet hangings, European tapestries, Madrid glass, desks inlaid with tropical woods, vellum-bound books, ivory figurines from the Orient, ceilings that sparkled with gold leaf, brass-studded zapote doors, tiles, sundials, bronze grilles, and fine paintings—but he could not go back to them, yet they meant so much to him because they signified that he and Don José had been civilized, cultivated gentlemen together and that they had been comrades in the appreciation of beauty as well as in all other things.

He began to think the other way. Slowly, he began the examination of the consideration of sending her away. He had to stop himself before he had fairly got into the conception because thinking about it made him numb. He was not able to understand anything he felt when he tried to imagine that she had gone away from him.

Frank Heller found him with a Mexican tracker who had been able to follow him as though his horse's hooves had been dipped in tar. The major was sitting disconsolately in front of a fire, his face strained and thin behind a straggly ginger beard. He had been gone five weeks. Heller told him the baby had measles, that the baby had been crying for him and asking for him.

He rode back to the ranch, thirty feet ahead of Heller and the tracker at all times. He thought of Don José. He thought of Maria de Lourdes. He could understand that she was gone and that nothing could bring her back and that it would be right, after such a long time, if he were to hold another woman in his arms, that it would be right if he could be allowed to love her and she to love him. What he could not understand was what was lodged most deeply within him: that Janine had been Don José's woman (even one of Don José's many, many women, but despite forcing himself to remember that he knew she had been the favorite of all of them); that Don José had been his greatest friend and benefactor, his most extraordinary benefactor. He told himself that he could not bring himself to take the woman of such a friend.

The major sat in the patio every evening for three more years, grunting if she spoke to him, staring at the smoke from his cigar.

One evening in the late spring of 1859 she did not come out into the patio.

She was not anywhere in the Big House the next morning. A large Indian woman was with the baby. He asked her where Juana was. She smiled and answered, "Juana gone to France." The major's legs nearly gave way under him.

"France?"

He got a horse away from a rider who was moving on it across the compound by pulling the man out of the saddle. When he reached Pickering House, Franklin Heller was alone up at the end of the bar nearest the door, polishing glasses.

"You see Janine?"

"No, sir."

"Where the hell is she?"

"What did they say at the ranch?"

"New woman with the baby said she'd gone to France."

"*France?*"

"Was there a stage outta here this mornin'?"

"That was near three hours ago."

"Get over there an' find out from that agent who was aboard her. Don't ask if she was aboard, you hear? Just tell him to show you the list."

Franklin vaulted over the bar like a water buffalo clearing the top of a steeple and landed heavily on the other side. "Didn't think I could do that, did you?" he said and winked at the major. The major glared at him so he made his face earnestly serious again and left the saloon.

The major stood at the bar with a cigar clamped

125

between his teeth and drank whisky at ten o'clock in the morning, staring into the many watery patterns of the deeply polished wood as though he could find the answer there but finding only a growing sense of panic. That he had to get her back he fully understood now. She was his living link with the great days of the Hacienda Vicuña, which had been the most golden days of his life. If she left him all of that would implode upon himself, and he would be standing again at the center of a honkatonk smelling tinhorns and murdering to keep an eighteen-dollar poker pot and his brass-spittoon honor. That was not the only way he felt but it was all he would allow himself to admit that he felt as to how much he needed her, and why he needed her, and still be loyal to the Vicuñas.

Franklin came back to the saloon.

"Abe Weiler put her on the stage with Mrs. Shady Masters, Judge Masters' wife, this mornin' an' she said good-bye to Charlotte Comfort, the school principal. She told Mrs. Comfort she was goin' to New Orleans then to France. Abe Weiler said she looked as sour as a toothache."

"Get me a fresh horse from the livery stable, Franklin. And tell them I want some kind of saddle canteen, then fill 'er up with bourbon."

"Bourbon?"

The major looked uneasy. "I'm not drinkin' Scots whisky for the time bein', Franklin. Now go get me that horse."

He just made it aboard the *Little Maerose,* throwing the reins of his horse and five dollars to a small boy and yelling for him to take Major Patten's horse to the livery stable, then leaping aboard the flagship of the one-vessel fleet old Cap'n Youngstein ran between Brownsville and New Orleans. It was seven o'clock in the evening. The major had had plenty of time to think, even if his reasoning had been mostly wrong, so he didn't waste any time mooning and gazing out at the water. He got her cabin number from the purser who was wearing a cream-colored Stetson, then he went to find her cabin and knocked heavily and insistently upon the door. It was opened instantly. She looked as

126

though she had been prepared to be angry at such rude knocking but when she saw him she sagged against the bulkhead and stared at him unable to speak. She wore a transparent yellow dressing-gown and the same scent which had moved him so many times before. Her wide, astonished eyes were green. Her soft, long, black hair had been brushed loosely to fall far down her back.

"Why did you do it?" he demanded.

"I was no longer needed."

"The baby needed you."

"The baby is eight years old. And what do you know about such things?"

"How can you say that?"

"Had you noticed that I had been training the woman who is with her now for six months?"

"Let me in. We can't stand here arguing like this for everyone to hear us."

"Why can't we? Why should you come in? What is there to say?"

His hands came up slowly and touched her soft arms. "There is a lot to say."

She stared at him with hope and wonder. She stood aside and allowed him to pass, needing to move closely in front of her. Facing her he closed the door softly and locked it. His arms went around her and his hands pressed into her. Her arms held tightly about his neck as they kissed, nine years and eighteen days after they had met. She stared at him transformed, limp with a rage of feeling for him. "Don José told me I was to cherish you," she said slowly. He was released from a cage.

They were married in New Orleans on 3 June 1859.

CHAPTER 3

In 1868, the week after spring round-up, Major Patten received a letter from his New York bankers, Dillon & McHugh, which he read twice but was not sure whether he understood it.

My dear Major Patten:

This letter will introduce Miss Marilyn Ridgeway, daughter of Admiral Cremony G. Ridgeway of Seattle, Washington, and the Brooklyn Navy Yard. Miss Ridgeway is a student naturalist. Due to her high scholastic achievement, her college has agreed to allow her one year of field study in southwestern United States where she will live with the Indian tribes, studying their customs, the flora and fauna of the region, and in particular she hopes to be able to observe at first hand the large-scale production of cattle because of her advanced interest in improving breeds and increasing beef production. The writer will be in your debt if you can make this last wish possible.

Very truly yours,
Edward J. Dillon, Jr.

"When did this get here?" the major asked Gimpy Morgan, his book-keeper.

"Just."

"How did it get here? There ain't no stamp on it."

"Young girl brung it."

"She there now?"

"Yep. Voice like a bird. Sets out there on the porch a-hummin' like an organ."

"Send her in."

Marilyn Ridgeway was a tall young woman who was extremely diffident yet so friendly that the major's first reaction was to flinch. She wore very large, round eyeglasses, beige leather gloves, a large hat with artificial grapes around the brim and a long veil which tumbled down over a brown silk dress, all of it based upon a foundation of stout orange high-buttoned shoes. The major greeted her warmly, if uncertainly, and asked her to sit down.

"Long trip, Miss Ridgeway?"

She nodded shyly and so rapidly that she blinked.

"Good trip?"

She nodded and smiled without showing her teeth.

"Meet any dangers?"

"Oh no! I entrained to St. Louis and just a few days north and west of there I made my rendezvous with the Blackfeet, which had been arranged by the head of our Biology Department. Blackfeet are nice. They were kind enough to pass me along to the Comanches, who were just darling, then they passed me to the Mescaleros, who gave me to the Lipans, who brought me almost to your very door." She spoke brightly and rapidly.

"The Comanches are on the warpath!"

"I know."

"The Mescalero Apaches massacred two wagon trains in the past eight days."

"They behaved absolutely awfully. And I told them so."

"The Lipans are the most murderous single Indian tribe on the North American continent."

"That depends, of course."

"Depends?"

"Well, I mean, I do speak their languages. I am conversant with many of the crafts of the Pacific and Atlantic coastal Indians, short cuts to useful skills they might not yet have overtaken themselves. I mean I was able to be some sort of small help to them so naturally I found them all *very* kind and *very* hospitable people."

"Ah."

"And here I am."

"We're glad to have you with us and we'll make you just as comfortable as we know. My wife and daughter will be right glad to see a fresh face, I can tell you that."

"Thank you, sir."

"Uh—this letter from Eddie Dillon—uh—it says you're interested in increasin' beef production."

"Yes, sir."

"Well, that's all right with me." He mopped his forehead with a large white handkerchief. "I can't say I know what you have in mind. A longhorn is a longhorn an' any other breed of cattle just don't seem to have ways to stay alive in country like this."

"I have a few theories which are not even worthy of talking about yet."

"When would you like to start lookin' around?"

"Would tomorrow morning be all right?"

"Sure thing."

"It is such a long trip out and back that I must budget my time. I hope that doesn't seem rude. I have promised the Lipans that I would spend a few weeks with them in the fastnesses."

"Great toads and sandstorms," the major said. "Eddie Dillon didn't give you a letter of introduction to that blood-drinkin', murderous Tortillaw, did he?"

She laughed gaily. "Tortillaw? Murderous? Why, Major Patten, if you could take the time to really know him you'd find him one of the truly delightful Indian executives in the country."

Jim Street was probably the only vegetarian cowman in the cattle industry. Others may have followed him but he was the first. The vegetarian ethic—whether sung by Ovid, taught by Buddha, or moaned by Rousseau—is a foremost part of maximum idealism. Percy Shelley claimed that because Prometheus stole fire to cook meat the vulture of disease fastened eternally upon his liver. Seneca indicated the vast numbers of lives one stomach absorbs as representing "the devastatión of land and sea." Emerson admonished that to eat meat is "complicity" in murder. Pythagoras, Hippocrates, Plutarch, and Schopenhauer were vegetarians, and Leonardo da Vinci. Alexander Pope wrote of such a man as any of these: "No murder clothed him and no murder fed."

However, in a most terrifying manner, murder clothed and fed the vegetarianism of Jim Street. He loved cattle in a deep and mystical way which flew back to the night of horror when the Lipans had burned the pueblo and he and Irish had been saved by huddling against the forelegs of steers at the center of the herd. He could not eat meat for the least idealistic of reasons: the roasting smells of human meat and the final memory of his mother.

He most emphatically did not object to others eating the flesh of cattle. As he saw it, to be eaten was the cattle's proud destiny; to bring health to children and strength to the working man, just as they had, most impassively, brought safety to Irish and himself. He saw the cow's transmogrification into steak as the noblest mission of all.

After one day of escorting Marilyn Ridgeway

around the ranch, Jim was very nearly ready to sign on as her slave. He said to Irish the first night, gripping his forearm tensely. "I have found my ideal woman, Irish."

"No! Where?"

"Turns out she was a-sittin' and talkin' in the major's office. I don't know how it all has happened. Major Patten sent for me an' there she was."

"Maybe you better go to church like I been telling you."

"I cain't wait 'til you hear this girl sing harmony. Why, she can even take the bass part, an' I'm tellin' you, Irish, she knows as much about cattle as ole Doc Vicuña."

Jim had been repairing leather gear when the major sent Gimpy Morgan to find him. She was sitting there as he went in and the smile she made for him near stopped him in his tracks.

"Miss Ridgeway," the major said, "this here is Jim Street, the man most interested in beef cattle in the whole state of Texas."

"How do you do, Mr. Street?"

"This here is Marilyn Ridgeway, Jim."

"Howdy, ma'am."

"Jim, Miss Ridgeway is studyin' at a school in the East to be a cattle expert an' I'm askin' you to show her anything she wants to see on the Patten spread."

"Yes, sir."

"You got yourself a real stockman, Miss Ridgeway. Jim can tell you anything about a steer 'ceptin how to eat one."

They walked in silence towards the number one corral. "Where'd you like to start, ma'am?"

"Anywhere, Mr. Street. Just anywhere you think best."

"I'll get us some horses."

Miss Ridgeway had changed to a buckskin riding outfit which she had bought from the daughter of a Comanche medicine man, but she wore the same orange high-button shoes. They rode away from the ranch for two or three miles without talking, which impressed Jim a great deal. As they stopped for a moment on a knoll of the prairie she said, "I would like to explain my work."

"Yes, ma'am."

"I suppose you have heard the Mesopotamian anecdote about Noah and his ark?"

"Yes, ma'am."

"It was offered to satisfy early man's curiosity about the origin of the animals around him."

"Yes, ma'am."

"However, when the natural sciences identified more than two million separate forms, living and extinct, it became incredible that even the Ark, with its 450,000 cubic cubits could have carried such a cargo. Why, the weight of all species of birds alone on the roof of the thing would have caved it in."

"Yes, ma'am."

"I am studying to be a natural scientist. I will have my degree in two years; then I intend to work with cattle and make the production of beef my field."

"Why?"

"Why?"

"You must have a reason. I mean, it's sort of a new kind of work for a woman."

She smiled at him brilliantly and blinked thrillingly. "What a perceptive man you are!" she said. "Yes, I suppose there is a reason. I never knew for the longest time but the Dean asked me to think hard about why I needed to go into such a different field. Oh, I had the usual reasons. I mean, the vital need to increase food production for a nation growing as rapidly as ours. In the end I satisfied her questions, but I never gave her the real reason because it seemed too *silly*."

"I'd sure be proud to hear it, ma'am."

"When I was little everyone in the family loved beef tea. There was never enough to go around. I mean enough to satisfy everyone. It had to be imported and it was expensive and I suppose if every one of us weren't so mad for it that we would have had our small single cup and that would have been that. But we *adored* it. We looked forward to Sunday lunch, home in Seattle, which was the only meal of

132

the week we were allowed to have beef tea. My sister and I would talk about its flavor all through the week. My grandfather and I used to sit together on rainy days and try to describe to each other why we loved it so, enchaining each other with memories of its taste. I must have vowed then and there that someday I was going to do something so that everyone in the world could have beef tea if they wanted it and as much as they wanted of it. Then I found myself being pulled toward the natural sciences and, at last, here I am."

"Yes, ma'am."

"Do you like beef tea, Mr. Street?"

"No, ma'am."

They walked the horses slowly forward. Miss Ridgeway let her eye rove over the few hundred long-horns in the immediate foreground, sixty to a hundred yards off.

"So many names were given to the first cattle, which we know as *Bos primigenius* and which is why so many cows are called Bossy, incidentally. I mean the *Bos* came from Greek and Latin, as you know, with the genitive *bovis,* from which are derived our words bovine, beeves, and beef. The Germans said *Ochs,* the Danes said *oxe,* and somehow these got themselves combined with the Sanskrit word *ur,* meaning forest or stony place, and suddenly we had *urochs* or *aurochs,* meaning wild cattle."

"Yes, ma'am."

"These aurochs, according to paintings on the walls of caves in southern France, show a close resemblance to the longhorns brought to Mexico and Texas by the Spaniards. Cattle just like these," she said, waving her quirt in an arc to indicate the herds around them. "These cattle, just as they look now, go all the way back to the middle Pliocene, which was three to five million years ago. They lived through four glaciations of the Ice Age. Don't you think the whole develop-ment of beef is wonderfully romantic?"

"I sure do."

"The Prodigal Son gorged himself on roasted veal. Did you know that the Pharaohs had riders put their own brand on their cattle?"

"The faro who, ma'am?"

133

"Oh, the Egyptians were *marvelous* cowhands! The tombs of Deir show a picture of a *huge* longhorn being roped and thrown. There's one showing a rider bulldogging a steer. I mean, actually twisting his head and muzzle!" She leaned over the saddle and squeezed Jim's forearm. "That was over five thousand *years* ago."

Street took a deep breath. "I bulldogged my first steer when I was twelve years old," he said burningly. "He threw me like a catapult, but I climbed on the horse and they ran him again and I threw him to the ground. A full-grown steer. That horse was the best old horse I ever rode. Six years old. He was an all-round horse, good on the road and in the brush. Sure-footed in rocks as a mountain goat. Never stumbled. And could he cut? After a while he got so good I'd just ride him into a herd, show him the critter I wanted to cut out, take off the bridle and let him go it alone. No matter how that animal would dodge, old Bricks would take him right out of the herd. I never hit him. Why, I never more than even barely touched spurs to his sides. He'd come to me if I called his name or whistled. When we stopped all alone on the range at night, I never had to fear his leavin' me. Bricks was sure a fine horse." Jim was near to panting when he finished the speech.

Miss Ridgeway looked at him with new eyes. She realized all at once that that speech had been an extreme vote of confidence for her, and something more. It was a commitment. It was a warning. It was a clear statement of his intentions. She felt warmth climb her. Her cheeks grew rosier and rosier.

"You are an extremely handsome man." It was an involuntary admission. It was instinctive. It corroborated his drift.

"Huh?" Most men are not as quick to catch emotional nuances as most women. That is elemental, except in cases to the contrary.

"You have excellent bones and a most trustworthy appearance." He caught on. Lust began to stir deep in his stomach. He swayed slightly in his saddle.

"You're pretty good lookin', too, ma'am," he answered hoarsely.

She blushed more deeply, looked away from him, felt her own innards contract and expand, contract and expand, cleared her throat and said, "These cattle are direct descendants of the *Bos primigenius* from the wide lowlands between the Sierra Moreno mountains and the Guadalquivir River of upper Andalusia. The summers are hot there and there isn't much water, which is so much like this country, isn't it?"

"Yes, ma'am."

"Have you ever *tried* beef tea?" she asked suddenly.

"No, ma'am."

"Why not?"

He had never told anyone the story before. He had never been able to form the words. He told her about his mother and about the night of the destruction of the pueblo seventeen years before. He told her he was a vegetarian, but that he felt as deeply as she did about somehow finding a way to make more and better beef. When he finished her eyes were misty. She gripped his hand tightly, leaning forward in her saddle, then she took a deep breath and plunged. "Mr. Street, my eventual goal in naturalism has been to make an opportunity to work and study on a large cattle ranch, such as this. I want to learn everything there is to know about all cattle from *Mammalia,* the milk givers, to *Ungulata,* which have hooves, to *Artiodactyla,* the even-toed ungulates, to the *Pecora,* or cud-chewers, to the *Cavicornia* and the *Bovidea*—oh, all of them; ox, antelope, chamois, goat, and sheep. I want to be one of those who feed the world!" Her voice rang out. He stared at her with what can only be termed adoration. "That is one of the finest things I ever heard a woman say," he told her warmly, his voice breaking. "And you said it for me, too, when you said it."

"I can't do it all until I graduate. I promised Dad," she said huskily. "Two years seems a long way off to be so far away from—from—from all this."

"You got to learn all you can," he said harshly. "I don't know nothin' an' I need for you to teach me."

"You mean—you'll wait for me?"

"Wait? Why I'd wait fifty years for a chance—a

135

chance to—a chance to better our stock and and build better beef." They were holding hands.

"I knew you would understand!"

"You did?" He seemed dazed.

"I saw it in your walk and in your eyes. I am a burningly practical woman, Mr. Street. I have a bitter urgency about what my destiny can do to eliminate the longhorn from our herds.'"

"*What?*" He flinched as though struck.

"Oh, I know it is hard to see at first, but I must make you see it."

"I'm willin' to see it, but what about Major Patten?"

She spoke fiercely. "The longhorn as we know him today has got to go! He does not deliver enough beef for the size of his frame."

He stared, utterly hooked.

Her eyes burned with zeal. *"I care not who writes my nation's hymns,"* she said, *"if I may breed beef."* He never forgot those words.

She left after six days with him. They were six days of ecstasy, days of torrential description or sharing information of the powers of Herefords and Brahmans, of Angus and Guernsey, of feeds, patented troughs, of ticks and the problems of watering.

On the seventh morning a party of Lipans waited on their horses three hundred yards off from the ranch buildings. It was dawn.

Jim and his girl shook hands, staring at each other levelly.

"I will be here again in 1871," she said. "In July."

His jaw fell. "We said *two* years!"

She looked at him bravely. "I have decided to take a doctorate."

"A veterinary?"

"No. But the highest degree in the natural sciences."

"Then—then it's worth it."

"I hope we're right."

"I'll be right here, waitin'."

"Will you answer if I write to you?"

His face flushed. "No."

"No?"

"I cain't write nor read. But I'll tell you what I can

do. I can go across the river and get an *evangelista* to write for me."

"A gospel preacher?"

"No. A professional letter-writer."

"No."

"Why?"

"It wouldn't be the same. I wouldn't feel that I was communicating with the inner you."

"They're very serious. They never laugh even when a letter is supposed to be funny."

"No—Jim." It was the first time she had ever called him by his first name. He reddened. She spoke from under lowered lashes. "We could think of each other at nine o'clock every night—wherever we were."

"Oh Marilyn!"

"Remember there is a two-hour time difference. It will be eleven o'clock where I am."

"Ain't that kinda late to stay up?"

"No. Not really. Is nine late for you?"

"Well, sorta."

"Shall we make it eight?"

He nodded dumbly, enchanted.

"Good-bye dear. Good-bye for three years," she said.

"Farewell until July 1871."

He could not speak. She rode out to meet the Lipans. Halfway, she turned and blew a kiss which hit him like a stone, then she rode off with the Indians.

CHAPTER 4

As MAJOR PATTEN said, his face a tight, tough mask, "Maverickin' is one thing, but cow-stealin' is a man stoppin' by to borrow a rope around his neck."

Everybody used the old-time rule for counting cattle. The only controllable reckoning was the number of calves branded every year. Experience showed, because cattle generally matured before they were sold, that for each calf branded there were five other cattle of the same brand on the range. If a man branded five thousand head, he had twenty-five thousand.

From the beginning of the cattle business in Texas, the range code required that every stockman should brand all the calves he rounded up, but they were all supposed to be branded with the same brands carried by their respective mothers. When everybody played fair, all outfits picked up the natural increase on their own cattle, no matter how many miles the stock might wander. It became the custom when cattle were sold off to sell any other cattle of like stock which had been found, and the fixed fee for the finder was a dollar a head. The difference on the sale was handed over to the owner of the cattle. It was easier to bring home money for a steer that had strayed sixty miles than to bring the steer home.

However, what with some folks being lazy and others being greedy and the range and the plains as wide as any ocean, things began to change a little bit when more and more outfits began to work. A natural development called "mavericking," named for the calf—called a "maverick"—which strays from its mother or the herd, came about with riders putting their own home brand on anybody's unbranded stock, instead of the owner's brand which had been burned like a big sign into the mother's hide. In the beginning the losses were small and things tended to equalize themselves. Major Patton's riders branded that way, the same as everyone else's.

In 1867 a new outfit headed by Whisperin' Leon Roth and Marty Ragaway moved into the range west of the major's pre-emptions, and they began to brand mavericks wholesale.

It was a blue, whistling day when Irish and Jim went out to talk to Roth. Roth was on horseback and Ragaway was on foot, having walked over from the chuck wagon. They all wore heavy woollen shirts cut to fasten high around the throat for days like that. Their boots extended well up the calf of the leg. Irish had his custom-made, and the boot tops were sewn ornately and embellished with different kinds of leather. Jim was too stingy to spend money like that. He wore the store-bought Star Brand. They all wore woollen pants with Levis over them. The pants were stuck in the boots. Yellow slickers were tied securely behind the cantle of each saddle.

Street looked at Roth and spat. "Two months ago you was so flat broke you was buyin' feed an oat at a time for your horse."

"Pretty close to true," Roth said.

"Now I see you got yourself near to three thousand head of young cattle."

"Yes, sir," Marty Ragaway piped, "an' they all come from a yoke of old oxen we drove in here from the north."

"You just never woulda thought them two oxen could be all that prolific," Roth drawled.

"They all have fresh brands," Irish said. "Major Patten said to tell you he hopes your herd doesn't keep growin' younger."

"Why does he hope that way, friend?" Roth asked.

"Because if your herd keeps growin' younger someone is going to say, 'Leon Roth is a bad man on a good horse and that horse might just lose its owner.' " Irish brought his quirt down hard on Roth's horse's rump. The horse screamed and streaked away with Roth almost tumbling off him. Marty Ragaway stood staring at the two riders with a hard face. They wheeled their horses and rode away east. It began a blood feud which ended at four graves.

The major had established one brand as the property of his daughter Evaliña. It was called the Open Ear brand and it was recorded with the county clerk, as required by law, in the stock-record book. The brand was a nest of reversed *C* marks. Major Patten had been building up the herd for six years with his best bulls. It was this herd of little Evaliña's which had been so carefully fenced with wild-rose hedges so that scrub bulls couldn't get in and upset the breeding balance. It was a prize herd. It was the major's pride.

This side of being caught red-handed, Leon Roth and Marty Ragaway might have been able to go on indefinitely with their mavericking because the major's stock holdings were so enormous and his calves so ubiquitious that it would have been hard to prove that a new brand wasn't a true brand, but Roth and Ragaway had moved up into straight cow-stealing. The method they had developed was simplicity itself.

They studied the brand on Evaliña's cattle, then devised an overbrand which created an entirely new brand, one they had already registered in the county stock-record book, thus making things seem entirely legal—after the fact. This new brand was called The Butterfly. They burned a nest of normal *C* marks facing and touching the Patten brand of reversed *C* marks. They stole six thousand head of cattle by working the Patten brand into their own.

Major Patten was all horns and rattles when he realized how far the stealing had gone and how tightly legal they had made it. He called out all hands and the cook, as the saying goes, and he offered fighting wages to anybody who could stop Roth and Ragaway. After half a night of talking, Irish and Jim said they could whip the cow thieves if he wouldn't get delicate about how they did it.

"Delicate?"

"We're a-goin' to fight fahr with fahr," Jim said.

"Tell me about the delicate part."

"Roth and Ragaway has bought three thousand head on the other side of the Frio. They put a clean and legal Butterfly brand on them just to make their outfit look prosperous. After our stock was stole they just added it into that herd."

"Well?"

"We aim to steal Miss Evaliña's stock back, plus all of their legal stock, so's when we're through them boys is plain ruined."

"How?"

"We'll give their whole herd a chance to fill up with calves; then, in the late winter just before they start droppin' them calves, we'll go into their range with a whole outfit an' rework their Butterfly brand which they worked out of the Open Ear brand."

The major bit off the end of a black Cuban cigar. "Go to it, boys," he said.

They registered the Double Targets brand in Evaliña's name. Then they took off to the west with a full outfit of hands and cooks, rounded up the Roth and Ragaway stock and burned in another

Butterfly next to the reworked brand. They made Evaliña Patten a profit of thirty-seven hundred head of cattle. Roth and Ragaway didn't have as much as a T-bone steak left. They were mighty riled.

Late one afternoon, red-faced and filled with murder, Whisperin' Leon Roth himself, with Mike Segal and Chuck Moses, rode up to Jim Street in the Patten west hundred section.

"We lost a herd of beeves," he said curtly. "We'd like to cut yours." This was common practice. An outfit could request permission to cut their own cattle out of the herd of a neighbor and the request was seldom turned down.

"Sure, boys," Jim said; "help yourselves." The cow thieves rode through. They found nothing but the Double Target brand. They rode south, sullenly. They were back with the same request the next day, then the day after that. The third time Jim stared them down. He slid the carbine out of his saddle pocket and held it across his lap. "No damn greasesack outfit can trail cut a Patten herd three times runnin'. Get movin' and keep goin'."

Working themselves into desperate exhaustion because they didn't have any hands to call on, not the way the Patten spread could call them out, and working in a running blizzard for a cover-up, Roth and Ragaway rounded up and stole as much Patten stock wearing the Double Target brand as they could find. They reworked the Double Target by adding another full set of concentric matching circles of facing nests of *C*s placed directly below the two targets and registered this in the stock-record book as the Round Triangle brand. They were able to reclaim only twenty-seven per cent of the stock stolen from them because Irish and Jim had driven the rest of it off the west range and because of the terrible blizzard.

Irish and Jim let Roth and Ragaway keep that twenty-seven per cent long enough to get another fill-up of calves, then they registered the Four Roses Brand with the county clerk, burned in the fourth set of Butterflies, and the cow thieves were ruined and humiliated—the laughing-stock of the Southwest. There was no more room to work or rework or re-

141

work brands on the sides of the cattle. If those cows had been touched with one more hot branding iron, the major said, there would have been thousands of medium rare steaks walking the range.

When the operation seemed to be over, Irish rode out through the western pastures for a final look-around. He saw Willy Davis, a Roth and Ragaway hand, riding toward him. Willy was a kid, follyful and fancy. He hardly cared whose side he was on if there looked like there could be a fight in it. Standing on foot between them, as Irish came over his rise of ground, was a tall, impassive Indian dressed in leggings and mocassins. Willy twirled his rope, grinning like a hyena, caught the Indian around the neck, and upset him in the dust. Willy guffawed. He was having a fine old time.

The Indian was on his feet instantly. He was calm. He moved quickly. He grabbed the rope to create a slack. He ran with it around and around Davis' horse, entangling the legs. He began climbing the rope to the rider.

Irish galloped forward, a hundred and fifty yards between them. He saw the flash of the tomahawk. He yelled, "Shoot him! Shoot him in the belly!" but Willy didn't know what was happening, it happened so fast. The Indian brought down the hatchet on the top of Willy's skull and the boy was dead.

The Indian leaped off the horse and stood his ground while Irish galloped to him, drawing his gun and knowing exactly what he was going to do.

"I am Tortillaw, chief of the Lipans," the Indian said in Spanish. "I am your sister's husband."

CHAPTER 5

IRISH rode beside Tortillaw toward the rim of the mountains. They did not speak. This was the chief who had taken Jacaranda away with him on the night of the raid seventeen years before. The range of mountains ran from northwest to southwest. They crossed the range. Fifteen miles beyond that, a second line of mountains ran in the same general direction. They crossed it and rode toward the southwest, following the valley and riding toward a third range of mountains, watching its color change to whitish chalk. They made their way up a canyon with great boulders littering its floor, picking their way with much difficulty. In time, the canyon's steep walls widened out and the south side grew less and less steep. They were on a sloping mesa which was the Lipan fastness.

Never among the savage peoples of history, excepting the white man, has there been any equal to the ferocity, the intelligence and the wanton destructiveness of the Apache Indians. They were wholly non-productive, subsisting entirely on plunder and game; incapable of sustaining any continuing logistical effort to maintain a large number of them for a week or more, they were scattered in small bands throughout the west of Texas, the whole of Arizona, part of New Mexico, and in all the northern portions of the Mexican states of Chihuahua and Sonora.

Tortillaw was chief of the Lipans, the large and merciless tribe of Apaches who roamed west Texas and northern Mexico. The single difference between the Lipans and the main body of Apaches was in their tribal organization. The Apaches would not accept chiefs, preferring the system of every man for himself and striking collectively only when the chance of loot looked tempting enough and a greater number of warriors was required. The Lipans served under regular chiefs whose decision was final and to whom total obedience was paid. Tortillaw was that chief.

No amount of hunger or thirst, cold or heat, seemed to have the slightest effect upon Tortillaw. He was relentless and inexorable when carrying forward the plans for a raid. Ten Lipans would undertake a raid and a series of murders which would stagger the valiance of any warrior of any other Indian nation. Mercy was unknown to them. They were educated from childhood to take pleasure from inflicting pain. They took birds and animals alive and gave them to their children to torture. Proud Lipan parents were filled with pride if their son showed ingenuity in ex-

143

tending pain widely and deeply, looking on approvingly while Mother gave a helpful suggestion now and then.

Tortillaw was a large muscular man who very early in his career had established himself as having strength, bravery, endurance, and intelligence unequalled by anyone in his tribe. He was a great killer of men, a gifted hunter, an effective diplomat, a firstclass thief, and a wily and wholly dishonest leader.

He had an enormous head and broad shoulders. He was a shading under six feet tall. He had a large mouth, cruel and uncompromising; a hawklike nose; and a jutting potato chin. Aside from the flashes of intelligence in his beady eyes his face remained expressionless. He combined many elements of greatness with an indescribable gift for cruelty and the pursuit of horror.

He had taken Jacaranda Reyes when he had been nineteen years old and she had been twelve. When he was twenty-two and she fifteen he married her, shucking off at her insistence three Lipan wives like so many garments. The fathers, brothers, and uncles of the cast-off wives took exception to the decision. Tortillaw settled the matter by challenging any of them and all of them. Three accepted. He fought them one after another on the same night before the fires of the assembled tribe with long knives. He killed them all. Had one of them killed him, Jacaranda would have been murdered.

Irish found his sister on a pile of skins in the largest hogan in the fastness. She had become enormous. Chins spilled upon chins. Her thick black hair had been oiled with bear grease and was coiled on her crown in a unique manner which, combined with her pouched black eyes and sallow skin, made her seem more Indian than anyone in the tribe he had seen. Her mouth was puffy and seemed grossly discontented with its place on her face, as though sure it belonged above the left eyebrow.

"Benito, I would not have recognized you. How you have changed since you were seven."

"That is life," he said. "But you look exactly the same."

"Really?"

"I like your hair that way."

"It's a change. I have a little Hopi woman who does it for me. You met my husband?"

"Yes."

"He is chief. A very big man."

"He was killing a cowhand just as I came along."

"He probably had to do it. Believe me, Benito, Indians are not as bloodthirsty as people like to say. Did you happen to observe the circumstances?"

Irish nodded.

"Would you say he had provocation?"

Irish shrugged then nodded again.

"That's good. I have told him over and over: they shoot at you, you shoot at them. They hack at you with a hatchet, you hack at them with a hatchet—but don't start it. Killing can be vulgar, I try to explain to him. *Tortillaw!*" Her voice rang out and her husband appeared in the doorway, seeming more diffident to Irish than before.

"Yes, Jacaranda?"

"I was very pleased to hear from my brother that you had to kill the man you killed yesterday."

Tortillaw nodded at Irish. He smiled and gulped. "I was minding my own business when he tried to maim me for life."

"That's all, dear." Tortillaw withdrew.

"He certainly must look back fondly on the day he kidnapped you, the way you've improved him."

"Still, I miss the finer things. Tortillaw senses that."

"Well, it was nice seeing you, Jacaranda."

"Would you like a surprise?"

"A short one?"

"You are an uncle. Twice. Two boys. Marvelous boys, real Mexicans if you know what I mean. Some surprise, hey?"

"Well, in a way—no. You have been here for almost seventeen years."

"The male point of view. He wanted to have a bigger family, too, but I said to him when the men have children that's when we'll have more children. It's no picnic you know, I told him. The methods here aren't exactly like when we were surrounded by a lot of trained midwives on the Vicuña hacienda. I didn't ask you to kidnap me and murder my family, I said to him. If I were some wild Indian squaw and not a civilized woman maybe it would have been a little different and besides you should see these two kids. Real chiefs. I raised these boys to be proud of their Mexican heritage. They know they are basically too civilized for this kind of life but they are boys and boys like the outdoors."

"I'm sorry, I'll miss them," Irish said.

"Listen, he can be very proud of these kids. Rafeito, the oldest, was only eleven years old when he killed three United States Army officers. Officers. And there isn't a kid in this fastness who can torture a prisoner the way he can." She shook with laughter. "He does a stunt that is the funniest thing you've ever seen. He ties a prisoner up. Then he pops out one of their eyeballs, sitting right in front of them, then he chews the eyeball very, very solemnly, staring at the prisoner without cracking a smile. It is *hilarious!*"

"I'd sure like to meet them," Irish shuddered, "but I'll have to be moving. I have a lot of work to do and it's a long ride."

"Long ride? Two days!"

"Still—"

"Tortillaw!"

Her husband appeared at once. "Lover, Benito has to get back home now."

"I'll send Iron Legs and Bear Fingers with him."

"You'll take him yourself. You brought him here and you'll just see that he gets back safe and sound, you hear?"

"I don't need a guide," Irish said. "Really. I can find my way."

"That's what you think. Anyway, it's a question of civilized manners. And—oh—by the way. How's Papa?"

"Dead."

"Well, there you are. Here today, gone tomorrow. Time certainly flies in these fastnesses."

Tortillaw cleared his throat. "If I take him he'll have to wait two days. We have the big annual rain-dance festival beginning tonight and—"

"And *nothing!* You always have an excuse. You always have some kind of outlandish story when it comes to something *I* want, so let me tell you something, my fine Indian friend——"

Irish was returned to the ranch by Tortillaw. They did not speak much on the ride home until Irish said that if he were Tortillaw he would hit Jacaranda across the side of the head with a stone axe, and they became good friends.

Major Patten thought he had been killed. Jim was out gunning for Ragaway and Roth, who had blamed Willy Davis' death on Irish. Weeks later, the Patten ranch heard that they had disappeared into California where they got into show business by holding up box offices in Fresno and Sacramento.

Before they left, Ragaway and Roth left word for Irish and Jim. They said they would be back to gun them down if it was the last thing they ever did. They returned to Pickering City, as good as their word, in 1868.

CHAPTER 6

MNEMONICISTS state that interest is the key to memory. The philosophers tell that interest is the key to life. Memory and life are one, each visited at a different time, simultaneously. More time has been spent in the attics of memory than in contemplation of the mirrors of the present. The world is an army marching backward in martial array, following back-stepped leaders who have convinced them that they are going forward. It has always been a world of wistful opisthoporics who know that memory is the greatest compensation for living because it tolerates time and permits the great, gone moments to be held for ever.

Evaliña Patten was seventeen years old when she first consciously set eyes on Irish Reyes and Jim Street. Just as oddly, Irish had seen her for the first time the day before. Jim Street had set his eyes on her for the first time two days earlier. Each man had reacted differently. In Reyes' case the sight of her had made him

147

physically hungry. He had seen her some forty yards away, had stared at her swaying like a flagpole in a hurricane, and had broken into a run for the cookhouse to plead with Mat Sun for quantities of huckydummy and marrow gut, which he stuffed into his face to chew with a dazed expression. Jim Street had happened around the corner of a ranch building the day before that, seen her advancing with her stepmother well across the compound, and had had to totter off to sit in the darkness of the smokehouse for many hours mumbling. He was found in there late in the day. His eyes held that steely something to be seen within the eyes of carved cigar-store Indians who later guarded retail tobacco shops in the cities of the Atlantic seaboard.

Evaliña Patten was more beautiful than any man could ever adjust to. Her grandfather's and her mother's hair, aided by her father's ginger coloring, had melted then rushed a soft golden redness on her head. Her eyes were great and shining and black like the tips of a city policeman's shoes protruding from under an ivory satin drape. She was as tall as her father, which put her ten inches shorter than Irish or Jim. Just beneath the thrillingly banal expression upon her glorious face, in random repetition (just as a breeze may tease the surface of a summer pond to disappear almost instantly) there glowed and faded untold, untapped riches of wistful, ineffable lust. Even though she was only seventeen years old, her architecturally impossible bosom projected that same lovable quality. She had the behind of a dainty young mare.

At seventeen years of age, Evaliña's whole state of being conveyed her need. She did not seem able to sit still upon any chair. It was as though she were roiling the spring of some deeply held sediment, always revolving some rapturous mechanism directly beneath her seat.

Until that warm late-summer morning Irish and Jim had never met Evaliña face to face. It is possible that she had seen them before, but unlikely due to the extraordinary sensation of electrocution which lighted suns at the base of her stomach when all at once she turned, looked, and they were standing there.

148

The night before, the major and Janine had stayed up almost until dawn talking earnestly, if not desperately, about what was the right, the fair, the necessary thing to do regarding Evaliña and her right to knowledge concerning the Aztec curse on the Arias family. Evaliña and Janine were to leave in two days for Brownsville, where they would embark for Vera Cruz, thence to proceed by rail to Mexico City where Evaliña would begin her three years of traditional instruction by the women of the Arias clan. The major was ready to fall to his knees and to pray for guidance.

"In the end, Don José didn't think there was a curse," the major said.

"There was a curse."

"His last words in this life, spoken right to me as I held his head in my arms, were: 'If the child is a girl you must never tell her about the curse. I no longer believe there was a curse.' Then he died."

"I know." She lowered her eyes. "But there *was* a curse. I know that because of him. You know that because of his daughter."

"That could be the Latin blood, my dear," he said gently.

"Latin blood?" She touched her chest. "I have Latin blood. Was it the same? Am I like a tigress eating a lamb? Am I like the force of a sledge crushing rocks? With me is there a feeling that perhaps there is another part of life to be lived?" He would not look at her and he would not answer. She went on, "You cannot know what Don José required. I could not possibly convey what it meant by telling you numbers and measuring the time he gave to it. There was a curse. Oh, yes. And it is your duty to tell the child about the curse."

"No!"

"Then you must let me tell her."

"I cannot and will not. I have told you what Don José said and you know what Patricio said."

"Patricio was a *charro,* as wise to the ways of the world as—as—as Irish and Jim."

"They had given the matter great thought."

"Major! What can you be thinking of? Here we can

149

watch her and help her, but she is very much a full-grown woman even though she is only seventeen years old and in Mexico—"

"In Mexico she will be even safer. The Arias family has been coping with this for twelve generations."

"Major. Suppose—just suppose—that someone should grab her and kiss her. You *know* what that means. You *know*."

"No one will grab her and kiss her here because they know I'd kill them. No one will grab her and kiss her in Mexico because they are ready for anything; this is an old story with them."

"But on the stage. On the boat. On the railroad from Vera Cruz?"

"She'll be safer there than any other place—on this ranch or in Mexico."

"Why?"

"Because you will be with her."

The major rode into Pickering City with Irish and Jim, moving at a steady canter for the full two miles. After the three months of intensive work with the major they had two days off coming to them before they would separate for the first time when they began calling out the boys on either side of the Rio Grande.

They stopped with the major at the Pickering Academy for Females and got last-minute instructions from the major. Evaliña saw them for the first time from the window of her room in the senior dormitory. Her hips moved ever so slightly. She had never seen two such beautiful young men in her life. She had never actually related herself to young men before, she realized. She felt now that she had only imagined that she understood what they were for. She studied Irish, then Jim. She wished they could be chained to the hitching post so she could look at them for hours and hours. The first thing she said when her father came into the room was, "Pa, who are those men who rode in with you?"

Her father was preoccupied with the sorrow of seeing her leave the next day, beginning a separation of three years.

"The new foremen. Jim Street and Irish Reyes."

"Where do they come from?" She offered the question as though she were confident his off-hand answer would be that they were just visiting from heaven.

"The time is almost here, sweet lamb. This time tomorrow."

"Oh, Pa! Do I have to go?"

"We got to think of it as somethin' we're doin' for the honor of your Mama."

"Yes, Pa."

"Did you ever know your Mama could whistle Handel's 'Water Music?' "

"Yes, Pa."

"You're about to learn how to do that, too."

"Oh, Pa!" Evaliña cried out fiercely, flinging her arms around his neck. "Don't you ever get to thinkin' that I'm not goin' to miss you, too!" He held her close, patting the top of her head and thinking about the curse.

When they left the major, Irish and Jim proceeded directly to Pickering's Paradise, the recreational wing of Pickering House, and plunged into an executive-type holiday. They slammed through the swinging doors, yelled for whisky, and within the hour were shooting the suspender buttons off the principal gunmen of the region. By midnight they were having a smashing time. Some young ladies who had been imported from Panama by the management on a sort of exchange-student basis, which was so profitable at the time, had joined them; young alert girls for each chap. They all played a fun game which called for much trooping up and down stairs. Selfishly perhaps, Jim and Irish barred anyone else from entering the place, so content were they with the obliging young women, the whisky, the shooting at fixtures, the occasional fist fights with each other, and with Franklin Heller's deft service as *maître d' hôtel* of saloon.

It was a beautiful saloon. It was a place which, years after leaving it behind, men could close their eyes and see before them—smell the booze, the beer, and the sawdust, the free lunch (the later item being an innovation from the East) which had scented their finest days. The bar had been imported from Dublin, Ireland, from a public house which had very nearly been a private club as it had catered to rich Episcopalians.

Each panel of the back bar, the setting for the great mirror which had been cut from the largest rhinestone ever dug in the County Clare (the salesman had said), was of lustrous rose mahogany, as was the massive, memorable bar itself, polished like the face of a mountain lake in the moonlight. All around the bar, in the elegant dining area called the Forum of the Twelve Aldermen, were oil portraits of the twelve succeeding political bosses of Hoboken, which the salesman had released to the major for a song.

The bar had heard many songs. Jim Street played the banjo now and then, for two or three hours at a time, singing songs which at times became so sad that one or another of the exchange students would spring into his lap, pound her little fists into his chest, and cry out that he was too young and too beautiful to sing of such pain and sorrow, but he would go right along with such wringers as "I'll Find My Ole Dawg Up in Heaven" and "Johnny's Gone For Soldier," never once repeating himself.

Jim had learned to play the banjo from a traveling minstrel man named Joe Sweeney who, in order to look like the natives of the town, had rented a Colt pistol and a holster rig (wearing it across the chest in the manner which was later to be adopted so effectively by John Wesley Hardin), only to be challenged by a drunken cook and shot in the left foot before he knew what had happened. Jim had repaired the bullet hole in the actor's shoe and, in return, had been taught to play the banjo. He had even mastered the seven-finger strum which had become such a wild rage when Jolly Roger Lewis' United Musical Artists massed seventy-five banjo players in Zouave uniforms for torchlight parades in the East, although Jim had never heard them. His singing voice also lent the effect of a larynx under a seven-finger strum. His tremolo was enormous, serving up each individual note on a half-shell of quaver, a professional effect Mr. Sweeney had taught him. During the later hours of the evenings in which he sang there was seldom a dry eye in the house.

Irish, less musical but with all that perhaps more of a dreamer, devoted passionate hours to convincing Franklin Heller that a man with a burro, a pickaxe, a shovel, and a large sack could make himself a fortune in gold from the hills south of Monterrey, or he tried to sell the bartender a complicated drawing he had made on oilcloth which he represented as a design for an endless-belt square-taco machine.

In between the financial schemes, the singing, the whisky, and the troopings up and down the stairs with the sequin-toothed girls, they gave themselves up wholeheartedly to furniture-wrecking and mirror smashing, to stud poker, and to the gayer native dances.

At seven o'clock the following morning, fifteen hours after Irish and Jim had begun drinking in Pickering's Paradise, Whisperin' Leon Roth, Marty Ragaway, Mike Segal, and Chuck Moses got ready to settle their most bitter score. Roth, shouting at the top of his lungs, a conversational peculiarity which had earned him the nickname he bore, laid out the plan of action on the floor of the livery stable, which was directly under Evaliña Patten's room at the Pickering Academy. As he shouted the details of how he wanted the gun-fight arranged, little Evaliña was on her knees packing a large case with the clothing for her journey to Mexico on the ten o'clock stage that very morning. She heard that clarion voice speak the names of the two men she loved. She pressed her ear to an open knothole in the floor, listening intently. Everything concerning Roth's caricature of cow-stealing in the past fell into focus instantly. The story of the humiliation and the pledge for vengeance was one of the legends of the Patten ranch. Besides, these were the men who had tried to steal her own cattle. When she heard that cruel voice tell that Irish and Jim were drunk and helpless in the Paradise and that these men would move out to gun them down, she acted.

She was just seventeen. Russet-colored curls framed her flawless face; her braced bosom which was as deep as a bass drum rose and fell with mounting fear for her men. She sped out of the room, down the rainpipe

153

beside the window in the corridor to avoid censure from Mrs. Comfort, and into the dark byways of the only street in Pickering City, to make it to the rear door of the saloon in time to give warning.

As she crept in the back door, coughing lightly at the fumes from the long *fête,* Franklin Heller was asleep stretched out on top of the bar, his huge boots making a great *V* for Vino through which the tremendous mountain of his stomach could be seen rising and falling with the tuckered pathos of a gluttonous mastodon.

Evaliña had never been in such a place before. She stared with fascination at the little heaps of Panama exchange students curled up here and there under the round tables, so colorful in their quaint short flared skirts, high black stockings, and numerous spangles. Shards of mirror glass enhanced the flooring. Many of the chairs and tables had been overturned. All the windows had been closed and the curtains drawn, but two odorous oil lamps were lighted. There was a sharp scent of commercial carnation water in the air remaining, mixed with cigar smoke as thick as marshmallows, the heavier bouquet of one-hundred-and-twenty-proof bourbon, and the pungent sting of vintage males.

Jim and Irish were seated at a large poker table in the center of the large saloon under one of the two swinging lighted lamps. They were drinking bourbon out of unbreakable tin cups and Indian wrestling. That is to say they were not wrestling with a group of Tlachugan braves, but were facing each other, gripping each other's hands which were held perpendicular to their elbows, whch rested upon the green baize of the table top. They were trying to force each other's forearms backward until one or the other touched the table top. The cords of their necks stood out like pistol barrels. They had been in that motionless position for some time. It was an excellent game because it held them erect. They seemed slightly booze-blind although, of course, the young girl could not recognize that.

"Hello there, boys!" she sang out with her pure treble voice.

Their heads turned very slowly but at the same

time. They saw the vision of her. Their jaws dropped together as though supreme mopery were part of the choreography they had rehearsed. It was not only her incredible beauty which caused them to disengage their hands in slow motion and reach for the bourbon bottles; the Pickering Academy uniform, with its silvered middy blouse, scarlet bloomers, and turquoise Confederate Army hat, startled them as well. She moved closer to them, sensing that she should reassure them before she warned them.

"Never mind, boys," she said. "I'm real. Don't bolt. But have you ever seen a more ludicrous school uniform?" Irish and Jim had never seen any school uniform, so they did not comment.

"Boys! Boys!" She lifted her pink little fingers as though to keep the young riders at a conscious level. "I am little Evaliña Patten, the major's daughter. I am not being forward, accosting you in a saloon." For a scalding instant Street looked as though he feared she was going to punctuate that explanation with a grind and a bump. Irish flinched.

"Irish! Jim! Listen to me! You are in terrible danger. Roth and Ragaway have bulged out of nowhere!"

Irish answered for both of them.

"Honey, you are one gorgeous thing," he said. Street inclined his head in full agreement, then lifted it again experimentally.

Meanwhile, back at the livery stable, four men with eyes like a cheap wholesale grade of domestic caramels steeped out into the main street. In forbidding silence they arrayed themselves from sidewalk to sidewalk across that street, evenly spaced with Moses and Segal flanking Roth and Ragaway in the middle. They began their grim walk. It was a stiff wooden-legged lurch which was to be imitated by so many gunfighters throughout the West as the years went on.

Abe Weiler, the only doctor in Pickering City and publisher-editor of Pickering City's only newspaper, the crusading *Times,* a monthly, saw them coming. Made spry by the danger and the circulation-stimulating story it presaged, to say nothing of the active medical opportunities which could follow, he rushed across the street and into the dry-goods store dead ahead.

Evaliña stood in front of the two young men and pleaded with them, trying to make them focus on their peril, trying to make them focus on anything. "Jim! Irish!" she said. "Ragaway and Roth are coming to gun you down *Irish! Jim!* Ragaway and Roth are coming!"

"Honey, I tell you you are an absolutely gorgeous thing," Irish said. Street bobbed his head up and down.

In despair she ran to the front window of the saloon and peered through the curtains at the direction of the livery stable. She saw the four men. She saw the eight guns on their hips. She saw the forty-eight pieces of lead but did not actually compute that far as they had not yet come to multiplication at the Academy. She knew only one way to stop them.

Street stumbled to his feet. He stared down at Irish. "Roth'n Ragaway," he said, "lookin' for sawdust in their beards."

"*Sí.*"

"Putcher boots on."

"*Sí.*" Irish bent over but kept going down. He sat on the floor and put one boot on. He could not find the other boot. He looked up at his partner helplessly.

"Who neez boots," Street interrogated.

"*Sí.*"

Irish pulled himself to his feet by clinging to Jim's pants. He was a heavy man desperate to right himself. The trousers ripped, but only in the back. Irish made it to his feet, but Street's whole rear section flapped as he turned.

"Whereza gunz?" Jim asked rhetorically. They scanned the room several times. Irish spotted Franklin Heller's gun belt hanging on a hook at the end of the bar. He started toward it, walking as though his right foot were in a shallow trench and his left foot on a minor shelf because he was unaccustomed to walking with only one two-inch heel.

Franklin Heller had never worn this gun belt because the outfit in East New York who had shipped it to him had mistakenly sent him one which was many sizes too large, and Heller had a sixty-one inch waistline to begin with. Irish took the belt off the hook and slung it around behind him reflexively. Street was standing directly behind his friend. He caught the end of the belt and passed it around in front of them. They buckled it. With cold eyes and a lot of death on each hip, their inside arms bound closely to their sides between them, they moved with the lithe grace of cowhands toward the door and what waited for them in the street outside, Irish limping somewhat badly due to the imbalance caused by wearing just one boot, and Jim chancing lumbago or worse due to the exposure of his lower rear section.

"Something's wrong here," Irish mumbled as they reached the door.

"We forgot our hats," Jim explained. "But the hell with that." Somehow they made it out to the center of the street.

Evaliña had found Irish's six-gun. She moved along, close to the building line toward the livery stable, her eyes never leaving the slow advance of the four gunmen. When she was directly across the street from the bank where her father was luxuriating in an all-night poker session with the bank president, the sheriff, and Frank Braden, the advance man for a stunt balloonist, she turned to investigate the sounds of Reyes and Street, bound together like Ishmael and Queequeg with one belt, two guns, three boots, and no hats between them as they staggered into the deserted street, their faces set in the iron mold of men who play to win.

She fired a snap-shot through the bank window. There was a shatter of glass and a shout of horror. The advancing line of gunmen halted uncertainly. Reyes and Street went for their guns, to learn confusedly that their inside arms were strapped in. Major Patten came vaulting out of the broken window, a gun in each hand. "Who shot the sheriff?" he yelled.

"*Pa!*" Evaliña cried out, diverting the disconcerted

cow thieves for an instant more. "It's Roth and Ragaway! They aim to kill our boys!"

Irish fired. Evaliña fired. Jim fired. But each shot followed four shots in dazzling rapid succession from the two guns of Major Patten. Four dead cow thieves were stretched out on the main street of Pickering City.

"They reached and they fumbled an' it was a fatal weakness," reported the major, holstering his guns. "Roth and Ragaway was a bad element."

"Oh Pa!" Evaliña wailed. "Did Sheriff Kullers lean on my bullet goin' past?"

"Never mind, hon," her father said proudly. "Yuh done real good. You'll do to ride the river with."

BOOK THREE

———

1871

CHAPTER 1

THE year 1871 was significant in many oblique ways. The Shriners founded themselves. Jesse James got away with fifteen thousand dollars from the Obocock Bank in Corydon, Iowa. Orville Wright was born. All Indians were made national wards. The first professional baseball association was organized. Whistler completed his mother's portrait. The word *vaudeville* appeared for the first time, and the great fire of Chicago (which destroyed A. Lincoln's draft of the Emancipation Proclamation) began when a cow kicked over a lantern at 137 De Koven Street.

Jim Street and Irish Reyes were cleaning their fingernails with hunting knives at the bar of the Paradise listening to Franklin Heller's analysis of a recipe for *Gebäckene Kartoffeln mit Parmesan*. Heller was breathing on glasses and polishing them as he talked. "Parmesan is a semi-fat cooked cheese with a slow maturing rate," he explained, "and if you buy any make sure it comes from the *right* bank of the Po River, or the *left* bank of the Reno."

Major Patten's outstretched hand hit the swinging door from the outside and he burst into the saloon, slightly wild-eyed. He walked rapidly to the three men at the bar.

"She gets in one week from today," he said excitedly, breathing hard.

"Who?"

"What?"

"Evaliña! My little girl. She'll be back one week from today and she'll be home for good."

"Why, that's wonderful news," Franklin said. He reached for a bottle of bourbon under the bar. He filled four glasses.

Jim wiped off his thin mouth with the back of his hairy hand. "She saved our lives, Major," he said, "and we never got a chance to thank her because we overslept."

160

"You'll have your chance," the major said.

"She risked her life for us, Major," Irish said.

The major set his jaw. "Get this straight, boys. Jan and me and Evaliña will line up on the porch of the Big House and them folks as wants to walk past and shake hands and all like that. That's all. Nothin' else. Nothin'."

Irish and Jim seemed confused. They looked at each other quickly but they did not speak.

"How do you want the Welcome Home organized, Major?" Heller said, moving in smoothly. "I got four hundred and twelve paper hats left over from Founder's Day. I can book Lem Berns' Philharmonica Band in here from Bracketville. The Reverend Howard Pearl is just about headin' this way on the circuit and he can make a glorious speech of welcome."

"Maybe we oughta get Mat Sun out here an' figure the food while we're settin' ever'thing else," the major said. "She'll step off that Brownsville stage at high noon an' I want to hear cannon goin' off, church bells ringin', tubas blowin', and be able to smell the barbecue and see the bunting five miles off when we ride on out to meet her rollin' in."

He turned for a moment to look balefully at Street and Reyes because they were twenty-eight-years old, too healthy, and suddenly too damn pushy about thanking Evaliña. They moved down the bar and looked away from him.

They missed the celebration.

The stage came in right on time, skidding like an iceboat behind the eight mules who always needed to be turned and headed to stop the coach. Two lines of twenty riders each had made a wild-running escort for the last five miles into town, and as the procession roared in with the stage coach bucketing wildly, the riders began to shoot off their guns and Professor Lem Berns had his assistant brush the hair out of his eyes so he could hit the downbeat. The rubas punched grunts out of the soft air, cornets blew hard enough to ripple the rows of bunting strung across the main street, and the tangy smells of barbecued meat, *salsa piquante*, and black coffee were sharp enough to hone a knife on.

161

The crowd had come in from five counties around. There were nine hundred, mostly Patten people, chewing and sipping, gulping and swallowing, and they all cheered hoarsely and well when the stagecoach door opened, but the round hairy sounds seemed to stop midway in their throats when Evaliña Patten appeared. She stood there for two or three minutes on the stage steps and waved her handkerchief at everybody.

The pandemonium was transformed into a hushed silence. She was so dazzlingly beautiful that they could only stand, popeyed and gaping. Then the women started weeping, thinking of their own youth and of their husbands who seemed fairly certain to get drunk that night, and the spell was broken long enough for Reverend Howard Pearl to yell "When the Lord giveth, he giveth with an open hand!" Everyone whooped with sensitive understanding and the major got so mad he kicked in the bass drum and fired two shots in the air. Folks toward the back of the crowd thought it was some kind of celebration signal and in no time two or three hundred guns were going off, causing the deaths of twenty-three chickens in Miss Kay Norton's barnyard one hundred and ten yards down the road.

It turned into a great party.

Evaliña and Jan held each other and cried a little when they first came together after three long years. A line of people that stretched for nearly half a mile got itself formed up and the Pattens shook hands with the whole county, making them welcome. The Paradise sold more whisky than any day since the Dred Scott news had come in in '57. Mat Sun was out there at the fires, cooking every ounce of the glorious eating food himself, his long pigtail white as a candle. By midnight, the word came through that two drunks had got themselves shot, but it turned out that they had only sat on some lighted fireworks.

The major seemed to have done staring at Evaliña piercingly by ten peeyem. Then at last, he and Jan and Evaliña were alone in the flame-tree patio. They spoke in Spanish, to hear Evaliña's considerable improvement.

162

"Good trip, honey lamb?" the major asked for the ninth time that day.

"Oh, fine, Pa."

"That's good."

"You look so well, darling girl. So lovely."

"Everybody was simply wonderful to me."

"She speaks right fine Spanish, too," said the major, who didn't.

"Pa, where were your two foremen tonight?"

"What two foremen?"

"Jim Street and Irish Reyes."

"What about them?"

"Where were they? They're still with the outfit?"

"Yes. They're here. Why?"

"They were so adorable. I mean they were so absolutely *predilecto*."

"Now lookahere, Evaliña—"

"This child has been traveling all day and anyone can see that she's worn out," Jan said. "It's long past bedtime for all of us. Say good night. We have all day tomorrow for talking."

The major undressed slowly. All thought of Patricio, Don José, and those two small boys he had sworn to protect had gone from his mind. He thought of calling them both out and gunning them, but he rejected the dream because it might upset Jan. He thought of riding over to see Paul Hochuli in Harris and persuading him to send for the boys to drive his cattle north because Hochuli was going to move beef toward financial ruination in Abilene that year—just like everybody else except the major.

The three years of separation and worry had just about pushed the major overboard. He thought about the curse until he built a fire of hate in his mind against it. He loved the two boys, but he loved Evaliña more. Evaliña wasn't only his son. She belonged to the sacred memory of Maria de Lourdes and Don José Vicuña de Arias. Don José had given the major his position and his respectability, which he may have valued above all else. All he could seem to hold in his mind was that one kiss could bring his world down upon him. He had just shaken his nightshirt over his

163

head when he looked across the room to see Janine, white-faced, closing the door, leaning against it after it was shut, her eyes wide. She tried to bring her hand to her mouth as though to stop the words she was about to say. Her hand was trembling violently.

"What—What is it? What happened?" he said harshly.

"She knows."

"Knows? Knows what?"

"The Arias women told her about the curse."

"Aaaaaah." Air escaped from Major Patten as from a limp balloon. He fell straight downward upon the bed and sat there numbly. He began to think of Maria de Lourdes' desperate melancholy which had begun the instant she had heard about the curse.

"How did she take it?" he asked dully.

"When she had finished telling me—"

"Yes? Yes?"

"She seemed delighted."

At a quarter to one in the morning, while the Pattens were still wide awake, something happened which made all discussion of the matter merely academic. They heard the heavy crash of two bodies hitting the floor of Evaliña's bedroom, next door to their apartment, following the chattering of shattering glass which could only have been the skylight the major had installed two years before when he had learned by letter that Evaliña had been studying the art of painting flora upon dinner plates.

Within seconds he had jolted open her door. He carried a large pistol. His voice snarled softly and wordlessly, like a puma's.

CHAPTER 2

THE major reached behind himself through the doorway and pulled a lighted lamp into the room. The light washed away bulky shadows. The large bodies of two men lay face down on the floor. Evaliña sat bolt upright in bed. The major moved forward. With his boot he turned over the nearest body. Evaliña gasped. It was Irish Reyes. She stared at him hungrily as though he were a huge *pambacito compuesto*.

Her long ginger hair chuted down behind her. One shoulder strap of the translucent nightshift fell. The promise it pulsed into the room for a fraction of a second could have, in the years following T. A. Edison, powered a generator sufficiently to have lighted the rooms and the factories of a city of sixty-two thousand population for three and one-quarter hours. Evaliña threw back the covers as though to bound out of bed.

"Back!" the major snapped with velvet hinges on his voice. She remained sitting on the edge of the bed. The major walked two paces and turned the other body over. It was Jim Street. The major began to kick each fallen man alternately on the soles of the feet, giving the vaudville effect of a stationary but spirited cakewalk. *"Up!"* he whispered with a terrible voice. "Up or I'll shoot off the ends of your ears." The two men scrambled to their feet. *"Out!"* the major snarled. They moved quickly and were gone. Evaliña grabbed a scent bottle and threw it with all her strength against the closed door. "Drat, drat, and drat!" she yelled. "How is a girl supposed to get back to sleep in a big, cold, empty bed after all that fuss?" She could still hear the sound of their heavy boots clomping away from her down the corridor.

With an oil lamp in one hand and the large gun named Big Max in the other, the major moved Irish and Jim ahead of him through the night to the smallest shed, which stood some sixty yards behind the Big House. The night was black and sightless. The big pistol waved them into the shed. The major closed the shed's door with his elbow and placed the lamp on a worktable. He kicked two tin buckets viciously at the men, his eyes glittering. The lamplight blinked at the bare walls. There was a place for everything and everything was in its place. The smell of kerosene and the smell of the wood mixed heartily with the metallic smell of the tools which were hanging everywhere. Street stood warily in a large black Stetson hat and blue jeans and a black wool shirt. Irish wore tight-fitting *charro* pants which gripped his calves and ankles and tied under his boots. He had big silver spurs on, a bright green shirt, and a tall, peaked sombrero whose brim swooped upward in the back. Despite the clothes they were wearing, an anthropologist asked to choose the Mexican of the two would have chosen Street with his olive skin, hawklike nose, and pencil mustache. In fact, a jury of W. B. Yeats, Padraic Colum, and Oliver St. John Gogarty would have chosen Reyes as the most Irish-looking owner of a Hiberian public house out of a convention of Irish public-house owners. The fact that most people choose not to look like what they are supposed to resemble has caused its share of trouble in the world.

The kicked buckets careered to a stop at the feet of the two foremen as they towered over the major. *"Set!"* the major ordered.

They up-ended the buckets and sat down gingerly, watching the gun.

"Never thought it would ever come to this, boys," the major said softly.

"It is all a big mistake, Major," Irish said.

"I don't know how you could do such a thing to me and to my family."

"It ain't exactly like it *looked,* now, Major," Street said.

"I seen you lyin' there and I thought you was both dead. I was right sorry to think that. You was both good boys."

"Still good, Major," Street gulped. "No use talkin' about us like we used to be."

"The little lady saved our life three years ago, Major," Irish said. "We wanted to thank her."

The major snarled like a cougar. Both men flinched.

Street and Reyes had acted independently of each other that night for the first time since they had been seven years old. Both men had been riled by the major's mysteriously truculent attitude in the saloon a week before. They had begun to talk to each other about the enormous, the ultimate, service Evaliña Patten had performed for them by saving their lives and as they talked they convinced each other that they had a right to thank her for that in their own way, not as part of the entire county lined up in front of the Big House porch to shake her hand and mumble. The brainwashing which was to last for a long time began right there. Each man felt the other had the right, and because they had always thought alike and for each other, after a bottle or two in the big welcome-home celebration each man had decided to act without telling the other.

They had been a little bit booze-simple, but they had known enough not to go up to the front door of the major's house at one o'clock in the morning, so they had simultaneously climbed opposite sides of the flame-tree patio, had seen the large, luminous glass skylight, had been drawn to it mainly by curiosity. Reaching it, they had stood up at the same instant, scared hell out of each other by finding themselves face to face, and through dismay had toppled over sideways through the skylight to crash to the floor of the room. That was how they chose to reconstruct it at the moment.

"You know whut all this has to mean for you boys?"

They decided not to answer.

"Well, boys, you're the two best wagon bosses I ever had, but as you stand there now you might as well be a couple of sheep rustlers. You compromised my little girl. She is the granddaughter of the greatest *hacendado* the whole world has ever known. That's mighty serious. If it hadda been just one of you, I'd of shot him down quick and clean, but you doubled the bet so's it won't look to the world as awful as if jest one of you had been found in that room. Yessir, boys, that's just what you did. You doubled the bet." The thought of a wager seemed to bolster the major.

Irish spoke softly and cheerfully. "Well—it's a good thing then, hey, Major? I mean you don't have to shoot us. I mean, it's a good thing Jim and I happened to meet on that roof and rassle a little bit, then fall through the skylight, hey?"

The major snarled again. He shot a hole through

the bucket on which Irish was seated. The boioinging reverberated through the small space so violently that all three men had to clap their hands to their ears like hyperausiacs in a thunderstorm. Gradually, the tintinnabulations faded. The major cleared his throat emotionally and went on.

"One of you will be as dead as a horseshoe by sunup, and the other man is goin' to have to marry up with my little girl."

Silence flailed at them.

Irish spoke first. "I think it would be a good thing to sleep on this, Major, I really do."

The major shook his head mournfully.

Jim cleared his throat. "Sun-up?" he asked mildly.

"Uh-huh."

"And—uh—you say—uh—one of us two fellers has to marry up with Miss Evaliña? Uh—little Evaliña?" He closed his eyes and waited for the confirmation.

"Uh-huh."

"Which one?"

"Why, hell—the one who revenges her honor and shoots the other down like a cur."

"Shoots? Down? Like a cur?" Irish cried out.

"I say no, Major," Jim blurted. "I couldn't draw on Irish, no matter what."

"Then I'll shoot *you.* And Irish marries Evaliña."

"But, Major," Irish cried. "My father promised me to Florita Peña fourteen years ago. You know that. You blessed the plan!"

"Let Guillermo Peña look out for *his* daughter and I'll look out for my daughter," the major answered flatly. "You goin' to shoot Jim down for what he done to Evaliña?"

"*Gracias,* Major. I could not."

The major's head dropped sadly. "Well then, boys, this is good-bye." He cocked the huge pistol which made a sound similar to that of a giant sequoia tree being split by lightning. "You won't feel nothin'. Just like a little poke in the left eye, but for keeps."

The door opened. Janine Patten stood in the doorway, Evaliña directly behind her. "No, Pa! *No!*" Evaliña yelled. She was wearing a calico peignoir. The décolletage was blinding. It gave the doomed men

168

even more to live for. It would have stirred an elderly military statue.

"Put the gun down, Major," his wife said. "Shooting people doesn't change anything."

"No, Jan. What I'm goin' to do has been an unwritten law for a thousand years."

"But you'd let either one of them marry her. You just said that."

"One of them. But there's two of them."

Evaliña rested her hand on her father's gun wrist. "Let's talk about it for a little bit, Pa. Please put Big Max down for just a minute?"

"If you killed these boys you would have to face Patricio and Don José someday, when your time comes," Jan said steadily. He looked at her in panic. "I know what you need to do to keep Evaliña's honor, and I agree all the way with you: it must be done."

His head was shaking many noes while his voice said, "You do?"

She nodded.

Everyone in the room stared at Janine. She, too, was beautiful with magnificent posture and silvered hair. Her shining dark eyes stared at her husband, grateful to heaven that she had a solution for him. She licked her full lips and said, "I think we have a chance here for the most exciting series of wagers ever placed in Texas or Mexico or anywhere else."

Major Patten's pistol arm dropped to his side. "How's that?" he asked softly and with much interest.

"We must plan some contests. Definitely. We will let everyone know about them from here to St. Louis and New Orleans. We will say that both of these young men have asked for your daughter's hand in marriage and that to be fair, to help Evaliña to decide between them, whoever wins the first three out of five contests will be her husband."

"Oh, Jan!" Evaliña barely breathed.

"Why, we'll bring perhaps ten thousand people to Pickering City with events like that with an appeal of a reason like that, and you'll be able to take all their bets in a betting bank that can run to half a million dollars."

"Well, think of that!" the major said. "But what kind of contests?"

"You'll think of those. They could race horses, or shoot at targets. They could rope cattle—"

"I could chalk up the changin' odds on big blackboards and hang the odds at the key points all over."

"They could box or wrestle."

"I could have teams of riders carry the odds and the results out to a five-hundred-mile circle every twenty-four hours." The major wheeled to face Irish and Jim. "I could telegraph to Brownsville and Corpus Christi—why, Jan's *right*—I could be taking bets as far away as New Orleans and St. Louis."

"You purely and surely could, Pa." Evaliña looked with wonderment first at Irish and then at Jim. The intensity of her gaze hit both young men as with the force of a power hose. They did not recover from that look and one became deeply resentful when she looked like that at the other. The smell of both women in that small space made the three men heady.

CHAPTER 3

A STAGECOACH pulled by eight brown mules, each seemingly racing the others, came tumbling off the hill. The driver used his long whip as though outlaw bullets were flying through his hair. Riding shotgun next to him, the messenger leaned forward tensely and with desperate earnestness. Neither man looked back and the mules surged forward as though they had a date with the golden oats of destiny.

Inside the coach a man was being thrown from wall to wall, from floor to ceiling, because every holding strap had broken and there was nothing he could use to keep himself upon the seat at that breakneck speed. Under the most normal conditions the mules pulling the light coach moved along at top speed. They needed to be circled by the driver and checked by the helper at each stage stand before they would stop. If a passenger wanted to come aboard or alight between stage stands, all the driver could do would be to circle the mules, reducing the speed somewhat while the passenger jumped as best as he could. Stage robbers could stop the coach only by killing the mules.

There was no circling or thought of stopping on this trip. The man cried out piteously, "Stop! In heaven's name, stop! You are killing me." His diction was flawless.

For one threatening moment his head was shot through the opened coach window, upside down, as though he were floating in the air on his back. He screamed again at the danger and he knew that they had heard him for the driver had stared directly down into the floating passenger's eyes from the high seat. The passenger, John Moodie, was given little time for analysis. Neck wrenched and body mangled, he was thrown back into the coach to bump and crash upon the floor. At that moment he heard sharp whoops from the driver's seat and supposed they were to be murdered by Indians but did not care. Either that or whatever they had been straining forward for had been sighted. Someone or something had weathered every rack; the prize they sought seemed to have been won.

John Moodie was about to enter Pickering City, Texas, because he had taken a wrong turn at Pittsburgh, Pennsylvania, traveling—as he did at that time —in surgical stockings for a firm long established in London, England. In Pittsburgh he had met a semi-retired soubrette, her heart still in show biz, but her presence firmly held in grasp by her mother, a redoubtable Pittsburgh dowager. They were an adorable family, Moodie suspected, and rumored by the daughter herself to be extremely rich. He had soon found himself participating, then sympathizing, with both sides of the argument between mother and daughter: *viz* the performing arts *versus* home and hearth, marriage and babies—which had been raging, the daughter had told him, ever since she had been summoned home from a position second from the left of a bouncing line of *artistes* called Myerberg's Sweet Hearties, a lusciously overweight troupe Mr. Moodie had first encountered in Winsted, Connecticut, where for the first time he had drunk New Jersey champagne out of this young lady's slipper.

He had learned upon meeting her again in Pittsburgh, where she was weeping in the back of a better type of saloon, that she had been called home to attend her great-aunt's funeral. Once home, the funeral done, her mother had soon made it clear that there was no hope of her ever returning to the living theater. She confided to Mr. Moodie that she had decided to run away from Pittsburgh, from her home and her mother.

There had been a series of beers, a few salutary pats; a squeeze here and a pinch there, while he had listened to her story. He then held her attention by moving very deliberately and spelling out the word M-O-T-H-E-R with beer foam upon the dark wood of the table within the curtained booth. He asked her to read the word carefully. "Only one of these precious things to a customer," he said wryly. "I never knew my mother. Where would you go for Christmas, my dear?" She had wept anew at that, and he had felt he had been of some help to her.

In the end, fastening her garters, she persuaded him to come home with her to talk to her mother, to try to explain with his wonderfully refined English accent how much The Dance meant to the girl. He had consented. Before they had left the saloon, she asked him to hold all of her money so that no matter what demon might possess her she would not be able to run off to New York or Paris. It had not seemed likely to him at the time that two dollars and forty cents would have taken her that far, but he tucked the money into his own fulsomely stuffed wallet, and the very act had brought color to the girl's cheeks and resolution to her tiny, shiny eyes.

He met Mother. It registered with him that the family mansion had most certainly seen better days but, knowing how eccentric were the families of American millionaires, he dismissed his own censure of the smell of hospital supplies and sour beer. He had not looked down upon the burden imposed by wealth before then, he told himself, nor would he begin to do so that day.

He was asked to wait in a terribly shabby room. He sat down upon a sagging bed. Mother came in at a trot and forthwith he began his gracious chat, hoping he could express the meaning and contribution of The Dance, what it could mean—deep down—to its practitioners, *et cetera, et cetera,* but Mother did not seem to wish to talk at all. She was extremely short with her daughter, pushing her out of the room, then shutting the door with a lurching crash. She did not ask Mr. Moodie if he would care to have a refreshment, but banged a black bottle down upon a small table, shoved a glass under his nose, and poured.

"Drink it!" she snarled.

When he awoke he had no purse, no money, no trousers, and was rolling about on the floor of an empty westbound freight car.

The experience had embittered Moodie. He could not return to London, of course, where he would be marked for ruin for ostensibly having absconded with the firm's funds and a large supply of the company's surgical stockings. He had been forged in that fire twelve years before his terrifying stagecoach ride to Pickering City. The shame of Pittsburgh had changed his life, causing him to undercompensate in his awareness of women. He had lost a certain tinkle in his laughter when, if ever any more, he bantered with the opposite sex. Suddenly he sat bolt upright on the floor of the stagecoach, gazing backward upon the events of twelve years before and it came upon him in a revolting wave that the woman who had drugged him *could not have been Mignette's mother.*

Somehow, surrounded by horrendous yells, the stage stopped. He sat in disarray upon its floor trying to reconstruct the past but he had been too sorely pummeled by his journey that day. He could only remember, as always, that those two women had taken his cash but, in his heart of hearts, he also knew that all women could not be that bad and that somewhere, someplace, there must live for him an adorable girl from whom he would be able to wrench his money back, in full or better, so that he could return home to England.

Since April 1866, Mr. Moodie had been traveling for Captain Hugh Fitz-Moncrieff's Hair and Mustache Tonic, a Yonkers, N.Y., firm. Nowhere was there a better advertisement for such a product than upon the person of John Moodie, Esq., himself. He was a handsome man, quite tall, slender, with a high color; he wore a black mustache which was luxuriant fur, not merely hair in the ordinary mustache sense at all. Long it was, thick and sweeping. It was his selling tool.

When the stagecoach almost tipped over to halt, the two men leaped down from their high seats but no one came to open the passenger door. Mr. Moodie picked himself up from the floor of the stage, bit by bit, still mentally dazed by the flash of memory which had told him that that woman could not have been Mignette's mother. He flung half of himself at the coach seat, then arduously and with agony pulled the remainder of his body to a slumped sitting position. His nerveless hand fumbled with the door-catch. Somehow it opened. He tottered out of the stage lacking verve. He found himself facing the swinging doors of a saloon. The smell of booze almost made him whimper with gratitude. He made his way up the three short steps to the verandah.

Noises behind him caused him to turn stiffly. He saw a Texas town street. Not fifty feet away, in street center, he saw assembled a great circular congregation of people, all staring intently within itself. He saw a perfectly beautiful woman seated upon a towering stepladder and wearing a look so disconsolate, so bleak, as to seem helpless. A man's raw voice was droning on and on, from somewhere within that circle of flesh. "I offer seven to five. The price is seven to five." Mr. Moodie turned away, leaned upon the swinging doors and almost fell into the comforting saloon. His painful rigor gave him the carriage of the late Duke of Wellington (1769–1852). He grasped the rail of the bar and held on, wincing spasmodically.

The bartender slid a bottle down to him along the top of the polished bar. It stopped directly in front of him. He reached a glass, poured a shot into it, and gulped it down. He poured another and sipped it; nectar it was, a wonderful medicine and a great whisky all in one. The bartender followed the bottle, walking slowly, polishing the ruby-red wood of the bar

174

with a large soft rag as he came. The saloon and the bar-room were amongst the most elegant Moodie could remember seeing for well over two thousand miles. Why—this barman might even be able to make a proper Fandooka, which Mr. Moodie had not enjoyed since a glorious evening in the Illustrators' Club in Calcutta, so many years before.

"Do you make a Fandooka, my man?"

"A what?"

"Fandooka. F-A-N-dooka. You know, Gum Arabic, seven parts *okooleeau,* a touch of falernum, six ounces of Holland Gin, a pony of slivovitz, a sling of arrack—"

"No."

"Ah. Thought you might. Looks like that sort of place."

"I fool around a little with new drinks on my day off but I never heard of that one."

"Whatever is all that outside?"

The barman stared at the bottle in front of Mr. Moodie. "Outside?" he asked.

"That congregation surrounding the smashing girl who sits so mournfully upon a pedestal."

"Stranger, ain't you?"

"Yes."

"I knew that for true."

"My—uh—speech?"

"No."

"My costume?" Mr. Moodie was wearing a battered but still elegantly tall beaver hat in one of the lighter chocolate shades. His lapels, upon a long-skirted coat, were of fawn over brick-color wool. He wore a paisley Ascot cravat. The effect was handsome in the extreme but no one, on the other hand, would have mistaken him for a local cowpuncher.

"I mighta noticed your suit later."

"How then? Because I do not understand what is happening outside?"

"No. It was the way you drank the furniture polish."

Moodie took two steps backward. *"Furniture polish?"* He beat his chest. "I?"

"First time I ever seed it done."

"But—you served it to me! I thought it was your crude whisky."

"No, sir. I did not serve it to you. I was polishin' my bar like I always do. I finished up at that end so I slid the bottle up to this end to work up here and you took it and you drunk it."

"But—it's delicious!" Moodie reached out and poured himself another shot. He tasted it carefully, rolling it over his tongue and washing it across his taste buds. "You may *say* this is furniture polish, sir, and you may very well *use* it as furniture polish, but let me say that it is absolutely delicious."

Charily, the bartender half filled a shot glass and drew it to his lips. He sipped. "You're right," he said with awe in his voice. "This here is wonderful stuff." Mr. Moodie refilled both glasses. "And very heady-making, too," he murmured.

They touched glasses and sipped.

"Now, do tell me. What was that commotion in the street and who, in heaven's name, is that lovely, lovely girl?"

"It's a long story, Mr.—"

"John Moodie, sir. At your service."

"Im Franklin Heller, Commissioner of Public Health." Franklin did not know why he had made it a point to put on rank. They shook hands tensely. "I represent that girl's father in all Tourism Industries of Pickering City. Have another polish?"

"Don't mind if I do. You too, please."

"This here stuff is a godsend," Franklin said. "Customers are always spillin' their drinks after a certain time an' this stuff'll actually be good for the bar." He filled the two shot glasses slowly. "What you seen out on that street is pure sadness, Mr. Moodie. First time in his life Major William Patten has started somethin' he cain't finish. Not only that, but the lifetime friendship of two good men has been broken, and the whole thing is slowly sappin' away his daughter's health and alienating the affections of his wife, a wonderful woman, whilst the people of this region are purely sick with gamblin' fever."

"My word!"

They sipped luxuriously at the red furniture polish. Franklin Heller began to talk as though he'd needed badly for a long, long time to get to say what he had to say.

CHAPTER 4

So much had changed since that starry night when two young men sought somehow, although slightly intoxicated, to thank a young girl for having saved their lives three years before.

Reyes and Street, after twenty-one years of virtual inseparability, had become surly with each other; then it got worse. Mat Sun summed it up for both of them. "Whatta matta? Whatta hell, you clazee?" Reyes had swept all the glassware off the table in front of him and had yelled, "Aaaaah, shut up or I'll shoot holes in your pots!" Street merely threw a full plate of stew at the ceiling, shattered two earthenware pitchers with a large axe, chopped up the planks laid across the sawhorses where he and sixty-one other men had been eating, then left the chuckhouse aloofly. "Allight!" Mat Sun yelled after him. "That ansuh me. You alla same clazee!"

The progression toward these murderous rages had been steady and sure. On the morning following the major's decision to solve the affair of honor with clean-cut sporting events instead of two murders, both Irish and Jim had been summoned to the major's office in the company building.

"Set down, boys," the major said genially. "I got this thing all figured out."

The major had not bothered to sleep since he had dismissed them the night before. He had plunged into the task before him like an ergomaniac: drawing charts, jotting certain arithmetics, creating promotion schemes and setting down ground rules. He had estimated his printing needs, his commercial larder. He had figured permutations and combinations of odds, had set plans for the construction of a new twenty-room extension, each room sleeping ten, to the Pickering House. He had worked with Franklin Heller all through the night. It had brought his youth back to him, the wonderful, exhilarating days when one hardly knew what pleasure the next chump would bring when life was a sure-thing gamble with a stacked deck. The cares and anxieties of three years, all the furrows in his psyche which had been pressed there by the curse, were gone. He was light-hearted. He was redeemed by the rich vista of old-time larceny which he saw before himself.

He and Franklin Heller had covered such contingencies as the methods of spreading the most effective false rumors for the greatest impact upon shifting the odds whenever it seemed most profitable; of the need to get word to Irish's sister to cancel any Indian raids which had been scheduled for the neighborhood; the problem of provisioning the influx of sporting population from farm and range which could well swell Pickering City's population ten-fold. The major chuckled as he worked, thinking of how such a proposition would have tickled his old father.

Franklin left the major at seven-twenty ayem to gather up construction crews and to send riders and orders to Laredo and Brownsville and ships to New Orleans. When he had all that under way he slipped on a *toque blanche* and, in his capacity as *chef de cuisine* of The Pickering House, he made himself a four-egg cheese omelette, some mozarella toast, and an All-American Bunny made with grated Gruyere.

When the two foremen shuffled into the major's office, their employer was relaxed and affable. He had his feet on his desk. He wore his large, soft black hat with its broad brim for shading his absence of expression around the eyes, snow-white linen, a black string tie, and a long, black, vented coat with many secret pockets. His close-cropped mustache was still clearly ginger-colored but it was as though powdered sugar had been sprinkled over the top of it.

"We got a lot of work out there, Major. I ought to be across the river."

"We sure ought to be out there with the men, Major," Street said.

"No more, boys. You're on leave now with full pay. Round-up's over and we ain't drivin' north. You just forget all that. Max Miller and Spanish Wally Heim is the new temporary foremen."

"But—"

"No use arguin', boys. Now—the rules." He pulled a large sheet of paper in front of him. "The first event'll be a shooting contest. We'll shoot at snakes."

"*Snakes?*" That was Irish.

"How?" Jim asked.

"I figure I'll put you two boys each standin' in a separate ring of sand, say about thirty feet across. You wear your guns but you don't wear no boots. Then we let three diamondback rattlers into each ring, each one comin' at you from a different direction at the same time."

"*Rattlesnakes?*" Irish repeated incredulously.

"That's it."

"I *hate* rattlesnakes."

"At a signal from me. Not right away when the snakes come out, because the folks will want to get their late bets down, botha you draws and fires. Feller who kills all three snakes first wins the event. If a feller shoots before the signal he loses."

"Major," Irish said unevenly. "I don't think you heard me."

"I heard you."

"Major, snakes make me very, very nervous. I can't explain it. I can't have anything to do with snakes."

The major shrugged. "Then you forfeit the first event, unless Jim refuses to have anything to do with snakes."

"I like the idea fine," Jim said with mean arrogance. "Nice, easy event. Just a shootin' contest an' I can beat Irish shootin' any day of the week."

"People know about the way I feel about snakes," Irish said. "We should have another contest which is an equalizer or your odds will be all wrong."

"What kind of equalizer?"

"I honestly think the second event should be wrestling in twenty feet of water." Jim Street went as pale as if all his veins had been opened. The major watched closely.

"It'd be a good idea if we could ever find twenty feet of water," the major said.

"We can bring it down from the spring at Fort Clark."

"Yes, we could," the major mused.

"It must be a terrible thing to die by drowning."

"Well, it's a purely horrible thing to die with a slimy snake wrapped around your leg," Street barked.

"Boys," the major intoned. "You have some right hard times comin' up. This thing has to make you bad friends until it's settled, maybe longer. That's somethin' you'll have to sort out yourselves, because when you sullied the honor of my little girl you lost any chance for my help. I woulda shot you last night. An' I'll shoot you for sure if you try any sneakin' around in the day or night tryin' to sweet-talk Evaliña. You hear me?"

He stared at them hard. No one spoke.

"One more thing. If I find you shootin' at each other or fightin' each other annaplace but in my ee-vents, I'm a-goin' to put a bullet through your knee bones, an' a stiff-legged cowhand don't set no saddle."

That evening in the patio, Janine Patten established that if Irish and Jim were competing for Evaliña's hand in marriage they must be considered engaged to her. If they were engaged, considering all the risks they were about to take they had a right to court their fiancée.

The major balked furiously but he lost. He was backed up into agreeing to one hour of courtship by each man, each week, providing it was understood that he would be sitting right there with them while they courted.

Evaliña beamed at her stepmother.

CHAPTER 5

FRANKLIN HELLER rode sedately up to Peggy Flinn's place in Ciudad Hochuli, about two hundred and eighty miles east of Pickering City, at about six o'clock in the evening. Peggy was tending bar, smoking a short black twist, with a red rose behind each ear and, as usual, the brass knuckles of her hitting hand studded with Alaskan diamonds and Oregon rubies. She had white hair worn in a Dutch-boy short cut. She wore a low-cut scarlet evening dress and wooden sabots. She was so delighted to welcome a fellow saloon-keeper that she got down on her hands and knees behind the bar and wriggled out a bottle of extraordinary rye whisky from an iron chest.

"How come you're ridin' this far east, Franklin?"

"Long story an' a sad one, Peg."

"Pour it out, Franklin."

"Hochuli riders still come here?"

"Ain't no place else they could go without they did two days of ridin'. That's Cap'n Paul Hochuli hisself at the end of the bar."

"Fine-lookin' man."

"Yes. He is. Come on along and meet him."

"No, Peg. Looks like a case of mumbles is about to come on him. I'll be content to talk my heart out to you, Peg. Maybe you kin tell the other boys later on."

"What happened, Franklin?"

He gulped the rye, then stared straight down into the glass after that. "You remember Irish Reyes an' Jim Street?"

"Remember? Them boys was the wildest an' finest spenders ever to pleasure a calico queen. I—why, I was a little sweet on them boys myself and three of the little Official Hostesses here folleyed them boys all the way to Pickering City, as you well know." She stopped. She put her jeweled, brass-knuckled hitting hand over her heart. "But they're Patten's wagon bosses. What're you askin' me for?"

"They was always together. Always both. Never just one of them boys alone, always the two of them." He stared at her mournfully. His lower lip bobbled a little. Peggy drew back so suddenly in shock that one of the eight-ounce emerald-and-lava ear-rings snapped off and crashed to the floor, waking an exhausted prospector who had been slumped across a table near the rear of the bar. Franklin gripped her non-hitting hand, which lay on the bar between them. "Peg," he

181

said, "Jim Street an' Irish Reyes is out gunnin' for each other."

"No!" It was almost a shriek.

"Yep."

"A woman?"

"Yep."

Peggy Flinn began to cry. She cried like a trombone. "It ain't right! Somebody's got to stop it!"

The Ciudad Hochuli Exchange Center was a huge square hall one half of which was a honkatonk with a bar, girls, and a running red-dog game, and on the other side a general store selling such items as apples, bullets, chili, and sheet music. When Peggy began to wail, men looked up in alarm. The stopped hefting sacks of flour. They lifted light-boned girls from their laps. They turned to gape at something no man had seen since Ralph Austrian, her sixth husband, had run off with a barbed-wire demonstrator. Peggy Flinn was crying. She was beginning to splinter the top of the bar with her jeweled knuckles to emphasize her grief. At last, because somebody had to do something, and because leadership was called for, Cap'n Hochuli himself tottered along, holding the bar rail firmly as he came.

"Guess you better speak up, stranger," he said ominously to Franklin Heller.

From directly behind him, Franklin heard another hard voice say, "Whatever you done to make Peg cry, stranger, you're a-goin' to pay for with your hide." All at once, a semicircle of tall lean men, all wearing guns, ringed him. When one of the men took hold of Heller's shirtfront and pulled him around, Peggy leaned across the bar and broke his grip with a heavy wallop. "Take your hands off my friend, Herman Addison," she shrilled. "That's Franklin Heller. He's from the sober side of the bar over to Pickering City." She took a deep breath to keep from bawling again then she exhaled slowly. "Irish Reyes and Jim Street is gunnin' for each other," she said slowly. Earl Keate was the first man to recover.

"It cain't be!" he yelled.

"What happened?" Cap'n Hochuli said grimly.

"Both boys get theirselves engaged to the Major's

young daughter and it made for hard feelin's." The crowd buzzed.

Heller told the story. He told about the projected contests. When he had the crowd worked up to an excited pitch he told about the gala wedding celebration to which they were invited one and all, and about how folks they hadn't seen in years would be coming up from Brownsville and down from the San Saba and in from west of the Pecos River.

"Franklin," Cap'n Hochuli said, shaking his hand. "There's not a man or woman here who'd miss ridin' over to see them contests and that weddin' for annathing in Texas."

Mat Sun handled his end of the sales promotion with similar aplomb in the southeastern areas, the country around Laredo and Brownsville. Within two weeks he was able to place four frontpage stories which were picked up by newspapers in St. Louis, Dallas, and New Orleans, capturing the certain interests of the sporting element in those communities.

Major Patten handled northern Mexico personally, where he was the greatest landowner and deeply respected. He organized straw bosses on his own range in Chihuahua and Coahuila and sent them out with colorful, impelling information and instruction as to exactly how they were to spread it. He visited the *hacendados* himself. When he finished he returned via Fort Clark, spreading the word sympathetically among the big ranchers, the riders, soldiers, and gamblers. He also organized the shipment of the water supply for the wrestling tank for event number two.

The gold mine had been salted.

CHAPTER 6

IN their limpid innocence, hardly equalled since Narcissus first played peek-a-boo with the forest pond, Irish and Jim had nothing to fall back upon beyond the instincts and race memory Carl Jung had not yet even put there. Originating from different sets of loins

183

and dreams, they approached the quandary in which they stood as though it were newly patented, triple-gooey flypaper and yearned towards the shrine of romantic love from diametrically opposite directions.

On the Sunday morning after his new destiny had been cast Irish sat on the opry-house rail of the Number Three corral and pondered. As he sat there, Jim left the bunk-house and went looking for him, as sullen as a mule in a mudhole. Irish was exerting a tremendous effort of will to move the vision of Evaliña (dressed, undressed, half-dressed, redressed) off to the far side of his thoughts. He began to consider the tradition of honor into which he had been born.

He would have been among the first to acknowledge that birth was merely the beginning of an inextricable involvement with the past. A long time before, he mused, a Major William Patten, citizen of the United States, had married the only daughter of Dr. Don José Vicuña de Arias, a citizen of Mexico. As a natural consequence of that act an enormous portion of Mexico had become the property of a foreigner. It followed, therefore, that if a present citizen of Mexico were to marry the daughter of the owner of these combined holdings, one day most of the states of Chihuahua and Coahuila would revert to hallowed Mexican ownership including—indeed—a large portion of the United States of America. In this manner of reasoning he was slowly able to see that his father would surely have forgiven him for having turned his back upon Florita Peña, whom, he told himself, he did not know very well in any event and whose marriage to him could hardly be seen as so gloriously benefiting the Republic as would his marriage to Evaliña. He saw clearly that it was his destiny to bring about this gigantic international realty transfer. It was true, from the warm love and deep affection of their long lives, that Jim had been the best friend any man had ever had, but none the less he could now detect other elements to their relationship which had sinister overtones. Jim was continually trying to get the men on the Texas side of the ranch to work better than the *vaqueros* on the Mexican side of the ranch and,

184

viewed in the present international or patriotic light, that was not a very friendly thing to have done.

On his side of the river, Irish had devoted himself from the first day, as had his father before him, to getting facts through the thick heads of every *vaquero* in his charge and to making them understand that they were engaged in something more than just a job. He made them understand that every day they must remind themselves again that the Mexican *vaquero* had invented the U.S. cowboy, had taught him all he knew, and that it was their unceasing duty to Mexico to maintain the highest standards, to live *muy charro,* and altogether show those stumblers across the river what it meant to work a cattle ranch properly. That Jim had grown up beside him on that very ranch was hardly pertinent to the issue. Jim Street had been born in New Orleans He was no Mexican.

Irish suddenly grew dizzy and very nearly fell off the fence as, in scene after scene passing across the screen of his imagination, he recalled Street's gape every time Evaliña's name was mentioned or the few times she had crossed his view. He began to understand that Jim might actually think he was the man for Evaliña.

The girl was a Mexican!

If Jim were allowed to fool himself that he had even the slightest chance of success of winning Evaliña, he would be capable of plotting a gringo conspiracy with Major Patten, employing chauvinistic, distasteful nationalistic tricks and prejudices, by urging that all the cattle, the land, and the girl be held in title of the United States side of the river. The thought made Irish so furious that, as a wall-eyed stallion ambled past him in the corral, he kicked the horse vigorously on the side of the head. It was simply too much to be forced to think about: a gringo conspiracy to steal land from Mexico and to separate him from the woman who had been born to be his.

This ceased to be a light or conjectural matter. When it came to his country, Irish told himself, he was a very serious man. It was a time, above all other times, when a man would be required to be *muy charro.*

When Jim Street had awakened that morning he had been able to assure himself that they had both been duped into allowing themselves to be used as chips to feed the gambling mania of a mean old man. Sure, Evaliña Patten was a right fine girl and a beautiful hunk of calico but there just wasn't a woman in the world worth coming between two old buddies. Hell, he thought, they'd been hanging around the Patten ranch long enough. Time they spilled over into California or headed up toward Wyoming.

Such thoughts remained the sole currency of his reason for over two minutes.

Suddenly an icy wind of memory passed chillingly across Street's mind. He began to finger the legend of Major Patten marrying the daughter of the richest rancher in the world. If a little shrimp like the major could get away with a thing like that, Jim felt sure that if it had been a choice between him and a foreigner like Irish Reyes, he could know instantly who the next owner of the Patten Ranch would be. By ten more minutes of such inner indignation and such a tenderly felt need to protect Evaliña and Major Patten from Irish, he sprang out of bed, dressed, and went out looking for Reyes with cold lights in his eyes.

"Don't you kick any horse in any corral on this side of the river, son!" he snarled up at the figure of the brooding man seated on the to rung of the fence. Irish turned and stared down at him with bitter contempt.

"If you wasn't a midget I'd be happy to kick you in the head," he assured Street.

"I'm boss here, Sonny. You'll watch your language and you'll cut outta here real fast."

"To the dopey Texans you are boss. To a Mexican you are another half-assed cowhand, and to a *charro* you are nothing."

"Get down an' get out. Get over the river with them other little brown peewees who ain't fit even to shoo goats."

Irish leaped to the ground. They stood, nose to nose, glaring. Jim put a heavy hand on Irish's shoulder as though measuring him for a punch.

"Take the hand away, farmer."

186

They each kicked the other simultaneously, square on the ankle, then each one grabbed his own injured foot and began to hop, yelping. Major Patten fired from forty yards away. Each bullet shot the heels off the hopping boots and each man fell heavily into the dust. Major Patten walked towards them slowly and stood looking down at them coldly.

"I told you boys that when you fight you'll fight for me and the punters. Now vamoose across the river, Irish, and stay there till I tell you it's your courtin' night."

CHAPTER 7

A BIG, soft moon, its features to be providentially lighted by reflections from the great black eyes of Evaliña Patten, had been bowled to its center position in the sky. Jim Street, wearing his fumafiddle and forfaraw, his hair shining with a secret pomade, his knees knocking together, was in his place in the enclosed garden patio. Evaliña appeared at the end of the garden walk, accompanied by her dueño, Major Patten, who was wearing two guns.

She wore a white lace mantilla over a comb of green jade held in her soft copper-colored hair. Her large black eyes challenged the jade. They were soft, shining, and erotic. The moonlight rested gratefully upon her flawless skin, filtered magically by the lace, then brushed off like silver powder by sudden sweepings of her great eyelashes to fall softly around her. She wore a white woolen *quexquemtl* over her shoulders. He had never seen anyone as beautiful. The white lace, the white wool, and her patent, ever-pleading offering of herself as she came toward him, made her seem like an enchanted bride from an ancient legend. As she came nearer he rose to his feet, actually believing he was getting up slowly and with dignity, but in fact achieving an ascension which was to be only 1.0145 inches short of the record vertical leap attained by Lan Adomian during the second performance of the ballet *Le Maréchal* at the Paris Opera House on 16 February 1870.

187

Evaliña whispered, "Gracious, Pa, did you see *that?*"

Jim returned to the ground with a clump which caused him to lose his balance.

"Evenin', Jim," the major said.

"Why, Jim Street! Hello there and good evenin' to you," Evaliña said, extending her perfect arm which had been punctuated with a white glove. He began to conquassate. He held her fingertips for an instant and for a measure of support, then dropped them as though they were burning him.

Major Patten pulled a piece of twine out of his coat pocket. "This string is exactly fifteen feet long," he said. He tied one end of it to the leg of the double summer seat, then walked the other end to the string's full length. "Fair is fair," he said loudly and sat down on the garden chair he had pulled over, keeping his back to his daughter and her co-fiancé. "You got one hour, Jim," he announced. "Start courtin'."

Evaliña pulled Jim down upon the summer seat and held both of his hands in hers. Her mind was whirring. She had a man beside her at last. She was hardly sure of the features the man's body was wearing but she thought of that pulsing, virile frame as being half of a unit composed of one half of her promised men and the other half a part of the other fellow, her other true beau.

"I want you two boys to know that I consider it very touching and very sweet for you to have made Pa see the truth that if we were engaged we were entitled to court."

Jim tried to speak but it was useless.

"What I mean is—isn't it *fun?*" Her huge eyes sparkled. "Just think of it! Four nights a week for me, and two nights a week for each of you. Unless the contests have to start much sooner."

Street's expression grew even more addled.

"Don't you boys start getting jealous of each other, now, and spoil everything. Oh, just *try* to imagine what it's going to be like after one of you boys wins those contests!" She beamed her innocence upon him. "Would you care to kiss my ungloved hand?" she asked.

Jim slumped downward upon the summer seat like a sack of wheat from a broken pulley. At that instant the major whirled, his eyes narrowed, not knowing what he might see.

"Is that boy all right?" he asked.

"He's just wonderful."

"Is he—uh—awake?"

She giggled deliciously. "It's hard to say."

"That boy looks dead to me."

She stared at Jim. His head had fallen forward on his chest. She grabbed his nearest hand. "Pa! He's cold as ice!"

The major darted forward. He knelt beside the stricken man and felt his pulse.

"Oh, Pa! Is it his heart?"

The major stood up. "Now, hon, the boy just fainted. A pretty girl is a kind of new thing to Jim. I'll ask you to go into the house now, honey, and send Mat Sun out here."

Lifting her skirts, Evaliña ran along the garden walk and into the big house. The major knelt beside Jim and loosed the new kerchief which was knotted at his neck.

The following evening Irish Reyes rode from his wikkiup across the river to the Big House, dressed in formal *charro* costume for maximum wooing effectiveness, carrying a large guitar slung across his back. Seventy-one silver buttons rode up and down each side of his tightly black-trousered legs. The trousers hugged his ankles over glistening black boots. His silver Chihuahuas were as enormous as spurs could be while still permitting him to walk the few steps which might be necessary. His black vest, brocaded heavily with silver and scarlet rosettes, clung to him over a flowing black shirt. His vaudeville Irish face, under the steeply conical sombrero which was corded with heavy silver, was a difficult one to reconcile with the magnificent indigenous clothes and that impatient guitar.

As he rode, he revelled. Everything was going his way. Mat Sun had let slip what had happened to Jim the night before. One had to have a tradition to survive in such matters as these, he thought happily. Poor Jim simply could not cope with the matters which he, Benito Reyes, a Mexican *muy macho,* understood instinctively. What a ludicrous failure for a man to suffer at the very first moment of courtship of such a woman, and how happy it made him feel.

He thought of the events of that very morning when he had walked quietly past Jim at the chuck wagon where he was chambering a meal and had said, "Good morning, great lover." Jim had screamed like a wounded cougar, if that was the correct expression, and had gone for his gun but he had had no gun belt on. He had let out such a tremendous cry of rage that two of the cowhands who had been leaning over to get more coffee had fallen into the fire. Running like heel-flies had been after him, Jim had picked up a huge log and had tried to brain Irish with it, but Irish had danced ahead of him murmuring, "Careful, lover, careful. When you get excited you faint," and this had so blinded Jim with rage that he had run through cookfires, horse teams, bunches of astonished riders, grabbing desperately at belts for a gun, tearing at the canvas of a wagon to get at a rifle, and no combination of restraining men seemed to be able to hold him. He was stopped when Major Patten had slammed him behind the head with the butt of a big fifty.

"He must be sick," Irish said, staring down at his friend and grinning evilly. "The instant he saw me he went crazy."

"More hair in the butter," the major had said sadly; "true love can sure change a man."

And now here he was, Benito Reyes, riding through the softening night to court his beloved, the most beautiful woman who had ever lived.

He moved through the moonlight across the patio at the big house. He put his left foot upon the summer seat, facing the path which led through the flowers to the house. He pulled his guitar into position and struck the first stirring chords of "The Warm Cathedral Walls of Cordoba" and began to sing softly.

The moon had returned to its center position in the sky and the cosmetic it had chosen for that night was orange tinted with Chinese red. He had swung into the chorus of "The Roses Climb the Jail at Carabanchales" when a light went on through the window behind the balcony on the second floor, which he knew to be Evaliña's room. He drew his breath sharply and abruptly changed the tune to the dedicated "There Is an Altar in Parangaricutirimicuare." His strongly pleading voice crept along the garden walk, then climbed the side of the house, seeking the wonderous object of its adoration.

The blacony window opened. Evaliña stood there in the softest center of the warm light and she seemed more thrillingly, more wildly beautiful than ever before. His song kissed her. The strings of the guitar resounded within her youth. By the time he reached the last line he could hardly breathe from what he felt. He disengaged the guitar and left it behind him on the summer seat. As he approached, she sneezed.

"I hab a berry, berry bad cold," she sniffled, then blew her nose. "I'b afraid dweel hab to make the courding sub other nide." She sneezed again before she withdrew into the room. The light went out. He stared upward at nothing from the darkened garden. From behind him, on his left, he heard a man's coarse horse-laugh ring out raucously.

CHAPTER 8

THE chivalric pageantry had captured the emotional attention of the entire Southwest and much of northern Mexico. The first fifteen hundred visitors to The Games arrived in Pickering City six days before anyone was expected.

As the number of visitors swelled, they showed a variegated character. *Hacendados* as massively prominent as Don Eduardo Jaffe, salesman from Oklahoma City, gunmen from Colorado, at least one unfrocked clergyman, and among the gamblers from St. Louis and Fort Worth there may have been even more. There were cowhands from everywhere west of the 98th parallel, cavalry officers, infantry soldiers; active, retired, and semi-retired dance-hall girls. The fortune-teller, Madame Arlyne Weininger, set up a small dark tent and helped to settle the direction of the betting for the more indecisive. Also present were one entire medicine show from its winter quarters in Havana, Illinois; two wagon trains carrying settlers and orange seeds to California; and an *enclave* of Swiss-Italian waiters.

Their average age was thirty-one years. Their average cash money availability was ninety-two dollars with a credit extension point, the major had calculated, of five times that amount because he believed that all people were basically honest if it were merely proved to them that the creditor would go to any lengths to get his money back, including shooting.

To his gross estimate of $298,431 as the total possible cash value per each five hundred visitors, the major added his estimate of their worth in livestock, vehicles, chattels, clothing, real property, jewelry, religious articles, unentailed inheritances, reward money, and insurance at twice that figure—swelling the over-all potential, per each five hundred visitors, to $896,237. At the height of the festivities, when Mat Sun estimated that 2,492 new-comers were visiting Pickering City, bringing with them a potential income of $4,481,000, he pointed out to the major that he could not expect to beat them all out of every last cent. However, even at the override of ten cents a shot on whisky and twenty percent on beds and Official Hostesses, on food and billiards, it offered a most agreeable prospect for profit before the actual events ever got under way. The major was already beginning to consider that it might be really worth while to make the thing an annual event if he could only figure out a continuing reason to provide the main mechanics.

The weather for the first day of The Games was exceptional. The visitors had found shelter in tents, in and under wagons, in The Pickering House, boarding with residents of the city and among the young Panama exchange students at Pickering's Paradise. Thoughtfully the major had posted his ruling that gambling games other than the events themselves would be permitted at the Paradise but that the municipal government would find it necessary to assess each hand played at five percent and would rigorously enforce its displeasure at any other sort or site of gambling arrangement. Mat Sun's crews set up separate kitchens at each end of Mildorf Street (named for Zelda Mildorf, the first woman Pony Express rider) operating out of six chuck wagons selling S-B stew, marrow gut, prairie oysters, and barbecued beef or pork. The intensive population growth brought with it soaring inflation but the major was able to hold down the swollen price indices to a three-hundred-nineteen percent increase.

The courthouse square was a dead-end street which backed away from the town's main artery at its center, putting out or in between the livery stable and the slaughterhouse. The courthouse was a two-story frame building which made up the dead-end base of the square. To its right was the art school (Dir. José Muñoz de Medina) and the Institute for Botanical Studies (Dir. James Fagin Ryan), followed by a side of the livery stable. To the left of the courthouse, extending again toward the main street, was the smithy, then the profile of the mustard-color slaughterhouse. Many of the buildings in the square were two stories high and had balconies as well as roofs from which the spectacles might be viewed from above. The major offered these places at a mere five dollars a location and had stationed roving betting commissioners (Mat Sun's younger brothers) to service the areas.

In the large dust-paved square itself there was room to pack in approximately eighteen hundred people; for places in this area no charge whatsoever was made. On its north side, in front of the Institute for Botanical Studies, the main Jim Street betting booth had been erected. It was under the supervision of Mat Sun. The main Irish Reyes betting booth was directed by Commissioner Heller on the opposite side of the square. Between the two at square center were the two golden-sanded Contest Circles, the elevated Referee's Box, and the high, solidly anchored stepladder on top of which the Grand Prize, Miss Evaliña Patten, had been seated. The sun was bright and hot.

Evaliña seemed metaphysically beautiful as she looked down on the two thousand flushed and admiring faces. Her full mouth, with its undeniably Arias lips which were like shaved pink mice; the perfect arch of her brows; the huge fringed jewels which were her eyes; and her extraordinary ginger-copper hair dominating her even more extraordinary figure seemed to inspire the betting eagerness of the crowd. The betting had at no time been desultory, but when she climbed to her place upon that pedestal it became frenetic, perhaps seeking her approval but always moved by her meaning.

She wore a canary-yellow linen duster over an apple-green blouse and a long yellow skirt. Black gloves had been pulled up to her elbows. Upon her exciting hair, over her inciting face, she wore with pleading symbolism the stuffed white dove of peace.

The noise was constant and excitable and enormous. The crowd was bidding and betting, yelling to children or guffawing with high spirits. Dogs barked. Lem Berns' Philharmonica Band—working with two cavalry bugles, drums, a tuba, and a fiddle—played "Alongside the Sante Fe Trail" and "Little Joe, the Wrangler" six times each. Everyone was dressed in their Sunday best. The women from north of the river wore their go-to-meetin' black. The women from south of the river wore their go-to-meetin' oranges, violets, peacock greens, and electric blues. Everybody kept moving so as not to miss what all the other folks were up to. Hundreds moiled about the betting booths, peering up at the large blackboards on which the odds had been posted.

10—1	Accidental snakebite
20—1	One death by accidental snakebite
50—1	Two deaths by the same

These posted prices never changed. They were mere accommodations for punters unable to resist long shots.

1—1	Street wins snake shooting
7—5	Reyes wins snake shooting
125—1	Draw

The knowledge of Irish's pathological fear of snakes had been carefully planted with the crowd and they bet heartily against him. However, the flood of money from the riders who knew Irish, inside money that knew how *charro* this man could be, stabilized the betting and held it to those late prices. Strete had opened at 1—5. Reyes had started at 8—1 until the equalizing money had been put down. The odds on a draw were another of the major's magnets for true suckers.

5—1	Forfeit by either side
10—1	Forfeit by weapons failure
25—1	Shooting of contestant by other contestant

Although that particular panel had been chalked up to add variety and color to the action, it represented the area of Major Patten's thinking, although he had not yet decided how he would place his personal bets. Since he could not very well lose, or even win, by betting with himself, he had come to an arrangement with Mat Sun. They were to be private bets so as not to affect the public odds. After twenty-seven years of service with the major, Mat Sun had more than enough funds to meet the major's play.

Mat Sun moved across the dusty, noisy square and stood directly in front of the official Referee's Box where the major sat alone. He did not speak. The major chewed his lips and made mysterious estimates with a pencil and paper, perspiring heavily. He saw Irish start through the crowd behind his honor guard of *vaqueros* led by Pepe Ferrer. The major's eyes darted quickly to Mat Sun, then away. He saw Jim Street emerge from the Institute of Botanical Studies to move slowly through the crowd behind an honor guard of his own boys. He made up his mind.

"All right. I want twenty-five thousand dollars on a Reyes forfeit, and I'll cover with a ten-thousand-dollar bet on the shooting of either contestant by the other contestant." Mat Sun wrote that down carefully. He held the paper out for the major to sign.

"What's this? Don't you trust me?" Mat Sun shook his head slowly. The major swore horribly in a low tone, but he signed.

The fourth large blackboard on either side of the square placarded bundle bets, whereby punters could wager on whole series in the competition with one bet. At that moment the odds were 5—1 that either man would win the competition in three straight. The other prices on the bundle bets varied.

Either man — 3 straight   5—1
Either man — 1st two 3—1
Both men — all draws   200—1

Money poured in from everywhere. The major shook with the excitement of so much gambling opportunity. A line of four nervous men stood in front of the official Referee's Box talking eagerly to the major, one at a time, in dry whispers. Each man had substantially the same thing to say. They shared the gamblers' disease with the major; they were the natural losers of the community.

"Mr. Heller said I'd have to arrange credit with you Major."

"Glad to help, Frank."

"A hundred?"

"Why sure. What will you back it with?"

"Two strings of work horses?"

"Better make her three, Frank."

"Three she is."

The mayor peeled off the money and pressed it into the loser's hand and the man was off, snaking through the crowd to get his bet down.

The mayor had a large turnip watch on the sawhorse table in front of him, but he didn't ever seem to look at it.

"Pa!"

"Huh?" He looked directly over his head, absentmindedly.

"The boys are out there and ready. When are you going to start them?"

He stared at her resentfully. "I don't know who told them boys to come out," he said sourly. "It's only twenty minutes after twelve an' folks is still fighting to get their bets down."

"You *promised* we'd start at noon. I'm getting sunstroke and the boys are just about ready to pass out from stage fright."

"Five more minutes, honey."

"No!"

"Two more?"

"No!" She kicked her feet furiously against the sides of the stepladder. It seemed to sway. The crowd moaned.

"Aaaah!" the major cried. He fired Big Max into the air. The even bellowing of the crowd dropped to an even shout, the shout fell to a roar, the roar descended to a rumble, the rumble dropped to a whisper.

"Shoot 'em up, boys!" Doc Weiler yelled from the balcony of the courthouse. *"Yippee!"*

The two contestants stepped forward into their respective rings which were directly beside each other. The bleached sand would give optimum viewing contrast when the snakes glided in to strike. The contestants did not look at each other or at the crowd which completely surrounded them. They examined their guns then holstered them. Their Levis had been rolled up to their knees and they were without boots.

Irish was still and white. When he examined his guns his hands shook. When Jim looked up soulfully at Evaliña and bowed formally in the silence, the crowd acknowledged the bow with a sudden cheer, and Irish jumped with taut, reflexive terror. He kept staring downward at the sand, as though expecting the dreaded snakes to emerge from it. His hands kept pillrolling, forefingers upon thumbs.

The major's voice rang out. "As Major of Pickering City, Presiding Justice of the County Seat, President of the Board of Selectmen, and Official Referee, I welcome y'all here today. Most of all I welcome you as the father of a little Texas lady—" he removed his J.B. and held it over his heart "—who is a-sittin' an' a-blushin' right here over my head." Nine hundred and twelve men in the crowd silently removed their Stetsons and placed them over their hearts. "It is for her hand and for the honor of the great state of Texas that these two fine young men, boozum friends since boyhood, will contest today."

"Let 'er rip, Major!" Abe Weiler yelled, hiccupping and holding aloft the liniment bottle he had been drinking from.

"These here are the rules for today's contest," the major shouted. "When I fire Big Max, three full-grown rattlesnakes, all fat an' sassy, will be moved into each contestant's ring from different directions."

Irish swayed.

"Neither man will be allowed to draw an' shoot until I fire the second shot. The man who draws an' hits all the sand eels first is the winner. Are you ready, boys?" The jammed courthouse square was as quiet as a winter midnight.

The three cowhands holding bright green wooden boxes were at north, east, and south positions of each sanded ring, six men in all. They were half-kneeling. Jim and Irish stood tensely, their arms hanging loosely at their sides in contradiction to their corded necks and clenched jaws. Evaliña bent away over, peering down at them intently. The major raised Big Max and fired one shot. The end walls of the green boxes were lifted slowly. Six snakes, each four feet long, moved slowly out into the intense sunlight. The six handlers withdrew, pulling their boxes with them, to hunker in front of the first row of the ring of people which was two hundred and fifty feet across. The chant of the bookmakers began again, but more softly, to compensate for the silence of the crowd. The snakes moved indolently across the hot sand towards the statuesque contestants.

Irish looked as though he were going to retch. If he fainted he would fall on, or beside, one or another of the snakes. He breathed shallowly. He could not look at the ground. They were seven feet away and coming in at him from three directions.

The major fired the second shot.

Irish drew fully a half-second before Jim, but instead of defending himself he shot the head off the rattler in Jim's ring. Without showing a flicker of sur-

198

prise, Street killed a snake in Reyes' ring. Irish shot the rattler in Jim's north position. Jim killed the snake behind Irish. Simultaneously, as though they had drilled through the maneuver for years of public exhibition of this sort of thing, each man shot and killed the remaining snake at his own feet, at the same instant.

"Muy charro! Muy charro!" Doc Weiler shrieked from the balcony. Two hundred and four Mexican sombreros were thrown into the air. Eighteen hundred people yelled with one voice. Irish fainted. Evaliña got to him first by jumping. The Official Referee, at a cost to himself of thirty-five thousand dollars from personal bets and an amount which only heaven could presently calculate from public bets was forced to call the contest a draw.

CHAPTER 9

FRANKLIN HELLER sighed. "That was two months ago," he told Mr. Moodie. "Every contest since then, all eleven of them, turned out to be a draw."

"Every contest?"

Franklin nodded sadly and filled two more glasses with furniture polish. "You take that second contest. No one would ever figure it for a draw, but it sure was."'

"A horse race?"

"No, sir. Bring horses into a contest and you ain't just bettin' on two men any more, the major says."

"A duel with epées?"

"No, sir. It was water-wrestlin'. Major pulled the water in all the way from Fort Clark. Everybody knew that Jim Street was as scared of water as Irish is about snakes. Why, they darn near have to throw him into his monthly bath. Odds were ten to one against him. Major bet twenty thousand dollars on Irish and the public bet a whale of money on a draw at 125-1."

"What happened?"

"A draw."

"My word."

"They didn't wrestle much. Turned out Irish was grabbed tight around the neck and they sank like stones and if it weren't for Evaliña jumpin' in offen the high ladder to save their lives they woulda been drowned for sure." He opened the cabinet at the back bar and took out another bottle of furniture polish. "We had a big tourist book here for awhile," he said. "Sold a lotta whisky. Major's lost over a million and a half dollars, not that that's a lot of money but his pride was hurt. Crowd lost interest after awhile. They had to git on with what they was doin'. The big crowds is dwindled down to about forty fever gamblers. The boys, both of them, is all drawn out with hate for each other. That beautiful young girl sets there gettin' bitter an' old before her time, but her daddy purely won't give up and his wife won't talk to him any more. The end has to be near. He cain't think up any more contests because there ain't any and even if there was they ain't anybody left to bet."

"But how will the whole thing be decided?"

"Code of the West, Mr. Moodie."

"I don't follow."

"Major found them two boys in his daughter's bedroom late at night, didn't he? He gave them an honorable way out and they didn't take it, did they?"

"Yes. I mean no."

"There's only one thing the major can do. He's goin' to have to shoot them boys."

"Why, that's preposterous!"

Heller looked over Mr. Moodie's shoulder. "Here comes the crowd now. Must be over." He raised his voice. "How'd it go, Goodson?"

"Draw," a huge man with dank hair and a severe cast in one eye answered.

"Them boys is sure well-matched," Franklin said, almost to himself.

"What was today's contest?" Mr. Moodie asked with a bewildered voice.

"Well, there's a lot of petroleum oil around here," Mr. Heller said, "and it's a nuisance if you're lookin' for water. The major give both boys a shovel an' when he fired the pistol they started to dig, an' the first boy to strike oil—"

"Strike oil where?"

"Out there on Mildorf Street. They probably hit two gushers." He shouted across the room. "Todson, what dig did they strike on?"

Todson was a toothless man wearing a racoon hat and a fur canteen who carried a sack of flour. "Number four dig. Ole Mildorf Street's a mess. They cain't stop it gushin'. Oil over ever'thing."

Mr. Heller shook his head disapprovingly. "Sometimes Texas is just too much," he said to Mr. Moodie.

"Now look here, Mr. Heller," Moodie said hotly. "How can any man of goodwill say that he has run out of ways to compete when murder is the only alternative? By heaven, something has to be done here!"

"How'd you go about doin' it, Mister?" a deadly voice said, directly behind him. Moodie turned.

Mr. Heller said, "This here is Major Patten." He coughed mildly. "This is Mr. John Moodie, Major."

"How do you do, sir," Moodie said coldly.

"I do fine."

The major was considerably stained and spotted by the oil. His hands were black, his face was smudged and his shirt front ruined but his ginger-gray mustache burned brightly and his narrowed eyes shone blue. A group of ten or twelve other oil-stained men filled the area around the major and Mr. Moodie, all listening intently.

"Well, it is perfectly clear," Mr. Moodie said emphatically, "that you are living upon the natural frontier between two countries. For a truly large-scale conception of a contest, that would be your starting line. The frontier happens to be some one thousand miles away from the national capital of one of the two countries." He suddenly grew professionally affable. "It is my eventual destination. I am the sole North American representative for Captain Hugh Fitz-Moncrieff's Hair and Mustache tonic." This was not entirely true.

"I'll take ten cases," the major said, as though to save time. "Now, keep talkin'."

"Ten cases! My dear fella, if you ever used ten cases of Fitz-Moncrieff's you'd be tripping over your mustache." The major didn't answer. "Well," Mr. Moodie said, "starting from that frontier, you have the two men race to Mexico City. On horseback." There was no group response.

"No horses," the major whispered. "We're bettin' on men, not horses." He started to turn away.

"The horses are no factor, sir! After all these men will not be galloping along a broad highway, will they? They'll need to be keen hunters to find food, because settlements and cities are few and far between. They'll need to be able to survive the attacks of savages and somehow to best the heartlessness of the Mexican bandit. All sorts of things like that. Mountain ranges eighteen thousand feet high, sir. The ability to recover from tequila. They would be traveling alone and separately over a most dangerous and changeable route. By boat where they chose, by train where they desired, and not at all only by horse, Major Patten. Oh I tell you sir, this race—such a race—could be the sporting event of the century!" His excited eyes moved across the semicircle of faces. The expressions had changed. Excitement was beginning to affect the die-hard gamblers. Every man watched the major tensely.

"Stranger, what're you drinkin'?"

"Why—uh—furniture polish, I believe."

The major winked to denote appreciation of the joke. "Fill 'er up, Franklin," he said. "Drinks on me all around."

"Were you—uh—serious about the ten cases of the product, Major Patten?" Mr. Moodie asked tentatively.

The major nodded. "I like to do things big for the sake of Texas," he said. "And this race idea you give me is the biggest thing we've had here yet."

CHAPTER 10

"Ladies and gentlemen, fellow Texans, good visitors—tomorrow is a fateful day for the Patten family. I've been over all the ground of the race with the two boys and they maybe know the risks better'n I do but they're all ready to let 'er rip tomorrow. Now, some of us might be inclined to feel that these two boys are a little too

202

evenly matched just because they tied each other in eleven straight contests. Well, from now on that does not purely hold. They both know the terrain well, but if either one of the boys has picked his route, they ain't told me. Now, as Official Referee, I will travel from here to Monterrey by stage, taking with me the Official Judges: Mr. Franklin Heller, your able Commissioner of Public Health, and Mr. Mat Sun, a well-known and inscrutable Oriental. Furthermore, to complete this commission of judges I have see-lected an absolute stranger, a man who is a complete foreigner to everything we hold dear, an Englishman name of Mr. John Moodie, who happens to be headed for Mexico City and who could not care less who wins this great race. The Grand Prize, accompanied by Mrs. Patten, will travel with us. At Monterrey we will pick up the railroad and ride her south all the way to the capital.

"The startin' point, at sun-up tomorrow, will be down by the river, at the foot of Mildorf Street. After they get their start, the rules is that both riders is got to check in with the Official Judges at any one of the two check points along the road. The railroad route, that is. The first one will be at Santa Carmen de Barajas in northwest Zacatecas, and the second will be at San Luis Potosi. Each man has to check in at one of the two points or he's ruled out of the race, but if he gets there before we do, he don't have to wait for us— just tell the stationmaster.

"The distance for the course runs to about twelve hundred miles, which is a right good race when you figure some pretty big mountains, some fairly hot and dry desert country, and then the extra runnin' to lose Indians and bandits, plus the toll tequila takes. The Official Judges has allowed that the boys oughtta be able to do fifty miles a day, good days and bad, until they get up there on the big mesa where the altitude and the thin air can slow the horses down a little bit. So, with givin' and takin' a little bit if these boys fail to ride up to the finish point in the big plaza in fronta the church in Mexico City by thirty-four days, then they both lose and," he sighed heavily, "all bets is off."

It was growing dark. Bonfires were starting all over

the mild slope which led down to the river. The comforting smell of barbecue was everywhere. Lem Berns' Philharmonica Band had started to play "The Zebra Dun." The night knifed in like a banjo chord.

CHAPTER 11

TWENTY-SIX hundred people from five states of the two countries were lined up along the Río Bravo del Norte at dawn the next day. Two clergymen had offered to conduct special services absolutely free but the major opposed the plan. Fortunately Commissioner Heller was able to bring him around to good sense. "Hell, Major, this is the kind of thing that puts gold edges on history. It'll heighten reverence for the event, yet increase the betting."

"You're right, as usual," the major replied. "Let both them preachers work. The good Lord sure poured in your brains with a shovel and nobody joggled his arm."

The ladies of Pickering City had been sewing handsome blue pennants with white letters which said PICKERING CITY VACATIONLAND and which the major had made arrangements to sell for twenty-five cents each. From across the river came two thousand chorizo sausages, each neatly wrapped in a tortilla. Mat Sun's men had made seventy-five gallons of coffee which was strong enough to be the first vegetable substitute for benzedrine. All the food was laid out at four o'clock in the morning on long sawhorses in the area behind the spectators facing the river. The printer at San Antonio had not been able to meet the deadline to print the Souvenir program after Doc Weiler had tripped and fallen into two large fonts of type at the newspaper. It meant a loss of fifty cents per program to the major, but it was the single disappointment of the day.

The date was 17 July 1871. The sun appeared at 5:10 a.m. The sky was clear. There was a light, invigorating breeze. Two young jinglers led the two horses for the race along the river bank and were rubbing them down self-consciously before saddling. One horse nickered and one horse whinnied but Mr. Moodie was not able to designate which was which at the request of a schoolteacher who was visiting Austin, Texas, from Chicago. The leading preacher, the Reverend Dr. Morton Cubit, had been the victim of a puzzling mistake in the mails that morning. He had ordered one dozen thumb-indexed hymnbooks from a religious-supplies house in Atlanta, Georgia, but instead he had been shipped a complete set of vestments of the sort used at baptisms of the infants of royalty and lawyers. It came complete with a mitre, an elaborately embroidered cassock, and ankle-length white robes of Chantilly lace. Once Dr. Cubit had decided that it was his duty to wear them, it made the day. He was a tall, thin man with teeth like a disordered lumberyard and black eyes with the polish of insanity. At the moment he went into his first holy fit, Franklin Heller knew they had made the right decision.

Lem Berns' entire ocarina section accompanied Dr. Cubit at his work, playing "The Trail to Mexico." Doc Weiler went larruping through the crowd, hollering out the chorus:

> "I made up my mind in an early day,
> That I'd leave my gal, she was too gay,
> That I'd leave my home and roam for awhile
> And travel out West for many a mile."

John Moodie bet every penny he had in the world, the sum of one thousand dollars, that neither man would win. There was a slight delay while Mat Sun sought a definition of terms from Moodie, who stated that he was not betting on a draw, which would be impossible in this instance anyway, he felt. He was not betting that neither man would finish, which would be entirely possible. He felt in the event of either of these two instances his bet should be refunded. However, he was willing to bet that neither man would win Evaliña in marriage and felt therefore that the odds should be even higher than those for a draw. Mat Sun conferred with Major Patten, who happily laid a price of 150—1.

Both contestants had been put up in rooms on opposite sides of the Big House. At four-thirty in the morning, dressed and ready, Irish received the *evangelista* he had ordered. The man was an important figure in Mexico, the public letter writer. He carried a large pad and a pencil with which he would rough out the message, to be refined and made more elegant later with a pen. He peered over thick, rimless glasses. He was small and bald and spoke with a profound basso.

"Good day, sir," he said briskly, marching into the room as soon as Irish opened the door. "I am your friendly *evangelista,* here to serve you with a smile and at new, low rates."

"We'll see about the rate," Irish said. He closed the door and began at once. "This is a letter to Señorita Evaliña Patten." The little man sat down and arranged himself. "This letter is not to be delivered until one hour after the race has started."

The *evangelista* made a note of that condition. "Proceed."

"My Glorious One—"

"Hey?"

"The letter. I am dictating. To Miss Patten."

"Ah! Proceed, proceed."

"My Glorious, Incomparable Evaliña," Irish began in mellifluous Spanish, "I am about to leave your side, the warmth of your imponderable smile, the mistiness of your shining beauty which glows always in my heart of hearts. *Hmm.*" He paced with his hands behind his back, studying the pattern in the carpet. *"Ah*—Neither of us knows, nor will we know until the moment when my weary horse carries me across the Plaza de la Independencia, whether we will ever meet again. I may fall—*uh*—I may fall under the naked knife of a savage—"

"Not so fast, not so fast."

"Take your time."

"Go ahead."

"I may be shot down in the flower of my youth by some bandit's gun." He clasped his hands in front of him. "Whatever happens, what I feel for you at this grave moment in our lives I will feel forever, now and for always, my adorable lady." When he finished the *evangelista* was sniffling.

"I have been a leader in the Mexican communications industry for many years, sir," he said. "I do not think, however, that I have ever heard any message as lovely as that which you have just given me to write."

"Thank you."

"Oh no, sir. What a rare privilege. That will be five dollars please."

"I've dictated letters twice as long as that for thirty-five cents."

"Oh? Very well, sir. Thirty-five cents it is."

As Irish paid him he asked if the *evangelista* could find a man named Jim Street.

"Is he of the ranch?"

"Yes."

"I can find him."

"Well, he can't write either. And—well—he may have something to say to her—in farewell. Go to him and give him the chance."

"How much may I charge him, sir?"

"Charge? Charge him what you always charge. Five dollars. Go!"

Jim dictated to the *evangelista*.

"—and furthermore I know where we can get the Hereford stock, quick and cheap considering what they'll bring to the longhorn stock. If you don't take me seriously on this thing, please take my word, Major, that you will be forced out of business in ten years' time. Very truly yours. Sign it *James Howell Street*."

"Is that all, sir? Just one letter?"

"That's all."

"That will be ten dollars, please."

Jim paid him twenty-five cents from a deep sack, then moved out of the room, eager to get started.

CHAPTER 12

IRISH was riding his best horse, an *appalusa* stallion, a blue horse with gray splotches of bold contrast. He wore skintight trousers, a short jacket over a dark-green shirt, a sombrero of waxed straw with a brim wide enough to go over Niagara upon. The trousers were all of one piece from belt to instep; it would have been a heartbreaking job for a man filled with ardor to try to peel them off in a hurry. His saddle was a frame of soft wood, more comfortable than the Texas saddles; well hollowed in the right places and much lighter. Long, wide stirrup leathers hung down for protection against the *huizache* thorns which could go right through a boot. He sat carelessly, with the easy authority of a horseman, his left forearm out at right angles and keeping loose contact with the horse's mouth. His bedrolls lay under the rings and snaps of the tarpaulin behind his saddle; eighteen-ounce tarp to protect the soogans and blankets. Whatever incidental supplies he had decided he might need had been fitted into the *alforjas,* bags hanging down from the saddle like lumpy legs. He pulled no pack horse. He was a hunter and he would live off the land. He carried two six-guns holstered in his saddle and rode with two more in his gun belt. A carbine wasn't much use to a moving horseman pointing at a moving target. Four six-shooters with five beans in each wheel could hold off a lot of trouble for a man who was traveling light. Not that he was without the carbine. He was a hunter. Sometimes he would shoot while still.

He looked forward to coming upon the small lake, actually more of a river-fed lagoon, where he would have his fill of pleasure catching ducks as he had with his father in the old days.

He moved across the green-tufted plain. It was baked earth. It lifted itself as it moved leagues ahead of him. All around him were surely what must be the mountains of the moon which had fallen to earth one night before history. If Lucifer grieving in Hell had stretched his arms toward Heaven in agonized beseechment, his horned fingers pushing up from under the earth's crust from the darkness of hopelessness, this, too, could have caused these incredible shapes upon the earth. The sun shared its light with everything. It had not yet crossed over to the west by two hours. When it was two hours in the west he would be at the small lake, enjoying his game with the ducks.

All at once he sighted an old landmark. It was a cairn of stones his father had raised ten years before to commemorate the point in the state of Coahuila precisely parallel to the breweries of Monterrey, one hundred and ten miles to the east. When he reached the cairn, Irish climbed down from his horse and stood with head bared for two silent minutes, in appreciation of the beer which went all over Mexico from those miraculous breweries.

Jim Street moved along at a lively, patient pace. He rode only in daylight. He had had to kill three Indians the morning before. They had come at him as he had left the tip of a small pine forest on the high plateau. He had pulled up the *bay coyote* horse under him, a dun with a stripe up its back. The pack horse had stopped patiently in direct line behind him. He had shot three of the war party of seven Indians with three shots, standing stock-still and using the carbine slowly. The others had wheeled their horses and run.

He carried four six-guns. The Spencer was behind him on the pack horse with his banjo.

He moved ahead on the strong, striped horse, followed obediently by the steel-gray pack-carrier, going at a scheduled rate across the vast land which was monitored closely by white cloud tufting an infinity of blue, always moving slightly ahead of him through the long valleys filled with willows and streams, endless valeys with escarpments buffered by the wind into fantastic shapes.

"It's mighty easy for us in this rolling coach," said Franklin Heller. "But I have to feel pity for the hardships of them two boys riding along out there."

He spoke from a window seat, riding backward, of

the Official Judges' coach. He faced Major Patten. Evaliña rode backward at the other window, facing Janine Patten. John Moodie sat between the major and his wife. Mat Sun faced Mr. Moodie. It was a tight fit. If anything, the springs of the carriage made the coach ride more uncomfortable. The major looked shrewdly across at Mat Sun.

"What odds will you lay," he asked, "that Irish Reyes is waiting for us at the first contact point?"

"Two to one."

"Why not thirteen to five? That's what I would have given."

"Two to one."

"All right. I bet you five thousand dollars. What odds that Irish's horse comes up lame?"

"Twenty-five to one."

"I bet a thousand." He puffed his cigar contentedly, feeling he had hedged the first bet. He stared out the window. Over the rise, eleven Papagos came screaming on painted horses, over the ridge to the left of the coach, shooting carbines as they came.

"Hey, looka that," Mr. Heller said with astonishment. "Ever' one of them Indians is ridin' a paint horse!"

The major shot steadily and carefully with a six-gun. Evaliña sighted her Sharps .50 across the bridge of Mat Sun's nose and fired. The others watched—excepting Jan Patten, who preferred to look out of the other window because she was feeling a little wagon-sick.

"What odds that Jim is attacked by Indians and Irish ain't?" the major shouted over his shoulder to Mat Sun as he shot.

"Two to one?"

"Ought to be better'n that." He fired and hit again.

"Two to one."

In a short time nine of the Indians were dead and Sig Shore, the stagecoach driver, shouted down his congratulations on the fine shooting. There were two live Indians left sitting stock-still on their piebald horses, receding into the distance as the coach moved forward.

"Well, give me five thousand worth."

The major calculated swiftly to himself. If he lost the twenty thousand on Irish's appearing at Santa Carmen de Barajas, he could still win five thousand net if the horse came up lame, so that even if Irish were attacked by Indians he would still break even, and if he cashed every bet, of course he'd be ahead seventy-five thousand, if he didn't lose them all. So goes the mind of the gambler. Even their figures are always wrong.

The jouncing passengers watched the mesquite go by.

"Damndest thing I ever saw," Mr. Heller mused. "Where'd eleven Indians get eleven paint horses?"

"It's funny to think that we'll soon be ridin' in a luxurious railway car," the major said. "Progress is all right up to a point, but this whole part of the world is gettin' a mite too modernized. Shoulda seen this mesa twenty years ago."

Mr. Moodie peered out at the endless plain which was stubbled with cactus and mesquite, looking for the changes. His eyes blinked in the acrid blue gunsmoke which filled the coach.

CHAPTER 13

IRISH found the small lake which was actually a river-fed lagoon. It was surrounded by evergreens which sloped upward and away from it. The air was clear and smelled of balsam. Far off on the other side of the lagoon, just as he had known they would be, just as they had been when his father had first promised them fourteen years before, sat a large platoon of wild ducks. Irish dismounted at a clearing near the shore. He unsaddled his horse and rubbed him down well. He left the horse to munch on the sweet grass, then went off to find the cache of gourds he and his father had used and hidden.

It was a small, very blue lake. It was quite round and about a half-mile across. When he turned his back, it changed its color archly from cobalt blue to a handsome dark green with little effort at all.

The cave behind the cleft rock, on the slope two hundred yards above the lake, was as they had left it. He rolled the rock aside and looked in upon the gourds.

He pulled them out, one and two at a time. In all, he counted thirty-six. He laced his *riata* through the top of each one and carried them all down the slope, making his way to the windward side of the lake. He unlaced them, dropping each one in its turn into the running stream which ran across the lagoon toward the sitting ducks. He watched until all thirty-six were gently carried by stream and breeze across the lake and through the duck colony, disturbing them, sending them in panic toward the sky to circle in the air while their leaders watched and then judged the gourds and worried over the feeding ground. Slowly, in small groups, they returned to the surface of the lake.

Irish walked leisurely around the rim of the lake. He waited on the other shore, ensconced in serenity, until the gourds floated to him. Again he laced them together with his *riata,* carried them back to the starting point on the windward side of the lake, and set them adrift once more, this time in bunches. He watched as the current and the wind took them through the ducks. Many fewer were disturbed this time, perhaps twelve ducks out of ninety. He kept three gourds.

He undressed slowly. Then, naked as a *xoloizcuintle,* he fitted one of the gourds over his head. It covered his face and neck and had holes at the front for seeing through and breathing. With a sack in one hand he walked into the lake until he was completely submerged, then moved forward slowly, pushing the two empty gourds lightly ahead of him, imitating their bobbing motion with the gourd over his head. He reached the edge of the flock. One after another, he caught three ducks by the feet and dragged them under the water to drown them silently and stuff them into his sack. He swam back to shore smacking his lips over the feast which was about to start.

CHAPTER 14

SANTA CARMEN DE BARAJAS seemed bigger than before to Jim after nine days alone on the mesa. He rode up to the railroad station ten minutes after the train carrying the Official Judges had arrived. Being that close to a talk with the major away from the diversions of the ranch, Jim was deeply preoccupied. He moved along behind his plans as automatically as his pack horse followed him. His mind was seething with new approaches to the production of beef which for a moment, like a flash of lightning, brought him piteous yearning for Miss Ridgeway. As he thought about Miss Ridgeway, the major, and beef it is possible that the hamburger sandwich (as the United States of America knows it and loves it today) may have been born, amid the litter of sinewy dreams which shouldered and crowded each other, lowing and mooing, across Jim's stimulated conceptions. He knew somehow that when the banner of his victory had been raised over the enormous Patten holdings it would have been raised wherever steak was ordered or wherever people trudged through the snow on a northern night to bring calf's-foot jelly to a sick friend. He saw himself far forward in a revolution which would strike until the longhorn had disappeared for ever from the earth.

Heller and Mat Sun strolled back from the only hotel, where the major, his wife, and the Grand Prize had been established to check the stationmaster's office for news of contestant check-in. Jim had slung himself off his horse at the station, unseeing in his absorption, and he was nearly broken in half by the greeting Heller slammed into his back with hearty force. Inside of three or four minutes he was breathing nicely again. They half-carried him across the dusty street to the adobe hotel, where they found the major seated within the surprise of a beautiful green-grown patio.

"What happened to the boy? An Injun arrow? A coward's bullet?"

"I don't know," Franklin said. "Must be exhaustion. I seen him standin' there, said hello, an' he went down like his legs was broke."

Jim found his voice. "Anybody but you done that to me, Franklin, I'd shoot him down. You ever do that to me again and you better strap on a gun afore you try."

"Well, son," the major asked warmly. "How's the race goin'?"

"Fine, I reckon."

"Siddown, siddown." The four men sat in wicker

chairs surrounded by the sounds of fountains. They accepted cigars from the major.

"Run into Irish?"

"No, sir." Mat Sun caught a waiter's attention.

"Where's Moodie?" Heller asked. Mat Sun mumbled steadily to the *mozo* concerning food.

"Lookin' at the sights, I guess. First time in Mexico."

"I sure got a lot to talk to you about, Major," Jim said, concentrating hard.

"Go to it."

"I jest crossed your Mexican ranch. Man, you don't get but about fifteen per cent outta that scrawny longhorn cattle."

"Now, fergoshsakes, Jim!" Major Patten said irritably. "Let's not start up with that. It's been a long, hard trip. Trains ain't like ridin' on a horse, you know."

"You must be sun-happy, Jim," Franklin said. "Your own financee right here yearnin' to talk to you an' you want to sit around an' talk cattle?"

Jim sat up with a jolt. "Oh, yes. Evaliña. Well, I mean, where is she?"

"Mighty dusty ride, son. She's ablutin'. Be down for lunch."

"Think we oughta send up word I'm here? Just tell her, sort of?"

"She'll be down, son. Got to eat, ain't she?"

The *mozos* charged the table with food. All talking was suspended in the face of such smells and such frenzied activity. In a progression of lightning moves every square inch of three tables pushed together had been covered with something to eat. Spread before them were *quesadillas potosinas,* golden cheese decanted into capsules of the lightest crust; *chalupas estilo puebla,* tissue-thin tortillas spread with green sauce; *chilis* in walnut sauce; an enormous bowl of *mole negro oaxaqueño,* with its texture and color of boiling chocolate, throwing off a cinnamon steam, within which floated tender chunks of turkey, peanuts, pecans, almonds, spare ribs, and raisins; a fire bowl of *salsa piquante*; four stacked quires of warm *tortillas;* hot maroon *frijoles rancheros* and enough *mochomas,* captured within a ring of *guacamole* the color of springtime, to satisfy the hunger of a war party of Lipans.

214

The smells alone could have nourished a sedentary worker. They were warring smells. Each was willing to welcome other, infidel smells into his congregation if they would accept it as the only true smell, the smell of smells.

The major dealt out four hands of tortillas as though they were round playing cards. Each man leaned forward and attacked the food. Mat Sun nodded constantly and ecstatically as he chewed. No man spoke, unless his mouth was full to bursting.

"Majuh?"

"What?"

"You bet twenny thousand dollah. You lose again."

"What?"

"You bet Ilish come Santa Carmen de Barajas. Ilish no here. You bet Jim no come Santa Carmen. Jim here. You lose twenny thousand dollah."

"Oh, that. Yes."

"Sign here, preez. Li'l markuh." The major scowled and scrawled his name. Then he smiled in a smarmy way. "He said he was attacked by Indians, didn't he? You owe me the five thousand I bet at two to one."

"No."

"What?"

"You bet Jim attack, Ilish no attack. We no yet talk to Ilish to find out he attacked." The major bit off the end of a new cigar and spat it violently into the calla lilies. "What about them longhorns?" he snarled at Street. Jim hitched forward in his chair eagerly and began to talk.

Upstairs in the large high-ceilinged room, Evaliña read the note in her hand for the sixth time. She had been over it twice with Janine Patten, who watched her reflectively. Evaliña's lovely cheeks were flushed. Her eyes were bright with a new kind of excitement. She bit her lower lip hungrily as she read.

My dear Miss Patten:

Have I offended you in some dumb and sightless manner? From the moment we met at the outset of this sad train journey, aside from your murmured repetition of my name as you acknowledged the

215

introduction, you have never again spoken to me. I am sure you have never thought about this condition, nor about me as a fellow traveler or in any other more intimate manner, steeped as you are in the conjectural future. How very conjectural! More perhaps than any other young woman's, I must say, for you face the destiny of marrying a man whom you cannot love or, worse, if the winner of this dreadful travesty of dreams of youth should be the man whom you secretly believe you wish to marry, then you would need to wonder for the remainder of your sweet, sad days if it might not have been the other you would have chosen had you been allowed a normal courtship—those dearly remembered, wholly cherished, thrilling days and nights which are the gift of time to all other girls.

I have tried to burn my message into your mind with my eyes, but you are not able to see me. I have tried to will my thoughts for you into your consciousness so that you would perforce need to turn to me to hear me, but I was not able to penetrate the serene thoughtfulness of your most exquisite beauty beyond being allowed to see the ancient and enthralling excitement in your eyes.

What did I wish to say to you? I cannot tell you in these pages. Indeed, I may never unlock such burning words unless you free me from the bondage of your preoccupation with times which have not yet happened and may never happen.

Just show me that you see me, dear Miss Patten! Only flicker your eyes to show that you know I am on this planet with you! Save me!

Yr. ob'd't servant,
John Blue Moodie

Evaliña's bottom was roiling rapidly upon the chair. Her breathing seemed to come more rapidly, but not out of indignation. She did not seem to condemn him out of hand for his impertinence. She was greatly puzzled, partly fearful, but she regained a grip upon herself and jerked herself backward from the kneeling image of Mr. Moodie in her mind—oh, that lustrous mustache; oh, that pendulous pink under-lip!

She made herself see Irish and Jim standing and walking, riding and shooting, drunk and sober, eating and roping. She fancied for an instant she could smell them both and if she had been standing close to them she would have reeled. Strength and purpose sluiced through her. She had memorized and had gloried in every inch of those two men which had, so far, been permitted to her view. She loved them both, and if she were to marry one of them, that would be as it was meant to be, and in time—who could tell—but other more extensive arrangements she pushed off to the future.

She looked down at the letter, folded it, and started to tear it in half, but discovered she could not. She folded it one more time then tucked it into her gravy-brown reticule. She did not know whether she had missed the courtship which he had said was every girl's right. Surely, she was able to tell herself, when men went off to war, a thousand girls had had to cast aside dear dreams of courtship to marry their men. Was it her right to lift the nostrils of her psyche and sense the approach of yet another upwind male? She thought of the curse then, for a moment, but she knew she was safe to think this way because there could be no commitment until there had been a kiss, then that commitment must be for ever. They had taught her that over and over and over again for three years in Mexico City. Did she desire poems, flowers, and a gloved hand at the small of her back during a waltz? She did not know but her thighs trembled as she remembered the words from the story books which had told of other girls who had been wooed.

"What are you going to do, my darling?" Janine asked softly, her small fist clenched in her lap, tense with concern.

Evaliña stamped her foot. "Oh, this Mr. Moodie is a puling fool!" she said and strode out of the room, slamming the door with self-exasperation.

When she reached the patio and saw Jim Street sitting there, talking volubly and in dead earnest to her father, silent and serious, she was moved because she knew that Jim had never before spoken to anyone with such ardor and passion. He was so intent upon his address that she was able to stand at his shoulder without his knowing she was there.

"—more pounds of pure beef for steer and a job for all the other parts, I tell you. Don't you see what this can mean, Major?"

Franklin Heller nudged Jim's knee. Jim turned, looked up, and scrambled to his feet.

"Why, uh—gosh. Hello there, Miss Evaliña."

She had grown white with fury. "Where's Irish?"

"Jim said he's probably callin' on some old friends of the family over to Lalotorres."

She stared at the four faces in disbelief. "Why!" she gasped. "I do believe you've all had lunch!"

"Very good," Mat Sun said professionally.

"Have you had lunch, too?" she asked Jim fiercely.

"Why—why, yes ma'am."

Her eyes filled with tears. She took a white glove out of her reticule, pulled it on silently, weeping without a sound. "How gallant and lover-like, you are," she said and turned to walk back across the patio the way she had come.

CHAPTER 15

JIM moved along easily with the two horses. In the distance he could see a great herd of antelope feeding. He moved cautiously along the slope. He was downwind. He dismounted and picketed the horses. He went forward on foot carrying the Spencer carbine. Soon, not thirty yards away, some yards off from the herd itself, a sentinel buck antelope was standing in the shade, partly screened by chaparral. He aimed carefully.

Suddenly, to his numbing shock, the stag stood up on its hind legs and, waving its forepaws with desperate fear, cried out. "No, no! No! Don't shoot! Oh no!" with a musical female voice in the English language.

Jim was immobilized. The rifle dropped. He stood as still as a stone before the entreating advance of the antelope. Ten feet away from him, the buck took off its hooves, then removed its head. The blonde head of a young woman wearing an orange velvet beret appeared. "Oh, Jim!" it said. "What a close thing that was!"

"Marilyn!" he gasped. "Miss Ridgeway!" He sank slowly to the ground of the hillside. She knelt upon one shapeless deer-camouflaged knee and felt his pulse. "I hope the novelty of this reunion hasn't upset you," she said, genuinely concerned with his sudden weakness and with the lighthouse wildness in his eyes.

"It sorta jolted me havin' a buck deer talk to me like that. An' in such a high voice."

"That rifle certainly frightened me."

"But what happened?"

"Oh, it's just an old Ojibway device," she said deprecatingly.

"No, I mean—us—I mean the ideas we had about beef. You said you was comin' back to the spread in July."

"I did?"

"You did."

"Well—I—I was just a part of the crowd. I—I heard about your wedding plans. It was just that—that I thought you'd be much too occupied to have time to talk about crossbreeding."

"You see, Marilyn—"

"Please don't explain. Besides, I'm Dr. Ridgeway now. I am to be part of the Museum of Natural History of the City of New York. I was lucky enough to have a room mate whose dad had a friend who knew Albert Smith Bickmore." Three gliding hawks marred the perfect blueness of the sky. The antelope munched on. A lizard who seemed to be late for work darted from under a rock beside Dr. Ridgeway to a rock beside Jim.

"Should I call you Doc?"

"Please don't." She bit her lip. She cast her eyes away from him. "Call me Marilyn—just—just as though nothing had changed."

"Well, you see, Marilyn—I think that's the prettiest name I ever did hear—what happened was this —I—"

"Jim! Please!"

"But she had saved our lives and we was only there

tryin' to thank her, then the glass roof broke and Major Patten came in with Big Max—"

She took his hands in her hands. "I beg you not to try to explain what has happened," she said. "We knew each other so briefly. Three years apart is such a long, long time and I mean—what I am trying to say is: I understand and that is all. Please, let us never never talk about your—your marriage again." Her voice broke. She turned away from him quickly, throwing her brown hind legs wide. The plains around them stretched out to make a violet-wrapped valley with peering heads of amethyst hills wearing their peaked hats and staring back at him.

"We could talk beef," he said, deeply stirred himself. She reached out and took his hand. "I have learned so much," she said. "More than ever before I know now that the longhorn must disappear if we are ever to find the great yield of pound for frame."

They sat, huddled closely together, talking about breeding, when they were taken prisoner by a patrol of the forces of General Enrique Jorge Molina.

CHAPTER 16

IRISH had traveled at an easy pace from five o'clock in the morning until three in the afternoon. He had rested himself and the horse whenever they saw shade. He had crossed into northern Zacatecas and was perhaps four hundred and fifty miles on his way. In twelve more miles he would be facing Don Guillermo Peña B. He had ridden fifty-five miles out of his way to do this because he had to do it. But it was such a demand of honor that it made his hands shake and gave his stomach the feeling that it had digested its own bottom. He was not able to permit himself to imagine what was going to happen when he explained the facts of his present life to Don Guillermo. From all information he had been able to glean along the way, Don Guillermo Peña at sixty-eight years old was still the fastest gun in Mexico.

As he rode into Lalotorres he saw that nothing had

changed and he remembered that each time he and his father had traveled through these same streets nothing had changed before. He inhaled the charcoal smoke. He heard the sounds of the women slapping tortillas. He saw the red roofs, the golden walls and the dark-brown streets. The amazing pink seventeenth-century church still dominated the pueblo under a Meissen blue sky. The cows and the goats chewed on cactus. The torpid tickbirds sat in the trees, black and somnolent. The circling turkey buzzards planed again across the solid blueness and Irish moved in dread of the duty he must soon perform.

Don Guillermo saw Irish before his horse had taken four dainty steps into the plaza and nailed his attention with a great shout. Grinning wanly, Irish rode to him. He dismounted at the cantina where the great man sat in the sun.

Don Guillermo was a deep brown. His drooping mustache had turned white. He was not at all stooped; tall and thin made taller still by the great sombrero, and his merry eyes were as hard as diamond chips.

He called for pulque, then he and Irish squatted back on their heels after an *abrazo* which had nearly cracked Irish's ribs.

"My boy, my boy," Don Guillermo said, "as always it makes me want to weep with joy to see you— son of my greatest comrade."

"I wish he were here with us now," Irish said, feeling he could use an extra set of guns on his side.

"No," Don Guillermo answered after some silent thought, "that would not be good. If he were here with us now perhaps he would not be as lucky as he was. He was a horseman who died in the saddle, in the heroic manner accorded to great men."

"That must be someone else you speak of, Don Guillermo. My father died in bed at the *casco* of Don José Vicuña de Arias."

"No, no. I speak of your father and if I have lived my life well and with consistency, I may be allowed to hope as a gunman that I will die by the gun."

"Except, if I may say so, there is no one living fast enough to beat you."

"That is true. And extremely reassuring, but after all,

my boy, we are given but one chance to die. We must study that chance well. If your father were here with us now he might be cheated of a fine, clean death in the plunging saddle and end by slipping on a piece of fruit, or in bed like some priest or an old woman."

"That is true, as you say it," Irish said.

"I hope I am as lucky."

"There is always the hope that you will be shot from behind."

Don Guillermo shook his head emphatically. "No, no. Not at all. If I were shot from behind the sentiment which would outlive me would form the opinion that I had made my great reputation by shooting others from behind. It won't do, Benito."

"I was joking, sir. It was an idiotic thing to suggest."

"My son, if you are an idiot, may we some day be blessed with a governor of this state who is such an idiot."

"The Republicans are in again, hey?"

"Yes. *Pfui!*" He went back to the core subject abruptly. "Tell me, son, do you know of any really great guns—I mean guns in or near my class—in your travels?"

"Well, hardly. But Major Patten himself is phenomenal."

"Oh, a very good man. Oh, excellent. I saw him take Armando Sotres and Ronaldo Luster in Hebronville in '47. They were fast men themselves but they never had a chance with him."

"Is that so?"

"Of course, he is something of an old man now. Their reflexes go."

"He is still fast."

"How fast are you, Benito?"

"Regular."

"Ah, no. It is modesty. My son Hernando saw you work when you and your friend Street took those four pimps at Fort Frankenheimer. He said you were first class."

"Hernando, as we all know, is a very kind and generous boy."

"That is true."

They hunkered silently for a while, enjoying the

few sights of the small *zocalo*. When Marco Reuben, the innkeeper, showed himself again they had more pulque. They sipped and enjoyed the sun, frequently having more pulque. They were there quietly for an hour or more.

Then it happened.

"And now you have come south to get married, hey?"

Irish was astonished at the old man's philosophic acceptance of such a dramatic reversal of a cherished plan. "Yes, sir," he answered with brisk relief, "but how the news got this far south so fast beats me."

"I got the news the instant your horse set foot in this *zocalo* today," Don Guillermo said, smiling benignly.

"Every year I conceive greater and greater admirations for you, sir," Irish told him humbly. "Who ever would have thought you would take this so well! After all, sir, as we all know, the fathers of daughters are the most peculiar animals and this one, I told myself, is a most dangerous one. Great God, when I think of the extent of the wedding plans alone!"

"They have been vast," Don Guillermo said, nodding and smiling.

"And yet, before I could summon up the courage to tell you that what must be, must be—and I do what I am doing for the sake of Mexico—"

"Of course, of course."

"—you have somehow had the wisdom to perceive it in the gait of my horse and, with your understanding, knew that youth must be served, that life must go on, *et cetera, et cetera.*"

"By God, you talk like your blessed father, rest his soul," Don Guillermo said, slapping his bony thigh. "You have that gift of making the other fellow seem graceful and deft for some such diminished act as burping after breakfast. How loveable a quality that is! When I think how many years, nay centuries, that it has been a foregone conclusion that young men shall ride out to carry off the beautiful young women as their brides so that our nation may grow stronger— and yet you have managed to turn this inevitability with such open, honest charm as to make it seem as though the issue were at any time in doubt—that it would be possible that I would, or could, oppose your course while gallantly ascribing inevitability to wisdom and understanding on my part—well, my boy, I wish to say to you with a full heart that it is good to be an old man after a life such as mine and to know that there are young men such as you who will carry on."

"Thank you, sir."

"We must have some tequila."

Irish made a strangling sound.

"I realize it is early," Don Guillermo said, "but the timing is always more important than the time."

"How true."

"We will have some tequila then we will find Florita."

"Florita?"

"Yes."

"Your daughter Florita?"

"Whom did you think—my cook Florita?"

"Do you think we should?"

"Why not?"

"Well, it seems sort of—sort of—"

"Abrupt?"

"Exactly. Even unfair."

"By God, I never thought the old superstitions would outlive my generation, but I must say it is charming."

"I did not mean it so much from a superstitious point of view, sir. Girls do have feelings, after all. For me to come here and ride roughshod over her most delicate sensibilities only because I have committed an impulsive act on behalf of the Republic—well, it would be wrong, sir. If you will permit me to say so."

Don Guillermo stared at Irish for some time then nodded ruefully. "Of course it would be wrong. I forget. It was so long ago for me. You must feel that I have contempt for the most vital and necessary ways of youth. As though I were suggesting that we merely burst in on her and say, after fourteen years of waiting, "Look here, my girl, Reyes has come by to marry you." No, no. You are right. She has earned the right to have a handsome young man come riding to her window, to greet her with the sound of a guitar, and the words of a warming, warning love song."

"And so shall she have such a man!" Irish responded warmly, instantly. "It is what she deserves and what she would have had long before this had I not been such a ninny and a dolt!"

"Don't chide yourself, my son. I am not one for early marriages on either side. The future is the proper place for Florita's courtship and marriage, as you say."

"May her courtship and marriage be of instant moment!" Irish cried out, lifting his glass of tequila high, his eyes shining with appreciation for Don Guillermo's almost saintly forbearance.

"Do you really mean that?"

"Mean it? It is a wish I would gladly die for!"

"The day after tomorrow?"

"If I had my way it would be tomorrow."

Don Guillermo shook his head. "Too soon. I couldn't possibly get the town ready. But the day after tomorrow is her departed mother's saint's day and if I have to keep everyone in the pueblo working day and night, I think I could have a bang-up wedding party ready by then."

"I know you could."

"Shall we say—at noon?"

Irish shrugged. "Ask Florita. It's her wedding, after all."

"Of course. Forgive me. Those are the decisions for the woman." To their surprise they discovered they had finished a bottle of tequila. The plaza had grown dark. Don Guillermo suggested that they move inside *La Cabaña de Tio Marco, La Casa Absintio,* which was the name of the *fonda.* A table had been made ready for them near the hearth fire. The warmed room smelled as it should: of old booze, great hunks of food; it had chairs and tables but no barn animals were permitted inside unless accompanied by their owner. The two men sat down carefully.

"I will explain how I happened to be here this afternoon," Don Guillermo said, hiccupping slightly. "My sister and Florita detest the look, the smell, and the taste of pork in any manner of serving. I have never eaten anything so satisfying as roast pork. We have worked out a compromise. Once a month Tío Marco cooks for me the most succulent, the most tender, the

225

most greasy suckling pig in the style of New Orleans. Tonight, my boy, you are going to share that feast and then you may get on with your courting."

Irish nearly blubbered. "Don Guillermo, sir," he said brokenly, "I tell you, you are the most generous, warm-hearted, live-and-let-live human being I believe I have ever known."

"Come, come, my boy. What we both need is a drink." He ordered another bottle of tequila, then inquired with extreme solicitude as to the condition of the dear little porker he had entrusted to Tío Marco's care, who pronounced it "the finest little dollop of a piglet I have ever prepared in the style of New Orleans" and promised that in one hour he would serve them the meal of their lives.

"The man is a wizard," Don Guillermo murmured. "He does a little sauce which will make you sob when you think of it ten or twenty years from now." From the kitchen Tío Marco broke into a haunting *cante jondo.* "He is singing the *azules* of old New Orleans, which can break your heart with their folk meanings, if authentic." They belted the tequila in silence, neither man wishing to pay disrespect to the singer, and when the song was ended another bottle of tequila was gone.

"Another bottle?" Don Guillermo asked. "Ordinarily, I would say that three quarts of tequila before dinner could get at the appetite. But not with a pig like this little pig. Oh no, sir."

"Cernee, another boddle," Irish mushed. "No pig like this little pig." He tapped his chest in deliberate measure.

The dollop of a little pig was served. In lieu of napkins each tucked a serape under his chin. Within seconds it was as though their hands had been in heavy cold cream, or axle grease, up to the elbows. Their eyes glimmered far back in their heads as they popped sweet shreds of the thrilling little porker into bubbled wafers of tortillas, applied frijoles, *salsa piquante,* and guacamole, then dipped all of it, up to the wrist, into the golden-red *salsa nostálgico,* chewing with far-off gaze and salivating like open hydrants. When the exquisite tortillas had been consumed, when the more obvious portions of the darling little pig were gone, Don Guillermo broke in half what was left, gave one piece to Irish, held the other himself, then called Tío Marco to roll up their sleeves.

Don Guillermo sank his teeth and face into the pale indigestibility and Irish crushed and crunched away across from him. They could not pick up the jars of tequila because with the slightest squeeze to hold and lift, the glass would go skittering away from them, ejected violently because of the inches of deep grease on their hands. Tío Marco stood by and held up the tequila for swallowing. "Always insist upon the aged tequila," Don Guillermo advised, "for if tequila has not been aged at least three days it can be like lowering a hungry crocodile into your brainpan."

They heard the rushets of flamenco guitar come into the room from immediately outside the main door of the *cantina*. "I hope you will enjoy a little music, Your Honor," Tío Marco said. "I have persuaded a debtor to sit outside and play some *paso dobles*."

"I am going to make a toast." Don Guillermo stood up slowly, clutching his portion of piglet, swaying dangerously against the draught of the room. "To Benito Reyes—son of a great horseman and my dear friend—"

Irish decided not to try to stand, but his spirits held high none the less. "To Don Guillermo Peña, alcalde of Lalotorres, and the most awe-inspiring gunman of all time, whose endless killings have become part of the song and story of the region—"

"Papa?"

Both men turned slowly to view the tiny, lovely lantern-eyed, boneless girl who stood in the doorway, surrounded by guitar notes. Irish struggled to his feet, not making it once. "Papa, it is very late. I have brought the hay wagon to take you home."

Irish gaped. This was little Florita! What had happened? What incandescent magic had transformed her into such an incomparable realization? He stared at the moving lights in the blackness of her lovely eyes. He goggled at her dismaying lines from scarlet flowers in glistening hair to her indefectible ankles. With delicate perception he realized that he had not shaved for six days. He remembered that he could not offer to

227

shake her hand because his was covered with inches of pork fat.

She stared at him as she stood there like a clubbed oaf. With a great effort of will she was able to hold back tears.

Her father looked at her owlishly; which is to say he was gray, he blinked frequently, and his nose seemed to hang down over his lips. "My dear Florita," he said, careful not to break any of the vowels by biting down on them, "may I present your future husband, Señor Don Benito Reyes y Splendor?"

Irish felt himself sobering up at an enormous rate of speed. He began to ratiocinate like a fictional computer, reprocessing every sentence he and the terrible Don Guillermo had said to each other that night, and his head alternately cleared and fogged with the horrors known to all indulgers of the double life. His peril defined itself with pristine clarity.

Don Guillermo had NOT forgiven him. Repeat. Now hear this. Now hear this. Don Guillermo believed that he, Señor Don Benito Reyes y Splendor, was to be married on the day after tomorrow to this enchantment who stood before them. *Aaaiiii! !*

With an anguished wail Florita turned and went out the door, not even pausing to slam it heavily. The guitar notes describing the *paso doble* still showered all over the floor from their outer source. Irish fought his own bent as a fantast. Could this breath-taking girl be the extended development of the child which had spoken in rusty door-hinge tones? Should he run after her? He felt a slippery bar of pig being slipped into his hand. Tío Marco Reuben pressed a jar of tequila to his lips.

"We will drink to your marriage, day after tomorrow," Don Guillermo said solemnly as they faced each other across the stout wooden board. Irish took a deep breath. He stepped forward over and into the abyss of duty.

"The day after tomorrow? My marriage?" he squeaked. "Why even if everything goes well I can't get to Mexico City for almost a week." He coughed. "Maybe more."

"Pardon?"

"I say how can I get married day after tomorrow when I won't get to Mexico for over a week?" His arms hung at his sides like hounds' ears.

"What has Mexico got to do with anything?"

"Why—the bride-to-be will be waiting for me in Mexico."

"The bride-to-be is here. You just saw her."

"Impossible, Don Guillermo. She is riding with her father now, on the train from Ciudad Juárez." Tío Marco had begun to back away towards the kitchen.

Don Guillermo's face had changed considerably. It was rather horrible. "I am her father. I am here."

"You are here. Undoubtedly, sir. But you are not the father of the bride." They were seated on the wooden chairs. Only four feet of table between them.

"What is the name of the bride, my boy? I must be sure about this thing."

"Evaliña Patten."

Don Guillermo overturned the table. He kicked the chair under him away from him, and his grease-packed fingers threw the pork bone. Irish moved a fraction of a second behind him, kicking his own chair as far away as possible, and backing up rapidly as Don Guillermo backed away from him. Irish knew he was about to die and thought, with a fleeting sense, what an honor it was to be shot down by a killer as legendary as Guillermo Peña B.

"Draw!" Don Guillermo roared.

They pulled guns. Irish never was to know that he had beaten the great Peña to the draw and would have killed him and walked away because all four of their guns popped with projectile force from the squeezing pork grease on their hands, the way a clutched bar of soap will sail out of the bath tub. The guns crashed to the floor four feet away from them, equidistant from both.

They sprang forward, reaching the weapons almost simultaneously. Their hatless heads clanged together, sending them staggering backward to the opposite wall as though they had been rammed by goats. Each step and movement of the grim duel was in precise synchrony with the rhythm of the *paso doble* "El Gato Montes" being played on the debtor's guitar. Dazed and battered, each man made it to his feet and started uncertainly towards the inert guns again. This time, as though as the result of exhaustive rehearsals, they tripped and skidded upon their fallen pork bones, sending both forward headlong, passing each other by as in a major movement in a folk dance, each to crash head-first into opposite walls of the *cantina*. This time the old gentleman stayed down, snoring softly. Irish stared at him foggily from across the room. Marco Reuben was at his side instantly, holstering his guns for him, then washing his hands and arms with soap and water, drying them with his shirt. "Ride, señor. Like the wind. When he comes to, he comes to shooting." Tío Marco pushed Irish to the door.

Irish paused to buy the debtor's guitar. He found his horse and galloped along the moon-silvered road in a muddle of confusion, in a lavender mist of chagrin and regret without remembering quite what it was he regretted until, in a flash of puce and green, he remembered Florita's beauty as she had stood in the doorway of Tío Marco's. He knew why he had bought the guitar. He spurred his horse suddenly, veering to the right and charging up the long hill which led to Guillermo's house on the remote Calle Faro. He dismounted in the shine of moon before the patio, tying his horse to a flowering vine. He stood under the only window which showed a light, fifteen feet above him. He struck the opening chords and sang softly:

"My heart is caught
Behind the bronze bars of a purgatory
Which is the memory of you.
It torments me, this dream of you,
As you glisten, the rain of my love
Upon your haunting face.
I am imprisoned in that time,
Caught for ever by these thoughts of you."

He waited, staring up at the light.

Something touched his arm and he jumped away ten feet or so, shrieking. It was Florita. She was hooded and cloaked in the darkness, her face like white marble.

230

"I heard. I listened and I heard," she said.

He could not answer.

"Why did you do it?"

The only thing he could think to say was, "I did it for Mexico. I wanted to make all of that land Mexican again."

"You have hurt me and harmed me. Now you must help me. You have no choice."

"I would do anything for you."

"I cannot stay here. The shame would be too great. For fourteen years my father has been talking about this wedding everywhere in the state. You must take me with you."

"But—"

"You will take me as far as Mexico. From there I will go to my mother's people in Spain. You can do no less. You will take me."

"I will take you."

CHAPTER 17

IT was cool and beautiful on the high mesa. The light moved at will, unchecked by dust or smoke or heavy layers of atmosphere. It burnished the mountains, painting their slopes with hymns of light and shadow, and with terrible strength flung shadow far across the openness of the plain through tufts of strained grass and mesquite. The floor of the mesa lifted, raking sharply uphill. At the center of the vast plain, embracing a number of buildings and many corrals sat the present headquarters of General Enrique Jorge Molina.

General Molina, *cabecilla* of the region and sole authority over an area which included parts of Durango, Zacatecas, Aguascalientes, and San Luis Potosi, the four central states of the Republic, held his power by virtue of the loyalty of his troops. Men had flocked to his standard when he had decided to enter the political arena because three years before he had ransacked a great shipment of costumes of the Blenda Isbey Opera Company as it was being shipped to Quito, Ecuador, from Detroit, Michigan. In this

231

manner the general had obtained three hundred and ten Polish hussar uniforms, gorgeously frogged, and their appearance had been so effective that in time he had ordered five hundred more of the same style from a theatrical supply house in Kansas City, Missouri. He further held the loyalty of his men because he took a kindly view towards looting and pillage and employed the best cooks.

He was impatience itself to become part of good government, as are so many wealthy men. He held no powers from the federal government or from the governments of any of the four states he dominated but he had a plan to catch the attention of the central government to gain him the appointment to a governor's chair. He had been successful in sustaining a civil war in all four states while he had set to work to stamp out the wave of terrorism and unrest which he had caused and felt surely that it would be only a matter of time before the grateful central government saw to it that he gained a senior appointment.

His base headquarters was on the borderline between Zacatecas and San Luis Potosi. At the moment of the capture of Jim Street and Dr. Ridgeway, General Molina was bucking for the governorship of Zacatecas. That goal could be changed quickly, however. The general was a mercurial man. He had been faithful to but two concepts in his lifetime: power, and the memory of his fiancée, Esperanza Toledo-Arnall, deceased.

No matter where the general bivouacked while campaigning—in a tent on the mesa, in a mansion in the town, in a cave in the hills—he would fasten to that residence a temporary street address: *Camino a Toluca 325,* once the home of the little girl to whom he had been affianced in the Federal District when she had been twelve years old and he fifteen, some forty-one years before. She had passed away at her own twelfth birthday party, having choked on two enormous chili peppers which her father had popped into the *huichepos* as a special treat and a surprise. The loss had broken the young man's heart. It had turned him against both *huichepos* and society. He had never married. If he saw a child while he happened to be drinking tequila he would weep so desperately that his men would not be able to hold him upright in the saddle but would need to lay him across his horse's rump face down in order to get him away and assuage his grief.

The general was an anomaly of pedestrian locomotion in that he was both widely bow-legged and extremely pigeon-toed, a startling effect from the rear. He tilted downward at the left shoulder. This combination of postures had caused him to transfer out of the Mexican infantry early in his career. He was at one with any horse he rode, and it made him considerably taller, which he needed. His horsemanship had been so superb that he had been attached to the Mexican embassy to the court of St. James's. He had lived in London for six years. His leadership aura was one of unmitigated menace. This was no paltry achievement for a man who had soared to the rank of general from a height of five feet one inch, shod. His lack of platform was exaggerated by his weight, two hundred and forty pounds without his guns.

For a man with such a bulky body, General Molina had an unexpected shaped face. It was long and thin. Everything upon it dropped downward as though in use in a charade which continually demonstrated a bunch of bananas. His skin was bright yellow. His eyebrows were concave. His nose plunged almost to overshoot his large sagging mustache, which overhung his down-pulled mouth like ferns in a rain forest. His chin was pointed and carried a startlingly black wart. Because he was stone bald and there was always wind on the mesa, he wore a high sombrero whose brim curled dramatically behind him. This added somewhat to his height, indoors and out. His eyes were brown and yellow, as were his teeth.

General Molina's father, a top undertaker in his time, had named the boy after Henry George, founder of the single tax. That philosophy conflicted excessively with the general's own fiscal policy. To date, in his provinces, he had invented over two hundred new taxes for his people, creating a system which was so wringingly grotesque in an internal-revenue sense that it is not likely that even the most sardonic of his people would have been able to smile had they been told the significance of his name. For three months after instituting a five per cent tax on pulque, the milky beer made from maguey, so much turmoil had been caused that it was rumored that he would be made governor of Hidalgo within a month. He had found it necessary to shoot seventy-one conscientious objectors to the tax, which was a shocking and brutal thing excepting that they were all confirmed pulque drinkers and their executions had lowered the incidence of alcoholism in the statistics for the region.

Dr. Ridgeway and Jim Street were brought into the headquarters area at five-thirty on the afternoon of the forty-first anniversary of the passing of the general's fiancée. Purple crêpe had been fastened over the doorway of *Camino a Toluca 325* and its lintels were framed by blankets of calla lilies. Sentries paced with wool-muffled boots. Everyone moved very slowly and carefully lest General Molina be disturbed because, of all days, this anniversary made him most keenly aware of death. At eleven that morning he had turned upon his Scandinavian Intelligence Chief and Bandmaster, Captain Loki Berquist, and had shouted through his sobs, "Why should little Señorita Toledo-Arnall be taken away to the angels when a dog like you is permitted to roam the world?" and had shot him down. The body was still in there with the general. At last, in time to spare his reason, the hour for the first executions of the day came round. Eleven subversives who had been proved to have entertained thoughts of a two-party system were to be shot. All of them had had a fair trial by means of a chat with the general himself, which was standard operating procedure to insure that justice would be done; they had been found guilty. The new prisoners, just arrived, were to be arraigned before him immediately. The general's headquarters were in the sprawling main house of what had been a large sheep ranch. It was a large room. Wildly colored serapes were strewn on walls and floor. Each of the six straight-backed chairs in the room had gun belts hanging from them. The air had been tinted a distinguished gray-blue by cigar smoke. When the prisoners were brought in, General

234

Molina was sitting with his back to the door, his face buried in his hands, deeply depressed.

"What is it?"

"Two new prisoners, sir."

The general did not turn to look. He merely waved one hand. "Guilty. I find them guilty as charged."

"Guilty of what?" Dr. Ridgeway said indignantly, and at the sound of a female voice, General Molina turned.

"Ah. Gringos."

"I demand to know why we are here," Dr. Ridgeway said firmly.

"Do you speak Spanish?" General Molina asked in Spanish.

"I refuse to answer any questions in any language whatsoever," Dr. Ridgeway said, in English.

"Then we will speak English and you will do as you are told. What is your name?"

"Dr. Marilyn Ridgeway."

"A physician?"

"I am a natural scientist."

"What is your name?"

"Jim Street."

"What are you wearing on your back?"

"A banjo."

"Is it like a guitar?"

"No."

"Play something."

"He will do nothing of the kind."

"I ain't playin' nothin'. I got dragged here against my will an'—" He saw the corpse on the floor, eight inches from his foot, bullet hole at base of nose. "What would you like to hear?" he asked. He used his eyes to drag Dr. Ridgeway's eyes to the body.

"Something sad. Sad but brave."

" 'Just before the battle, Mother'?"

"Sad? With wisps of gallantry?"

"Yes, sir."

"Play it."

Jim made a few peg adjustments and, clearing his throat reflexively, he went into the introduction sweepingly with his haunting tremolo, fingers moving the patented pick as though it were a homeward-bound humming-bird. He was in unique voice. It seemed to be shot through with marzipan or silvered with the dandruff of the gods. He pressed all glottal stops relentlessly to produce a heart-breaking, wavering quiver of sound:

> "Farewell, Mother, you may never
> Press me to your heart again;
> But, O, you'll not forget me, Mother
> If I'm numbered with the slain.
> Hark, I heard the bugles sounding,
> 'Tis the signal for the fight!
> Now may God protect us Mother!
> As he ever does the right."

Dr. Ridgeway had taken up the second part with sure, pure alto, staring at the body on the floor and singing with fervent hope and belief.

> "Hear the battle cry of freedom,
> How it swells upon the air;
> O, yes, we'll rally round the standard
> Or we'll perish nobly there."

"Beautiful," the general sobbed. "Very, very beautiful and enormously gallant. Play it again. Oh yes. Play it again."

CHAPTER 18

THE train carrying the Official Judges' committee and the Grand Prize moved smoothly across the State of Zacatecas at its eastern frontier, where it joined San Luis Potosi. It was loaded with freight but running at half passenger capacity. The new passenger cars were comfortable. The new wooden benches shone. The floor was carpeted in green. Each window was not unlike a moving picture-postcard of the moving plains and the stubble of short pines which grew amid bare places in conversational groups.

That morning Mr. Moodie had decided that there

could be but one procedure if he were ever to be able to wrench some ecstasy out of his life. He had become emboldened by the fact of the decision. Suddenly he knew that this, today, was to be either the beginning of the end for him (it had taken just twelve years to recover from the humiliation of Pittsburgh) or the end of that beginning which had so tragically barred him from returning to England. If he were to walk out among the angels while he still clung to the garment of his youth, he must plot and dare. He knew he was not robust enough to break across the bass garrulity which was spinning about their heads in connected and unconnected loops of sound.

"Jim says to me he don't want nobody to say he's right an' nobody to say he's wrong. He says he can prove his case against the longhorns. He was right a few years back when he predicted them new laws in the North against the fever tick the longhorns carry. I asked him if he was tryin' to make himself head cheese."

"Speakin' of cheese, you'd like a German cheese called *Nieheimer Hopfenkäse*. It's a sour-milk cheese cured between layers of hops. They make 'em into little cakes an' let 'em ripen for about eight days, then they break 'em open an' put in some caraway seed and some beer. Dee-licious!"

Evaliña sat across the aisle from Mr. Moodie, but facing him. Her stepmother was beside her, staring out the window. Mat Sun had retired to the rear of the car with a bottle of warm, new zotol and a pack of cards, waiting for a chump. He sang to himself in Cantonese and gazed out of the window, smiling.

Mr. Moodie began to project a concentration of himself upon Evaliña's youthful sensibilities. He felt he should have a chance to succeed. She was young. She was healthy. She was inexperienced. He stared intently at her eyes, although not at her gaze, willing her to become aware of him. It took him two hours to break through her fortress of reverie, which concerned the delicious events leading away from her forthcoming marriage. She was deep within a fantasy of passion, a condition most favorable to Mr. Moodie's purpose. More and more this was becoming her favorite game and she knew she would have to find a way to curb it lest one false, unthinking, impulsive mood bring down the curse upon her head. Two hours of intensive concentration, as Mr. Moodie was applying it, would have tried the strength of the great masters of Yoga.

At last she looked absently in his direction. She recoiled, then found control. She was pinned by the intensity of his stare. She would have to change her seat, she told herself; but she could not. More and more her eyes, helpless to do otherwise, would dart to his. Neither changed expression any more than do the facing stone gargoyles on the Cathedral of Notre Dame. Deep signals were emitting excitement and gyrating mystery. She *had* to tear herself away but she could not. She needed to find something which could absorb her consciousness, to wrest her racing imagination away from those piercing, possessing eyes. What were they saying to her? What did they want from her? Where was his smile? Men were supposed to smile when they were pleased. Was he displeased with her? Such a thing had never happened to Evaliña, blessed as she had been by being the most beautiful female in history up to her time.

Her mind thrashed about in a welter of conflict. Her sweet, small bottom rolled at a quicker pace in an imperceptibly wider set of circles, but no one noticed this exept the attuned Mr. Moodie—causing him to tremble from each elbow to the wrist.

CHAPTER 19

IRISH moved more slowly traveling with Florita. He was much more careful of the heat. They had not spoken since the last words in front of her father's house.

He stopped at three that afternoon and picketed the horses, directing Florita to the shade of a clump of madroño trees. She moved spiritlessly. Her face was drawn downward into a haggard mask. For three nights they had slept within four feet of each other. They had not spoken. He had produced the food and had cooked it. She accepted the food and ate as much of it as she could.

The horses were in luck. The picket pins were planted in a field of fine grass, for that country, and because they had been spared each time he had spared Florita (as well as he could within bounds of conscience) so they were fresh and strong.

Irish lay near them in the shade. He was suffering. The only salvation for him was to push onward into complications of the delusion that he was marrying Evaliña Patten for the sake of Mexico, to bring those vast holdings under Mexican ownership where they had been for almost four centuries. He had not been able to lift his eyes to look upon Florita. But when he did see her and was struck by the sadness in her face tied in by the lines of sleeplessness and utter shame, it made him grieve for her and for himself. The day had been intensely hot.

Grazing horses make a kind of musical sound. As they crop the grass and grind it, the sound becomes something which men whose lives have depended upon horses seem to be able to hear, awake or asleep. Irish was dozing when the musical sounds stopped. He turned over. Both horses had their heads up and ears pointed toward the range of mountains to the west. Irish looked. He saw a thin string of dust rising. It swirled high into the air as though it were being churned. It seemed to be coming toward them.

He saddled the horses with rapid skill. He checked the wheels on all four guns. He holstered two and stuck two in his belt. He untied the serape which had been lashed to the after part of his saddle and, doubling it, passed it over his head and shoulders where it landed in loose folds, jammed his sombrero on top of his head and the upper part of the serape, and tied it under his chin with a buckskin thong.

He called to her curtly. "Florita!" She made a snap turn. She sat up to stare at him with angry eyes. She had been resting in the shade for an hour and a half and she had not moved but she had not been sleeping.

"I told you nver to speak to me again," she said.

"Indians." He threw the blanket at her. "Arrange your serape as I have arranged mine."

"I want nothing to do with you or anything you do," she said, "even if I am to be scalped and burned at the stake."

He shrugged. "Arrows can make a girl's skin look pretty bad," he said. "Five or six arrows sticking out of your head and the complexion is ruined. If I were you I would arrange your serape the way I have arranged mine."

"But why? It looks terrible."

"Arrows don't stick on a loose serape."

"You mean you really think it's Indians?"

He turned again and watched the column. He could make out the forms of the horses and riders now. "I know it is Indians," he said, "and worse, they could be Apaches."

She quickly threw the serape over her head and shoulders and tied it down with a scarf. "What else must we do?" she asked.

"Ride like you've never ridden before," he said to her softly. "I will take care of everything else."

The horses seemed to sense the danger. Irish rode a great horse and had to hold him to stay abreast of Florita's horse at its top speed. The Indians screamed as they saw their quarry get under way. They entered the road two hundred yards behind them. It was a war party of more than sixty braves.

Four arrows were sticking in the folds of the serape around his head and shoulders. Florita had not been touched. An arrow had grazed his right arm and another had creased his left thigh. He decided they must be after his horse. For sixty warriors to waste time over the saddle bags of two people didn't make any sense. They would kill him when they caught him, and Florita too, but the chance of blood was secondary. They wanted the horse.

Irish had raised the horse from a colt. He had hand-fed him. He had trained him with gentleness and not four months before he had been offered one hundred and twenty-five mustangs in exchange for him. Irish had refused. The Mescalero who had made the offer had been outraged by the refusal of such an unprecedented offer in trade. Irish had said he could take care of one animal without feeling any strain but if he took on one hundred and twenty-five the Mescaleros would steal them back at first grazing.

The pursuit led through a series of low hills with deep ravines. It was seven o'clock. They had been running for two and a half hours. The moon was up. There were no clouds. When Irish looked behind the gullies were empty. The Indians seemed to have given up but it flashed across his mind that they might know how to cut him off by a short road. He grasped Florita's bridle and dug into his tired horse with his spurs. He brought his quirt down hard on Florita's horse's rump. He held that speed for almost twenty minutes, then suddenly he heard the Indians screaming close behind them. He looked. They were within thirty yards. There was a sound ahead of them. Another war party came galloping over the rise ahead. Irish wheeled his two horses sharply and headed up the hill into a canyon whose floor was littered with boulders. There was a steep cliff ahead behind clumps of madroño trees mixed with oaks. In the moonlight they were squat, crooked trees but with the boulders they gave the two horses and riders running sanctuary from the Indians who were too close behind them. Irish turned and this time he fired. An off-side Indian fell. He saw a canoe-shaped rock ahead of them under a great overhang of granite, making an open yet almost protected cave in the side of the hill. He rode them into it, then leaped off, pulling the carbine with him. The moon was bright. The first shot sent the Indians off their horses to cover. What had started as an in-passing theft of a horse had become as a fire in them, because he had shed much of their blood. They would wait for him until they had killed him with arrows or knives, or by starvation or thirst. They had nothing but time. He reloaded. Once he thought he saw something move from the shelter of one boulder to another. He fired and was rewarded with a scream of pain.

CHAPTER 20

Jim concentrated on remembering the layout of the sheep ranch as he had seen it from the rise of the hill when the Molina patrol had brought them in. Through the window behind General Molina's head he could see the large, filled sheep pens in the moonlight. Using the hourly executions as a timetable, he estimated that it was just before eleven o'clock.

His hands were gnarled from constant banjo playing. Dr. Ridgeway was quite hoarse from incessant singing. His chording fingers had begun to bleed long before and because the blood made them slide on the metal strings the General, with considerable solicitude, had insisted that he wear a supple riding glove on his left hand. Jim had been playing for six hours. The only interruptions, every hour, on the hour, had been the executions which they were permitted to enjoy through the far window. His extraordinary voice, trained to be heard over the lowing of cattle, had become a broken thing. His stentorian tones, once so sure, had been reduced pitiably, but he had to sing on. Through it all he was sustained by the quality of the parts singing of Dr. Ridgeway. She would switch, to give him pleasure and variety, from tenor to alto to soprano to bass, each one tone-perfect. General Molina clutched a jar of home-made cactus whiskey, out of which the hangover-causing impurities could not possibly have been strained, and stared with poignance at the meanings behind the lyrics of each song.

"When I left home, my mother for me cried,
She begged me not to go, for me she woulda died.
My mother's heart is aching,
Breaking for me, that's all
And with God's help I'll see her,
When the work's all done this fall."

The general wailed and buried his face in his arms on the desk, then leaned far back in the swivel chair with his eyes closed and beat on the arms of the chair with his fists.

> "While riding in the darkness
> So loudly did he shout,
> He tried his best to head them,
> To turn the herd about,
> But his saddle horse did stumble,
> And on him did fall;
> That boy won't see his mother
> When the work's all done this fall."

The music the two singers made, toward the end, was like the sound of thistles falling into thick soup from a great height. As Jim croaked on he stared out of the window to his left where the last remaining prisoners were having their hands tied behind their backs and slammed up against a brick wall. Defiantly they refused blindfolds. The front line of riflemen knelt and aimed and the second line pointed their rifles. The lieutenant's sword went up. The two singers faltered. The sound of the banjo stopped.

"Go on!" the general bellowed.

The fusillade was fired. The three men crumpled and fell.

> "Boys, send my mother my wages.
> The wages I have earned,
> And tell her not to wait for me,
> The last steer I have turned.
> I'm going to a new range,
> I hear my Master's call
> I won't get to see my mother
> When the work's all done this fall."

"What is your name again, sir?" the general asked.

"Street, sir." He could hardly be heard.

"Street—no, no, I must not be impolite." The general looked at Dr. Ridgeway blearily. "What is your name again?"

"Dr. Marilyn Ridgeway." She had to whisper.

"You have a beautiful voice."

She nodded her appreciation dopily.

"I am going to make you the leader of my Woman's army. Rank of major. You will organize the women of each new bivouac into choirs. It will have a decided effect upon the men. A thirty-year contract. You will retire a full colonel."

"I would like—a drink—of water."

"What was your name, again?"

"Street."

"Street, I have an opening for an intelligence chief who can also double as bandmaster. You will start as a major with the full thirty-year contract I give to all my people, and you will retire a full colonel."

The general shot off his pistol through the ceiling. An orderly appeared. The general ordered dinner for three.

There was a scraping of boots outside the door and three resplendently uniformed officers came into view. "Ah!" the general said, nodding to Dr. Ridgeway and Jim. "Your comrades-in-arms. My General Staff."

First in was Colonel Francis Winikus-Garnet, a rosy-cheeked yet sinister soldier of fortune who had Montague Square written all over him. The three officers were dressed in apple-green uniforms frogged with black silk, each man under white epaulets and canary aguillettes. They wore yellow gauntlets, flared apple-green breeches piped heavily in black, and high, shining, black boots with brass spurs. Each man held his shako under his arm, insignia facing outward.

"Gentlemen, I present to you Dr. Ridgeway and Mr. Street, who will join us. Dr. Ridgeway will head my new Women's army. Mr. Street will replace Captain Berquist," the general gestured to the body on the floor, "who, as you all know, passed away this morning."

The officers bowed.

"Dr. Ridgeway and Mr. Street, which we will call them until they can be sworn in, are genuine artists and fine musicians. I am not only pleased that you are here to meet them, but I want you to hear them perform." General Molina nodded to Jim. "If you please."

His throat torn, his fingers raw, Jim attempted "I Gave One Eye for Winfield Scott." As he sang, Jim knew they were a grotesque failure. Their voices had the broken texture of potato salad. There was a generally wet silence in the room when he finished. The general quaffed another jar of cactus whisky and applauded heavily crying, *"Bis! Bis!"* so that the others were obliged to pat their hands together softly. "Are they not marvelous?" the general asked with genuine appreciation.

"I believe I rather preferred Loki Berquist's tuba, myself," Colonel Winikus-Garnet said. The tall, languid officer next to him stared hopelessly out of the window. The third picked his teeth with a stiletto.

The orderly entered with a tray which had been covered with a white, concealing cloth and set it down on the general's desk. "Ah," General Molina said, lifting the cloth, "a little snack!" He may have seemed to be articulating with great difficulty but that could have been due to the several jars of cactus whisky he had drunk during the long day. On the tray was a warm stack of tortillas and four small plates which held an assortment of *chili* peppers including *furias, infiernos, terrores, sensaciónales, avispas, torridos,* and *frenesís,* in green, yellow, and fire-red separations. "Be careful," General Molina said, passing the tray to Dr. Ridgeway and to Jim. "These are chilis which can blow the head off your shoulders with their powers and melt all of your food pipes. They are brought to me from Colima."

"They may help the throat," Dr. Ridgeway said, holding the tray under Jim's chin.

"You—you think so, Marilyn?"

"The Argurules, who are the greatest singing tribe in Mexico, in Central Tabasco, train on *furias* and *sensaciónales.* Seenotro, their leader, lives on *torridos.*"

"Then I think I will pass them up."

"Jim, dear. Please eat. Your throat is about to close up on you." He was so moved by her words and by the way she looked at him that he reached over, and moving too quickly for anyone to stop him, grabbed four fat, burning capsicums, popped them into his mouth, bit down hard and began to chew.

"No! No!" shrieked an officer.

"Street, for the sake of heaven, man!" Winikus-

Garnet cried out. It was too late. Street's eyeballs began to protrude beyond the end of his nose. Tears fell down his cheeks and sweat collected in great gobbets in his eyebrows. His face broke out into dozens of dead-white spots with tiny blue centers, like a bandana handkerchief. Two clown buttons of rouge appeared on each cheekbone. His frightfully stung lips and his eroded gums and tongue were yet too paralyzed by the searing alkaloids to permit him to speak, but he was able to nod to Dr. Ridgeway that he had survived.

General Molina clapped him on the back. "You were superb. Tomorrow you will skip a grade to lieutenant-colonel. I have never seen a gringo eat *chilis* like that."

"By golly, Marilyn," he said in clear, unmangled tones. "You were right! I think I got my voice back with them *chilis*. *Mi, mi, mi, mimi*—" The tones were magnificent. He offered her the tray. She accepted one *chili* each of the three different colors and chewed excitedly while she listened to him vocalize. She seemed to have no reaction whatsoever. "Yes, yes!" she said. "Oh, isn't it wonderful! It was only something Dr. Agassiz happened to drop in conversation when I was going with a Harvard boy. Oh, Jim! If such a thing were possible I would say your voice is even better than ever."

He stared at her adoringly.

He began to play and to sing as though he were back in Pickering's Paradise on a Saturday night and softly Dr. Ridgeway joined in with him. His tremolo quivered like a great gong, shimmering exquisitely upon each note then breaking, as light breaks upon an ocean, into warped and tortured vocal tones of a thousand shades. Their two voices rose over their audience with an artistry which met the deep grief of the inspired lyrics with transcended understanding. The audience was transported. There was not a man among them, as the duet progressed onward through dozens of verses, who was not reminded of some pure streak of goodness in his life. There was not a man there who was not made far, far better for the duration of that moving song.

"Comrades, gather closer
And listen to my dying prayer.
Who will be to her as a brother,
And shield her with a brother's care?
Up spoke the noble Rangers,
They answered one and all,
'We will be to her brothers,
'Til the last one does fall.'
One glad smile of pleasure
O'er the Rangers' face was spread,
One dark convulsive shadow
And the Ranger boy was dead."

As Jim Street and Dr. Marilyn Ridgeway howled
out the sixty-fifth and last stanza of that hymn to self-
lessness, the four military men were wracked with
choked sobs.

"Far from his darling sister,
We laid him down to rest,
With his saddle for a pillow
And his gun across his breast."

"That settles it!" General Molina said in a loud,
stirred voice. "You and Major Ridgeway will accom-
pany us on the major operations we will move upon
tomorrow. Give them the details, Colonel." The general poured out another jar of cactus whisky and sat
back watching his two precious new acquisitions
through pleased, narrowed eyes.

"We shall derail the southbound train which is traveling between Monterrey and Mexico City," Colonel
Winikus-Garnet said crisply, "tomorrow at three
peeyem. The derailment will occur just beyond the
railroad tunnel between Joaquin and La Strada. Sur-
viving passengers will be shot or bayoneted and the
freight cars—three in number—now loaded with new
rifles and ammunition in quantities sufficient to supply
an army will be transferred to our pack trains. Actually, I think you'll enjoy it. Plenty of blood."

As Jim gaped at them, stunned and speechless at
such casual treatment of a planned massacre of his
friends, each officer in turn shook his hand then Dr.

Ridgeway's, thanked them for a touching experience, and filed out of the room.

General Molina was almost asleep. He stared at them, trying to find the words to order them to play on, but was unable to keep his eyes open. His head fell to the top of the desk. They watched him steadily. Within seconds he was snoring.

Jim touched Dr. Ridgeway's wrist and pointed to the window behind the sleeping general. He grabbed the general's pistol from the desk, gave it to Dr. Ridgeway to hold, then made the rounds of the gun belts hanging from the empty chairs, snatching four guns—two for his holsters, two to be stuck in his belt. Systematically, he stripped bullets out of the gun belts and stuffed them into his pockets. Dr. Ridgeway had opened the window silently. Jim slipped out into the blackness. She could see his hand motioning. She slipped her legs over the window-sill and let him catch her under the arms to bring her down slowly. "Be very careful," she whispered. "I am very, very ticklish." She smelled delicious. He grabbed her hand and pulled her behind him through the moonlight toward the sheep pens. He could now see the horse corrals beyond the pens. They went under the fence and kept to the ground under the sheep for twenty or thirty yards, talking in low voices as they moved. The strange new smell frightened the sheep and they began to baa and mill nervously. A sentry's voice yelled, "Who goes there?"

A chair crashed through a window far behind them. They heard General Molina's voice yelling, "Shoot them in the legs! Stop them but don't kill them. Colonel! Colonel Winikus!"

They reached the horse corral. Jim whistled softly. He pulled Dr. Ridgeway along beside him as they walked crab-fashion along the high fence rail which separated the pens, trying to peer into the corral.

"You see, I just thought you forgot about our July date, Marilyn," he said. "Man, I really sweated it out."

"We agreed not to talk about that."

"Hell, Marilyn, if you'll have me I want to marry you an' what I'm trying to tell you is—"

"Jim!" Her voice was so intense he thought she'd been bitten by a snake and he wheeled. Her arms caught his head in a tight lock and pulled it down to her mouth. She kissed him as he had never been kissed before: with appetite, with skill, with extraordinary promise of what lay beyond that, and—because she was trained—with some natural science. He fell against the fence when she released him. "I accept," she said fervently. "I have thought about you at ten o'clock Eastern Standard Time every night for three years. You are in my blood and I could never let you go!"

"Why, honey—! I feel the same, only maybe even more so, because I been alone a lot." A shot rang out. They became aware of the boots of troops moving over the cobblestones of the compound. Colonel Winikus-Garnet's voice rang clear. "Come out, Street, and bring the woman. You haven't got a chance."

Jim kept hold of Dr. Ridgeway's hand. They moved slowly along the fence, Jim whistling. Soon the *bayo coyote* worked his way through the other horses and found Jim. Jim patted him softly and spoke to him in a low voice. "Hold him, honey, an' I'll get you a horse an' some gear."

More soldiers were being broken out on the double, moving noisily in all directions on the compound. Above all the noises there was the shrillness of the general's tantrum-screaming that they take the prisoners alive.

Jim found saddles just where they were supposed to be in a Mexican corral, slung across the third fence rail. He pulled them down, with blankets, one at a time and saddled his horse and a jet-black horse for her. He ran his hands along six fence posts, but he could find no bridles. His eyes had become accustomed to the darkness. He could see the three rings of infantry being deployed around the pen and the corral; one holding eighteen hundred sheep, the other holding four hundred horses. Their contrasting smells and sounds filled the air around him. The dust they had raised covered him.

Working frantically, he found two lariats in the saddles. He got dizzy with his luck. He had found two wranglers' saddles and not those for cavalry. He fashioned a hackamore in the darkness, forcing himself to work deliberately. He formed a loop on the offside of the black horse and tied a bowline on the near side to form a noseband and the headpiece. He cut strands of the rope to make the brown band and the throat latch. He set the come-along hitch, then ran it backward and secured it to the saddle horn. Then he repeated with the *bayo coyote*. Colonel Winikus' voice brawled: "You are surrounded, Street. - You cannot escape. General Molina will give you five minutes to come out, throwing your arms out ahead of you. If not I will send in a company of mounted men to stampede the animals. You will be seriously hurt. Come out now like a good fellow, and throw your arms out ahead of you."

While the colonel shouted, Jim slipped under the rail to the sheep pen. He held Dr. Ridgeway's lovely head in his hand and almost pressed her ear to his mouth. He told her what they were going to do and she nodded, delighted. He kissed her ear, then moved as fast as he could through the sheep and the darkness, carrying the joined ropes with him, dragging rams with him where he went. Working his long rope, he lashed the first ram's left horn to the next ram's right horn until he had lashed the strongest sheep together in a thirty-yard parallelogram; a live fence of lashed rams along the front, two rows of lashed rams fencing the sides. It was a great box of wool which would move all together on seventy-two hundred legs.

Dr. Ridgeway tied the black horse to the saddle of the *bayo coyote*. The bleating of the sheep was so frantic they could no longer keep track of the activities of the soldiers. Jim unlatched the sheep-pen gate, lying on his stomach, while Dr. Ridgeway unlatched the corral gate. Both faced into the compound, now filled with soldiers. They were unlatched but not opened. General Molina's shrill voice yelled, "There he is. He's trying to come out at the sheep gate. Don't shoot to kill that man. Don't shoot to kill!"

Jim made his way back to Dr. Ridgeway. "Here goes, hon," he said, "an' if we make it let's have a dozen kids." He kissed her this time. Then he picked

250

her up and slid her across the backs of the sheep, following her. They worked their way to the backs of the sheep at the center of the flock. Jim fired four shots into the air, then lay face down, grabbing wool and gritting his teeth.

The horses started forward first and came thundering out of the corral at the soldiers in a blind movement of four hundred horsepower. The sheep moved out as one sheep, crashing into the gate of the pen flinging it open, taking fence down with it. Soldiers were thrown, trampled, and scattered away from the line of stampede of the twenty-two hundred animals. The packaged mass of mutton and wool thundered across the compound surrounded by neighing frightened military horses on all sides. The splintering push of the movement knocked down all torches which the colonel had had staked to illuminate the area and everything was in blackness, routing General Molina. One hundred yards away from the compound Jim looked up to see the *bayo coyote* moving easily ahead of the charging sheep, trailing the black horse. Jim whistled shrilly three times and the horse began to head the sheep, moving slowly back and forth ahead of them, slowing them down until they had almost stopped. Jim pulled Dr. Ridgeway to her feet, then waded forward through the sheep as a man would walk through hip-deep water. They climbed over the horns of the leading line of rams and mounted. They rode hard, heading south. Jim tried to remember the old prayers as he went. He had to find that train before General Molina did.

CHAPTER 21

JUST before dawn, after a night of watching every tree and rock and expecting it to move, Irish decided they would have to make a run for it if they were to have any chance at all of staying alive. Three times during the long night he had spoken to Florita but she had not answered him. When he had decided they must run, he tried once more.

"When the dawn comes we are going to try to ride through them."

She shrugged.

"It is the only way. There is a chance we will make it, but if we stay here, we will be killed."

She shrugged again.

"It is a good chance that we will die together this morning, Florita. I say that to you so that you will know that what I say will not be a lie. You have been the woman of my thoughts for fourteen years of my life. Now you are the woman of my eternity. There has never been any other woman but you."

She began to sob but she did not look up to him or even gesture that she understood him or would forgive.

"I can say it now because it will bring no shame to a fine girl—to Evaliña Patten—but if I had not agreed to marry her—if Jim Street *and* I had not agreed to undertake endless contests to marry her— we would have been shot by her father."

She wheeled around where she sat on the ground and looked up at him with her enormous dark eyes, which had filled suddenly with hope and with a will to live.

"It is not what it seems. It was an accident which I would tell you about if we were to have a little time to spend the rest of our lives together, but since I would be killed if I did not agree to marry, I began to tell myself that I was not a coward, which I was, that I would be serving Mexico by reclaiming the land of Mexico from a foreigner but you must see that I must have known that it was all a silly joke because I came to your father to talk of it and I came to you." She was on her feet.

She shrugged.

"It is the only way," Irish said. "There is a chance we will make it but if we stay here we will be killed."

She shrugged again. She suppressed a yawn.

"I am telling you there is a good chance that we die together this morning, Florita," he said irritably.

"Some joke."

"Some joke?"

"For fourteen years I have been dreaming of how

we would live together, only to come to the point where you offer a chance to die together."

"Death is very serious."

"Oh come, Benito. But so was our life and what did you do with it?"

"Are you willing to concede that death is very serious?"

"Have you lost your mind?"

"Answer me!"

"Yes. Death is very serious. Particularly when someone wants to talk you to death while you are surrounded by fifty or sixty murderous savages."

"All right, then. You realize that at such a time even the worst villain would not tell a lie?"

"I suppose not."

"Then I say this to you, Florita, there has never been another woman but you. This unhappiness—this present involvement—it was a freakish accident. I love only you, Florita."

"Oh, Benito!"

"I want you to know that and to cling to that now that death is near."

Florita grinned and the whole world changed around them. "Those Indians will have to change their plans," she giggled. "This is no day for being killed. Now, tell me once more. You are *my* man then?"

"Now and tomorrow, now and for ever."

Her hands went around his neck. She pulled him to her. They kissed as though there were no Indians and as though death were not a very serious thing. Then she said, "Eh! Let us mount and ride through them and you can tell me about the freakish accident when we have been married for a year." A carbine was fired. The rock next to Florita's cheek was splintered by the bullet.

Irish ran and got the horses to their feet. He threw Florita upon her saddle, then mounted his. *"Aaaiii! I feel so wonderful,"* he yelled and, holding her horse's bridle, moved them both out from under the shelter of the overhanging rock.

Two-fifths of a second before he could dig his spurs into his horse's side, the Indian fell on him from the shelf twelve feet overhead, slamming into him heavily and slamming them both upon the hard ground. Florita screamed and threw herself off the horse. "Back! Back!" Irish yelled to her. "Put your back to the wall and hold a gun."

The Indian was on top of him, facing Florita. The horses were gone. She could get no gun. As they had fallen the sharp point of the long knife in the Indian's right hand was deflected by Irish's silver belt buckle. Irish was able to pull his own knife out of its leg scabbard with his right hand while gripping the Indian's knife hand over his head with the other. They thrashed across the ground and made guttural animal noises from deep in their throats. Despite the total darkness which followed the false dawn, he knew the Indian was naked except for a loin cloth. The body was heavily oiled, making it nearly impossible for Irish to hold a grip.

Irish took the chance he had to take and dropped his now-greased hand into the sand to gain some friction from the sticking sand. At this instant the Indian struck with the long knife. Irish stopped it within a fraction of an inch of his throat. This time he had a firm grip on that wrist and his sanded hand held on. With a sudden roll and a body feint Irish was able to break loose and leap to his feet, feeling that at any second he would be struck from behind in the blackness. They circled each other to the right, just able to make out each other's forms. The Indian lunged. Irish stopped it and brought his own knife up from under in a ripping arc, but it was stopped. They stood as a frieze, Irish holding the savage's hand high over their heads, the Indian pulling Irish's knife hand down below their knees. Unable to cope with the body grease any longer, Irish tripped his opponent with a violent pass of the right foot, but the warrior brought Irish down with him and twisted himself on top of him before they struck the ground. Helplessly, Florita stared and screamed. In an instant the crazed Indian had won. He held Irish down with his mass and weight. He pinned down Irish's knife arm with his left knee and his right knee fastened the doomed man's left arm to the ground. It was over. The long knife went high,

254

then started downward just as the sun threw its light upon them.

"Tortillaw!" Irish screamed. The knife stopped. The blood brothers stared at each other. The Indian gasped and scrambled off Irish's chest, then helped him to his feet. Florita rushed in and put her arms around Irish. Tortillaw began to talk fumblingly, his breath coming in gasps. He began to brush off Irish's clothes ineffectively while Irish began to climb into a panting, towering rage.

"This clown is my sister's husband," Irish said, pushing Tortillaw's ministering hands away. He stood there glaring at the Indian, growing angrier and angrier. "Now, Benito," Tortillaw said. "Take it easy. It is all a terrible mistake. How could I know it was you?" His hands were extended in entreaty. Many Indians had begun to appear from out of nowhere at all. They seemed bewildered.

"How could you know it was me?" Irish yelled, his face stuck so close to Tortillaw's face that their noses almost touched. "What kind of Indian chief are you? You're supposed to have eyes like an eagle in your kind of work. You're supposed to be able to read the date on a centavo piece from the top of a mountain, you painted ape! You chased me for thirty miles. How can you have the gall to stand there and say you didn't know it was me?"

"I wasn't there!" Tortillaw bleated.

"Oh, sure—sure." Irish held Florita's hand and shouldered his way through the mob of hideously painted Indians, striding toward his horse, Tortillaw trailing directly behind him, plucking at his sleeve and talking as persuasively as he knew how. "I just got here. I was nearly sixty miles on the other side of the valley when I picked up the fire signal from my boys."

"Oh, sure—sure."

"Please believe me, Benito. If Jacaranda ever knew what happened this morning—" Tortillaw gulped as though swallowing one of the boulders.

"What are you doing this far into Mexico in the first place?"

"We will join war parties of Mescaleros, Yaquis,

255

Opatahs, and Pagagas. There will be five hundred warriors. I will lead them."

"Where?"

"We will take the smoking train which rides from the north to the south."

"The train from Monterrey to Mexico?"

"Yes. It carries four thousand rifles and a great store of powder and bullets. There is no guard."

Irish shut his eyes to close out the horror. It would be of no use to stop Tortillaw and his Lipans. The other tribes would carry out the attack. In his spent imagination he could see the charred bodies of his friends laying across the twisted tracks with their throats cut and their hair lifted.

"But how can that many large war parties meet then find a train over thousands of miles of track?"

"We will form where we will strike, a half mile after the train has come through its tunnel between the pueblos of Joaquin and La Strada, when the sun is *there*," Tortillaw pointed at the sky between noon and the horizon; at three o'clock.

"Well good hunting," Irish said off-handedly. "We'll be moving along."

"I am deeply in your debt," Tortillaw said.

"It is nothing, Tortillaw." Irish stared at him, waiting.

"Just the same. I owe you much."

Irish helped Florita into the saddle. "Well, perhaps some day I will need your help."

"On that day you will ask for it freely and I will give it freely."

"*Adiós,* brother."

"*Adiós,* brother. *Adiós,* amigo." Irish guided Florita's horse through the boulders and the madroños. When they were in the clear they broke into a canter, heading south toward the railroad tunnel between the two pueblos.

"Benito?"

"Yes, my darling?"

"If the father wanted to shoot you before, why will he not wish to shoot you now when you tell him about us?"

"He will—naturally."

256

"What will you do?"

"I must give him a chance to shoot me, just as I gave your father a chance to shoot me. Fair is fair."

"Yes," Florita said, sadly. "Fair is fair."

CHAPTER 22

"My mother was a militantly gentle woman," John Moodie said to Evaliña as the train moved across lower Zacatecas, "and so very much a woman. She was like you to a startling degree although you, to me, are Woman in her most modern meaning. The old-time softness, yes. In fullest abundance. The shyness, the psychological peeking forth into the physiological, hopeful that the emotional will yield dangers in tramping, sweating, trampling men."

Evaliña shivered. Janine watched Moodie's lips moving from the window across the aisle, but she could not hear what he was saying. She knew what he was saying from the look upon Evaliña's face. Her eyes moved to the major and Franklin Heller. They were both asleep with their hats down over their eyes.

"The elemental sweetness is there, too; a tender and a golden rarity. A gallantry and an understanding tolerance of two worlds clearly mingles within you. The mind which reasons with the subtlety of Arab and Moor, with the anagogic restlessness of Spain, Mexico, and Indian America, to combine with the more forthright creativeness of the Anglo-Saxon is a force to hope upon." Evaliña's underpinnings churned. She gripped her lower lip between her teeth.

"Serenity is youth; coda. You are not you. I am not me. We are our quest." It was as though Mr. Moodie had set the dials which would receive the sounds emanating from a mental institution upon Mars. "It is a different time we are forced to seek in every age we live in. Time-tainted eyes look downward from the slopes of middle age to see, for the first time, the wondrous scented valley they had left behind. We each try to tell ourselves that we are able to climb back again into the golden valley, but unless we are flown

257

there within the arms of a love young and unused we cannot go back. With this prescience I have measured out my life from this day forward. Time cannot be stopped. The mind cannot be stopped. But I saw that if emotion could be suspended, then time and mind could have no meaning, for it is the feeling we spend which is the currency of living, not the minutes and not the futile thinking. Passion and its explosive anarchies are the way to youth. You must use Now. Is youth a time for waiting, as the old would have it for them? No and no! I prove this with the alchemy of my own years. I have waited here for you within a cocoon of wistful lust, protected by this monomania from the rips and pulls which are hooked to the flesh of other men. I walked through this world with a sealed vow. I held my dreams as the breathing of a great bear in hibernation diminishes until it almost breathes no more. I stepped daintily out of the scarlet garments of my passion, folded them neatly, and stored them behind the lock of my ideals. By divesting my flesh of my passion I have suspended my youth. But I was merely waiting. This was not a clod, hat in hand, in the anterooms of a life. This was the purest kind of pure seeking. My youth slept on, perfectly preserved until I should, at last, choose to back my carnality. *You* were my quest." Evaliña's pink, pink mouth lay slightly open. Her bosom rose and fell with accelerated regularity. She licked the lips of her open mouth.

"Do you see the sweaty footprints of my passion as it encircles you, drawing nearer and nearer? Will you spring at it and bring it down, like a mindless, scented tigress?"

Major Patten snored softly across the aisle of the speeding train as it moved into the tunnel between Joaquin and La Strada, his feet up on the seat in front of him. Commissioner Heller dozed beside him. Their colleague was in what was by now called the Mat Sun Office, playing cards at the rear of the car with a matador, a soldier, and a shovel salesman. Sunlight had gathered at the back of Evaliña's head, illuminating the copper glow of her hair.

"Oh, Mr. Moodie," she said.

CHAPTER 23

THE tunnel ended six miles below the pueblo called Joaquin. The mesa sparkled out in all directions away from the mountain like a green-stubbled sand pancake sliding toward horizons of blue china. The land had been climbing frantically as though a flood had been following it, away from the flatness of Texas and away from the seas. Where the tunnel had ended the land had ascended to six thousand feet. It was hot, but a chill waited within the nearest shadow. The land marched upward ahead of the train; moving higher still; higher, then higher again.

The seven-car train plunged out of the tunnel like a playful land-locked porpoise. Engine, tender, two passenger cars, and three freight cars came out into the sunlight. The train's course was flanked by four hard-riding horsemen, two on each side of it, dashing toward it from ninety yards away, at a long angle. The horsemen could not see each other, blocked by the train. Both sets had come round the wide mountain from a different side at the same moment. Their horses were lathered and straining. Each horseman fired a pistol simultaneously to gain the attention of the people on the train.

"It's Jim!" Major Patten shouted. "Who's that with him? By golly, it looks like that college girl Eddie Dillon sent me three years ago."

"It is," Janine said. "Yes, yes. It is!"

"Jim?" Evaliña cried. "Jim Street?"

"Drat, drat, *drat!*" Mr. Moodie said.

Mr. Heller was staring from the train window on the other side of the car. "Jim Street?" he yelled. "Are you goin' blind? That's Irish Reyes an' you know it, but I never seen the girl with him before."

"Irish! Irish Reyes?" Evaliña cried. "Where?"

"Dammit, dammit, *dammit!*" Mr. Moodie snarled.

"Blind?" the major shouted indignantly. "You ever see Irish wear blue jeans and a flat John B?"

259

"I never did, an' he ain't wearin' 'em now," Mr. Heller yelled back. Depending upon which side of the car they were on, the passengers were aware of only one rider, except Evaliña, Mr. Moodie, and Mat Sun—who left the Mat Sun Office and ran like a streak to the rear platform, his pigtail flattening out behind him in the breeze he made, to the rear platform of the car where he grabbed the upright wheel brake. Riding hard, Jim Street saw what he wanted to do and yelled at him, "No! Don't slow 'er down. No, no!" then disappeared from view.

Each rider rode a desperate parallel course to the first freight car, which followed the second passenger car, but as they came in they faded back to the second freight car before they could climb aboard. Each rider swung off his saddle, kicked the stirrups away, and grabbed a rung. The men went first, clinging to the side of the bucketing train so they could pull the women to the ladders. When they were all fast they began to climb to the freight-car roof. At the same moment, Irish's head and Jim's head popped up facing each other across the roof. "No!" Jim yelled.

"Mother of God," Irish cried, "are we going to play to another draw?"

They clambered up to the roof of the car and pulled the women after them. They were all haggard from exertion.

"Florita," Irish panted, "may I present my oldest friend, Jim Street—and Miss Marilyn Ridgeway? Miss Ridgeway! What are you doing here?"

"We just happened to meet on the mésa."

"How do you do?" Florita gasped.

Jim could hardly pull air into his lungs. "How do you do? You're Florita Peña?" They were all sitting on their hams, trying desperately not to fall off the roof of the car.

"Yes," Florita answered, "I have heard so much about you." The girls expanded and contracted like bellows.

Irish fell over on his side, panting. "Listen," he said with a great effort, "It's about time you two met."

Jim had jammed his fist into a stitch in his side. "Incidentally, what happened?" he gasped. "How come you're here?"

"Lipans, Mescaleros, Yaquis, Opatahs, and Papagos are riding in to take the train," Irish wheezed. "Five hundred warriors. The train is carrying guns and ammunition and they want it. Why you here?"

"The same guns. General Molina wants them. They've ripped up all the track ahead to stop the train."

"What time they come?"

"Three o'clock."

"Indians too."

"It'll be pretty busy."

"What'll we do?"

"Go to back the train up."

"You tell the train driver."

"Where you goin'?"

"I'll get the major. We'll break out guns from the freight car an' make every passenger a soldier. We got enough bullets to hold off Napoleon."

Jim stood up and looked as far ahead as he could. "Them tracks is out, all right," he said. He suddenly pointed off to their right. "Irish, look! Here comes the goddam cavalry!"

Irish looked out across the mesa. At about five miles out he could see the green, gold, and black uniforms of the horse troops glistening in the brilliant sun, about eight hundred strong. Forage wagons were strung out behind them and a line of burros brought up the rear.

They held a war council on the platform of the second car. They stared out at the approaching cavalry as Irish reported.

"Here come the Indians!" Franklin Heller yelled. They spun around and stared across the open plain with slit eyes. Above the tumult caused by five hundred hordes and the occasional glitter of war paint they could see the high, feathered lances of the warriors. The line of march of both attacking forces was such that the train masked the cavalry from the Indians and the Indians from the cavalry.

Irish explained what he knew about the Indian plan of attack.

"Let's break out them rifles and bullets," the major said.

The fireman almost shot Jim as he jumped from the roof of the first car into the tender, but Jim was able to land a foot on the fireman's chest as he fell. The train driver went for his gun. "Hold it!" Jim said in rapid Spanish. "Look out to your right."

They looked. They turned to Jim.

"Molina?" the train driver asked. Jim nodded.

"We're cooked," the fireman said.

"The hell we are."

"Stoke her 'til she blows," the fireman said. "Here goes nothing."

"The track is out ahead," Jim said.

The train driver peered forward. "So it is. What do we do now?"

"We stop and back her up as fast as she goes, right through that tunnel."

"That's all?"

"You handle the drivin' an' we'll handle the fightin'."

With a joyous shout the fireman cried, "We stoke her 'til she blows! Here goes nothing!" The driver slammed the train into a fifty-foot stop. Behind him, every passenger was thrown eight feet forward, including Father Luis Aguilar who released any number of rude and unexpected oaths.

Jim climbed to the roof of the passenger car, then raced as fast as he could go before the train began to move in the reverse direction, until he found the war council on the passenger car platform.

Colonel Winikus-Garnet had just lost a heated argument with the general. The colonel had been trained as a cavalryman since he had been a boy. He insisted it would be unthinkable for the regiment to attack a moving train without dismounted covering fire, known tactically as the pivot of maneuver. He had argued to allow the assault force to be made up of two squadrons attacking in waves, with a third squadron to be held in regimental reserve. He had deplored General Molina's decision to leave the units of horse artillery behind. He had demanded that the attack be made as nearly as possible at right angles to the pivot of maneuver in order that they might take advantage of the covering fire until the ultimate moment of impact.

The general had rejected every plea. "I may be governor of this state one of these days," he had said. "Do you think I would be able to terrify my own people if they knew I reduced every risk when I had attacked a few passengers on a helpless train?"

"Civilians be damned!" the colonel had said. "It cannot be possible that you would consider asking any professional soldier to take part in such an action as you propose."

"I do not ask you. I order you." That had been the end of the resistance.

General Molina watched the train through a telescope. "Look there," he said, "I believe that's my bandmaster running along the top of the objective. Hmm. But why is the objective running backward?"

"Perhaps the driver has seen the bit of ripped track, sir. As planned."

The general swung his glass to that part of the railroad track which lay to the rear of the train, near the tunnel. He watched two squads of his men removing the track on the train's only escape route. "The driver won't be able to see *that* bit of ripped track very well, will he gentlemen?" General Molina said and smiled horribly. "My congratulations. Good staff work."

Tortillaw signaled the great war party to a halt two and a half miles east of the train as he watched it slam into an abrupt stop. They watched the small figure of a man sprint two car lengths, then climb down and stand on a crowded platform with other figures. Tortillaw's keen eyes swung along the length of the train, then past it to the stretch of track where sixteen soldiers were busy ripping up the road, and he knew that there were other hunters after the same prey on the other side of the road. Suddenly, the Indian force seemed to melt into the landscape, disappearing utterly as though five hundred horses and warriors had not been there such a short time before.

Jim lowered Irish by the ankles from the top of a moving freight car. Hanging upside down, Irish held a gun in his right hand and shot the locks and the hinges off the freight-car doors on the side facing away from the cavalry force and therefore beyond their view.

When Irish came up again, Major Patten and Mat Sun prised the flat door open and let it fall with a crash. Irish and Jim swung themselves from the car's roof to its interior. They broke open the gun cases and ammo boxes. They lashed together fasces of eight rifles, took the line the major lowered from the roof, and secured it to the first gun packet. Hawks swooped low over the train. The sun poured heat on. The buckety-buckety redundancy of the car wheels gave the only sound.

As the major looked up along the line of cars which were speeding backward, he saw the newly gutted section of track ahead of them.

He hightailed it along the roof of the train, leaping across the chasms between the cars, running against the inertia with difficulty. As he reached the head car he fell. He caught himself just as he came to the edge and pulled himself up again. Lying on his stomach, he yelled down at the engine driver, "Track out ahead!"

"What the hell do you think we're backing up for?" the engine driver answered.

"You mean *behind?*" the fireman asked.

"He said ahead."

"Never mind the ministrel chatter," the major snarled. "I mean behind and ahead. You got about two hundred yards."

"St. Christopher pray for us!" the driver yelled. He slammed the brakes on. "This General Molina sure knows how to rob a train," he cried. What Father Luis Aguilar was saying at that moment is best overlooked.

"What do we do now?"

"Reverse her," the major ordered. "Drive her forward four, five miles, then stop an' reverse her again."

"And for this we came off the Vera Cruz run!"

"Stoke her 'til she blows!" the fireman yelled. "Here goes nothin'."

"I am not pleased by the way those people are taking this catastrophe," General Molina said to his staff. "They are showing too much initiative. They should be paralyzed by fear and uncertainty by this time."

"Perhaps they are just too sticky to show it, sir," Winikus-Garnet suggested.

"Unknown Indians are massacring the derailing party, sir," Captain de la Mure reported languidly.

"Indians!" the general showed the affront he felt. He snatched the glasses out of his aide's hands and sighted. "Oh, barbarous! Oh, the swine!" he moaned. "What heinous cruelties! Ugh! Oh! These are indeed atrocities and not mere propaganda." He handed the glasses to Winikus-Garnet. "What do you have to say for yourself, sir?"

The colonel studied the scene. "I'd say there is a lot we could learn from those aborigines, sir," he said at last.

"Never mind the war college talk. I want to know why your reconnaissance reports showed nothing like this."

"Our very *thorough* reconnaissance reports, sir, as late as yesterday afternoon revealed only nine squaws in the entire region—berrypickers—and two rather elderly Indian gentlemen."

"Is it your professional estimate then that the entire group of savages who are murdering our men out there are merely an isolated party which is passing through the region?"

"It is, sir."

"I concur on that, sir," Captain de la Mure said, yawning.

"And I, sir," put in Major Wchzychas. "Everything is entirely in order and proceeding as you had planned it."

"CHHHAAAARRRRRGE!!!!!" the general cried, spurring forward. The first cavalry assault on the train was launched at M hour plus .013.

The terrain favored the train if nothing else did. When and as the general's force decided to close in and board they would need to conquer a fourteen-foot, thirty-degree grade which also led to further masking

265

of the Indians. Boarding cavalry would also find an irritating bottleneck at the passenger-car platforms, and each window was well guarded with several rifles. To cope with these possible delays, the general decided to burn the passenger cars to the ground after the freight cars had been uncoupled from them. A set of fire wagons waited sedately behind his lines for the command decision. Should any of the charred passengers be capable of tottering away from the holocaust the general had decided that these were to be bayoneted, not shot. "Waste not, want not," he reminded his staff.

"What a grand governor he will make," Winikus-Garnet said warmly to Wchzychas. "Give me a soldier at the helm and I'll show you a crusader for the people every time."

Major Patten had divided his riflemen into four forces, split between the two passenger cars. Within each car was an eastern and a western front, installed to cope with the Indian force and the cavalry respectively. The main defense force was deployed behind each of the twenty-eight windows of the two cars facing west, toward where the cavalry had begun its charge. On the eastern front were Father Luis Aguilar, aged seventy-one, who was returning from a visit with twelve nieces and twelve nephews in Monterrey; a girl of six who refused to have anything to do with her rifle because it was covered with storage oil which could have soiled her new pink dress; and a gold prospector named Colorado Bill Prass who had struck it rich for the first time in a twenty-six-year career and who was heading into Mexico City to spend as much of it as possible on new pickaxes and bacon, then to get out into the mountains again. The lookouts had not yet sighted any Indians.

Mat Sun was in charge of Services of Supply; Irish and Jim were the supply force, reconnaissance force, and commando unit. Major Patten was commander-in-chief, Franklin Heller his second in command, in charge of car number two. Mr. Moodie was liaison between the two cars and all units. The three girls worked in the small conductor's office, rolling *tacos de carne con cebollas crudas*. The odors of

266

onions, hair pomade, and hot plush filled the air. The cavalry charged in as a long line on a suicidal right-angle course.

As they ranged in position at each of the train windows, the defenders were as dissimilar a group as any other three or more people anywhere. There was one professional soldier on leave, resentful that he would be required to shoot people while off duty. There were three competitive shovel salesmen; seven farmers; two wholesale kerosene men; four dance-hall girls who had rolled their last drunk in Saltillo before running to catch the train; an unlicensed kosher poultry butcher; four matrons; a hay fever victim; a Catalan matador and cuadrilla; and an extremely dour Scots governess and her two small charges. The major had not planned to include the latter three among the defenders but the governess kicked him in the ankle when he orderd them away and told him that if the children didn't see anything how could they learn anything.

No defender was hit in the first assault. However, they killed thirty-six attackers and wounded sixty-one. The holes the bullets made in the uniforms and the stains upon them caused by the bleeding, enraged the general. He re-formed the horse troops out of rifle range and addressed them in a fury, galloping back and forth along the line, shouting at the top of his voice.

"How can you permit a ragtag of commercial travelers and country women to hit you like this? Have you any idea what this has done to the uniforms? Now hear this. Now hear this: If any more of you allow yourselves to be shot for the remainder of this engagement I am going to take those beautiful uniforms away from you, officers and men. Now hear this! If any man of you allows himself to be hit, soiling those magnificent uniforms such as not even the federal troops are issued, you will be making the charge after this one in your underwear."

The men sat at silent attention. The general reared back his charger.

"CHHAAAARRRRRGE!!!!" the general shouted, spurring forward. The second assault upon the train was launched at M hour plus .595.

Major Patten's inspection examined the bullet stockpiles at intervals along the aisles of each car. The piles of glittering brass jackets were stunning in their contrast against the long green runner. There were eleven loading stations on either side of the ammunition dumps.

In Franklin Heller's car the four soured dancehall girls worked as a team. Two loaded and two fired, then they switched and the loaders stepped into the front line to turn the big trick. Every time Franklin approached them with counsel or a word of godspeed they would snarl, "Aaaah, shaddup." The oldest blonde, with eyes like a kewpie doll in a ring-toss joint, could shoot the straightest but she insisted upon shooting the horses. Heller caught her at this twice and finally, when the first assault was spent, he swung her around and walloped her across the chops. "Aim at the man!" he thundered. "Can a horse shoot you?"

Her friend, a ketchup-colored redhead, picked up the fallen rifle and shrugged. "She can't help it, mister," she explained. "To Hortense evvey guy is a potential score and you don't go around shootin' your market."

The air in both cars was thick and blue from the smokeless powder and as acrid as cheap white wine. As the second assault was launched, the major ordered that all defenders hold their fire to draw the cavalry closer to the train; they were to fire on signal. The line of cavalry rode closer and closer. At a point seventy yards from the moving train General Molina issued his order to open fire (from his observation post at six hundred yards) to Colonel Winikus-Garnet (at three hundred yards) who signaled the order to Major Wchzychas on the line.

Eighty-four troopers were killed in the attack, forty-six uniforms were badly torn on the wounded, or otherwise bloodstained or marred. Major Wchzychas, who tore his tunic quite accidentally while galloping past a yucca tree, shot himself rather than face the humiliation of the consequences. Fortunately, no one aboard the train was hit or hurt and the train reached the end of its southern run, stopping just thirty yards short of derailment.

"We're shore whipping the tar out of them," Commissioner Heller crowed.

"Maybe we're winnin', but it cain't keep thataway," the major answered.

"Why not?"

Irish and Jim climbed down from the freight car.

"Because no matter how dumb the general is he's goin' to start his attack when we're stopped at one end of the line or the other and second because they're goin' to start to use fire on us and these wooden cars'll go up like tinder."

"What'll we do?" Jim asked.

"Well, what he wants is them freight cars an' the Injuns want 'em, too. If we cut the freight cars loose they might get fightin' over the loot an' we might get a chance to reset them rails up ahead."

"No Indians would match themselves against any armed body in an even fight, Major," Dr. Ridgeway said. "They will only hit if they can have the advantage of surprise or numbers."

"They have numbers now."

"No, sir, Major," Jim said flatly, "that'd be against the general's stated policy of no survivors. It could muddy up his whole campaign for governor if the people knew he had went chicken an' let as much as one person go."

"You mean he'd loot, then try to kill us, too?"

"He'll kill first, then loot. He's put a lot of time an' blood into the governor campaign, Major."

"What do you think, Irish?"

"I think we'll beat all of them. I'll tell you how."

Dr. Ridgeway, standing at the open mouth of the freight car, inhaled deeply, then poured out the scream of a puma, closing it off with the Lipan signature which resembled the sound of a grieving armadillo mother being strangled by the pressure of a water buffalo's hoof upon her larynx.

Far out on the prairie, Tortillaw leaped to his feet. Cupping his hands around his mouth he emitted the enormous amplification of the sound of an alligator in labor, ending the call with the Lipan answering signature of recognition and welcome, which closely resembles the cry of a pterodactyl as it makes a mistaken landing in darkest night upon the opened mouth of a tyrannosaurus rex.

Two Indian riders bareback on ponies darted across the mesa to the train. Dr. Ridgeway was pulled aboard the lead horse. Irish leaped on the second. They were ridden directly to the war council seated in deliberative circle.

DR. RIDGEWAY: How?

FONSECA: How? she asks, when she practically wrote the book.

TORTILLAW: You come well, Sister and Brother, which is to say you are welcome.

DR. RIDGEWAY: I hear you, Brother.

IRISH: Also me.

TORTILLAW: You what?

IRISH: I hear you.

FONSECA: How's tricks, Sister?

DR. RIDGEWAY: Consider this trick. Do my brothers know the pinah weed—straight, tall, and dry?

FONSECA: Of course.

DR. RIDGEWAY: Did you know that wherever you find the pinah weed you will find potatoes?

FONSECA: Is that so?

TORTILLAW: Hmm.

  [They were seated in a deliberative circle, each member of the council cross-legged.]

IRISH: How is my sister Jacaranda?

TORTILLAW:: A few hot and cold flashes and occasional dizziness but otherwise fine.

  [Fonseca produces a civilized lady's hat. It is made of black straw, molded in the image of a hen with pink and orange feathers.]

FONSECA: How do you like this?

DR. RIDGEWAY: Oh, stunning. How smart!

FONSECA: Gorgeous, hey? I promised my missus something from this trip and luckily we ran into a chance for a little massacre on the way down, but when I look at it I'm tempted to keep it for myself.

IRISH: Let us get ourselves with it.

MATOUK: Ugh.

FONSECA: It is well.

IRISH: I come with a great present for my brothers.

The warriors of the great tribes have gathered to take the guns which are stored in the fire horse, but the paleface soldiers want to take them, too. We do not want the soldiers to have them but want you to have them. If you accept them as a gift, none can be hurt.

TORTILLAW: We hear you, Brother. But how can you make the gift? You are fighting the soldiers. To accept the gift we would have to fight the soldiers. We do not know if we can safely accept such a great gift.

FONSECA: You can say that again, Brother.

MATOUK: Ugh.

IRISH: Everything is not always as it looks to the eye of the eagle. We have fire sticks of great power to blow up the horses and soldiers. Our guns have already killed many. We can show you the way to lift the hair of all the soldiers. We lack horses. We must stay on the train. That is why we offer payment of guns to the great chiefs in return for small assistance.

TORTILLAW: It is no longer a gift? It is a payment?

FONSECA: He's beginning to level anyhow, the momser.

TORTILLAW: I hear you, Brother.

IRISH: Two days ago, in the north, my brother, chief of the Lipans, husband of my sister, said he would grant me any wish within his power.

MATOUK: Ugh.

IRISH: I will now tell my brother my wish.

Major Patten capped the sticks of dynamite very carefully. He was seated on the last seat of the second car. He placed each finished stick, to the number of four, in Mr. Moodie's cradling arms. Mr. Moodie walked stiffly to the car platform in the manner of a regent transporting an infant emperor upon a cushion. Major Patten kept capping, placing the next batch of sticks, one at a time, in Commissioner Heller's arms. They were sweating exceedingly.

"Ticklish, ain't it?" Franklin said.

"Remember one thing, Franklin. If annathing goes wrong we'll never know it."

Mat Sun stood beside the train driver in the cab of the engine. The train had been stopped at the northern end of the run. The fireman was stoking. They stared out at the cavalry formations assembled far across the mesa.

"What are they doing?" General Molina asked querulously. "Why has the train been stopped this long?"

"I suspect they may be low on fuel, sir," Winikus-Garnet said smoothly. He and the remaining officers mounted on their war chargers surrounded the general in the manner of an oil painting commissioned by a cognac firm. They were dressed only in their underwear, some of it extremely disreputable, but wearing their high-shining black boots. The troopers, in strictest discipline, were mounted in serried ranks behind them. They had been stripped to the underwear. Neat piles of brass-buttoned tunics and starkly tailored trousers had been stacked in wagons behind the lines.

General Molina wore his field marshal's regalia: salmon pink with white satin lapels, facing a bold magenta stripe down the sides of the white trousers. Eight rows of medals and decorations sparkled upon his pigeon chest. He had switched his false teeth to the entirely-gold set for the final assault.

"How many fire wagons will make the attack?"

"Three, sir."

"You deem that sufficient?"

"Entirely so, sir."

"Are they deployed?"

"Yes, sir."

"*Chhaaarrrrge!!!*" the general bellowed, and the line shot toward the railroad tracks just as the train began to move along its southward course.

The third assault on the train began at M hour plus 1:37.

The train moved resolutely along its north-south course because it was on rails and had no other choice. The cavalry, with its three well-placed fire wagons, came toward the train at full charge from a mile and one half away; far behind them, from his command post, General Molina's buttons glimmered and gleamed. The wind carried the sweet, exciting jingle of the horses' gear ahead of them. In the first line, each trooper carried a torch. The second line came on with carbines at the ready, to cover the fire throwers. The outlandish visual effect of total warfare in its underwear did not detract from the determined intensity of the scene.

On the other side of the train and wholly screened by it and by the rise of ground which held the tracks, five hundred painted and savage Indians rode a trisecting course with the train and the cavalry, riding from southeast to northwest at a pace calculated to keep the train between them and the consciousness of the cavalry commander.

Inside the train the defenders were at their window posts; rifles held and rifles stacked and loaded.

Directly over their heads on the roof of the train were Jim Street, Mr. Heller, and Irish Reyes on the rear passenger car; then Major Patten, Mat Sun, and Mr. Moodie on the first car; spaced toward the engine in that order at fifteen-foot intervals. Evaliña, Florita, and Dr. Ridgeway were crouched over the live dynamite sticks between the two passenger cars. They watched the line of cavalry charge forward with narrowed eyes. Irish stood slightly sideways and watched the silent Indian force come nearer and nearer. Except for the jingling of the cavalry and the tlocking of the iron wheels on the rails, everything was silent.

From his command post six hundred yards to the rear of the action, General Molina signaled his order to Colonel Winikus-Garnet, who was a mere four hundred yards behind the cavalry line, who passed it along to Captain de la Mure, an infantry aide who had no idea why he was where he found himself. As the brass-edged orders to fire the train came down in relay, Evaliña handed up one package of dynamite to her father and Florita handed another to Irish. They in turn passed each package of four sticks along their lines on top of the train. As the horse soldiers came in, gripping torches and screaming thirty yards from the train, and as the second line of riders opened fire with their carbines, each man on the train's roofs lighted the short-fused dynamite sticks with the burning rope ends at their feet.

"One . . . Two . . . *THROW! !*" the major shouted, and each of the men sent his dynamite stick out in a long, low arc. They exploded in front of the line, in the fire wagons, and between the two lines. Rifle fire from the passenger-car windows began to cut down those who had not been unhorsed by the explosions.

While the others made ready for the second throw, Irish and Jim went running along the roof to the end of the second passenger car. They were running almost abreast of the Indian force trotting decorously beside the train. The two men leaped down into the opening between the last passenger car and the first freight car. Grunting and straining, the two huge men uncoupled the connection between the passenger and freight cars. It came clear. The passenger cars drew away rapidly, creating a widening gap, and the horde of shrieking savages shot through, across the tracks, to explode within the ranks of the remaining cavalry. The carnage was total. Only General Molina and Colonel Winikus-Garnet made an escape, having a four-hundred-yard start, driving the three uniform wagons ahead of them.

Major Patten stared out over the bloody field which receded behind them, watching the Indians hack away at the scalps of living and dead. He turned to Mr. Heller and with the steely tones of the pioneer said, "I seen a lot of things in my life, Franklin, but we have just witnessed—for the first time and maybe the last time in the history of the West—a war party of savage Injuns riding out to rescue the white from a massacre by the cavalry."

"It must be horrible to go in your underwear," Mr. Heller replied.

Janine Patten folded her book closed. During the battle she had been reading the published letters of Madame Calderón de la Barca. The noises had abated somewhat, or seemed to have been stifled by the distance. She strolled through one car, where everyone was hanging out of the windows, looking backward, into the next, then straight along its aisle to where the commando group stood, staring agape at the Indian massacre of the cavalry.

En route she stopped and spoke to the wizened priest, Father Aguilar. He seemed perplexed by what she had to say, but he rose and followed her.

She stood directly next to Mr. Moodie and said, in loud, emphatic tones, "I have brought a priest with me, Major. The time has come to settle this."

The major reacted like a stranger in town because his mind was still filled with the action they had just survived. "Settle what?" he asked reasonably.

"Settle Evaliña's marriage and settle it without any more childishness."

"How're we goin' to do that without the race is started all over again right from here?"

Every face turned on snapped necks as the speakers addressed each other. Mr. Moodie, Irish, and Jim stood on Janine's left. Evaliña, Florita, and Dr. Ridgeway stood on her right.

"What are they saying, Benito?" Florita asked in Spanish, for the Pattens were speaking in English. He told her. Her eyes went wide with horror. Dr. Ridgeway and Jim seemed frozen.

Janine looked directly into Mr. Moodie's eyes, as she answered the major with everyone dreading her answer. "Irish and Jim will toss a coin," she said. "A coin has only two sides and if they each choose a different one there cannot possibly be a draw this time and the winner will marry Evaliña here and now!"

"Now, jest a minute, Jan—"

"No! A coin. Now!"

The major drew a silver dollar out of his vest pocket. He looked tentatively into every face around him. Every face was jelled into an expression of dread.

"Well—what do you call, boys?"

No one answered.

Janine stared hard at Moodie. He seemed to read something in her eyes. "Irish takes heads. Jim takes tails," she said firmly.

"All right with you boys?"

"Toss the coin, Major," Janine ordered.

The coin went spinning into the air.

"No! No!" John Moodie shouted and, reaching over, he pulled Evaliña into his arms and kissed her passionately.

275

"Great horned toads!" the major shouted.

They stared at Evaliña, who had become utterly transformed. Gone was the withdrawn, innocent, girlish manner. She had thickened spiritually with one deeply-felt kiss into as close an approximation of an emotionally abandoned woman as any anti-débauchée would ever care to say. Her nostrils quivered. Her scarlet tongue licked at her lips as might that of a test baker at a patisserie, hungrily and incessantly. Her eyes were filmed with the daintiest lust imaginable.

Grasping Evaliña and Mr. Moodie by the wrists, Major Patten faced them to the little priest and said, "Father, do your duty." He put his head back and—looking toward heaven—he yelled "We always worry about the wrong things."

The fatal kissing had only begun. Four sets of shod feet began to rise slowly from the floor of the train in transfixed, romantic levitation. James Howell Street moved like a figure on an old town clock and took Dr. Marilyn Ridgeway in his arms. They kissed in the interested manner of a boa constrictor kissing a rabbit. Benito Reyes y Splendor went like a sleepwalker to Florita Peña de Valiant and reached out for her as a balloonist seizes ballast and they undertook mutual kissing of infinite meaning. Franklin Heller watched the locked couples as Father Aguilar read the marriage service over the almost Moodies.

"Looks like they're next," he said sagely to Mat Sun.

NEW FROM BALLANTINE!

FALCONER, John Cheever   27300 $2.25

The unforgettable story of a substantial, middle-class man and the passions that propel him into murder, prison, and an undreamed-of liberation. "CHEEVER'S TRIUMPH . . . A GREAT AMERICAN NOVEL."—*Newsweek*

GOODBYE, W. H. Manville   27118 $2.25

What happens when a woman turns a sexual fantasy into a fatal reality? The erotic thriller of the year! "Powerful."— *Village Voice.* "Hypnotic."—*Cosmopolitan.*

THE CAMERA NEVER BLINKS, Dan Rather
with Mickey Herskowitz   27423 $2.25

In this candid book, the co-editor of "60 Minutes" sketches vivid portraits of numerous personalities including JFK, LBJ and Nixon, and discusses his famous colleagues.

THE DRAGONS OF EDEN, Carl Sagan 26031 $2.25

An exciting and witty exploration of mankind's intelligence from pre-recorded time to the fantasy of a future race, by America's most appealing scientific spokesman.

VALENTINA, Fern Michaels   26011 $1.95

Sold into slavery in the Third Crusade, Valentina becomes a queen, only to find herself a slave to love.

THE BLACK DEATH, Gwyneth Cravens
and John S. Marr   27155 $2.50

A totally plausible novel of the panic that strikes when the bubonic plague devastates New York.

THE FLOWER OF THE STORM,
Beatrice Coogan   27368 $2.50

Love, pride and high drama set against the turbulent background of 19th century Ireland as a beautiful young woman fights for her inheritance and the man she loves.

THE JUDGMENT OF DEKE HUNTER,
George V. Higgins   25862 $1.95

Tough, dirty, shrewd, telling! "The best novel Higgins has written. Deke Hunter should have as many friends as Eddie Coyle."—*Kirkus Reviews*

LG-2